SEEDS OF LIFE
AND
WHITE LILY

Two Science Fiction Novels by

JOHN TAINE
(ERIC TEMPLE BELL)

DOVER PUBLICATIONS, INC.
NEW YORK

This Dover edition, first published in 1966, is an unabridged and unaltered republication of the following novels by John Taine (Eric Temple Bell):

Seeds of Life, as published in *Amazing Stories Quarterly,* Vol. 4, No. 4, Fall, 1931.

White Lily, as published in *Amazing Stories Quarterly,* Vol. 3, No. 1, Winter, 1930.

Library of Congress Catalog Card Number: 66-20328

Manufactured in the United States of America
Dover Publications, Inc.
180 Varick Street
New York, N. Y. 10014

CONTENTS

SEEDS OF LIFE

JOHN TAINE
(ERIC TEMPLE BELL)

DOVER PUBLICATIONS, INC.
NEW YORK

CONTENTS

I. THE BLACK WIDOW

"DANGER. Keep Out." This curt warning in scarlet on the bright green steel door of the twenty million volt electric laboratory was intended for the curious public, not for the intrepid researchers, should one of the latter carelessly forget to lock the door after him.

The laboratory itself, a severe box of reinforced concrete, might have been mistaken by the casual visitor as a modern factory but for the fact that it had no windows. This was no mere whim of the erratic architect; certain experiments must be carried out by their own light or in the dim glow of carefully filtered illumination from artificial sources. The absence of windows gave the massive rectangular block a singularly forbidding aspect. An imaginative artist might have said the laboratory had a sinister appearance, and only a scientist would have contradicted him. To the daring workers who tamed the man-made lightnings in it, the twenty million volt laboratory was more austerely beautiful than the Parthenon in its prime.

Of the thousands who passed the laboratory daily on their way to or from work in the city of Seattle, perhaps a scant half dozen gave it so much as a passing glance. It was just another building, as barren of romance as a shoe factory. The charm of the Erickson Foundation for Electrical Research was not visible to a casual inspection. Nevertheless, its fascination was a vivid fact to the eighty men who slaved in its laboratories twelve or eighteen hours a day, regardless of all time clocks or other devices to coerce the unwilling to earn their wages. Their one trial was the fussy Director of the Foundation; work was a delight.

About three o'clock of a brilliant May afternoon, Andrew Crane and his technical assistant, the stocky Neils Bork, gingerly approached the forbidding door, carrying the last unit of Crane's latest invention. This was a massive cylinder of Jena glass, six feet long by three in diameter, open at one end and sealed at the other by an enormous metal cathode like a giant's helmet. It had cost the pair four months of unremitting labor and heartbreaking setbacks to perfect this evil-looking crown to Crane's masterpiece. Therefore, they proceeded cautiously, firmly planting both feet on one granite step leading to the green door before venturing to fumble for the next.

Their final tussle in the workshops of the Foundation had endured nineteen hours. The job of sealing the cathode to the glass had to be done at one spurt, or not at all. During all that grueling grind neither man had dared to turn aside from the blowpipe for a second. In the nervous tension of succeeding at last, they had not felt the lack of food, water, or sleep. They had failed too often already, each time with the prize but a few hours ahead of them, to lose it again for a cup of water.

Crane planted his right foot firmly on the last, broad step. His left followed. He was up, his arms trembling from exhaustion. Bork cautiously felt for the top step. Then abused nature took her sardonic revenge for nineteen hours' flouting of her rights. The groping foot failed to clear the granite angle by a quarter of an inch. In a fraction of a second, four months' agonizing labor was as if it had never been.

Crane was a tall, lean Texan, of about twenty-seven, desiccated, with a long, cadaverous face and a constant dry grin about his mouth. He shunned unnecessary speech, except when a tube or valve suddenly burnt itself out owing to some oversight of his own. When Bork blundered, Crane as a rule held his tongue. But he grinned. Bork wished at such awkward moments that the lank Texan would at least swear. He never did; he merely smiled. Neils Bork was a true Nordic type, blue-eyed, yellow-haired, stockily built. From his physical appearance he should have been a steady, self-reliant technician. Unfortunately he was not as reliable as he might have been, had he given himself half a chance.

Viewing the shattered glass and the elaborate cathode, which had skipped merrily down the granite steps, and was now lying like a capsized turtle on its cracked back thirty feet away in the middle of the cement sidewalk, Crane grinned. Bork tried not to look at his companion's face. He failed miserably.

"I couldn't help it," he blurted out.

It was a foolish thing to have said. Of course he couldn't 'help it'—now. Only an imbecile would have deliberately smashed an intricate piece of apparatus that had taken months of sweating toil to perfect. Bork's indiscretion loosened Crane's reluctant tongue.

"You could help it," he snapped, "if you'd let the booze alone. Look at me! I'm as steady as a rock. You're shaking all over. Cut it out after this, or I'll cut you out."

"I haven't touched a drop for——" the wretched Bork began in self-defense, but Crane cut him short.

"Twenty hours! I smelt your breath when you came to work yesterday morning. Of course you can't control your legs when you're half-stewed all the time."

"It was working all night that made me trip. If you had let me take a layoff after we finished, as I asked, instead of carrying it over at once, I wouldn't——"

"All right. Keep your shirt on. Sorry I rode you. Well," Crane continued with a sour grin, "we shall have to do it again. That's all. I'm going to take a look around before I go to bed. Let's see if the baby can still kick."

Bork stood wretchedly silent while Crane unlocked the steel door.

"Coming?" Crane called, as he switched on the lights.

Bork followed, locked the door, and stood sullenly beside his chief on the narrow steel gallery overlooking the vast pit of the huge transformers. Forty of these towering giants, gray and evil as the smokestacks of an old time battleship, loomed up menacingly in the glaring light. Each stood firmly planted on its towering tripod —three twenty-foot rigid legs made up of huge mushroom insulators, like a living but immobile enemy from another planet. The whole battery of the forty devils presented a strangely half human aspect, and their massed company conveyed a sinister threat, as of seething whirlwinds of energy stored up against the men who had rashly created these hostile fiends. The two men, staring down on their half-tamed genii, felt something of this menace, although both were practical and one was daring almost to a fault. But in their present exhaustion, nature succeeded in making herself felt, if not heard, on a deeper, more intuitive level of their consciousness.

"Let's try out the two million volt baby," Crane proposed as a peace offering to the still surly Bork. "We haven't busted that, yet," he continued rather tactlessly, and Bork shot him a spiteful glance.

The 'two million volt' to which Crane referred was his first attempt to build a more powerful X-ray tube than any then in existence. By studying this two million volt baby minutely, Crane hoped to succeed with the full grown twenty million volt tube which he and Bork were constructing. Then, if theory for once should prove a trustworthy guide to the riddle of matter, they hoped to smash up the atoms of at least half a dozen of the elements. What might happen thereafter Crane refused to predict. He had seen too many ingenious theories exploded suddenly and finally by some unforeseen 'accident,' to have much faith in prophecies not founded on experimental evidence.

THAT no physicist had as yet completely smashed an atom from husk to nucleus, although many had knocked at least the outer shell of electrons off some of the less durable, did not deter mathematicians, who should have known better, from broadcasting depressing forecasts as to the probable outcome of drastic success. These gloomy prophets united in predicting an instantaneous outgush of energy, like a transcendent bolt of lightning multiplied upon itself a trillionfold, that would sweep the sun and all its planets, the unfortunate earth included, into everlasting annihilation. But, as the experimentalists pointed out, this might be merely another nightmare of the innocent theorists, which a single contrary fact—not a rival theory—would disprove forever. At all events it was worth a trial. Should theory prove right, the rash experimenter, puffed out like a feeble candle flame, would never live to hear the inevitable 'I told you so'; should the doleful prophets again be in error, the man in the laboratory would probably witness events of surpassing interest never before imagined by the human mind. Crane was resolved to try. Like the legendary Prometheus he would bring light to the world or perish.

"Step it up two hundred and fifty thousand at a time," he ordered Bork, "and be careful. We don't want to blow out the tube."

Again Bork shot him a resentful glance as if his bruised conscience accused him of being a hopeless bungler. Nothing was farther from Crane's mind. He was merely repeating the routine instructions of the laboratory. To prevent possibly fatal mishaps, the experimenters invariably followed a rigid set of rules in their work, testing every switch and piece of apparatus in a definite order before touching anything, although they 'knew' that everything was safe.

Bork threw in the first switch and turned off the lights, plunging the laboratory into total darkness. There was a metallic clang, and the black air began to vibrate ominously with a rapid, surging hiss. A sombre eye of cherry red stole out on the darkness as two hundred and fifty thousand volts flashed to the cathode of the X-ray tube; then, almost instantly, the red flashed up to a dazzling white spot.

"All right," Crane ordered, "throw in the next."

Under half a million volts the twelve foot tube flickered and burned with a fitful green fluorescence, revealing the eight metal 'doughnuts,' like huge balloon tires, encircling the glass. These constituted the practical detail which balanced the terrific forces within the tube and prevented the glass from collapsing.

The outcome of any particular 'run' was always somewhat of a sporting venture. Until the shot was safely over, it was stupid to bet that the tube would not collapse or burn out. Crane waited a full two minutes before ordering the step up to seven hundred and fifty thousand volts. Under the increased pressure the surging dry hiss leapt up, shriller and angrier, and deep violet coronas of electricity bristled out, crackling evilly, in unexpected spots of the darkness.

Bork began to grow restless.

"Hadn't we better step it up to a million now, and quit?"

Crane laughed his dry laugh. "Getting nervous about what Dr. Brown told us?"

Bork grunted, and Crane, in his cocksure ignorance, elucidated. "All doctors are old women. What do the physiologists actually know about the effect of X-rays as hard as ours on human tissues? I've spent at least thirty hours the past eight months working around that tube going at capacity—two million volts—and there isn't a blister or a burn anywhere on my body. I'll bet these rays are so hard they go straight through flesh, bone and marrow like sunlight through a soap bubble. What are you afraid of? If our bodies are so transparent to these hard rays that they stop none of the vibrations, I fail to see how the biggest cells in us are in any danger whatever. You've got to stop hard radiations, or at least damp them down, before they can do human bone, nerves or muscles any harm. All the early workers used soft rays. That's why they lost their eyesight, fingers, hands, arms, legs, and finally their lives."

"It takes months, or even years, for the bad burns to show up," Bork objected.

"Well," Crane retorted, "if there is anything in what Dr. Brown said, I should be a pretty ugly leper right now. Use your eyes. My skin's as smooth as a baby's."

"He said you will be sterilized for life," Bork muttered. "The same for me. I'm not going to live the next twenty years like a rotten half-man."

"Be a confirmed bachelor like me," Crane laughed, "and you'll never miss the difference. What's a family anyway but a lot of grief? Throw in the next switch and forget the girl."

Under the million volts, the glowing tube buzzed like a swarm of enraged hornets, and for the first time in all his months of work in the laboratory, Crane felt a peculiar dry itching over the whole body. As Bork stepped the voltage up to the full two million, the itching increased to the limit of endurance.

"Imagination," he muttered, refusing to heed nature's plain hint. "Hand me the fluoroscope, will you?"

Bork groped over the bench beneath the switches and failed, in the dark, to find what he sought.

"I'll have to turn on the lights."

"Very well. Make it snappy. I need my lunch and a nap. So do you."

Rather than admit that Bork's fears might not be wholly old-womanish, Crane would stick out his discomfort and delude his assistant into a false feeling of security by feigning an interest in the hardness of the rays.

Bork turned on the floodlights. Just as he was about to pick up the fluoroscope, he started back with an involuntary exclamation of disgust. His arm shot to his side as if jolted by a sharp shock.

"Short circuit?" Crane snapped. "Here, I'll pull the switches."

In two seconds the coronas were extinct, a succession of metallic clanks shot rapidly to silence, and the cathode of the two million volt tube dimmed to a luminous blood red. The tingling itch, however, on every inch of Crane's skin persisted. Bork for the moment was apparently beyond speech. In the glaring light his face had a greenish hue, as if he were about to be violently seasick.

"Short circuit?" Crane repeated.

"No," Bork gasped. "Black widow."

Crane failed to conceal his contempt. "Afraid of a spider? Why didn't you smash it?"

Bork swallowed hard before replying.

"It dropped off the bench and fell behind those boards."

"Rot! You're seeing things. It'll be snakes next. There have been no black widows found nearer than Magnolia Bluffs or Bainbridge Island—ten miles from here."

Crane's indifferent sarcasm stung Bork to cold fury. His nerves were undoubtedly on edge after nineteen hours' exasperating work and months of more or less steady, 'moderate' soaking. He succeeded in keeping his voice level.

"Snakes? Then lift that board."

Without a word, Crane bent down and contemptuously tossed the top board aside. "There's nothing here," he remarked dryly, turning the next board. In his zeal to discomfit Bork he deliberately thrust his hand into the narrow space between the pile of boards and the wall, sweeping it methodically back and forth to dislodge the supposedly imaginary enemy. The sweat started out on Bork's forehead. Death by the bite of an aggressively venomous spider is likely to be unpleasant even to witness.

"Look out!" Bork yelled, as a jet black ball, the size of a tiny mouse, rolled from behind the pile, instantly took energetic legs to itself, and scurried with incredible speed straight up the concrete wall directly before Crane's face. Crane's action was instinctive. He straightened instantly to his full height, gave a convulsive leap and, with his clenched fist, smashed the loathsome thing just as it was about to scud beyond his reach. It fell, a mashed blob of evil black body and twitching legs, plop into the eyepiece of the fluoroscope.

"You win this time," Crane grinned, turning the black mess over on its back. "She's a black widow. Here's her trademark—the red hour glass on her underside. We had better post a warning to the fellows to go easy in the dark. This is the ideal breeding place for the brutes—dry and warm, with plenty of old packing cases lying about. I'll have to ask Mr. Kent to get this cluttered rats' nest cleaned up for once. Well, shall we finish our shot?"

"What for?" Bork demanded.

"Just to prove that we haven't lost our nerve. Here, I'll remove the evidence from the fluoroscope before you douse the lights. Better save the remains for the Director," he continued, carefully depositing the smashed spider in an empty cigar box, "or he'll say we've both been hitting the bottle. Ready? Shoot; I've got the fluoroscope."

As the lights went off, Crane caught the dull flash of anger on Bork's face. "I had better stop prodding him," he thought, "or he may stick a knife into me. He's a grouch; no sense of humor."

CRANE was partly right. Bork, a poorly educated mechanic with a natural gift for delicate work, cherished a sour grudge against the world in general and against the eighty trained scientists of the Erickson Foundation in particular. They, he imagined, had profited by the undue advantages of their social position, and had somehow—in what particular way he could not define—swindled him out of the education he merited. He had been denied the fair opportunity, which a democracy is alleged to offer all comers, of making something of himself. Such was his aggrieved creed.

As a matter of fact a good third of all the scientists on the staff had earned their half starved way through high school, college and university with no greater resources at their command than Bork possessed when he was at the student age. That they preferred drudgery for a spell to boozy goodfellowship for the term of their apprenticeship accounted for the present difference between their status and his. One of these men, a great specialist in X-ray crystal analysis, had paid his way while a student by stoking coal eight hours at night in the municipal gas plant. Bork, in all his flaming youth, had done nothing more strenuous than act as half time assistant, four hours a day, to a pattern maker.

Bork had brains; there was no denying so obvious a fact. But he was short on backbone. Being Crane's technical assistant, he naturally, if only half consciously, stored up all his spite against life for Crane's special amusement. Crane was the one man in the Foundation who could have tolerated the grouchy Bork for more than a week. The rest would have discharged him without compunction. Crane's wry sense of humor gave him a more human angle on the dour churl.

Although he would have cut his tongue out, rather than acknowledge the fact, even to himself, Crane hoped to save Bork from his sourer fraction and make a man of him. This missionary drive lay behind his frequent digs at Bork's tippling. Crane sensed the man's innate ability. That all this high grade brain power should fritter itself away on peevish discontent and sodden conviviality seemed to him an outrage against nature.

The exasperations of this particular day, culminating in the wreck of the new cathode and the incident of the black widow, crystallized Bork's sullen irritation toward Crane into a definite, hard hatred. The uninitiated often marvel at the trivial grounds cited by the injured party in a divorce suit, overlooking the ten or fifteen years of constant fault-finding and mutual dislike concealed beneath the last, insignificant straw.

So it proved in Bork's case. Crane's superior contempt for his assistant's perfectly natural abhorrence of a venomous spider revealed the full measure of the stronger man's subconscious scorn for a weakling. Bork was no fool. He realized that although Crane had always looked down on him as a somewhat spineless parody of a full grown man, he himself had looked up to Crane, not with respect or affection, but with smouldering hatred and the unacknowledged desire to humble the better man to his own pygmy stature. And in that sudden flash of revelation, struck out on the darkness of his thwarted nature by a tactless jest, Bork saw himself as the appointed destroyer of his would-be friend and natural enemy. His bitter sense of inferiority was swallowed up in a yet more bitter certainty that his was the power to injure Crane in a way that would hurt. As he switched off the floodlights, and silently threw in the full two million volts in eight perfectly timed steps of two hundred and fifty thousand each, he resolved to get blind drunk the moment he was free of Crane's supervision. He would not dull the edge of his projected spree by foolishly indulging in lunch or supper. No; he would hurl himself and all his forces raging and ravenously empty on the crudest bootleg Scotch whiskey he could buy. What should happen thereafter would be up to Crane alone. In any event Bork would win, in his perverse way, even if it cost him a term in the penitentiary.

"How's that for penetration?" Crane demanded enthusiastically, holding his hand before the fluoroscope in the path of the rays. They were standing about a hundred feet away from the tube. Not a shadow of flesh or bone showed on the fluoroscope. To those hard rays, the human body was as transparent as rock crystal to sunlight. Bork gave a grudging consent that it was pretty good. To test the peneration further, Crane next tried to cast a shadow of the heavy iron rail, against which he was leaning, on the fluorescent screen. Again the penetrating radiation passed clear through the obstacle as if it were air.

"And you're afraid," Crane exulted, "that rays which will pass like these through iron can affect the insignificant cells of your body. They wouldn't bother to stop for such stuff." Nevertheless it cost Crane all of his self control to keep from tearing at his own tingling, itching skin.

"Well, let's call it a day, and go home," he said.

On emerging from the laboratory they found a knot of curious idlers gathered about the cracked cathode, vainly trying to puzzle out whose the huge 'helmet' might be.

"We had better rescue that," Crane remarked, "before some loafer finds out that it's valuable. We can't afford to lose several hundred dollars' worth of platinum on top of our other hard luck."

Crane's thoughtless allusion to their mishap was the last straw. With a smothered oath, Bork turned his back on the small crowd and strode off toward the street.

"See you tomorrow at eight," Crane called after him.

Bork made no reply. Grinning broadly, Crane picked up the cathode and started with it back to the workshops. The idlers, having thoughtfully selected choice souvenirs of broken glass, dispersed. Had Crane been as keen a student of human nature as he was of the physics of radiation, he would have followed Bork and let the crowd keep the costly cathode as a memento of a memorable blunder.

II. THE BOILING BOX

INSTEAD of hastily swallowing a meal and hurrying home to bed as he had intended earlier in the afternoon, Crane sped as fast as his long legs would take him to see his physician.

Dr. Brown, the specialist in radiology, who had already warned Crane of the possible consequences of exposing himself recklessly to the hard X-rays, lived within a quarter of a mile of the Erickson Foundation. Being a family physician to about half the staff of the Foundation, he understood their needs better than might the average doctor. More than once he had been called out of bed in the small hours of the morning to resuscitate some careless worker who had neglected the precautions of common sense and been jolted into insensibility, or to pick splinters of glass from hands and faces damaged in the pursuit of science. Brown himself specialized in medical radiology, and was expert on everything that an up-to-date physician should know about the action of cosmic rays, X-rays, and ultra violet light on the human body. As a hobby he kept abreast of biology in its less practical phases, particularly in a study of the protozoa.

Crane found the doctor in. Without preliminaries of any kind, he plunged into the middle of things.

"My whole skin burns and itches like the very devil."

"You've been working with your two million volt tube again? Without any protection, as usual?"

Crane nodded, extending his bare forearm for Brown to examine. The doctor studied the skin minutely through a powerful pocket lens and shook his head.

"If there's anything wrong, a microscopical examination of the skin may show it up. Everything looks perfectly normal through this. Sure it's not just your imagination running away with what I said the other day?"

For answer Crane, unable longer to control himself, began tearing with his nails at every accessible inch of skin on his body. Brown rose and filled his hypodermic.

"This will stop it for a time. Go home and take a starch bath. Then rub down with calamine ointment. If the itch comes back, stick it out as long as you can before calling me. I'll probably be within reach at home all the evening. If not, the housekeeper will give you the name of another man. He will know what to do."

As the powerful shot took effect, the intolerable itching became bearable, and Crane began to doubt that his discomfort was more than an attack of nerves. Nevertheless he carried out the doctor's instructions to the letter.

"Safety first," he grinned, stepping from the milky starch bath and reaching for the towel. In his eagerness to live up to the doctor's orders, Crane hastened to dry himself thoroughly and rub down his whole body with calamine before even pulling the plug of the bath tub. Having finished his rub, he turned round to let the water out, and stopped short with an exclamation of amazement. The water, milky white less than five minutes before, was now a vivid pink. Even as he watched, the color deepened from red to crimson. In ten seconds the strange fluid had taken on the characteristic hue of freshly shed blood. Crane flung on his bathrobe and ran to the telephone.

In his haste to call Doctor Brown, Crane forgot to shut the bathroom door after him. His landlady chanced to pass along the corridor on her way down to the kitchen, just as Crane, in the telephone alcove, took down the receiver. Like the good housekeeper she was, the landlady made a move to close the bathroom door on her way past. The bathtub full, apparently, of human blood, paralyzed her for two seconds before she screamed. As she fled shrieking from the house, Crane succeeded in getting his connection. Doctor Brown, listening at the other end of the wire, heard ear-splitting shrieks and a man's voice which he failed to recognize as his patient's requesting him to come at once to Crane's apartment. He banged the receiver back on the hook and grabbed his emergency kit. Crane, he imagined, driven insane by his torments, had attempted to commit suicide.

On reaching Crane's apartment house, the doctor ran slap into enough excitement to justify a dozen murders and suicides. The landlady, in hysterics, was being supported on the lawn by two sympathetic neighbors. Crane, gorgeous in a flaming orange bathrobe which flapped about his long legs, was doing his best to convince three motorcycle policemen and a clamoring mob of morbid sensation hunters that he had committed no murder, but had merely indulged in a late afternoon bath. The police had their hands full keeping the mob back from storming the entrance.

With the skill acquired from many adventures with crowds and accidents, Doctor Brown insinuated himself into the mob and quickly worked his way to the police.

"I'm the doctor they telephoned for. What's up?"

"Nothing," the officer replied disgustedly, "if that fellow in the kimono knows what he's talking about. Go in and 'phone headquarters to send half a dozen men to help us."

Brown joined Crane on the porch, snatched him into the house, and bolted the door. Then he telephoned to the police.

"What happened?" he demanded of Crane, on receiving the Chief's assurance that the riot squad was on its way.

"I followed your instructions," Crane grinned. "Come and have a look at the bathtub."

With dramatic effect, Crane ushered the doctor into the bathroom and gestured toward the tub. Then his jaw dropped. The water was as starchy white as when he had stepped from the tub. Not a trace of all that violent blood remained.

"Well?" the doctor demanded meaningly.

"The landlady saw it too," Crane began. "I'm not crazy."

"Saw what?"

Rather shamefacedly, Crane gave a short but complete account of the entire incident as it had seemed to happen. To his surprise, Brown did not laugh.

"You think there may be something in it?" Crane ventured.

Brown was non-committal. He suspected Crane of a nervous breakdown, but refrained from saying so. The landlady doubtless had been scared half out of her senses by some stupid practical joke on Crane's part. He might even have pursued her with his razor.

"Let me take your temperature."

Crane submitted. His temperature was normal. So, as far as Brown could judge, was everything else about him. The theory of a nervous breakdown was abandoned.

"Find me a clean, empty bottle or a jam jar. I'll take a sample of the water and find out if there is anything wrong with it."

While Crane rummaged in the kitchen, the doctor carefully salvaged the teaspoonful of starch remaining in the empty cardboard container. He was just conveying this to his bag, when the front door bell began ringing insistently. At the same instant Crane reappeared with a clean ketchup bottle.

"Don't answer the bell till I fill this. Otherwise the police may smell a rat and bring the reporters down on our necks."

Hastily stowing the bottle of starchy water into his handbag, Brown followed Crane to the front door. The instant the bolt was drawn, a hard-faced captain of detectives thrust himself into the hallway.

"Where's the bathroom? You show me," he suggested grimly, seizing Crane's arm.

"Sure," Crane grinned. "The whole city waterworks, if you like."

Deigning no reply, the captain hustled the suspect upstairs. Once in the bathroom he gave a disgusted grunt at the tub, picked up the rag rug, scrutinized it thoroughly, and finally inspected the articles in the toilet cabinet.

"Does your landlady drink?" he demanded sourly.

"Never touched a drop in her life," Crane gallantly assured him.

"Then she's bughouse. If she throws another party like this one, she goes to the asylum. Tell her that from me."

Turning on his heel, he quit the profitless investigation and clumped downstairs. In his cocksureness that he saw through everything, he overlooked the one clue of any value. It did not enter his head to quiz the doctor then waiting in the hallway till the quieted mob should disperse. What was a doctor doing in the house if everything was as it seemed to be? Who had called him? Why? For failing to think of these pertinent questions the skeptical captain deserved to lose at least one stripe. Brown, for his part, tried to make himself and his telltale black bag as inconspicuous as possible. He might have saved himself the trouble; his estimate of the captain's intelligence was several points too high.

THE moment the front door closed on the redoubtable captain, Brown darted for the stairs. He met Crane half way.

"If your skin starts itching again, come to my house at once. I'll give you a bath. Tell the landlady the heat affected her. I'll speak to her on the way out."

"You think——" Crane began.

"Nothing. But it will be worth while to analyze this water, or whatever it is. Well, I'm going before the reporters arrive. They will have got wind of this at the police station. If anyone asks you anything, leave me out of it. I can't afford this kind of advertising."

By the time Crane was dressed, the disappointed mob had dispersed, and the distraught landlady was doing her feeble best to fend off the persistent attacks of three able young reporters. Crane routed them.

"Beat it," he ordered curtly, entering the living room. "Can't you see that this lady is suffering from the heat? That's all there is to it. If you can make a story out of that you beat Hearst. Only," he concluded with a grin, as he bowed them out of the house, "the city editor will scrap what you write. It would be a slam at our beautiful climate. There's a dog fight down the street. Try your luck on that. Scat!"

Having disposed of the press, Crane returned to the sitting room to comfort the landlady.

"Is there anything I can get you?" he asked sympathetically.

"If you don't mind, you might bring me a little gin and water—not too much water. The bottle is on the top shelf of the kitchen cabinet."

The last information was superfluous so far as Crane was concerned. He had discovered the half empty bottle while rummaging for what the doctor wanted. He was careful not to ruin the landlady's pick-me-up by too much water. In fact he gave her half a tumblerful straight, which was just what she needed. As she sipped the fiery stimulant, the poor woman felt as guilty as sin. She resolved to make the present bottle her last. Bathtubs full of sudden blood are too high a price to pay for a quart a day. To her credit, she lived up to her resolution. This was a pity, as gin afforded the poor woman her one escape from her humdrum existence, and she had a constitution that sulphuric acid could not have corroded. When Crane learned of her self-denial he felt quite conscience-stricken. But he dared not tell her that her vision was a sober fact. Her first act would have been to eject him from his rooms, as an incurable of some particularly dangerous kind. Then, to square herself in the eyes of her neighbors, she would have confided the whole grewsome truth to the avid press.

Having seen to the landlady's comfort, Crane attended to his own. He slipped out to a restaurant, had a square meal, and hurried back to bed. By eight o'clock he was between the sheets, determined to sleep in spite of the faint prickling all over his body. It was beginning again gently; wondering whether he could cheat the enemy by falling asleep, Crane dozed off. He had won, for the time being.

THE moment he had finished his dinner, Doctor Brown settled down to analyze the starchy water. Not being a skilled chemist he had to try the only method in which he was expert—microscopic examination. Should this reveal nothing unusual, he would submit a sample of the water to a competent chemist for detailed analysis.

Brown approached his problem with an open mind. Having profited by an excellent medical training, he was not addicted to forming opinions in advance of the evidence. There might be precisely nothing strange about that starchy water, or it might give a patient observer his first glimpse of a new universe. The doctor was ready for either contingency, or for neither.

With matter of fact deliberation he prepared the slide and carefully adjusted the microscope. Long years of habit enabled him to come within a shade of the true focus without looking through the eyepieces. His instrument was a high-powered binocular, which threw up the minute objects on the slide into solid relief. Having adjusted the focus roughly as far as was safe, Brown completed the delicate operation while looking through the eyepieces.

The singularly beautiful starch grains swam into stereoscopic view and blurred out, as the slowly moving lens sought to bring up the light from still minuter specks within reach of human vision. On the extreme threshold of visibility, a new universe slowly dawned.

The silent watcher of that undiscovered heavens scarcely breathed. Hour after hour he sat entranced, far from this world, as the first acts of a titanic drama, never before imagined by the human mind, unrolled majestically in a drop of water so tiny that no unaided eye could see it.

While one man followed the dim beginnings of a new order in wonder and awe that fateful night, another, blind with hatred and ignorant of what he was doing, sought to destroy the instrument of fate which had thrust the unknown universe up to the light and life. True to his brainless vow, Bork got soddenly drunk as fast as bad whiskey would let him. A dispassionate critic from a wiser planet, if confronted with Brown, Crane and Bork, that evening, might well have doubted that the three were animals of one and the same species—*homo sapiens,* so-called. Brown and Crane he might easily have classified as sports from the same family tree; Bork undoubtedly would have puzzled him.

The vile whiskey, more like crude varnish and alcohol than a civilized drink, had an unprecedented effect on Bork's exhausted body. His customary experience after a full quart of the stuff was a feeling of general well being and a greatly inflated self-esteem. This spree was strangely different from all of its innumerable predecessors. Instead of experiencing the comforting glow which he anticipated, the wretched man felt chilled to the bone. The world turned gray before his eyes. He saw his own life, pale and ineffectual as a defeated spirit, wandering aimlessly hither and thither through a cheerless fog of unending years. Why must he endure it longer? The drink had made him deadly sober. A remorseless tongue, loosened by the alcohol, insinuated that he was an unnecessary accident, a dismal thing that should never have been trusted with life, and a mistake to be corrected and forgotten as quickly as possible. Crane was right, the unhappy man admitted, although he had never put his estimate into cold, precise perspective, as Bork's own silent accuser was now doing. The very unconsciousness of Crane's contempt was what stung.

Bork sighed, slowly extracted the cork from the second quart, poured out a tumblerful of the raw stuff, and sat meditatively sipping it. As the alcohol seeped into his tissues, the insane clarity of his mind increased.

By midnight he had disposed of three full quarts of alleged whiskey. This equalled his previous record. By one in the morning he had bettered his record by a quart and was ripe for his insanely logical action. In his normal state he could not have reasoned so coldly, so clearly, so consistently. Crazed by the drink, he became as rigidly logical as a hopeless maniac. Glancing at his watch, he rose steadily to his feet, and marched from his frowsy lodging to execute his purpose and to silence that persistent voice which said he was born a fool.

No one meeting him on the street could have guessed that he was not cold sober. That is exactly what he was. For the first time in his life Bork had discovered himself, completely and without the slightest reservations of false self-respect. He proceeded through the night with a firm, resolute step, like a plucky man going to the electric chair and determined to die game.

It was a few minutes past two in the morning when Bork silently let himself into the twenty million volt laboratory and locked the door behind him. His immediate business was too serious to admit a smile. Yet he almost smiled as he reflected that Crane would have the satisfaction of thinking—not saying—"that fool Bork has blundered again."

Crane's exasperating silence had given Bork the first inkling of the bitter truth. Now he, the despised assistant, the man who might easily have been chief had nature not loaded the dice against him, would prove that he was the better man in one thing at least—unanswerable destruction. Crane, the arrogant, strong man, whose vice was pride in his easy strength, should learn the meaning of frustration.

The man who can hurt his friend is, after all, the stronger of the two. Bork switched on the floodlights and prepared to prove his superior strength.

He set about his awful business deliberately, determined for once not to blunder. Having descended the steel stairs to the vast pit of the transformers, he made the necessary connections to link up the forty huge gray devils into a single unit. The forty were now ready to smite as one, with the full bolt of their twenty million volts, whatever accident or design might offer them to destroy. Like a callous priest preparing a peace offering to Moloch, Bork quickly and accurately made ready the pride of Crane's heart as a sacrifice to the forty united devils. The two million volt X-ray tube, Crane's "baby," was linked into the chain of destruction to appease the forty and prove Bork a better man than his tormentor.

His preparation was not yet complete. Not only must Crane be humbled, but the pitiless logic of his own subconscious mind must be refuted forever. He connected one end of a long, stout copper wire to that which was to feed twenty million volts into the X-ray tube, made a large loop of the free end, passed the loop over his left arm, and dragged the trailing wire after him up the steel steps to the gallery of the switches.

To secure the effect he wanted, all switches must be closed simultaneously, releasing twenty million volts in one flash. This presented no difficulty. The switches he must use were ranged in one horizontal line eight feet long. Temporarily winding the loop round an iron upright, Bork was ready for his problem.

First he all but closed the whole row of switches, bringing the eight foot line of ebonite handles into the same sloping plane. Then he glanced about for a narrow eight-foot board or strip. The pile of scrap lumber, behind which Crane had thrust his hand to scare out the black widow, contained just what Bork sought. At the bottom of the pile were several narrow lengths of white pine, the remains of large packing cases, from six to twelve feet long and four to six inches wide.

Taking no chance of encountering another venomous spider, Bork disengaged the desired piece of lumber with his foot before venturing to pick it up. Then, ashamed of his lack of courage in the face of what he was about to do, he propped the narrow board against the iron railing and turned to the bench beneath the switches. To prove himself not an utter coward, he put forth a steady hand and raised the lid of the cigar box into which Crane had dropped the crushed remains of the black widow.

She still lay there, black and venomous looking as death itself. Every fiber of her apparently was dead. As he stared down in cold fascination at the hideous, crushed thing, Bork detected not the slightest tremor in any of her eight long, smooth, black legs. All were curved stiffly inward, rigid in death, above the red hour glass on her mangled body. She was dead. To put his sorry manhood to a crucial test before joining the thing he instinctively loathed in death, Bork put out a finger and lifted each leg in turn. Six remained attached to the body, two dropped off.

"Dead," he muttered, closing the lid of the cigar box to shut out the sight of that repulsive corpse which he no longer feared worse than death itself.

His final preparations were brief. In a few seconds he had the copper loop fastened securely about his neck, and the long narrow board evenly balanced in both hands. He laid the board lightly along the eight foot row of ebonite switches. Then, with a convulsive movement of both arms, he shoved the board back and down, instantly throwing in the full battery of switches and releasing the irresistible fury of twenty million volts to shatter everything in their fiery path, himself included, to a chaos of incandescent atoms.

The instantaneous surge of energy missed one of its marks. A deafening report followed the blinding green flash where the copper junction of the wire which was to have electrocuted Bork vaporized instantly. Before the current could leap along its entire length the first twenty feet of the wire exploded to atoms in a cloud of green fire. Bork's efficiency in making the connection had saved his life; a looser contact would have let but a fraction of the current through the wire to destroy him before it consumed the conductor. He had blundered again. His grandiose project had nullified itself in a short circuit which he should have foreseen.

Dazed and uncertain whether he was still living, he stared uncomprehendingly over the pit of the transformers and upon the X-ray tube. The floodlights, on an independent circuit, still filled the laboratory with an intolerable glare. Not a trace of corona flickered on any of the apparatus. The giant transformers loomed up, cold, gray and dead. The echo of the exploded wire seemed still to haunt the oppressive silence.

Gradually the stunned man became aware of the X-ray tube. Built to withstand the impact of two million volts, it should have been annihilated under the surging shock of twenty million. Had it taken the full bolt, or had the half foot of wire from the cathode to Bork's too efficient connection volatilized before the current could leap the short gap? That it received at least a fraction of the intended maximum was evident, for the lower half of the tube quivered and scintillated in coruscating pulses of sheer white light. The upper half of the vacuum in the tube, from the cathode down, was as black as ebony. Impenetrable darkness and sheer light were severed from one another absolutely; no shadow from the black dimmed the upper brilliance of the seething light, and no pulse of the white fire greyed the massive black above the invisible barrier.

Whatever might be taking place in that tube, it was automatic and independent of any extraneous electrical influences. The wires connecting the tube to the feeding apparatus had burned out, and the entire laboratory, except the floodlights, was electrically dead. As Bork watched, the black crept slowly downward. The diminishing light, devoured from above by the descending void, increased in intensity, as if struggling fiercely to resist and vanquish the death which crept down upon it. To the dazed man it appeared almost as if a plunging piston of black steel were compressing the resistant light down to nothing.

Within three minutes but half an inch of dazzling white fire remained. Laboring against the last desperate struggle of the light to survive, the black crept down more slowly. The last half inch dwindled to a mere plane of light as fiercely brilliant as the furnace core of a star. Then, in a second, the last light vanished, and the tube, now wholly black, exploded with a report that rocked the laboratory like an earthquake and hurled Bork to the steel floor of the gallery.

When he came to his senses, he found himself staring up through a phosphorescent glow to the dimly visible concrete ceiling. The explosion which had stunned him had shattered the globes of the floodlights. He got to his feet and reeled toward the door, only to trip over the copper wire dangling from his neck. With a curse he freed himself and fumbled for his key. Some moving object impinged gently against the back of his hand, seemed to break silently, and dispersed, leaving behind it only a faint sensation of cold. Another struck him in the face, and again he sensed the outward flow of heat from his skin. He became aware that his hands and face were slowly freezing.

To escape from that silent place of horror was his one instinct. The key in his pocket eluded his clumsy, half frozen fingers. Still dazed, he did not seek to discover the source of those moving things that touched his bare face as gently as kisses in a dream and slowly drained his body of its natural heat. At last he managed to grasp the key and insert it in the lock. His chilled fingers refused to function. He began beating wildly with his numbed fists against the steel door, conscious that he was slowly dying. Almost together, two of the moving objects softly struck the steel above his head, lingered for a moment, and vanished into total darkness. He saw what they were.

The black air of the laboratory was alive with thousands of spinning vortices of faint light drifting in all directions, rebounding unharmed from one another when two or more collided, and dying only when they struck some material obstruction—walls, ceilings or apparatus. It was the mazy wanderings of this silent host which revealed the darkness against flickers and flashes of dim, tumultuous light. Their numbers diminished rapidly, for they seemed to seek their own extinction, quickening their motion as they drew near to solid substances and jostling one another in their eagerness to cease to be. In ten minutes the darkness would have conquered, but Bork did not wait to see its victory.

A slight rustling on the bench behind him made him spin round in anticipatory fear. Almost before the horror happened he sensed its advent. The lid of the cigar box, in which the crushed black widow lay, flipped up as if some frantic living thing were trying to escape. The lid subsided for an instant, then again flapped sharply up an eighth of an inch. Bork reached the door in one leap. This time his fingers functioned automatically. Glancing back as he flung open the steel door, he saw the dim phosphorescence of the expiring vortices, a sight that reached the very roots of his fear.

The lid of the cigar box was thrown completely back on the bench by a rapidly swelling black mass that foamed up explosively from the box like living soot. As he slammed the door with a reverberating clang he caught a last glimpse of the boiling black mass budding upon itself in furious vitality and overflowing bench, platform and stairs in one hideous deluge of unnatural life.

He turned the key in the lock and reeled off into the icy grey pearl of the stirring dawn, sane at last with an awful sanity such as he had never known.

III. REBORN

Bork roomed in a shabby house in a shabbier street, as the only lodger of a deaf and half blind old man, by the name of Wilson, who saw him only once a month to collect the rent. Old Wilson seldom knew when his lodger entered or left the house, and he cared less. What the old man had done for a living in his prime was more or less of a mystery. Report had it that he was a broken down Alaskan miner who had made and lost a dozen fortunes. Before going completely broke he had bought himself a shack of a house and invested his remaining capital in government bonds, on the meagre income of which, and the rent from the upstairs spare room, he eked out a Spartan existence. The place was ideal for Bork, who hated the habitual prying of even the most reserved landladies. Old Wilson never entered his lodger's room. Consequently it was cluttered with empty bottles shamelessly exposed in the most conspicuous spots.

In spite of his age, Wilson was not an early riser. He enjoyed his ten hours in bed best of the twenty-four. Doubtless the futility of being up and about, when he could see but little and hear less, impressed on him the wisdom of dozing away as much of his meaningless life as possible.

About half past four on the morning of his mad escapade in the laboratory, Bork stumbled up the rickety stairs to his room. The necessity for an alibi in case of investigations regarding the shattered tube was beginning to dawn on him. He knew that old Wilson would not hear him, so he made no effort to walk softly. The alibi presented itself ready made. At seven o'clock Wilson's customary hour for rising, Bork would hunt up the old man in his kitchen and pay the rent a day in advance. Then the old fellow could swear that Bork had spent the night in his room, and believe his oath. The early payment of the rent would arouse no suspicion, as Bork had frequently paid a day or two ahead of time.

Opening the door of his room, Bork found the light still on. A half quart of whiskey stood on the untidy bureau. It was but natural in his shattered state that he should take a bracer to steady his lacerated nerves. He poured himself a stiff jolt and raised it to his lips. As the reek of the crude alcohol fumed his nostrils he was overcome by a strong feeling of revulsion. Yet he imagined that he needed the drink desperately. His attempt to swallow it proved unsuccessful; his body simply rejected the proffered mercy. A healthy young savage almost invariably rebels against his first swallow of raw whiskey, whatever may be his reactions to his hundredth. Bork was in precisely the same condition, except that his aversion was a thousandfold more intense. To down a drink in his present condition was impossible. Instinctively he hurled tumbler and bottle to the floor, smashing three empties in the act.

"What a fool I've been," he muttered. "I must have been sick as a dog to like that stuff."

Aware of an indefinable sense of power, he clenched and unclenched his fists, watching the ripple of the firm muscles beneath the skin. Presently he started. His hands, ordinarily a pasty yellow, were tanned a deep, healthy brown. He might have been working for months outdoors beneath a tropical sun.

A startled glance in the shaving mirror above the bureau confirmed his half formed suspicion. His face was as swarthy as a Hindoo's, and his yellow, fine hair had turned jet black and as coarse as an Indian's.

Even these radical changes, however, failed to account for the utter difference between the face staring wide-eyed from the dusty mirror and the familiar features which he remembered as his own. A more fundamental alteration had transformed his appearance completely. Suddenly he recognized its nature. His blue, cold eyes had turned black and strangely luminous. With a terrific shock he perceived also that he appeared to have grown younger.

In silence he slowly began removing his clothes. Five hours before his body had been like a young boy's, smooth, white, and practically hairless. Now his skin was the same rich brown hue, from heels to head, as his face and hands. Moreover, his chest, arms and legs were covered by a thick growth of coarse black hair like a professional weight-lifter's. From skin to marrow he was physically a different man. No one who had known him intimately five hours previously could have identified him as Neils Bork. This was a different man.

"Who am I?" he asked aloud, reaching for his shirt.

No sooner were the words out of his mouth than he realized two further changes from the man he had been, each of the profoundest significance. The querulous voice of Neils Bork had deepened and become vibrantly resonant. It was the voice of a man with both strength and personality and an assured confidence in his power to use them to his own advantage. It also was a voice that would attract women. Second, he noticed a new trick of habit, that was to become instinctive. The hand reaching for the shirt drew back, and for a simple, natural reason. The shirt was soiled. To put such a thing next to his skin—Bork had never worn underclothes—was an impossibility to the new man.

From the bureau drawer he selected his best shirt, a white linen freshly laundered, which he had worn but once or twice. The shabby suit was discarded in favor of his single decent one, a gray tropical wool. This he had not worn for over a year. The cut was a trifle out of date. That, however, was of no consequence. The suit was wearable, having been dry-cleaned before it was put away. Clean socks, his best shoes and a plain black scarf, which he had discarded as being too tame after one wearing, completed his outfit. It did not occur to him to seek a hat; his thick, black hair afforded ample protection from sun and weather.

Although the dead Bork had been a heavy, consistent drinker, he was not absolutely thriftless. From a slovenly suitcase stuffed with soiled clothes and worthless letters from girls a little less than worthless, the new man extracted the "dead" Bork's carefully hoarded savings. These amounted to about six hundred dollars in ten and twenty-dollar bills.

By a quarter past five the new man was ready to face his dawning life. Thrusting the roll of bills into a trousers pocket, he started for the door. Then he remembered poor old Wilson's rent. Although neither alibi nor disguise was now necessary, the new man felt that it would be wise to dispose of the old forever. Having found a stub of pencil, he scribbled a note on the back of some forgotten girl's scented envelope.

"Mr. Wilson: The enclosed ten dollars is for the month's rent I owe you. As you will see from my room, I have been a steady drinker. The stuff has got me at last. Rather than give my boss the satisfaction of firing me, as he must sooner or later, I am firing myself. Give this note to the police. They will find my body in the Pacific Ocean if they want it, and if the crabs don't get it first.

Neils Bork."

On his way out of the house he slipped the envelope with the ten-dollar bill under the kitchen door. Old Wilson was not yet stirring. The new man took with him nothing but his money and the clothes he wore. No one saw him leave the house; it was still too early for decent workers to be going about their business. He strode briskly along in the clean morning air, conscious of a new vitality coursing through his veins like the elixir of life itself.

WHILE the man who had been Bork was confidently marching to meet his destiny, Crane lay tossing and muttering in his fitful sleep, tormented again by the prickling of his skin. Shortly after six o'clock he awoke fully and leapt from his bed. The itching was much less severe than the first attack. Nevertheless it was sufficiently distressing to make him hurry his dressing and rush to the doctor's house.

Brown had not gone to bed. The curious glance he shot Crane was almost hostile.

"What's up?" the latter enquired, feeling the doctor's restraint.

"That's what I want to know," Brown answered shortly. "Where have you been the past week?"

"At my usual stand," Crane grinned. "The workshop of the Foundation, the twenty million volt laboratory, at home in bed, and up the street three times a day on an average for my meals."

"Is that all?" the doctor demanded suspiciously.

"Sure. Where did you think I'd been?"

"I couldn't guess," the doctor replied slowly, "unless it might have been some low dive of Mexicans or Orientals. Whatever it may be that you've got yourself infected with is new to any science I know. Your case is unique. Itching again?"

Crane nodded. "Save the lecture till after you've cured me. Then I'll listen and admit anything you like."

"The cure will be easy enough. You must soak yourself in disinfectants till the last particle of scale or dust is sterilized and removed from your skin. It may be a long job. Take boiling hot baths and make yourself perspire freely before you rub down with the disinfectants. Then do it all over again two hours later. Keep at it until the itching stops completely. I'll write out the prescriptions."

"You seem sore about something," Crane remarked as the doctor handed him a sheaf of prescriptions. "Why don't you speak up and get if off your chest?"

"I will when I know what it is myself. You give me your word that you are telling the truth about what you have been doing?"

"Of course. Why should I lie? If you want to check up, ask the men at the Foundation and my landlady."

"Then," said Brown, "we are going to discover something brand new. By the way, I should like to examine your assistant—Bork, isn't it? Has he been working with you all the time?"

"In the shops, yes. But not in the twenty million volt laboratory. I must have put in thirty hours with my two million volt tube going at full blast during the past eight months. Bork hasn't been around it more than an hour all told at the most."

Brown considered in silence for some moments.

"Will you let me try an experiment with your tube?"

"Any time you like, if I handle the switches. I would let you do it yourself if you had worked around high tension apparatus. You give the instructions and I'll deliver what you want."

"Very well. How about one o'clock this afternoon? I must get some sleep first. You can go home and begin sterilizing your skin."

"That will suit me. I'll be in the high tension laboratory at one o'clock. Ring the bell and I will let you in. You can't give me a hint of what you think you're doing?"

"I could. But why go off half-cocked? Either this is the biggest thing in a thousand years, or I'm completely fooled. This afternoon will decide."

Doctor Brown's discovery was not, however, to receive its test so soon. The late Neils Bork had made that impossible. Many weary months of toil and speculation were to pass before Brown could recapture the first fine careless rapture of his glimpse at a new universe.

The doctor had intended going straight to bed the moment Crane left. Sleep, he now realized, was out of the question. To quiet his busy mind he must pacify it by consulting the voluminous biological literature that would at least eliminate the chance of making crude, ignorant blunders.

By good fortune the Aesculapian Society had a prosperous branch in Seattle with an excellent scientific library covering all phases of biology and medicine. Doctor Brown was local vice-president of the Society. His pass-key would admit him to the library at any hour of the day or night, a privilege not shared by ordinary members. He shaved, asked the housekeeper for a cup of coffee, pocketed the rough sketches of what he had seen under the microscope, and hurried off to the biological library. There he spent the five hours from seven till noon poring over biological atlases and massive treatises on the protozoa—those simplest of all animals.

With a sigh, as the clock chimed out a musical twelve, he closed his books and rose to prepare for his appointment with Crane. All his painstaking search had so far yielded no glance of a similarity between what was already known to science and what he had discovered. Thus far the outcome was encouraging. But the mass of ascertained fact about the humblest living creatures is so enormous that Brown estimated his good fortune at its precise value—nothing. A search of weeks would be necessary before he could assert confidently that he had made a vital discovery—if indeed he had.

His preparations for the approaching experiment with Crane were simple in the extreme. Having lunched at a cafeteria, he asked one of the girls behind the counter for a dozen raw, new laid eggs. Half of these were for the test, the other six to control the test. Part of the necessary apparatus he hoped to find in Crane's laboratory; the rest he must provide himself.

"Where can I buy a hen?" he asked the girl.

Thinking him slightly mad, the girl replied that there was a poultry market six blocks up the street. Brown thanked her and drove to the market. There he purchased the most motherly looking, clucking Buff Orpington on exhibit, a large slat coop to house her in, and loaded her on the back seat of his open car.

The spectacle of the well-known Doctor Brown threading his way through the traffic with an eloquent brown hen as passenger caused several traffic jams. However, he got his collaborator home safely and turned her loose in the walled back garden. Before leaving her to enjoy the tender young zinnia seedlings, he made a passable nest of excelsior in the slat cage and presented the prospective mother with half a dozen new laid eggs. With that attention to details which is half of scientific success, the doctor marked an indelible blue cross on each of the eggs, so that the 'controls' should not be lost among the mother's possible contributions.

"Do your stuff, Bertha," he counselled, carefully disposing three of the remaining half dozen eggs in each side pocket, "and I'll do mine. Good bye; I'm half an hour late already."

DURING the five hours that Brown was winding his devious way through mazes of the protozoa in the Aesculapian library, the man who had been Bork made rapid explorations into the wonders and mysteries of his transmuted personality. On reaching the main business street nearest his former lodging, he eagerly sought out a restaurant. The old Bork had always fought shy of breakfast, for obvious reasons. The new man was ravenously hungry. It was still very early. In his rapid walk he passed several cheap, all-night lunch counters, hesitated for a moment before each, and quickened his pace, to leave them behind as rapidly as possible. This swarthy young man with the strangely luminous eyes was fastidious to a fault.

At last he found what he wanted, a spotlessly clean, airy lunch room with white glass tables and a long cooking range under a hood and in full view of the customers. A girl in a white cap and clean white smock, her arms bare to the shoulders, was deftly turning flapjacks on a gasplate by the window. As the new customer entered, she glanced up from her work. Ordinarily a second's inspection of the men who passed her by the hundred every day satisfied her curiosity. There was an undefinable 'something' about this new man, however, which riveted her attention instantly. Unconscious that he was being watched, the swarthy young man walked to the far end of the room and sat down at a small table. A smell of burning hot cakes brought the girl out of her dream.

"That's somebody," she remarked to herself, but half aware of what she meant. She was right. This man was 'somebody,' not a mere 'anybody' undistinguishable in any significant way from tens of millions as commonplace as himself.

The 'somebody' was giving his order to an elderly man waiter who stood, pad in hand, trying to concentrate on his job. But he could not.

"Excuse me, sir," the waiter began diffidently, "but haven't I seen you in the pictures?"

"Pictures? I'm afraid I don't understand."

"The movies. I meant."

The 'somebody' threw back his head and roared with a deep, resonant laughter. It was an echo of the laughter of the gods. Early breakfasters turned in their chairs fascinated and amused by that hearty, good-natured shout, wondering what the joke was. Then they saw the young man's face and studied it openly, curiously. What was there about him that instantly attracted all who got a square look at him?

"He's not American," one man remarked to his companion.

"No, nor Mexican, in spite of his hair and complexion. Who and what the dickens is he, anyway?"

The embarrassed waiter stammered an apology.

"That's all right. No, you have never seen me in the movies, and I hope nobody ever will. Ask the cook to hurry that order, like a good fellow, will you? I'm starving."

Still unconscious of the sensation he was causing, the stranger casually inspected the simple decorations and general arrangement of the room.

"It just misses being good," he thought. "What's wrong? Everything is clean enough, and the fresco doesn't jar like most."

The day manager had just arrived and was taking up his position behind the glass cigar counter. Seeing a new customer, and a distinguished-looking one, apparently in need of attention, he walked down to inquire what he wished.

"Have you been waited on?"

"Yes, thanks."

"Is there anything I could do for you?"

"Probably not. It's too late now. I was just thinking that the architect missed a masterpiece by a mere hair-breadth. If this room were three feet longer, two feet narrower, and seven inches higher, the proportions would be perfect. The tables don't fit, even now," he went on, unconscious of the astonishment on the manager's face. "Don't you see," he continued earnestly, "what a stupid waste it is to bungle a room that might be perfect if only a little forethought—not afterthought—were given to its design?"

"Excuse me, but are you an artist?"

Again the answer was a shout of laughter.

"No," the swarthy young man replied, subsiding. "And I never will be so long as I keep what mind I have."

"Then may I ask what your profession is, Mr.——?"

The luminous black eyes seemed for a second to look back and inward. What name should he give himself? For the moment, although his mind worked at lightning speed, the new man had difficulty in recalling what his name had been.

Bork; that was it. Obviously it must be discarded.

His eyes roved to the cigar counter.

"De Soto," he said, slightly altering the name of a popular cigar advertised in red and gold on a placard behind the counter. The name would fit Portugal, Mexico, Spain or South America and definitely rule out the Orient. Some touch of the torrid south was necessary to explain his coloring. An Oriental in America might reasonably expect hostility in certain States, while Latins or South Americans would be accepted as human beings.

It was a wise choice.

"I hope you will drop in often, Mr. De Soto," the manager replied with more than the perfunctory courtesy of business. He meant exactly what he said, for he, too, felt a subtle attraction to this dark young fellow who was the picture of health, and who could laugh so infectiously.

"I shall be delighted, whenever I am in the neighborhood."

His breakfast arriving at that moment, further exchange of civilities was left to the future, and the manager retired to inspect the ledger.

" 'De Soto,' " he muttered to himself; "where have I heard that name before? Wasn't there an early Spanish explorer of that name? Still, this boy doesn't look Spanish, and he hasn't the trace of a foreign accent. He's somebody, whoever he is. I must ask him when he goes out what he does."

De Soto's breakfast was perfectly cooked and beautifully served, from the rare tenderloin steak and crisp French fried potatoes to the sliced oranges. It was the breakfast that a strong laboring man would have ordered—if he could have afforded to pay for it. No modern businessman or sedentary scholar could have looked it in the face. De Soto disposed of the last morsel. There remained only the black coffee—a reminiscence of the dead, shaky Bork. At the first sip De Soto hastily set down the cup. Even this mild stimulant reacted instantly on his perfectly tuned body. It was impossible for him to touch the stuff, and he finished his breakfast by drinking three glasses of water.

The sip of coffee had a curious effect on De Soto. Of what did it remind him? Someone he had known? No; that wasn't it. Everyone at the tables near his was drinking coffee and apparently enjoying it. Evidently it was a common and harmless indulgence. Then what was it that he was struggling to recall? It concerned himself, personally and intimately. Of that he felt certain. From the fast receding life which he had left behind him forever, a voice like that of a drowning man whispered "Bork". De Soto half remembered in a strangely inaccurate fashion.

" 'Bork'?" he muttered to himself. "Who was Bork? Ah, I begin to remember. He was the man—electrician, or something of that sort—who committed suicide some months ago by drowning himself. Where did he do it? I seem to recall that he drowned himself in his room, but that's impossible. I've got it! The Pacific Ocean. Was it that? How could it be—it's too vague. The Pacific Ocean might mean anything from here to——."

His thoughts broke off abruptly, baffled by his inability to recall "China". Not only his own past was being rapidly swallowed up in a devouring blank, but also much of his elementary knowledge of the world which he had acquired as a schoolboy. For a moment he felt mentally ill. He knew that he should remember, and wondered why he could not. Some silent comforter put solace in his way.

"I cannot have lost all of my mental habits," he thought. Setting his teeth, he reached for the menu. "Can I still read? If not, my intellect is gone."

He opened the elaborate card. The effect was electric. Instantly the long pages of close print registered on his mind as on a photographic plate. Without the slightest conscious effort he had read and memorized two large pages of heterogeneous, disconnected items in a single glance. He smiled and reached for the morning paper which the man at the adjoining table had left behind. As fast as he could turn the thirty-two crowded pages he scanned them at a glance, photographed every item, whether news or advertisements, indelibly on his consciousness, and digested the meaning of all. Curiously enough he believed that he had "always" read in this manner. An apparent inconsistency, however, caused him a moment's uneasiness. There was much in the morning's news about the fighting in China. Reading of China, he visualized instantly all that he had ever known or imagined about that country and its people. Why then was he unable to remember the name when he tried consciously to recall it?

"I must have the stimulus of innumerable associations to think about any one thing, I suppose," he mused. "What was I going to do when I came in here? Breakfast, of course. But what had I planned to do next? It was connected with that man Bork's trade. Electrician. That was it. I know now; I was on my way to ask for work where I can study electricity, X-rays, and all that sort of thing. Why, I have always dabbled in electricity. How stupid of me to forget. My stomach must be badly upset. Well, I'll dabble no longer. This time I go into it for all I'm worth. Where the deuce was I going?"

Suddenly the name Crane flashed into his mind. For no reason that he was capable of discovering, De Soto began to rock with uncontrollable laughter. There was a tremendous joke somewhere, but what it was all about he could not for the life of him say. Nevertheless he continued to shout with jovial laughter till the whole restaurant turned to stare at him. Aware of their puzzled faces, he made a pretense of reading the comic strips of the paper and controlled himself. It was time to escape before some shrewd busybody should guess the secret of his joke—which he did not know himself. That was the funniest part of it. Who and what was Crane? Whatever the elusive Crane might be, he was at the bottom of De Soto's haunting, mysterious joke. Calming himself, he beckoned to the waiter.

"Will you pay the cashier? I have no small change. Please bring me a telephone directory."

When the waiter returned with the change and the directory, De Soto tipped him generously and proceeded to look up Crane. There were several Cranes listed. Their first names or initials all seemed somehow wrong. De Soto closed the directory and let his mind drift. A single glance had sufficed to print the entire list of Cranes, their addresses and occupations, on the sensitive retina of his mind. One name, Andrew Crane, room 209, Erickson Foundation, seemed to stand out from all the others. Why? What was the Erickson Foundation? He decided to ask the manager on his way out.

"Can you tell me where the Erickson Foundation is?"

The manager gave clear directions for reaching it.

"What sort of a place is it?" De Soto asked. His tone implied that he wished to learn the public estimate of the Foundation, not what its specialty was. The latter, De Soto felt, might be a suspiciously ignorant question. Some monitor was prompting him to use caution; why, he could not fathom.

The manager, bursting with civic pride, enlarged upon the world fame of the Foundation, which was heavily advertised in the local papers. He even boasted that Doctor Crane had made the most powerful X-ray tube in the world, and was now nearly ready with a giant that would surpass anything the Foundation's jealous rivals could hope to produce for a hundred years—perhaps for two hundred. De Soto struggled again with that awkward impulse to burst out laughing. The manager concluded his booster talk by a direct personal question.

"Are you in the electrical line?"

"Only a student," De Soto replied instantly. "I plan to go into X-ray work as soon as I have finished my course." This straightforward reply seemed, to the man who gave it, to be the simple statement of an ambition which he had "always" held.

"Where are you studying, if I may ask?"

De Soto hesitated, nonplussed. Where, exactly, was he studying? Had he ever studied?

"Oh, I'm just reading by myself."

The moment he had uttered the words, De Soto knew that he had told a falsehood. Instantly he corrected himself. It seemed the only natural thing to do; the lie tasted worse than coffee.

"I meant to say," he apologized, "that I'm going to start my reading this morning."

"Oh," said the manager. Then, irresistibly attracted by this frank young man with the singularly penetrating black eyes, he added a word of heartfelt encouragement. "You'll make good. Some day we'll hear of you in the Foundation. Well, drop in again."

De Soto left the restaurant, followed by the hungry eyes of the flapjack girl and by those of every other woman in the place. Although he was now so far ahead of his past that to look back on Bork was impossible, he had a strange feeling of "difference". From whom was he different? The faces of the men and women he met gave him no clue. Many of the easy going Mexicans had hair as black as his, skins even darker, and eyes almost as black. Could he have remembered Bork's features to compare them with his own, reflected in the shop windows he passed, he would have noticed that his lips were fuller and redder than Bork's, and his nose more thoroughbred-looking than Bork's had ever been. His own nostrils were slightly distended, like those of a race horse eager to fill its lungs with all the fresh air blowing in its face, not close and pinched like Bork's. The whole "set" of the face bore not the slightest resemblance to that of the "dead" man. This was a countenance alive with purpose and the will to achieve it; the other was the peevish mask of a neurotic weakling. No feature of the "dead" man survived as it had been, and no trick of expression remained to betray the future to the past. But of this De Soto was wholly unconscious.

"Can you direct me to the Public Library, please?" he asked a traffic officer.

"Two blocks north—that way; three west."

He reached the library just as the doors were opened. At the reference desk he asked where the books on electricity and X-rays were kept. To his surprise the middle-aged woman in charge did not reply immediately. She could not. Something in this strange young man's face reminded her of a boy who had been dead twenty-five years. There was not the slightest physical resemblance between the features of this dark-skinned, singularly intelligent-looking young man and those of the boy whose face had almost faded from her memory. Yet the one passion of her desolate life flamed up at her again as if it had never died.

"I'll show you where they are, Mr.——"

"De Soto," he supplied, wondering why she fished for his name.

"Pardon me for asking, but are you related to the Stanley Wilshires?"

"Not that I know of. I was born in Buenos Aires, and all my people have lived there for generations. Why do you ask?"

"You reminded me of someone—not your face, but your look. I must have been mistaken. Here are the electrical books. The X-ray material is in the next stack. You may use that table if you wish."

"Thank you. I shall probably stay here all day, as I have a lot of reading to do."

The librarian walked thoughtfully back to her desk. "I could have sworn it was Frank looking at me again. How silly!"

Many a woman was to experience a like feeling on first seeing De Soto's face. What attracted them, or what recalled the men they had loved, they could not have said, for it was beyond simple analysis. It was not an instinct for sympathy, for De Soto's face suggested confident strength rather than sympathy. Possibly the secret lay in the message of superb, clear vitality that shone from his eyes, recalling the heightened manhood with which these starvelings, in the fondness of their imagination, had once endowed their lovers—before they learned that fact and wishful fancy are a universe apart. Here was a man who lived with his whole body, as they would have wished their lovers to live, not rotting by inches year after year into a lump that was human only in name.

While De Soto in the Public Library, and Doctor Brown in the Aesculapian, unaware of one another's existence, were unconsciously storing up ammunition for a grand assault on one of time's deepest mysteries, old Wilson precipitated the official suicide of Bork. On rising at seven o'clock to prepare his breakfast, the old fellow found the envelope with the rent. His eyes were still good enough to make out, in a hazy way, a ten-dollar bill. They also perceived that there was writing on the envelope. Poor old Wilson had a premonition of the truth: his precious lodger had decamped, and this was his heartless way of breaking the terrible news. Without stopping to get his breakfast he doddered over to his nearest neighbor's.

The obliging neighbor shouted the dire message, a word at a time, into Wilson's better ear.

"You had better tell the police at once."

"Eh?"

"The police. Tell them at once."

"You do it. I've got to find another fool to rent my room."

The neighbor obliged the old man willingly. The service would get his own name into print, a distinction which he had not yet enjoyed.

The ten o'clock "noon edition" of the evening papers gave the sublimated Bork a generous headline and toyed in audible whispers with the dead man's shocking allusion to crabs. They also, one and all, lamented the regrettable and undeserved notoriety which this suicide would bring upon the world-famous Erickson Foundation. For they had grown just a little tired of tooting the Foundation's siren for nothing, and decided now to recover their just dues by spreading some real news. To be worth printing, newspaper personalia must be spiced with more than a hint of scandal.

The Director of the Foundation first learned the facts from one of his enemies with a low taste for extras. This gentleman telephoned his sympathy—"I have just heard the distressing news. Oh, don't you know? One of your staff has committed suicide in a shocking manner—gave himself to the crabs. Who was it? Neils Bork. You say he was only a technical assistant? The newspapers don't mention that. This will be a terrible blow to the good name of the Foundation. Well, you may count on me to do what I can."

The Director preferred not to count on his friends. Instead, he got Crane on the telephone—following a long wait during which Crane hastily dried himself after his second stewing.

"What's all this about Bork committing suicide?" the Director snapped. "Suicide? I know nothing about it. You must be mistaken. Bork was all right when he left yesterday afternoon."

"The papers are full of it."

"Excuse me a minute. This is a shock."

Crane sat down suddenly on the chair beside the telephone and buried his face in his hands. In spite of his "kidding", he had liked Bork. For perhaps the first time he realized fully how deeply attached he had been to the surly fellow whom he had tried his best to make something of. Although reason convinced him that bad whiskey and not he was responsible for the tragedy, a deeper voice accused him relentlessly.

"If it is true, I'll see what can be done."

"Very well. Please come to my office as soon as you can. This will give us a black eye with the trustees unless we can hush it up."

"I'll be down in half an hour."

IV. THE WIDOW'S REVENGE

ON reaching the laboratory shortly after one-thirty, Doctor Brown found a note addressed to himself stuck to the steel door by a strip of adhesive tape. It was from Crane, stating that he was "in conference" with the director, Mr. Kent, and asking the doctor to come to Kent's private office.

Not having seen the extras featuring Bork's suicide, Brown wondered what was up. "In conference" usually meant a wigging for some unfortunate member of the staff. Brown knew Kent well and did not exactly respect him. Kent, whose talents were purely political and administrative, boasted only a high school education. For his particular job he was competent enough, although his outlook was essentially unscientific. In matters of unimportant detail he was a martinet of an extremely exasperating type. Being what he was, and not being what he wasn't, Kent found his domineering fussiness and his social cowardice hotly resented by the eighty highly trained men under his alleged control. But, as he was the chosen of the trustees, the scientists of the Foundation had to grin and bear him. In all fairness to Kent it must be admitted that he was highly efficient in the particular task for which the trustees had picked him. This was the rather ticklish job of coaxing superfluous cash from retired millionaires, who nervously foresaw their rapidly approaching passage through the needle's eye mentioned in Scripture.

The eighty under Kent's nominal kingship treated their malevolent despot with a mixture of amusement and contempt. As the least of them had three or four times the ingenuity and imagination that Kent could claim, they made of his life a very creditable imitation of hell. Baiting Kent became the favorite pastime of their idler moments. When research palled, these misguided men would put one of their number up to making some perfectly outrageous demand of the harassed director. Then, when Kent naturally refused, the petitioner would indignantly "resign". This always brought Kent to his knees instantly. To go before the trustees and admit that the Erickson Foundation was not a cooing dovecote of high-minded scientists, who were toiling only for the good of humanity under their director's brooding benevolence, was more than the poor man could face. Harmony and cooperation, service and uplifting self-sacrifice being the director's official slogan, he dared not confess that "his" men were a thoroughly human lot, with all the self-interest of the average man, and a perfect genius for making themselves, on occasion, as irritating as a pack of discontented devils. Kent would have been happier as manager of a five-and-ten-cent store, where he could have hired and fired with Jovian irresponsibility.

In spite of his tactlessness and his aggressive stupidity, Kent had one feature—if it can be called that—which redeemed him almost completely in the eyes of his subordinates. His nineteen-year-old daughter Alice, fair-haired, violet-eyed and altogether wholesome with her keen sense of humor, was adored by every man on the staff, from the tottering De Vries, seventy years old, but still with the mind of a man of forty, to the gangling youths fresh from the university and just emerging from their rah-rah, plus-fours stage of development.

But for the alluring Alice, it is doubtful whether a single member of the staff would ever have attended the tiresome teas and deadly dinners which Kent imagined it his official duty to inflict on his imagined slaves. Even a funeral or a college commencement, they agreed, would have been lively with Alice as hostess. Kent, for his part, worshiped her from heels to hair. It was rather pathetic to see the jealous care with which he hovered about her when some attractive young man seemed to be getting on too fast in her affections. The husband of Alice, if poor, futile Kent could choose him for her, would be so impossibly perfect as to be a mere platonic ideal. He secretly hoped that her disconcerting sense of humor would keep her a spinstress, at least until he was a handful of ashes in a white jar.

On entering the holy of holies, Brown found Kent and Crane glowering at each other across the broad expanse of a mahogany table that looked almost as if it were not veneer. Sensing that the interview was now at the resignation point so far as it concerned Crane, the doctor made a motion to withdraw, but Crane irritably motioned him to a chair.

"There's nothing private," he announced. "Mr. Kent and I have been discussing Bork's suicide. I'll be ready for your experiment in a moment—if Mr. Kent doesn't force me to resign."

"Bork's suicide?" the doctor echoed. Brown seldom bought an extra; the war had cured him of the vice.

"Yes. Last night. The facts seem to be clear. It's the ethics of the situation that are worrying Mr. Kent and me. I see it one way; he, another."

"You might compromise," Brown suggested. It was not the first time he had acted as liaison officer between Kent and his unruly staff.

"Precisely," Kent took him up eagerly. "We must cooperate. Doctor Crane, unfortunately, refuses to see the absolute justice of my stand."

"If he did," Brown smiled, "he would have to surrender, wouldn't he? I shouldn't call that much of a compromise. It takes two to dispose of cold crow, you know—one to dress it, the other to eat it. Who is the chef in this instance?"

Crane's long jaw set obstinately.

"I am," he assented defiantly. "Mr. Kent insists that the good name of the Foundation be preserved at all costs—even that of common decency to a dead man, who, naturally, can't speak in his own defense."

"Excuse me a moment," Brown interrupted, "but aren't you beginning to itch again? You see," he continued, turning to the glowering Kent, "Doctor Crane is rather irritable today. By working around his two million volt tube without even the precautions of common sense, he has got his skin and his temper into a very ticklish condition. Nothing serious, of course; merely hard on the disposition. So you will pardon his rudeness," the doctor concluded with a disarming smile, "if he forgets himself. Very well, Doctor Crane, go on; sorry I interrupted you."

"Mr. Kent has been listening to a lot of old wives' gossip. Somehow it had got around that Bork was a soak. Can you prove it, Mr. Kent? No? Well, then shut up. I mean exactly what I say," Crane continued, lashing himself into a passion and entirely disregarding the doctor's warning look. "If you dare to give the papers any such scandalous lie about Bork, I'll give them a better one about how you run this Foundation. You're not going to throw mud all over a dead man's name just to save what you think is the honor—it hasn't any—of this corporation. All the Erickson Foundation gives a damn about is the patents it gets out of its employees for the usual nominal fee of one dollar—and you know it. There is no question of ethics here. You have none, the Foundation hasn't any, and I don't know what the word means. Get the point? The best man—or the biggest crook—wins. That's all. This time I win; you lose. You give it out to the papers that Bork was temporarily insane from a nervous breakdown, or I'll resign and tell the yellow rags why."

CRANE had gone too far. His itching skin had betrayed him into a complete statement of the contempt—justified, perhaps—in which he held his job, the director, and the canny corporation for which he worked. The fact that he obviously meant every word he said did not lessen the enormity of his offense in the eyes of the outraged director.

"This," said Kent in a cold rage, "is insubordination. I would be quite justified in recommending your instant dismissal to the trustees."

Crane gave a short, contemptuous laugh.

"What do I care for your silly job? I can get a better one tomorrow. You know as well as I do that I'm the best X-ray man in the country. You see, I'm not fainting from false modesty. Call in your stenographer and dictate that letter to the papers. Otherwise you can have my resignation here and now. That's final."

"You heard him," Kent exploded, turning to the embarrassed doctor. "Is that a proper way for a subordinate to address his superior? I shall report him to the trustees. You are my witness."

" 'Superior' be damned," Crane cut in before Brown could attempt to restore diplomatic relations. "Are you going to dictate that letter to the press? Yes or no?"

"No," Kent snapped. But it was a half-hearted snap, such as an aged and ailing turtle might have given his persecutor.

"Then I resign," Crane announced, rising to his feet. "Explain why to your precious trustees. If you don't, I will."

"Sit down," the doctor commanded sharply. "You are both making fools of yourselves. The only excuse for you, Crane, is that you have let a little itching get the better of your temper. I know personally," the doctor continued, turning to the enraged director, "that Doctor Crane has the very highest regard for you personally and for your amazing success in running the Foundation. Can you afford to lose such a man—your most loyal collaborator? You know you can't. Why not compromise? Crane agrees to stay in exchange for a short statement from you to the press clearing Bork's name. Bork, I gather, has committed suicide in a fit of insanity brought on by overwork. Why not state the simple fact plainly, Mr. Kent? It is no reflection on the Foundation or on your policies. Hundreds of men work themselves to death every year in the United States alone. And why not? It's better than ossifying."

Kent glared at Crane, a hard, newborn hatred such as he had never before experienced toward his "subordinate" wrestling with his common sense. The thought that Alice seemed to prefer this lank, outspoken Texan with the uncompromising jaw to any of the other younger men on the staff, but added more fuel to Kent's cold, smouldering rage. By openly defying his nominal superior, and showing him up in the presence of a third party for the overstuffed effigy which he was, Crane had earned the director's lifelong enmity. Kent was shrewd enough in a shoddy, political way in dealing with human nature. He resolved on the spot to do everything in his petty power, by underhand suggestion and faint praise, to turn his daughter against this man for whom she had more than an incipient fancy. A dozen promising attacks flashed across his narrow mind as he scanned Crane's frankly scowling face, his own gradually assuming the bland benevolence of a well-steamed suet pudding. In more senses than one it was a historic moment, although neither man could possibly have foreseen the strange consequence of their mutual folly. Doctor Brown, mistakenly inferring from the director's expressionless face that the storm was over, managed to wink at Crane unobserved by Kent.

"I withdraw my resignation," Crane mumbled, rightly interpreting the doctor's wink. This row was to end as all such rows invariably ended, in a climbdown by the director. So Crane in his easy self-confidence imagined. As a matter of fact, he had not only cooked his own goose to a turn, but the unsuspecting Alice's as well.

Kent apparently swallowed the bait—again as usual. The magnanimous director rose from his swivel chair and walked clear round the table to extend to the contrite Crane the manly hand of forgiveness.

"And I," he promised with pompous solemnity, "will give the papers the simple truth that Neils Bork died a martyr to science, betrayed to death by his own zeal in the service of knowledge and the pursuit of truth." The director inflated his chest, and Crane smothered a grin. "As you have well said, Doctor Brown," he continued proudly, "the shoulders of the Erickson Foundation are broad enough, and strong enough, to support the truth, the whole truth, and nothing but the truth."

It was a rotund utterance, worthy of the fattest of the innumerable commencement addresses which Kent was in the habit of inflicting (by invitation of boards of trustees as progressive as his own) on successive generations of young skeptics, all over the United States, who have outgrown this particular brand of twaddle. Yet, such an indurated ass was the good director that for the holy moment he believed every word he said. What he truly meant, in his subconscious mind, was roughly as follows: "You, young man, have made a fool of me before this doctor friend of yours. I shall wait until your back is turned. Then I will stick my longest knife clear through you. And it will hurt, for I shall turn it."

Feeling that the honorable director was, after all, rather a slippery mackerel, the conspirators deferred their departure until Crane had the meticulously dictated lie to the press firmly in his competent right hand. As a further proof of their sound appreciation of the good faith of the born administrator, they lingered until the message was safely delivered to an eager reporter summoned by telephone. Then, and then only, did they venture to take their respectful leave.

"And to think," Crane remarked viciously, as the massive door of the inner sanctum closed noiselessly behind them, "that he is the father of Alice. It's impossible."

"Heredity is a theory," Brown admitted, "in this case, anyway, and environment an illusion. The Kent family alone would disprove half of our biological guesses. And I'm going to take a crack at the other half."

To Crane's wondering eyes the doctor complacently exhibited six large, clean hen's eggs.

"Here's my apparatus. You have heard of Watson's experiments with fruit flies? Well, I'm going to try something similar. Flies don't prove very much for human beings. Hens are nearer our own kind."

"But a hen is essentially a reptile," Crane objected vaguely, as some shadowy reminiscence of his high school biology flitted across his electrical mind. "Birds came from snakes, didn't they? And we branched off from monkeys."

"Go far enough back," Brown suggested lightly, "and you'll find our common ancestor where the mammals sprang from the effete reptiles. No matter how far back you look—provided you stop within a few ages of the protozoa, you won't find any of our cousins among the insects. We may not resemble hens very closely, but we are more like fowls than we are like flies. Watson's work was great as a beginning. It was tremendous. He discovered a new world. I want to take the next obvious step. Is your tube working all right?"

"It was when we quit yesterday," Crane replied, inserting his key in the lock of the green steel door. "What an awful smell! Do you get it?"

Brown sniffed critically.

"That's organic matter decaying. I should say——."

What he was about to add remained unsaid. A terrific odor gushed out at them, beating back their feeble assault upon the pitch darkness of the laboratory. Not to be defeated by a mere smell, Crane flung a flap of his coat over his nose and mouth, and groped desperately for the switch controlling the floodlights. The switch clicked its futile message.

"Dead," Crane exclaimed, referring to the lights.

"Check," Brown muttered through his handkerchief, imagining that Crane referred to the overpowering reek. "This is more than organic decay. Don't you get a metallic taste as well? What on earth——"

BROWN'S further observations were strangled in an involuntary croak of instinctive horror. He had followed Crane along the palpitating darkness of the steel gallery of the switches when suddenly, from the sheer blackness above him, eight clammy "arms", colder than the black death and slimier than a decaying tangle of kelps, descended upon his head, chest and shoulders in a loathsome embrace. Instantly he was out of the laboratory, struggling like a madman to free himself from that frigid abomination adhering to the upper part of his body with all the chill tenacity of a dead octopus. Crane followed, shaking from head to foot.

Once in the glaring sunlight, the horrified men saw in a flash what had descended upon the doctor. Crane tugged it from the doctor's shoulders and hurled it away with a shudder of disgust. It was a hideous knot of eight smooth, slimy black legs, each about four feet long, still adhering crazily to the tattered fragment of a huge black thorax on which the dull red imprint of an "hour glass" was plainly visible. The rest of the monster's body had already evaporated in foul decay.

In petrified fear they stood staring at the remains of this unspeakable abomination which seemed to contradict nature, but which in reality merely emphasized her commonest manifestation. The enormous size of those obscene legs was no more than the natural outcome of the sudden overthrow of a delicate balance holding normal growth in check. Destruction of certain glands in the human body, or misguided tampering with their perfectly adjusted excretions, might well result in a corresponding monstrosity of a man. What had suddenly shattered the mechanism of control in this instance? Neither man could guess, although Brown might have suspected, had he known the details of Bork's attempted suicide.

The full sunlight had a horrifying effect on the remains. First the smooth black legs swelled slightly, as if filled with an expanding gas. The crushed legs then stiffened and straightened slightly under the increased pressure, and the skin tightened. Was that horrible fragment trying to live and walk? The pressure increased, and the legs began to glisten as if recovering their vitality. Then the joints of all cracked simultaneously; the eight black husks collapsed under the escaping gas, and all rapidly withered, wrinkling in black decay, like the skin of a perfectly embalmed mummy suddenly exposed to the light and air after centuries in the cold darkness of its hermetic tomb. Within ten seconds only a tangled knot of shriveled wisps of skin remained.

The two men stared into one another's faces.

"Did you see it?" they panted together.

"I don't believe it happened," Crane muttered. "We're both crazy."

"But the smell? It's still pouring out of that door. We must see what is in there."

"Not without a light. I'll lock the door and leave you on guard. If anyone wants to get in tell them we have an experiment going, and say I asked that everybody keep out for twenty-four hours."

With shaking hands Crane locked the door and hurried off to the workshops. In ten minutes he was back, trundling an oxy-acetylene blowpipe with four cylinders of gas, half a dozen globes for the floodlights, and two electric torches. He had recovered sufficiently to minimize the danger.

"I thought we might want to clean up after we've seen what there is to see," he grinned, pointing to the blowpipe. "This will throw a four-foot jet of flame hot enough to scorch the devil himself. How are your nerves? The walk did mine good. After all there must be some simple explanation for whatever has happened. Anything that can be explained is nothing to be afraid of. Well, are you ready? We shall have to stand the smell." They knew that they were in an undiscovered world. Would either admit it? No. To be good sports in one another's eyes, they made light of their anticipated discovery. Such is science, and such is artificial human nature.

While Brown played one flashlight on the lintel of the steel door and spotted the other on the path that Crane must take through the darkness, the latter set his jaw and rolled the truck with the blowpipe up to the gallery of the switches. Then he hastily locked the door and left his key in the lock. The odor had decreased somewhat, owing to the partial airing the laboratory had received while the men stood viewing the dissolution of at least one of the dead enemy, but it was still foul enough. Tying their handkerchiefs over the lower parts of their faces, the two set grimly to work. Their first task was to obliterate every trace of nature's madness; theorizing on its probable cause would come later, if at all. For the moment they realized that nothing mattered but speed in sanitation.

Their first tentative moves were slow and cautious. Although the state of the air seemed to prove that no living thing yet lurked in the darkness, they did not rashly tempt death. Armed with the identical slat of white pine which Bork had used in his blundering attempt to electrocute himself, Crane cleared a path four feet broad for himself while Brown played the flashlights on the hideous things in his companion's way. In all sizes and twisted shapes of death, from balls of black legs no bigger than a rat to contorted monstrosities like enormous jet black spider crabs, the rapidly decaying victims of their own uncontrolled vitality cluttered every yard of steel galleries and cement floors, and depended in loathsome festoons from every railing.

A sudden thud in the darkness to their left, followed by a dry rustle, brought both men to an instant halt, their skins tingling with an unnatural fear. Sweeping his flashlight up to the ceiling, Brown saw what had happened. From every steel girder hundreds of the dead enemy hung in precarious equilibrium. Now and then one swayed slightly, its unstable balance shifting under the rapid progress of a ravenous decay that devoured the softer parts of the enormous body with incredible speed, and tilted the harder remnant of legs and carapace a hairbreadth downward toward the inevitable fall. Underfoot a thick, slippery scum of innumerable black bodies, from the size of wheat grains to mere specks barely visible, marked the sudden slaughter of a self-perpetuating host extinguished in the very act of seizing upon unnatural life.

How had they lived? On what had they fed? The long evil legs were mere distended sacs of skin filled with foul air. Had they swelled to their terrifying dimensions by assimilating the gases of the atmosphere and transmuting the dust particles of the air into the tenuous substance of their skins? It seemed incredible; yet, for the moment, no other explanation even faintly rational suggested itself. Presently Crane turned over two enormous black husks still intertwined in their death embrace. The hollow black fangs of each were sunk deep into the hard thorax of the other. Their first sustenance—whatever may have been its nature dissipated—the starving brutes had devoured one another.

"I killed a black widow in here yesterday," Crane remarked in a strained voice. "Or was it a thousand years ago? There must be some connection between that one and these. The mark of the red hour glass is on at least half of them. Those without it are the males. Look at those two—the bigger one has the hour glass, the other hasn't. The big one was the female; the other her mate. When she began starving to death, she tried to eat him, only he got his fangs into her, too. Then they both died. Does what I did yesterday explain this nightmare? You're something of a biologist; you ought to have a theory."

"I have," Brown admitted, "but it is worse than this nightmare. Don't go up that ladder! Some of them may still be alive."

Disregarding the doctor's horrified protests, Crane began climbing the vertical steel ladder against the side wall.

"Throw the light up ahead of me," he directed, pitching off two dangling carcasses from the fifth rung. "I've got to get up to the floodlights and stick in some new globes. Two will do."

He made his perilous way up to the steel girders, kicked a footway free for himself along the broadest, and coolly inserted a new light globe. As he screwed home the bulb, the light flashed on, revealing for the first time the full horror of that black shambles like a madman's dream of hell. Brown vented an involuntary shout, and Crane for a moment tottered as if about to lose his balance. Recovering, he walked coolly along the cross girder and screwed in the second bulb, about fifty feet from the second and directly over the pit of the transformers.

"Is that enough light?" he called down.

"Too much. I mean, I don't want to see it."

"You've got to, until we clean up this mess from floor to ceiling. While I'm up here, I might as well clear the rafters. You get a board and begin sweeping them into piles. There's a broom in the janitor's cupboard over there to the left."

For ten terrible hours they toiled in the noisome air of that nightmare tomb, sweeping the twisted black abominations into stacks, and applying the fierce white jet of the oxy-acetylene torch to each the moment it was ready. Nor did they neglect to spray the withering fire over every inch of the concrete floor. Some spark of vitality might still linger in the fine black sand of innumerable eggs, that had burst like capsules of ripe poppy seed from the bodies of the dead females.

At last, shortly after two in the morning, their gruesome task came to an end. Both men were sick from the foul, nauseating fumes, and exhausted of mind by their protracted battle with an enemy that had defied nature only to expire hideously.

"I dare not go to bed with that still in my eyes," Brown confessed.

"Nor I," Crane admitted. "Let's take a long walk and blow our lungs clean."

"That suits me. By the way, how is your skin?"

"Itching again. But I can stand it till morning. Anything would be bearable after that nightmare."

They emerged into the cool night air and filled their lungs.

"I never knew that air could taste like this," Brown sighed, exhaling and breathing deeply again. "Aren't you going to lock the door?"

"No. For once I'm going to break Kent's pet rule. This place must smell clean by morning."

"What about your tube? Somebody may come and tamper with it."

"That's so," Crane agreed. "Perhaps I had better lock up after all."

He reëntered the laboratory and turned on the lights.

"The tube's gone!" he shouted. So engrossed had he been in the business of destroying the enemy that until this moment he had not noticed his loss. "There's nothing left of it but the concrete stand."

Brown followed him down the steel stairs to investigate. They found nothing that threw any light on the mysterious disappearance of the two million volt tubes. Only a vitrified white patch on the flat top of the concrete stand hinted at some unusual disaster. An outgush of transcendent heat had fused the concrete into a glassy pillar. Glancing up, Crane saw the melted remnants of the connecting wires dangling from their support.

"Short circuited by some fool's carelessness," he muttered. "Whose?"

"Bork's?" the doctor suggested. "He would be the only man likely to experiment with your tube. None of the others have worked with it, have they?"

"No. Bork was the only man besides myself who ever touched it. If he did this, it was deliberate. No wonder he committed suicide. Probably he meant just to set me back a month or two and blew out the whole thing. Bork was always a bungler. This is what I get for trying to make a man out of a fool. Never again!"

They retraced their steps to the gallery of the switches.

"Look at that," Crane exclaimed, pointing to the long row of ebony handles pressed securely home. "He short circuited the whole battery of transformers, too. It will take a month to repair that fool's damage. He must have been drunker than usual. Then he committed suicide to escape going to the penitentiary. Well, he did one sensible thing in his life."

"What will you tell Kent now?" the doctor asked as they again emerged into the fresh air, leaving the door wide open. "Will you still stick up for Bork?"

"Why not? Calling him what he was won't restore my tube. And I shouldn't care if it did. Tomorrow I begin work on the twenty million volt tube. Someone will find the door open in the morning and report the damage to Kent. Then the papers will theorize that some enemy of the Foundation stole a key to the laboratory and did ten thousand dollars worth of damage at one swipe. I'll not contradict them."

They walked till sunrise, trying to purge their eyes and minds of the night's horror. The disappearance of the tube gave Brown a further clue to the mystery, but he did not confide it to Crane. Until he could learn more of the action of extremely short waves on living tissue he would keep his daring hypotheses to himself. In the meantime there was one simple check which he could easily apply.

Just as they sat down for coffee at an all-night lunch counter, Brown had a sudden thought which filled him with alarm.

"What did you do with the water in the bathtub after I left?"

"Let it down the drain, of course," Crane replied. "What else was there to do?"

"Nothing, I suppose," Brown admitted. "Only I wish you hadn't. It is probably diffusing into the salt water of the bay by now."

"You got a whole bottleful," Crane reminded him. "Wasn't that enough?"

"Plenty," the doctor muttered.

On reaching his house, the doctor carefully packed the bottle of water in his black bag and hurried with it to call on one of his friends, Professor Wilkes, a specialist at the university in the protozoa. Wilkes was one of those fairly venerable scientists who live on the reputations of their prime, do nothing, and look down their noses at younger, more aggressive investigators who accomplish something. His air was that of a once-nimble sand flea soured by experience; his once flaming hair had gone dull reddish streaked with gray, and his lean, angular body was a habitual protest against the radicalism—scientific—of the younger generation. The professor was just sitting down to breakfast when Brown burst in on him.

"Check me up on this, will you?" he began without preliminaries of any kind. "Either I'm losing my mind or this water is alive with microscopic protozoa new to biology. Until last night I wasn't sure of my guess—I searched all the books, but wasn't convinced by not finding any of these described. I might have overlooked known species mentioned only in out-of-the-way papers. Last night settled it. These things *must* be new—to the extent at least of being radical mutations from known species. Their life cycle is entirely different from anything yet described."

With a curious glance at his friend's face, Professor Wilkes abandoned his breakfast, gravely took the bottle of water, and preceded Brown into the study. Having carefully prepared a slide with a drop of the miraculous water, he then applied his eye to the lens and slowly adjusted the focus. For a full minute there was a tense silence, broken only by Brown's unsuccessful efforts to breathe naturally. At last the professor glanced up.

"Are you sure you have brought me the right sample?"

"Positive. Aren't they new species?"

"Look for yourself," the professor invited, rising and making way for his excited friend.

ONE look was enough for Brown. With a short exclamation he straightened up and rubbed his eyes.

"Have I dreamt it all?"

"Probably," Wilkes remarked drily. "Alter the focus to suit yourself. Take a good, steady look."

Brown did so, peering into the tiny speck of moisture which concealed his imagined discovery. In silence he prepared half a dozen slides and subjected them to the same pitiless scrutiny.

"I was mistaken," he grudgingly admitted at last. "That water is completely sterile. Unnaturally sterile," he added after an awkward pause, in which he reddened uncomfortably under the professor's sympathetic regard. "There's not a trace of organic matter in it."

"You boiled it and filtered it through porcelain?" Wilkes suggested kindly.

"If so, I don't recall having done so. In fact, I'm certain I did not."

"Perhaps your protozoa all dissolved of themselves," the professor hinted, with just a trace of sarcasm.

"Could *these* dissolve?" Brown demanded, suddenly exhibiting a sheaf of the drawings he had made.

The professor silently took the sketches and stood shuffling them through his long fingers, occasionally pausing with a faint smile to admire the imaginative beauty of some particularly exotic "animal". Without a word he handed them back. His manner plainly intimated that the interview, so far as it concerned him, was at an end.

"You think I never saw the originals of those?" Brown protested.

"My dear doctor, I think nothing whatever about them. My advice to you is to go home, go to bed, and stay there for a week. You have been over-exerting your mind."

Brown restored the despised sketches to his pocket.

"Would you ask one of your colleagues in the department of chemistry to analyze the water in this bottle if I leave it with you?"

The professor agreed good-naturedly, and Brown left him to finish his belated breakfast. The moment his eccentric visitor was safely down the steps, Wilkes carried the mysterious bottle into the kitchen, thoughtfully extracted the cork, and poured the contents down the sink. Then he threw the bottle into the waste can.

"Mad as a hatter," he remarked. "Poor Brown! It's a blessing he has no wife."

The professor's theory was partly confirmed by an amusing item in the morning paper. This was a hilarious account of the doctor's progress through the city with the voluble Bertha as his only companion. The writer concluded his graphic description with the hint that Doctor Brown, the hard-shelled bachelor, intended his triumphal ride as a gentle hint to the ladies of Seattle that he preferred the company of a fussy hen to their own.

"Mad," the professor repeated to himself. "I'm glad I never consulted him."

Crane was just about to retire after a thorough disinfecting, when the telephone rang. It was Brown.

"We actually did all that last night?" the doctor's perturbed voice inquired.

"I don't know what you mean by 'that', but I can guess. We did, if you have in mind what I have."

"Is it anything about spiders?"

"You might call them that."

"So it was real?"

"Real? I'll say it was. Until you loosen up and explain how it could ever happen, I'm going to think of it as the black widow's revenge. You said it fitted some theory of your own. Come over this afternoon and save my mind. I'll need you."

"Who is going to take care of me?" Brown demanded. "All that we did last night is nothing to what I've just done. I've proved myself a hopeless lunatic to the worst old gossip on the university faculty. It will be all over town by tonight."

Crane chuckled.

"We did such a thorough job in cleaning up that nobody will ever believe a word we say, if we let the least hint escape. You won't catch me letting it out. Better follow my example and sleep it off."

"I will, as soon as I have given Bertha her breakfast. By the way, what is the proper thing to feed a hen in the morning?"

"Spiders."

V. HIS JOKE

From the moment the librarian left De Soto alone with the electrical books till eleven o'clock at night, when the closing bell rang, the new man concentrated every ounce of his tremendous vitality on his self-appointed task. Had he been told that human beings—except a few of the most highly gifted—master the printed page a line or a paragraph at a time, he would have laughed incredulously. He himself had "always" digested the information in books by turning their pages as fast as his nimble fingers would let him, and taking in each page at a glance.

The first books, purely descriptive, that he photographed in this manner on his mind, irritated him almost beyond endurance. Why did the writers go to such tedious length to state what was trivially obvious? De Soto began to conceive a mild contempt for the science of electricity as expounded in college texts and popular treatises. In some indefinable way it all seemed an old legend dimly remembered from a forgotten life. The rudimentary knowledge of the universal forces of nature was as instinctive in him as breathing. Had he not 'always' recognized instantly the hidden interplay of natural things as intuitively as he perceived the noonday sun? Why then did these tiresome authors throw up an endless dust of words and irrelevant theories between themselves and the truth of nature that anyone but a blind idiot could apprehend? The amazing speed of his own vital processes made the laboriously acquired knowledge of generations of scientific men seem deadly slow and wilfully blundersome. Why could they not open their eyes and see what lay all about them?

It was only with the thirtieth book hastily sampled that De Soto's naïve conceit received a salutary check. He had just flashed through the massive bulk of Faraday's monumental "Experimental Researches" marveling at the man's painstaking labor to expound the obvious, when he encountered a new language, written in bizarre symbols, of which he could make out nothing. Exasperated by his failure to understand the writer's hieroglyphics, he glanced at the back of the cover to learn the author's name. It was Clark Maxwell, and the title of the treatise was "Electricity and Magnetism, Vol. I." De Soto rose from the table and went in search of the reference librarian. She greeted him at her desk with a welcoming smile.

"Are you finding what you want?"

"Some of it. Can you tell me what language this is?"

She glanced at the beautifully printed page and laughed.

"Higher mathematics, I should judge from its appearance."

"Have you any books on this sort of thing?"

"Several hundred. I'll show you where they are."

She left him to his own devices in a stack of shelf upon shelf of assorted mathematics, from beginners' arithmetics to appalling tomes on mathematical physics that were consulted, on the average, perhaps, once in two years by the patrons of the library.

"Do I have to read all these?" he muttered, turning the diagrammed pages of a descriptive geometry. "More stuff that need never have been printed. Why do they write it? Couldn't an idiot see that this is all so?"

In spite of himself, as he worked his lightning way steadily through modern higher algebra, analytic geometry, the calculus, and the theory of functions of real and complex variables, he began to become interested. Here at last was the simple, adequate language of nature herself. It was terse and luminously expressive in a highly suggestive way—unlike the ton or so of solid prose he had already digested against his will. What the italicized theorems left unsaid frequently expressed more than they purported to tell. De Soto found his own intelligence leaping ahead of the printed formulas, and revelling in the automatic interplay of the concepts their brevity suggested.

Gradually a strange, new light dawned on him. This beautiful language after all was but another shovelful of unnecessary dust thrown up by clumsy workers between themselves and nature. Why go to all this fuss to torture and disguise the obvious? Why not look ahead, and in one swift glance see the beginning and the end of every laborious, unnecessary demonstration, as but different aspects of one self-evident truth? All these imposing regiments of equations and diagrams, that marched and countermarched endlessly through book after book, were merely the fickle mercenaries of men too indolent to win their own battles. By a conscious exercise of its innate power the mind, if only it let itself go, might perceive nature itself and not this pale allegory of halting symbols. Did the writers of scientific books need all these lumbering aids to direct comprehension?

"The world must be full of idiots," De Soto sighed simply, putting back a profound treatise on the partial differential equations of physics. "Has it always been so? I can't seem to remember a time when I didn't know all this stuff by instinct. Still, as I have to live in the world, I must learn to speak its silly language."

There was nothing miraculous about De Soto's performance. A profound physical change in the structure of every cell in his body had accelerated his rate of living—or at least of thinking and perceiving—many thousandfold beyond that of any human being that has yet been evolved. He had not waited for evolution. A million years hence the whole race will no doubt have passed the point which he, by a blundering accident, attained in the billionth of a second. Whether language, mathematical or other, will survive to plague our descendants of the year 1,000,000, is doubtful. These feeble aids will have become as useless as the meaningless magic of our remote ancestors. De Soto was but a partial, accidental anticipation of the more sophisticated and yet more natural race into which time and the secular flux of chance are slowly transforming our kind.

Viewing the vast accumulations of lore which he had absorbed and spontaneously outgrown, De Soto felt old and depressed. What could he do in a world that still tripped itself at every step on its swaddling clothes? Although he did not realize what he was, he felt a chilling sense of poverty and isolation. Sobered in his exultant vitality, he turned slowly back to resume his pursuit of the mysteries of matter. He began where he had left off, with Maxwell's treatise. This was now as childish as the mathematics he had outgrown. Book after book of high speculation and curiously distorted fact passed under his lightning scrutiny, was mastered for what its author intended it to be, and tossed aside.

"Wrong, at bottom, every last one of them," was his somewhat presumptuous verdict as he closed the last, a modern masterpiece on theories of quanta and radiation. "Why will they not see what stares them in the face? The universe lies all about them, everywhere, and like impossible contortionists in an insane circus they succeeded in turning their backs on all quarters of it at once."

It was no harsher a verdict than many a man of science would pass today on the science of the Greeks, or even on that of three centuries ago. Are we as blind as De Soto imagined we are?

"What can I do?" he asked aloud. "If these are the problems they try to solve, how will they ever understand a real one?"

The jangle of the closing bell cut short his gloomy meditations, and he walked slowly out of the building. The crisp night air brought the blood tingling to his cheeks and forehead in a surge of stimulated vitality. Immediately he felt young again, and walked briskly down the brightly lighted boulevard leading to the civic center. The tide of night traffic brought some all but extinct memory of a former existence into momentary life. For one awful second he doubted his identity.

"Who am I?" he gasped, stopping abruptly before the plate glass window of a soda palace. "Am I insane?"

He caught his own reflection in one of the decorative mirrors of the window. It stared back at him, ruddy-lipped, swarthy-skinned, black-eyed and, above all, young with an air of perpetual youth.

"That is not my face," he muttered. "I was never like that. His hair is jet black. Mine is—." He stopped, unable to continue. "That man," he whispered, "is looking back on me from the farthest side of a grave where I was buried a million years ago—or where I am to be buried a million years hence. It is all the same. I am dead and buried, and yet I live."

THE 'lost' feeling dispersed as quickly and as mysteriously as it had come. De Soto turned from the window and walked with springy step toward a small park. Although it was now nearly twenty-four hours since he had tasted food, he experienced no hunger. He did, however, feel the need of sleep. Where should he lie down and rest? A glance at the unfathomable vault of the sapphire sky, ablaze with steady stars, convinced him that even the airiest room on such a night would be intolerably stuffy. His problem solved itself. A vacant bench under a fragrant chestnut tree, whose leaves rustled mysteriously in the soft breeze, invited him to rest. In five minutes he was fast asleep. The policeman in the park padded by as noiselessly as a cat, cast the sleeping young man a cynical glance, decided that he was broke but sober, and passed on, leaving him in peace.

De Soto slept about four hours, an even, dreamless sleep of complete refreshment. Waking fully and instantly shortly after four o'clock, he felt alive with energy and ready for a long day's work. It was still dark, without a hint of the coming dawn. The library would not open for nearly five hours yet. Suddenly De Soto realized that the library was not his goal, and never would be again. Of what value were all its dusty mountains of dead knowledge? He had mastered the best of its scientific offerings. If the rest—literature, philosophy, and art—was of no greater merit relatively than the cream of the science, it would not interest him. It was not worth inspecting. All of it must be like the science—the first, awkward effort of a race, that had discovered its mind but yesterday, trying to grasp the meaning of life, and failing ludicrously in the attempt. Libraries and all they signified belonged definitely to his irrevocable past—the gray age of a million years ago.

Hunger asserting itself, he rose to seek a clean eating place. He found what he wanted on the cross street opposite the park, a small place, but spotlessly clean.

Only the cook and one waiter were on duty. Neither gave him more than a casual inspection as he entered, for both were servants to the core without one spark of imagination to lighten their completely bovine lives. To such human beings all others appear as listless as themselves. The food was well cooked and neatly served. On these scores there was no complaint. Nevertheless, as De Soto sat sipping his final glass of water, he experienced a vague feeling of discontent. What had aroused his indolent animosity? Chancing to meet the waiter's eyes, he knew. It was the waiter and the cook.

"A pair of mistakes," he thought to himself. "What does either get out of life? They might as well be vegetables. Neither has any interest in his work or in his life. Why don't they do something different? Or why," he thought grimly after a moment's reflection, "don't they hang themselves? The cooks, the waiters, the manager and all at that place yesterday morning were different. They were alive, and enjoyed life—in their own way. But still they were enjoying it. That is the great point. These two are dead and they lack the genius to wish they were buried."

Without tipping the moribund waiter, De Soto paid his bill and left the place in disgust. His harsh judgment on the sad-eyed waiter and the harmless, bored cook was of a piece with his estimate of modern physics. They and it were alike useless, both to themselves and to any rational society.

Not only mentally but also physically De Soto was an entirely different being from the stupid, unhealthy Bork in whom he had originated. It is therefore no exaggeration to say that De Soto was only about twenty-four hours old when he left the discouraging cook and waiter, and stepped out into the cool, bracing air of the early morning. In appearance he was a strikingly handsome youth of twenty, with almost a preternatural intelligence shining from his black eyes and glowing from every feature. There was, however, a haunting 'something' about his whole expression which contradicted his vivid youthfulness. An elusive seriousness belied the faintly smiling lips, and a still less tangible shadow of extreme old age lurked behind the light shining from his eyes. It was as if he had seen everything that life on this planet will have to offer for the next ten thousand centuries and, having seen it, was ironically disillusioned by its meaningless futility. Another man having had a similar vision might have been lifted to ecstasy over the lightning progress of the human race; not so De Soto. It was merely a matter of temperament; the dead Bork had not been completely burned out of the living man.

"What shall I do?" he pondered, as his rapid stride hurried him through the darkness. "Is anything worth doing in a world like this? If everything seems stale to me, how can I make it appear fresh and desirable to others? There are too many of them—millions and millions and millions like that cook and waiter. They take everything and give nothing. Give them nothing and they ask for nothing, provided they be permitted to exist. Why permit them?" he continued coldly. Then, after a long blank in which he neither thought nor felt, his lips silently framed the unanswerable question, "Why should any human beings live?" The obvious retort flashed into his mind, "because they can and because they do." That, however, was not an answer to the 'why' as he meant it. His purpose was taking shape. Before many hours he was to decide what he should do with his inexhaustible health and his boundless talent. Rather, the transformed cells of his body were to decide. It was a decision such as our own distant descendants may reach some day—the verdict of an incredibly old and sophisticated man infinitely disillusioned.

He stopped abruptly in his walk, hypnotized by the strange familiarity of a massive, rectangular building, which loomed up forbiddingly before him in the graying darkness. Where had he seen such a building before? As if threading the shadowy mazes of a previous existence in a dream, he stole toward a sharp oblong of sheer black on the dimly visible wall. The door was open. Before he realized what he was doing, he had entered and turned the switch of the floodlights.

"Where have I seen this place before?" he muttered, staring down into the pit of transformers. Another memory struggled up from the wreckage of lost associations, but he could not place it. "There should be twelve lights up there, not only two."

His feet urged him to descend the steel stairway to the pit. The gigantic gray devils towering up on their rigid legs were familiar enough in a subtle way; he had seen pictures of similar monsters in the books at the library. Intuitively and from his comprehensive reading he knew immediately their evil powers and their uses.

"These are unnecessarily big and complicated," he remarked aloud, as if giving his considered estimate to some attentive listener. "Don't you see that you could build a single, compact one to do all that these forty can? All you need—." He launched into a rapid description, bristling with technicalities, of what was necessary for his projected improvements. For an hour and a half he roamed through the laboratory, examining every piece of apparatus, criticizing and contemptuously condemning each in turn. "A hopeless bungle," was his final comment as he ascended the stairs to the gallery of the switches.

Daylight was now streaming coldly in through the open door. De Soto walked to the switch to turn off the lights. The main switchboard controlling the transformers caught his eye, and he noted that the long row of ebonite handles were all down as far as they would go. This was no condition to leave a switchboard in, no matter if it was "dead."

As he opened the switches, his vision included the long bench beneath them. An empty cigar box lay open on the bench. De Soto picked it up, turned it over and over in his hands and finally set it down, his mind vaguely unsatisfied. It recalled nothing to him. Yet he had a chilly feeling that some incident connected with that box had marked the turning point of his life. With a sigh he left the laboratory.

"Where was I born?" he pondered, gazing up at the golden flush which presaged the rising sun. "When? Was it in Buenos Aires, as I told that woman in the library? How strange that I should have forgotten everything of my early life! This is what they call amnesia, I suppose. Well, what does it matter so long as I know who I am now? Yes, I must have forgotten. Let it go."

A neat inscription over the entrance to the building opposite him announced that this was the Erickson Foundation for Electrical Research, and a small tablet on the upper step added Administration Building.

"This is where I intended to ask for work," he remembered, as from a past inconceivably remote. Between this dawning day and its yesterday, when he had scanned almost in a glance the sum total of existing physical knowledge, lay an eternity in his maturing mind. The twenty-four hours had aged him so that he looked back on his yesterday's ambition as the uninformed dream of an eager child. Although he knew better now than to pursue his childish purpose—whatever it may have been—he adhered to his plan of working at the Foundation. Already his initial intention was more than half forgotten; his new purpose, he thought, would at least help him to pass the time.

No sooner was this resolve formulated than a queer echo made itself heard from the deepest recesses of his mind. "Will you pass the time," the doubter whispered, "or will the time pass you?" For a moment a chill conviction seized him that both possibilities suggested by his subconscious mind were to be fulfilled to the last letter, and that he was merely a helpless drifter on a black ocean without shore or tide. He quickened his pace to ward off the fingering chill that pattered over his whole body, determined to lose himself in vigorous exercise until he could call upon the director and ask for work.

WHILE De Soto was walking off his depression, Brown was endeavoring to sleep. All he achieved was a fitful nightmare till about ten o'clock in the morning. Giving up the attempt, he rose and made a deliberate effort to resume his normal habits. This morning should be like any other of his orderly life. He bathed, shaved and rang for the housekeeper to order breakfast. The doctor was an early riser—when he had not been up all night—and his first two hours out of bed were his time for loafing. No man, he was wont to assert, could hope to wake up fully in less than two hours. His period of relaxation was not wholly wasted, however, for he usually managed to read at least one article in the current scientific journals before going to work. For the moment he was determined to forget his nightmare in the laboratory and his own vanishing protozoa.

The morning paper was rather duller than usual, and Brown was just about to discard it in favor of the "Biological Review," when an unobtrusive paragraph on the last page caught his eye. "Fishermen report strange malady," the caption ran. The fish, Brown learned on reading the article, not the fishermen, were the sufferers. Moreover, only salt water fish were affected. The disease manifested itself in discolored blotches of all hues—blue, green, yellow, purple and red—on the skin and fins. The flesh seemed as firm and sound as ever. Probably, the report stated, the discolorations were harmless.

"Perhaps," Brown agreed, cutting out the paragraph. "More probably they are not. This must be looked into by the Board of Health. If the fish trust thinks it can get away with anything like this, it is badly mistaken. That story should have been printed on the front page."

A short conversation over the telephone set the appropriate machinery into instant motion. The Chief of Health promised to send out his squads at once to seize and destroy all spotted fish exposed

"That settles that," Brown remarked, picking up the "Biological Review." But was it settled? Only salt water fish were being affected. The doctor meditatively extracted the sketches of his despised protozoa from an inner pocket and stood thoughtfully regarding them. "Are they as mad as the professor thought? What if they are? Discoveries aren't made by 'safety first.' I'm going to do that experiment the minute Crane gets his twenty million tube built and going." He rang for the housekeeper.

"Will you make it part of your work," he requested the capable woman who responded, "to see that Bertha is well taken care of? It may be weeks until I have any use for her, but in the meantime I want her to hatch all the eggs she lays."

The housekeeper put a broad hand over her mouth and turned aside. When she recovered her composure, she ventured a practical suggestion.

"You might get Bertha a husband, if you want her eggs to hatch."

"Of course," the doctor agreed hastily. "Will you see to it?"

When she had retired out of earshot, Brown called up Crane's apartment.

"Hullo, Crane? Could you sleep? No more could I. How is your skin this morning?"

"Practically better. I can't understand——"

"Neither can I, yet. But I'm getting warm. Have a look at the last page of this morning's *Sun*. There's an interesting article on fish. By the way, when you take a bath hereafter, sterilize the water as well as you can before letting it down the drain. Better get a liberal supply of cyanide of mercury and put about a tumblerful into the tub when you are through."

"What for?"

"General precaution. That amount won't do any harm by the time it reaches the sea, and it may prevent a world of mischief before it gets there."

"Am I dangerously infected?"

"Probably not, in any mundane way. That's what makes you so interesting. Going to start work on your new tube this morning?"

"Yes, as soon as I have broken the news to Kent that he must spend about ten thousand dollars putting the transformers right again. Friend Bork did a rare job as his parting shot. I was just going down to the laboratory when you called up. By the way, never tell a soul about last night. I'm beginning to believe it never happened."

"I'm not advertising. If anything interesting happens, let me know."

On reaching Kent's outer office, Crane was greeted with ominous formality by the secretary.

"Will you take a seat, Doctor Crane," she said, "until Mr. Kent is ready to see you? He was about to send for you."

"Who's dead now?" Crane inquired flippantly.

The secretary ignored Crane's levity and merely stated that the director was "in conference" with the trustees.

"I guess I'm fired," Crane remarked to the ceiling. "If so, will you please tell Mr. Kent that I resigned last night?"

As the secretary deigned no reply, Crane moodily sat down and lost himself in brooding. The spectacular damage to the transformers, he guessed, was the inspiration of Kent's untimely session with the trustees. They would naturally blame him for having left the door unlocked. "Well, he could not prove that he hadn't. Let them do what they liked; he didn't give a damn. In spite of his assumed indifference Crane realized that a dishonorable discharge from the Foundation would cut pretty deeply into his self-respect. Moreover, now that he was about to be fired—as he imagined—he suddenly conceived a warm affection for the Foundation and for every member of its staff, except of course Kent. A resonant voice asking for an appointment with the director caused him to look up.

The secretary was staring in fascination at the dark, intelligent face of the man addressing her, unable, apparently, to follow his question. Like the librarian she was wondering where she had seen this striking man before, although she was in her early twenties with no disastrous love affairs in her past.

"Will you please make an appointment for me with the director?" that elusively musical voice repeated.

"As soon as Mr. Kent is free," she murmured, "I know he will be delighted to see you, Mr.——"

"De Soto."

"Will you wait here? Mr. Kent is in conference."

"Must I wait? I should prefer to see him at once, as I have a full day ahead."

"I'll see," she volunteered. Then it occurred to her that she did not know the young man's mission.

"Mr. Kent will ask me your business." She all but apologized for the indelicacy.

De Soto unfolded a morning extra and indicated the joyous headline: "ERICKSON LABORATORY DESTROYED." Of course the laboratory was not destroyed; the giant transformers were only disabled. To have stated so in cold print would have killed the story. On this occasion neither the director nor the trustees were reluctant to confide their misfortune to the press. The janitor early discovered the open door; a short investigation by members of the staff, summoned from the workshops, disclosed the extent of the damage. Too obviously it was the work of an enemy from the inside. Kent, at the moment of De Soto's appearance, was endeavoring to convince the trustees that Crane was guilty.

"He practically told me to go to hell," he vociferated. "And he said he cared nothing for what he called his 'silly job.' "

"Why not ask your secretary to call him, Mr. Kent, and ask him whether he did it?"

Kent was game. He pressed a button. The buzzer called just as De Soto unfolded the extra for the secretary's gaze.

"I have called about the damage to the transformers," he explained. "Please tell Mr. Kent that."

"I will," she promised, and hastened to answer the insistent buzzer.

All the time that De Soto stood parleying with the secretary, Crane studied him minutely. By one of those common but unaccountable quirks of human nature that often mystify us, he took an immediate and violent dislike to the swarthy young man with the peculiar voice. Possibly Crane's own frigid reception by the secretary, contrasted with De Soto's, may have touched the hair trigger of his masculine jealousy and self-love, although the secretary was nothing to him. Ordinarily he treated her as a pretty piece of furniture. Whatever the cause of Crane's instinctive dislike, the feeling itself was not to be denied. That it was primitive and irrational but made it more significant. Crane followed the young man's every movement and listened avidly to every changing inflection of his voice. Had he been capable of self-analysis he would have summed up his conclusions somewhat thus: "That young man impresses me as a thoroughly bad egg. I'm going to watch him."

When De Soto asserted that he had called about the damage to the transformers, Crane's curiosity naturally was aroused to the point of acute physical discomfort. Left alone for a few minutes with the young man, Crane decided to break the ice.

"You are an electrician?" he demanded of De Soto's back.

De Soto wheeled about sharply and found himself looking up at a rather grim, square-jawed face on which more than a hint of hostility showed. Before he knew what he was doing, De Soto found himself rocking in uncontrollable laughter. Do what he would to stop his rude mirth, he failed. What was the joke? Why did the man's face awaken the haunting sense of the ironically ridiculous? No ghost of a memory whispered to remind De Soto of his past. Yet, what he planned to do with his unbounded talents for the good of humanity seemed irresistibly ludicrous, and the humor of the situation was focussed in some mysterious way on the disconcerted face looking down into his own. Crane stood it as long as he could.

"If you'll tell me what's funny, I'll laugh too. Go on; don't mind me."

De Soto gulped and subsided—outwardly.

"I was laughing at you taking me for an electrician," he explained glibly. "In a way I am, although radiations of the shortest wavelengths—ultra violet, X-rays, gamma rays, and so on, clear into the region of the hardest cosmic rays—are my specialties. You see, I have graduated from electrical engineering. That is what you thought I was interested in, from my remark to the secretary about the transformers. That's merely to help me into a job here."

"You say you have worked in the cosmic rays, and even beyond?" Crane demanded suspiciously, scenting a quack in this plausible young man. "I don't seem to recall the name of De Soto in that field. Where did you do your work, if I may ask?"

De Soto submitted to the unwarranted cross-examination with a good grace.

"In Buenos Aires."

"At the Universidad Nacional de Buenos Aires?" Crane suggested skeptically. He knew perfectly well that the national university of the Argentine offered no work in the field De Soto claimed as his own. De Soto, however, whether from accident or design, sidestepped the rather obvious trap. Unknown to himself, he was lying and lying quite ably. The hastily imagined fiction of his birth in Buenos Aires, which he had invented but a few short hours previously, was already a fixed part of the life he had "always" known.

"No," he replied. "I did all my studying privately."

"Self taught?" Crane suggested in much the same bantering tone he might have used to Bork. De Soto ignored the hidden slur.

"Why not? What are books for?"

"So you never have worked in a laboratory?"

For a moment De Soto was at a loss. He *had* carried out electrical experiments. But where? Somehow the sure feeling of familiarity with electrical apparatus, of which he felt confident, did not date with the rest of his self-acquired education. Doubtless his inability to connect the two was but another trifling instance of the amnesia from which he seemed to suffer. Trusting that he was telling the truth, he gave what appeared to him at the moment as the only reasonable answer.

"I had a small laboratory of my own."

Crane received this in silence. Further cross-examination was postponed by the return of the secretary. She had been urging De Soto's priority over Crane's in the matter of an interview with Kent and the trustees.

"Mr. Kent will see you now," she announced, nodding to De Soto.

Followed by the suspicious eyes of Crane, De Soto disappeared into the inner sanctum. Crane favored the secretary with a sour look and resumed his chair. Whether they fired him or not, he was not going to leave until he learned De Soto's object.

Once in the director's sanctum, De Soto found himself the mark for seven pairs of questioning eyes. Kent rose from his seat at the end of the long table, his hand extended in formal welcome, while the six trustees turned in their chairs to get a better look at the newcomer.

"You are from the press, Mr. De Soto?" Kent inquired.

"No," De Soto laughed. "I came about this." He tapped the article about the damaged transformers. "The papers say there is a hundred thousand dollars worth of mischief done."

"Exaggerated," one of the trustees interrupted. "Ten thousand will cover it."

"What I propose is this," De Soto continued, acknowledging the trustee's remark with a slight nod. "For not more than a total outlay of five thousand dollars you can duplicate your whole battery of transformers. Now, this is what I suggest. Spend five thousand dollars, and I will show you how to do everything your high tension laboratory ever did, or ever could do—provided you were to repair the damage. Moreover, the entire apparatus will not exceed a cubic yard in bulk."

Kent glanced at the trustees with a wan smile. His irreproachable secretary, departing from her habitual caution, had admitted an impossible crank to disrupt a most important conference. The quality of Kent's smile slowly changed. It became puzzled. Why, precisely, had he and the trustees listened so attentively to this swarthy young man's preposterous claims? A trustee cut the knot.

"Can you make good on what you propose?" In spite of his shrewd business sense he was strongly attracted by this magnetic young fellow's personality and the strangely luminous, rational glow of his eyes. "If you are not talking nonsense, you should be able to convince experts. Want the chance?"

"Experts such as you have," De Soto replied with truth but unintentional rudeness, "probably wouldn't understand my plans. However, if you wish, I will try to explain."

"Ring for Doctor Crane," the trustee snapped. "I believe Mr. De Soto knows what he is talking about."

At the mention of Crane's name, De Soto controlled a strong impulse to laugh. When Crane entered, glum as a naughty boy expecting a reprimand, De Soto turned his back on him. All through the ensuing discussion the man who had been Bork never once looked his former chief in the face. Some uneradicated instinct held him back, although consciously he had not the shadow of a memory of his former enemy and would-be friend.

THE lively talk began with a trustee's suspicious questioning of De Soto regarding the young man's scientific training. De Soto repeated smoothly what he had already palmed off on Crane, adding several circumstantial details. The story, strange as it seemed, hung together. The trustee, unconvinced, let it pass at its face value. After all, what did it matter who or what the man was, provided he concealed an inexhaustible mine of diamonds under his thick black hair? If he could do what he claimed in the matter of the transformers, this attractive young man must be an inventive genius of the very first rank. At the rate of one dollar apiece for all patents taken out while a member of the staff, De Soto might well be worth several hundred million dollars to the Erickson Foundation before his contract expired. The worldly wise trustee was already rehearsing the terms of the ten-year contract which would sew up De Soto tighter than any dead sailor about to be slipped overboard ever was.

From personalities the discussion soon launched into a bewildering debate of technicalities between De Soto and Crane on the design of high tension apparatus, the construction of more efficient insulators, thinner than the thinnest tissue paper and, most important of all, an entirely novel process for attaining a perfect vacuum. Even to the untechnical trustees and the unscientific director it was evident that the best of the argument was De Soto's from start to finish. As Crane interposed one objection after another, only to have each demolished in turn by a short sentence backed up by a shorter mental calculation, De Soto began to lose patience with the slowness of the expert mind. Finally, turning to the director in exasperation, he asked whether there was one—only one—competent physicist in the Foundation. Kent silently pressed a button. To the worshiping secretary he explained that Mr. De Soto wished to confer with Doctors So-and-So, naming the cream of the specialists enslaved to the Foundation.

They dribbled in by twos and threes, until a full dozen found themselves involved in the most terrific battle of their distinguished scientific careers. By ones and twos they were eliminated temporarily by hard facts or harder formulas hurled at their heads, only to rally for the next attack and be again knocked flat. Whether De Soto was right on his new theories, or on his novel project as a whole, was beyond their powers to decide. There was no doubt, however, that he had all the classical theories and current experiments—old stuff, in his contemptuous phrase—at his finger tips. Lunch time had passed long since; the dinner hour came and went unnoticed, and still the battle raged. At last, shortly before midnight, De Soto had sunk his last opponent. On many of the details of his project they were still unconvinced, but they had shot their last round.

The signing of the contract followed as a matter of course. Departing from their invariable custom, the trustees guaranteed to De Soto royalties of one per cent on all inventions patented by him while a member of the staff, in addition to the usual legal dollar. Argument with such a man might prove more costly in the end than graceful submission. They gave in before he could have a chance of offering his talents to some less greedy competitor.

While De Soto was affixing his signature—Miguel De Soto—to the contract, Kent buttonholed the President of the Board, and poisoned that potentate's mind against the defenseless Crane. All of Crane's flippancy in the face of duty, his flagrant disrespect for decent authority, and finally his heinous offense in leaving the door of the high voltage laboratory open, and so causing thousands of dollars worth of damage, were poured into the President's exhausted ear.

"You want me to ask for his resignation?" the President suggested. "Is that what you're driving at? Give the word, and I'll do it. We have just taken on Mr. De Soto at ten thousand a year *plus* those robbing royalties. Why not save Crane's salary? He's of no further use to us that I can see. Mr. De Soto's field includes Crane's, I gather?" Kent nodded. "Then say the word, and I'll give Doctor Crane his walking papers."

"It might cause criticism if it got out," the cautious Kent demurred. He saw his chance of sticking his longest knife into Crane, and he determined to seize it. In fact, he had worked on the President with just this purpose in view. "Why not cause him to resign voluntarily?"

The President all but grinned. "How?"

"Tell him that henceforth he is to act as Mr. De Soto's assistant. Say that we all know how proud he will be to work for so great a scientist as this extraordinary young man has proved himself to be. Don't mention a word about salary. Put it on the purely scientific plane of service."

"Leave it to me."

De Soto stood talking to three of the trustees as the President descended upon Crane. Speaking in a loud voice so that none of the technical staff present should miss the obvious moral, the President delivered his honeyed ultimatum. The faces of the twelve men of the staff went blank; those of the trustees beamed. Here was Crane's chance to show his mettle. The technical experts prepared to offer their own resignations the instant Crane refused the insulting offer; the trustees wondered whose fertile mind had conceived this neat method of firing a faithful employee whose services were no longer as profitable as they had been. Crane's immediate response took all parties completely aback.

"Thank you, Mr. President," he replied gravely. "I shall be honored to serve as Mr. De Soto's technical assistant. And I shall never forget your generosity in giving me this opportunity of showing my loyalty to the Foundation and to Science."

Kent's jaw dropped. Crane's rounded speech of acceptance was a first class imitation of what his own might have been under similar circumstances. What did that long, lean devil of a Texan mean by it? Was he forcing them to fire him outright, like men? Well, they weren't such fools. They would put no shovel in his hand to fling mud at the Foundation. So much for Kent. The President shot him a spiteful glance as if to say, "You've made a fool of me. Two can play that trick, as you will find out before long." The members of the staff looked anywhere but at Crane. They would have backed him up to a man. Who would have suspected him of having a yellow streak? So much for Crane's former friends. De Soto extended his hand in friendly congratulation. Crane shook it vigorously. So much for the conventionalities.

What of Crane? He meant every word he said. That he had phrased his acceptance in fatter rhetoric than he usually fancied was merely the luxury he allowed himself of insulting Kent before the trustees. Crane knew exactly what Kent was trying to do, and he dared his petty tyrant to do it like a man. As for the coldness of his scientific friends, he felt that he could endure it as long as they. It was of no great moment. The one thing that sustained him was his instinct that De Soto was evil to the core, with a black, new evil, venomous beyond human experience. Did not any of the others feel what he sensed with every nerve of his body? No, he admitted; they probably did not. The trustees were blinded by the profitable bargain they had just driven with the new man, the technical experts by his scientific brilliance. All, Crane felt, might more sensibly have sold themselves for thirty cents to the devil. Their gain was a fool's. Although he had no definite feeling as to the precise way in which De Soto was a thing of evil, Crane knew that his silent estimate was just. Until he or the Foundation went under, he would stick by the ship and save all he might. His motive was not love for a corporation which had treated him scurvily, but intense dislike, amounting almost to hate, for the dark young man with the piercing eyes who henceforth was to be his driver.

On passing into the outer office they found Alice waiting to drive her poor, tired father home. Kent seized the opportunity of further humiliating Crane by presenting De Soto to his daughter with a great show of arch-fatherly effusiveness. Crane observed the comedy, nodded curtly to Alice, and strode out of the building. To overtake his departing enemy with a last barbed dart, Kent raised his voice and insisted that De Soto be his guest for a few days until he found comfortable quarters near the Foundation.

Two minutes later Kent's car overtook Crane. Alice was driving; Kent was spread out on the back seat. De Soto, sitting up in front by Alice, seemed to be progressing rapidly with the director's daughter.

"That fool!" Crane muttered. "Can't he see what De Soto is? I don't mind being snubbed. But it is a bit thick when he uses Alice to do his dirty work. Well, if she is that kind, I'm not a sentimental sap. She can go to——."

An hour later, De Soto stood as still as a rock on the cork mat of the bathroom in Kent's guest suite, staring with unseeing eyes into the mirror. He had just enjoyed a luxurious bath. The director had kindly lent him a suit of pyjamas, smelling faintly of lavender, and a soft shirt and socks of his own for morning. De Soto had explained that his things were in his room at a distant hotel. In the morning he would lay in a complete outfit. For the moment he was lost in thought, or rather in an ecstasy of pure existence which was neither thought nor sensation. The warm bath had stimulated his circulation, and he was, for the time being, a perfect animal and nothing more. No spark of human intelligence kindled the black eyes staring into his own from the plateglass mirror.

Presently he sighed. Realization of his circumstances and of what he had accomplished during the past twenty hours overwhelmed him like a whirlwind of fire. The eyes in the mirror leapt into life, flaming up from the dead blackness of incredible age to the piercing gaze of intelligence incarnate in perpetual youth. His purpose came back to him. No longer merely a faultless animal, he had remembered his humanity and all that he intended for his fellow human beings. He remembered also the trustees and the director, and the bargain they had driven with him. For an instant his face clouded with fierce scorn. Then he began to shake with silent mirth. His secret joke, multiplied a billion-fold, had returned to comfort him.

"Millions and millions and millions of them," he thought, "like that cook and waiter, and millions more like Crane, those trustees, that director, and his daughter."

Still shaking with suppressed laughter he stole into the bedroom as noiselessly as a tiger and went to bed.

VI. DISCHARGED

SIX months after he began work at the Foundation, De Soto found himself world-famous. Although he never read a newspaper, he could scarcely avoid seeing his name at least once a week in the headlines as he passed the newsstands. He had out-edisoned Edison and out-invented all the electrical inventors of the past seventy-five years—according to the press. Remembering that the papers made a hundred thousand dollars worth of damage out of a paltry ten thousand in the matter of the transformers, we may safely discount these early reports to about ten per cent of their face value. When, some months later, De Soto began doing things of greater significance for humanity—things that could not be evaluated in terms of dollars and cents—the press was dumb, and for a sufficient reason. As long as the new so-called luxuries and conveniences of living which De Soto created, seemingly in his sleep, inspired the journalistic tongue, reporters and editors were on familiar ground. But when De Soto, tired of playing Aladdin's lamp to millions who rubbed him the wrong way, turned to the higher and more difficult parts of invention, the world simply did not realize what was happening to it.

DE SOTO'S masterpiece was new in human history. To find its peer we should probably have to go back at least as far as the beginning of geologic time. The human race, in De Soto's vaster enterprises, was merely a rather minor indiscretion on the part of mother nature. But for the first six months of his dazzling career as the king of inventors, Miguel De Soto lived up as best he could to what, he sensed, a somewhat pampered world expects from its geniuses. They asked him for bread and he gave them cake. The necessary physic after such a debauch of sweet stuff was to come later, when they were surfeited.

In extenuation of his subsequent career, it should be remembered that De Soto suffered from a blind spot in his mental vision. Like many men of great talents he at first had mistakenly believed that the world sincerely wished to better itself. If so, why shouldn't it be eager to reach the best possible state in one quick stride, instead of blundering this way and that like a drunken imbecile and getting nowhere in a thousand years? De Soto here made the usual mistake of the super-intelligent in thinking that his own clear vision would satisfy the blind.

The first six months at the Foundation passed like a Persian dream before the half closed eyes of the purring trustees. Without the least suspicion that their brilliant young employee was feeding them all this unnecessary wealth for purposes of his own, they squatted like drowsy bullfrogs on a warm summer day in their golden swamp, expanding their already enormous business and swelling to the bursting point with financial pride. The fatter they grew the faster they bloated. But De Soto, like the true artist he was, deferred the adroit pin prick which would deflate them all, until power had become a fixed habit with them and inordinate expenditure their means of keeping alive.

One example of De Soto's methods will suffice. It is already a classic the world over, but its retelling here may throw some light on his general campaign, which even now is not well understood outside of a very narrow circle. His first great financial triumph was a mere byproduct of his toy transformer and storage battery—the project which got him his appointment to the staff of the Foundation. He had undertaken to emprison twenty million volts in a small box, and to control his trapped devil in any way the trustees desired. In short, he promised to put the elaborate twenty million volt laboratory, and all of its rivals, completely out of business, and to do it for an expenditure not exceeding five thousand dollars. When the trustees remembered that their high tension laboratory had cost close on three million dollars, they saw the most obvious commercial possibilities in a flash. Although there was as yet no practical use for such a devil box as De Soto promised to deliver—unless the military and naval authorities might be tempted to flirt with it, the trustees had faith enough in pure science to believe that somehow, some day, the dollars would gush out of that evil box. Some young man as brilliant in a practical way as De Soto seemed to be scientifically would come along like Moses with the right kind of stick in his hand. Then, with one resounding smack, he would smite the useless black box, crack it wide open, and let the golden deluge drown the trustees in dividends.

De Soto did not wait for a greater than he to enrich the Foundation beyond its thirstiest dreams. He did it himself, almost in his sleep. One detail must be settled before the box itself could be constructed.

This was a revision of the whole theory and practice of insulation. The huge strings of earthenware mushrooms that made the long distance transmission of high voltage possible obviously would not do. The high tension lines from the mountains to the cities carried but a paltry two or three hundred thousand volts; De Soto must handle twenty million. To insulate against such a pressure with glazed earthenware, or with any of the known substitutes, would require a mass of dead material equivalent to several hundred times the small box into which De Soto planned to compress his entire apparatus, insulation, transformers and all.

Following a hint he had absorbed in his exhaustive reading, he saw that the true way out of the difficulty was not the building of more and more massive resistances of earthenware and the rest, but the practical construction of material films thinner than the most tenuous soap bubbles. These must be manufactured cheaply and deposited directly on the wire carrying the high current as an invisible sheath not over a few atoms in thickness—the thinner the better. With Crane's help, De Soto had perfected the working drawings and specifications of the process three days after he joined the Foundation. The plans were turned over to the technical staff for practical development, and in two weeks the Foundation had staked out its first El Dorado.

To their surprise, the trustees discovered that De Soto was an adept in the finesse of service as understood by them. It was his campaign that they launched against their innocent competitors. The Klickitat Lake Municipal Power Company, having just completed its giant power plants in the Cascades, was calling for bids on the insulation of its three hundred thousand volt trunk line. De Soto saw the Foundation's great opportunity and, incidentally, his own. The Power Company belonged to the people of Seattle. It was a public enterprise, supported entirely by taxes. By eliminating dividends to stockholders, the public hoped to obtain its power and light at a cost much below the current rates. Why not, De Soto suggested to the trustees, donate the required insulation to the public? The trustees saw the light and smothered their indecorous grins. By presenting the public with a few thousand dollars worth of the new insulated wire, and saving the oppressed taxpayers several hundred thousand, the Foundation would net an incalculable amount of free advertising and the good will of the people.

The engineers of the Municipal Power Company came, saw a four days' demonstration, and were conquered. High steel towers, tons of insulation, and expensive copper cables were all replaced by a thin wire sheathed in the new film and suspended from trees, telephone poles or broomsticks as convenient. In the words of their chief, it was a knock-out. It was. In five weeks the Erickson Foundation had a monopoly on insulation the world over, and one great corporation after another, from San Francisco to New York, from Manchester to Brussels, went flat.

This was but the beginning. De Soto, with Mephistophelean ingenuity, talked the not ungenerous trustees into trebling the price of the new, simple insulation the moment their strongest competitor collapsed. Having created a new necessity of modern life, the Foundation had the electrical industry at its mercy. To their credit it should be recorded that the trustees did not yield without a short struggle to De Soto's cynical importunities. Their profits already were outrageous; why make them sheerly indecent? De Soto could have enlightened them in one sentence, had he felt inclined. But the time for the dazzling revelations of the surpassing splendor which was to burst upon the trustees was not yet ripe; first they must be educated. They could not withstand this frank young man's magnetic charm. One and all they agreed that he was irresistible. He was.

All that De Soto asked in addition to his modest salary and rapidly mounting royalties was the time occasionally to undertake a piece of pure, unpractical research. As these short excursions into science for its own sake always resulted in some radical improvement of existing luxuries that sent whole businesses to the wall, the trustees humored him. There was the little matter of high vacua, for example. De Soto begged for a ten days' holiday in which he began his explorations of the hardest cosmic rays. First he must obtain a practically perfect vacuum. The so-called vacua of hard X-ray technique, where billions of molecules of gas remain in each cubic inch after the diffusion pump has done its utmost, were of no use in his project. He needed a tube from which all but a hundred or two of the ultimate particles of matter have been withdrawn. Again Crane and other members of the staff helped him with the mechanical details, and again he triumphed completely.

As a byproduct he revolutionized the industry of making electric light globes and radio tubes, cutting down the cost of exhausting these to a fraction of a per cent of what it had been. The trustees beamed on him, and told him to take a year's vacation if he wished. With a subtle smile, which they failed to interpret correctly, he refused. Later, he said, he would take a real holiday. They thought he was merely modest in a decent, humble way, like all good scientists—of their rather uninstructed imaginations. De Soto had a withering contempt for science and all its works as evidenced by the age in which he was condemned to live and be bored. But his frank geniality would have blinded almost anyone to the smouldering volcano which it concealed.

In addition to the commercial byproducts of his earlier genius, another, of a purely social character, was to have far-reaching consequences for himself. Partly to spite Crane, and partly because he had no insight into the more morbid aspects of human character, Kent insisted that De Soto occupy the guest suite in his house indefinitely. De Soto consented, chiefly because he disliked the bother of hunting up suitable quarters for himself. He breakfasted with Kent and Alice, but took his other meals out, except for an occasional festive dinner in honor of some new triumph of his commercialized genius. The inevitable happened. Alice fell hopelessly, degradingly in love with him. Before the irresistible charm of his resonant voice, his perpetual high spirits—they seemed high to her—and his vibrant vitality, she abased herself utterly. His careless words of greeting became her treasured pearls of seraphic wisdom and celestial love. She is not to be unduly censured for her blindness; De Soto might have had any girl he fancied for the trouble of asking. But he never bothered to ask. He saw what had happened to Alice and it did not even amuse him. Nor did it move him to intercede in behalf of her father when the lightning struck him.

The President of the Board of Trustees was blessed with a long and accurate memory. His spite against Crane evaporated and condensed on the hapless director. Kent, he remembered, had proposed the plan for forcing Crane to resign. It had resulted in making the President feel foolish—a disagreeable sensation to any self-respecting man. Accordingly, when De Soto began conquering the electrical industry, the President decided that Kent was no longer necessary to the prosperity of the Erickson Foundation.

"How would you like to be director?" he jovially inquired of De Soto on the morning of exactly the hundred and eightieth day of De Soto's contract.

"How about Mr. Kent? What will he do?"

"Go fishing," the President hazarded with a slow smile of doubtful sincerity. "You see eye to eye with me in this matter," he continued, and De Soto did not deny the allegation. "Mr. Kent is no longer necessary to us. What do the trumpery eight or ten millions a year that he begs from old paupers amount to, anyway? The royalties from your new oil switch alone—the cheapest thing you've done—make all that Kent brings in look like a Mexican dollar. You take hold of things and show the world what a real, up-to-date business administration is. Accept now. There's a good fellow."

De Soto lazily stretched his arms and yawned.

"All right. I'll quadruple your profits in a week."

The President was about to shake the new director warmly by the hand when the latter, for no apparent reason, doubled up in an uncontrollable spasm of laughter. Thinking De Soto was enjoying the joke on Kent, the President joined in the whole-souled shout. The harder he laughed the worse De Soto became. At last, after a severe tussle, the swarthy young man gained control of himself and stood gazing with humid eyes at the President.

"This is rich," he gasped. "You will tell him, of course?"

The President nodded, and De Soto went soberly to the workshops to supervise the construction of the last unit of his cosmic ray generator. That afternoon Kent broke the news to Alice.

"I have saved practically nothing," he confessed bitterly. "Well, I can peddle life insurance till some place offers me a position. We shall have to vacate this residence within a month. It will be De Soto's now. He's director; I'm down and out."

"Perhaps he will ask us to stay here until we get settled," Alice suggested, a sinking at her heart.

"Impossible! To accept hospitality from a man who has stabbed me in the back? Never!"

But he did, that very evening, when De Soto, in response to a humble hint from Alice, indifferently invited Kent and his daughter to stay as long as they liked. They were to manage the house; he would pay the expenses. Things were to go on precisely as before. De Soto did not care whether they stayed or went, and the considerable expense of keeping up the establishment would not make even a dent in his weekly royalties. Should the Kents finally decide to leave, he would have a housekeeper. All he asked was that he be spared the bother of settling down to a new regime.

The morning after the disaster, Alice rose much earlier than usual and waylaid the generous protector of the poor before he entered the breakfast room. The utter self-abasement of her thanks seemed to rouse De Soto's smouldering contempt.

"Are you a human being?" he demanded roughly.

She failed to comprehend the blasting sarcasm of his brutal question.

"Of course," she laughed.

"Well, then—" he began and stopped abruptly. A brilliant idea for an experiment had just flashed into his mind. His harsh tone softened, and he laughed in the mellow way that he knew was music to the deluded girl's soul.

"What I was going to remark," he continued, "was simply this. You are human; so am I. All that I have done for you is nothing. Nothing!" he repeated with furious emphasis. "If human beings can't do so little as nothing for one another, and not have to be thanked for it, they are no better than hogs. Or," he added after a reflective pause, "than a certain cook and waiter I saw about six months ago. So please never refer to this matter again. Stay here as long as you and your father wish and let things go on exactly as they did before. I'm comfortable; why shouldn't you be?"

His generous words, whose acid sting she missed completely, turned her blind love to dumb adoration. She was his whenever he wanted her. But he did not want her—yet. First he must perfect his generator.

ALL through the spectacular months of De Soto's rocket rise to world fame, Crane served his superior as faithfully as he could in the tasks that fell his way. Without the slightest twinge of jealousy, professional or personal, Crane admitted that De Soto's mind soared above his own a universe away. The young man never seemed to think out his problems or to reason painfully from one verified guess to the next, as even the greatest scientists do, except in their two or three flashes of blinding genius. The beginning and the end were alike to him; the beginning was the wish to accomplish some bold project, the end its accomplishment. De Soto's method was like a continuous streak of lightning. For all that Crane could see, nature offered no puzzle more perplexing to De Soto's easy skill than breathing is to a normal man. Thus far Crane was one with the rest of the staff. Where he parted company with them was deep down in his secret thoughts.

Crane's first impression of De Soto remained as vivid as ever. Outwardly the two men were on the friendliest terms. What the young king of all inventors thought of his technical assistant he kept to himself; Crane's opinion of his chief was too dangerous to be shared with the rest of the staff. Brown was his one confidant. Their common nightmare with the black widows in the laboratory had established a bond between the two that nothing could break. They seldom referred to their unnatural adventure, but both knew that it was at the bottom of their unreserved friendship. Nor did Crane ever allude to the great discovery which the doctor announced that he had made with his microscope.

On the evening of Kent's dismissal from the Erickson Foundation, the doctor dropped in to spend an hour or two with Crane.

"Wilkes called me up this afternoon," he began, when Crane had made him comfortable.

"Wilkes? Oh, yes, I remember. He's in biology over at the university, isn't he?"

"Up to his neck in it. I doubt if he's deeper in than that. Did I ever tell you about my little spat with him six months ago?" Crane shook his head, and the doctor freely confessed the humiliating episode of the vanishing protozoa. "Wilkes thought I was crazy drunk that morning. He told me this afternoon that he poured that priceless bottle of your historic bathwater down the kitchen sink the moment I was out of his house. He had promised me like a gentleman and a scholar that he would get one of the chemists to analyze it. When I asked for a report some ten days later, he assured me the chemist had found nothing but pure water with the usual traces of organic matter and minerals—lime, and such stuff—that are in all tapwater. Like a fool I believed him. Now he's kicking himself for the scurvy trick he played me."

"Why?" Crane demanded, scenting a clue at last to the incomprehensible mystery of the black widows.

"It's a long story. I'll cut it short. You remember that poisoned fish scare we had six months ago?"

"When the fish in the bay turned up all spotted, and you asked me to sterilize my bathwater?"

"Yes. And you remember how it passed off in a day or two? The fish seemed to recover completely, or else all the affected ones died. Anyhow, no biologist in this part of the world had curiosity enough to ask the Health Department for one of the spotted fish to examine. I don't blame them—I didn't think of it myself. Now here comes the fortunate part. Some crooked inspector in the department, instead of destroying the fish seized in the markets as required by law, sold the lot to a Japanese cannery down the coast. Some of that canned fish found its way to the table of Professor Hayashi, the expert in parasitology at the Technical College in Tokyo. The discolorations on the skin caught his eye at once. To cut a long story short, Hayashi's microscopical examination of the diseased skin revealed myriads of protozoa—the most rudimentary forms of animals—of species totally new to science. Being a German-trained Japanese expert on parasites, Hayashi went without food or sleep until he had prepared an exhaustive series of microphotographs of these strange new beasts."

The doctor paused long enough in his story to extract half a dozen beautiful photographs and the same number of his own hasty sketches, made the night when he examined Crane's bathwater, from his pocketbook.

"Compare the photographs with the sketches. The photographs are Hayashi's, the sketches mine. Professor Wilkes gave me those specimens of Hayashi's work this afternoon. It seems that Hayashi picked on Wilkes as being the likeliest man to recognize the protozoa if they were known. The fish had been canned a few miles south of here, according to the label on the can. Hence, Wilkes, being professor at the university here, and presumably not dead, would know all about what lay at his own back door. Unfortunately, Wilkes had poured the most conclusive evidence, and my one chance to be famous with it, down the kitchen sink. He called me up this afternoon to ask what is to be done about it. I have several suggestions, but I'm not going to share them with him. He's too fond of his kitchen. Well, what do you think of my sketches? As true to life as the microphotographs, aren't they?"

"You copied Hayashi's?"

The doctor laughed. "No, I drew them from what I saw under the microscope in that bathwater I got from you six months ago. It's a great pity that you recovered as quickly as you did from that unique itch."

"I may be able to oblige you again, in a day or two," Crane grinned. "But go on. You were going to say something."

"Only this. I fell for the biggest fool on earth. By the margin of a single stupid mistake, I have lost a new universe. If I had not gone over to see old Wilkes that morning, I should have kept on believing in my work. Now Hayashi will get whatever credit there may be in it. This stuff is brand new, I tell you!" he exclaimed, warming to his beloved protozoa. "These things could never have evolved from anything we know. Structurally they are entirely different from any that have ever been described. And to think that I saw them living and multiplying under the lenses of my own microscope!"

The doctor lapsed into moody silence. "Well," he concluded. "it's too late now. Still, Hayashi doesn't know the whole story. Until he or someone else explains why those prolific little pests stopped multiplying in the sea, we haven't even begun to explain them. I should have expected every fish in the Pacific Ocean to be as gorgeous as a rainbow two months after the infection started in our harbor. But it stopped suddenly and absolutely in a day. Why?"

"Ask me another. I'm not good at riddles. Want to see some more blood red bathwater?"

"Where?" the doctor exclaimed, leaping to his feet.

"In the bathtub, of course."

"Lead me to it!"

"It isn't there yet. But, if De Soto and I have any luck tomorrow, I'll brew you twenty gallons of the reddest water you ever saw. He and I have about finished his first two million volt X-ray tube. It's no longer than my forearm. Built on entirely new principles. So, if my exposure to the hard X-rays had anything to do with the infected state of my skin, we should know it by tomorrow night. What do you think?"

Brown looked depressed. There were so many factors that his

optimistic friend had overlooked that the doctor dared not feel enthusiastic.

"You forget the time element," he said. "One exposure, even of thirty hours, may not be sufficient by itself. Why did those fish suddenly recover? No; there is something beyond hard X-rays at work in all this. Your luck six months ago may have been only an accident due to a concurrence of causes that won't happen together again in a million years."

"Cheer up. We can only try, you know. This time tomorrow I may be wishing I were dead."

"I hope so," the doctor replied absently, dreaming of his lost universe. "In case an accident does happen, we must be prepared. You say De Soto's tube is built on entirely new principles?"

"New from beginning to end, from anode to cathode—like everything else he does. Lord! I wish I had one per cent of the brains that kid has."

"Then you might never duplicate that scarlet bath. It was the most brilliant thing you ever did. The very blunders of your own two million volt tube may have been responsible for what happened."

"Possibly," Crane admitted. "X-rays were discovered half by accident. It begins to look as if my precious tube may have been in the same class. Something that Bork and I did in spite of ourselves touched off a real discovery—which we succeeded in smothering between us."

"And I, too," Brown sighed, "missed the essential thing. Well, we must be prepared. Will you take half a dozen of Bertha's eggs with you to the laboratory tomorrow? Don't let De Soto know about them. Keep them wrapped up in the pockets of your working coat."

"Don't you think," Crane suggested, "it is about time for you to give me a hint of your theory? I won't steal it."

"You'd be insane if you did. Even I haven't the nerve to talk it over with a biologist. Very well, here goes—your itch, my protozoa, and our black widows."

For an hour and a half the doctor defended the shrewd guesses and bold theories which he had devised to account for the apparently unnatural adventures in which he and Crane had participated. To Crane's frequent interruptions that the physics of the explanation, at least, was too wild for any sane man to listen to, the doctor retorted that only a hopeless pair of lunatics could have witnessed what Crane and he saw with their own eyes in the twenty million volt laboratory. Was that a fact of experience, or was it not? Did they see black widows by the hundred as huge as spider crabs, or didn't they? Well, then, the doctor continued somewhat irrationally, if nature can upset her so-called facts to suit herself, why can't she equally well break the puerile laws which we imagine for her discomfort? Hadn't all of the great generalizations of Nineteenth Century physics been scrapped or changed out of all recognition in the first three decades of the Twentieth?

Yes, Crane admitted, but why try to answer the old insanities with new ones even more insane? To which Brown replied that when in a lunatic asylum—meaning modern physics—do as the lunatics do; namely, cut your theories according to your facts.

It was a wild argument and a merry one. The climax was a roar of laughter from both disputants simultaneously. For it occurred to them that they were but slightly parodying the proceedings of two recent world scientific congresses which they had attended—Crane in physics, Brown in biology. No layman could have detected the slightest difference between their fantastic arguments and the profound debates that will make those great congresses forever memorable in the history of science.

"That settles it," Crane gasped, wiping the tears from his eyes. "I'll take a whole crate of eggs to the laboratory tomorrow."

"Don't!" the doctor implored. "Half a dozen, no more. I don't want a man as brainy as young De Soto is to suspect what I'm up to. The least hint to a man of his intelligence and I'm dished. He would go into it for all he's worth and clean it up from beginning to end in a week."

"Perhaps he has already," Crane suggested quizzically. "By the way, all our crazy talk made me forget my real bit of news. Kent's fired."

"What! When?"

"This morning. De Soto told me all about it. The trustees, it seems, decided they didn't need Kent any longer, now that De Soto is bringing in the money by the trainload. So they kicked him out."

"The low hounds!"

"Oh, I don't know. Business is business. They made De Soto director."

"And he accepted?"

"Why not? They had no further use for Kent. Live and learn ethics, doctor. All professions aren't like yours. I only wish they were. Even De Soto seemed disgusted with humanity in general and with the President in particular. It was the first time I have seen him show any human feeling. He was quite glum all the afternoon till about six o'clock, when we finally managed to put his new tube together. Then he yawned—he's always yawning—and began laughing like the devil. I mean it; he laughed exactly as a good fundamentalist thinks the devil laughs when he sees some nice boy downing his first drink of bootleg whiskey. It made my flesh creep. I don't like that young fellow."

"You still distrust him?"

"Yes, and I don't know why. Sometimes I have a feeling that he is about five million years old."

"Absurd. You had better be going to bed, and so had I. Don't forget to call for those six eggs on your way to the laboratory to-morrow."

"I won't. How's Bertha, anyway?"

"Fine. She and Roderick have done nobly. My back garden is full of broilers now, and I haven't the heart to eat one of them. The housekeeper threatens to give notice unless I sell a dozen. She can go if she likes. Bertha is a joy, and I wouldn't hurt her feelings to pacify fifty housekeepers. Well, I'm going. See you in the morning."

Crane duly called for the six new laid eggs the next morning and joined De Soto at the laboratory at eight o'clock sharp. For once in his life De Soto seemed to be laboring under the strain of repressed excitement. Usually he was somewhat indifferent about his brilliant work, not to say bored by it all; today he could scarcely wait for Crane to begin trying out the new tube.

"Put on these," he ordered, handing Crane a long shroud of crackly transparent material, with overshoes, gloves and hood of the same. He himself was already armored for their dangerous work. The crackly stuff, not unlike the thinnest isinglass, was another by-product of De Soto's incessant inventiveness. It had grown out of the work on insulators, although dependent upon different principles, and was sufficient to block completely all rays hard enough to penetrate forty feet of solid lead. Against the X-rays Crane expected to generate in the new tube it was more than ample protection.

The walls, floor, ceiling and window panes of De Soto's small private laboratory were closely "papered" with this thin, transparent ray insulation. It would not do to have stray radiations penetrating into adjacent laboratories and deranging delicate electrical apparatus.

Crane waved the proffered garments aside.

"No, thanks. I've worked around rays as hard as these, and I'm still kicking."

"Better not try it again," De Soto advised, with just the suspicion of a threat in his voice. "Put them on."

"Sorry, but I must decline," Crane replied with a defiant grin, his square jaw thrust slightly forward. "You see, I want to do a little experimenting myself."

For three seconds that seemed to Crane to stretch to three eternities, De Soto's blazing black eyes fixed upon his. "What is happening to me?" Crane thought. "I feel as if my brain were being torn to pieces."

"What experiment are you going to do?" he heard De Soto's voice asking in tones of deadly calm.

"Nothing much," Crane replied. He felt sane again. "I just wanted to verify my guess that rays as hard as these cannot affect human cells."

"Human cells?" the deadly voice echoed, slightly emphasizing the first word.

"Yes—the units from which our muscles, bones and nerves are built up. You know what I mean."

"I know what human cells are," De Soto said slowly, with deliberate ambiguity. His tone implied that he suspected Crane of an interest in cells not human. "Put on these things, and let us get to work."

"I have told you I prefer not to."

De Soto's eyes flashed ominously.

"Don't make it my unpleasant duty to discharge you for insubordination as my first action as director."

CRANE hesitated. For a second he was tempted to defy the new director and take his medicine. Then he remembered why he had swallowed his pride in the first place when Kent had tried to make him resign. He also thought of Brown, and the disappointment of his friend should he fail in the matter of the eggs. Without a word he shed his working coat and hung it on a hook behind the door. De Soto followed him with his burning eyes.

"Why did you take off your coat? This material weighs very little. You won't be too warm with your coat on under this. I'm wearing mine."

"I'll feel freer without so many clothes," Crane replied off-handedly.

"You have something in the pockets of your coat that you wish to be exposed to the full effect of these rays. Take out whatever you have, and destroy it. There's an oxy-acetylene torch by that bench."

Crane tried to bluff it out. Going to his coat, he extracted the half dozen new laid eggs and casually exhibited them for De Soto's inspection.

"My lunch," he explained.

Without replying, De Soto took one of the eggs and held it up to the light.

"You eat them raw?"

"Are they raw?" Crane asked in well feigned astonishment. "That girl at the lunch counter must have done it as a joke on me—or else she was rushed and made a mistake."

For answer De Soto took the six eggs, one at a time, and smashed them against the wall behind Crane.

"I'll take you out to lunch," he laughed good-humoredly. Suddenly his whole manner darkened. His eyes blazing, he shot an accusing question at the pale face before him.

"Did you come back here last night after I left?"

"I don't get your drift."

"Do you know what kind of a tube this is?"

"A two million volt X-ray, if it's the one I've been helping you build."

"It is the same one. Could you make another like it?"

"How could I? You made the cathode and the anode yourself. I don't know the first thing about their construction. And I have no idea what that thing like a triple grid in the middle is for. All I know about your tube is what you've told me. You said it was for hard X-rays. It's all new to me."

"It might be a device of great commercial value?"

"For all I know it might."

"Go to the office and get your time. You are discharged."

Crane turned on his heel and walked out without a word.

VII. WARNED

CRANE did not bother about his pay check at once. It could be collected later. For the moment a matter of greater importance pressed. He sauntered into the small chemical laboratory where tests of materials were carried out in connection with the electrical work. Only one man, a technical assistant, was in the laboratory. Looking up from his work he greeted Crane with a curt nod. Like the rest of the staff he treated Crane coldly since the latter's degradation in rank.

"I'm coloring a meerschaum pipe," Crane volunteered. "Got any beeswax or anything of that kind?"

"There's some in the drawer under the bench—there by the window."

"Thanks," Crane helped himself to four cakes and walked out. On reaching his own office, he locked the door, and proceeded to take impressions of all his keys to the laboratories and workshops of the Foundation. It would be a simple matter to have duplicates made at some obscure shop in another quarter of the city. "They may put me in jail before I finish," he grinned to himself. "Anyhow, I'll give them a run for their money first."

In the business office Crane explained that he had come to collect his pay.

"But it is only the fifteenth of the month, Doctor Crane," the clerk objected. "Of course, if you want an advance, I daresay it can be arranged. I'll have to ask the head bookkeeper."

"Don't bother. I'm fired."

"Fired? What for?"

"Being too smart for our new director. Make out the usual month's bonus for discharge without notice."

"Sorry, but I can't. We don't give any bonus now."

"Since when?"

"The new rule went in yesterday, before Mr. Kent was discharged. The trustees made the rule before they elected Mr. De Soto."

"I see. They don't overlook anything, do they? Is the President of the Board anywhere about?" The clerk nodded. "All right, call him out, will you? It's the last favor I shall ever ask of anyone connected with the Erickson. Here are my keys."

"But I can't do that. He's busy."

"Never mind. Tell him I'm here with an urgent message from Mr. De Soto. Honest; I'm not fooling."

The clerk was fooled. Presently the high potentate himself hurried out of his lair to receive the urgent message in person.

"Yes, Doctor Crane? Perhaps you had better come into my office."

"Perhaps I had."

"Now, what is it?" the President demanded when the door was closed. Crane looked him squarely in the eyes.

"You can go to hell!" he said.

"I shall ask the Director to discharge you," the President roared when he recovered his breath.

"Too late. He just did it. I meant that message from myself to you personally. You're a pretty cheap sort of skate. Nevertheless, I'm rather sorry for you and the rest of this firm of pawnbrokers. De Soto is making you all multimillionaires in record time, isn't he? And he loves you all better than if you were his brothers? Fine. Take it from me, he hates every last one of you worse than a rat hates rat-poison. I know that young fellow; you don't. Look out that he doesn't leave you flat. That's all."

The President's face went a pasty yellow. For the first time it dawned on him that De Soto might have been laughing at him, not at the unfortunate Kent, when the latter was so swiftly fired. That laugh, in retrospect, had a peculiar quality. Swallowing what remained of his pride, the President motioned to Crane to be seated. Crane declined, and the President affected not to have noticed the rebuff.

"Of course, I should be very angry with you," he began jovially, "for what you said when you first came in. However, boys will be boys, eh? Now, don't get sore because you think you've lost your job. Perhaps you haven't. How would you like to be my technical secretary? I get hundreds of letters from all sorts of people that I can't answer properly. You know how it is in my position. What about it? Fifty per cent increase in salary, of course."

Crane slowly shook his head. Business was business, as no one understood better than he. The President's purpose was evident. But Crane was not to be bribed into the dangerous job of spying on De Soto while an employee of the Foundation.

"I'm afraid it wouldn't do," he said. "The Foundation can't afford to antagonize its new director."

The President regarded him long and thoughtfully before replying.

"You're loyal to us, aren't you?" he remarked with evident sincerity, as if the discovery surprised him—as indeed it well might.

"I have some pride in my profession, if that is what you mean," Crane admitted.

"Am I to infer that you think Mr. De Soto lacks professional pride?"

"De Soto is too brainy to take pride in anything. That's the trouble with him."

"H'm. You think he may be playing a game of his own?" Crane nodded slightly. "What sort of a game?"

"As De Soto has several thousand times the mind that I have, I can't guess what his game is. It may all be my imagination."

THE President paced the carpet in silence. Coming to a halt before Crane, he went to the roots of his doubt.

"Why are you telling me all this? Can't you see that it may be to your own disadvantage?"

"That's easy. Because I hate De Soto. I know," he continued with a dry smile, "that men don't hate one another nowadays outside of the movies. It simply isn't done—in the way that I hate De Soto. Still, I do, and that is the plain fact."

"Why do you hate him?"

"How can I tell? It may be repressed professional jealousy, for all I know. More probably it is based on fear—or cowardice, if you like to put it so. I'm afraid of what he may do to me, and to the Foundation.

"What do you suspect?"

"Nothing definite. Everything about the man, except his scientific ability, is vaguely rotten. My guess is that he is planning something brand new to take us all by surprise. We probably shan't know what has happened to us until it is all over."

"Would you care to act as my agent to keep an eye on things? No one need know that you are connected with me or with the Foundation in any way."

"I'm not a detective. Still, in case I get into trouble, I may as well tell you that I intend to keep an eye on Mr. De Soto on my own account."

The President touched a button. When the clerk appeared, he requested him to make out a check to Doctor Crane for the amount of five years' salary, "as a token of appreciation," he added for the clerk's misinformation, "for his excellent services to the Foundation in the past." Crane did not object; he felt that he might need the money before settling with De Soto. It was a worthy cause.

"Now, Doctor Crane, perhaps you can be more explicit. What do you plan?"

"Just what I have told you. If I were rich," he added with a grin, "I should go right back to the laboratory now and shoot De Soto. Then I'd hire the best lawyer in the country to get me off. Your new Director is more dangerous than any mad dog in the country."

"In what way dangerous? You are making pretty serious charges, you know."

"I can't tell you definitely, because I don't understand myself. But I can convince you, or any other business man, that De Soto had better be handled with care. The Erickson has sent quite a few businesses to the wall recently, hasn't it? The whole industry of insulation as it was a short time ago, for example. We all saw how it was done. Has it never occurred to the trustees that the Erickson might go the same way?"

The point was obvious, and the President saw it. A clammy perspiration prickled out on various parts of his body. He felt quite ill.

"But Mr. De Soto is under contract to us for ten years," he protested weakly.

"What of it? He won't have to break his contract to break you."

"He can't be so unscrupulous as you suggest. Who ever heard of a scientist turning crook like that? All the men on this staff are as honest as the day is long."

"Perhaps it is the other way about. De Soto may have been a crook before he took up science. According to his story he comes from Buenos Aires. I've pumped him. He never saw South America. As to contracts, he has as little respect for them as he has for—I don't know what. Why shouldn't he leave you in the lurch tomorrow, if he likes, and go over to some of your competitors? Before the courts had settled the row, you would be flat broke."

The President was now perspiring freely. If De Soto could lie about his native country, why not about business matters? The possibilities of a broken contract were too obvious and too awful to be contemplated in silence.

"What would you do in our case—provided your suspicions are justified?"

"Sell out to my nearest competitors. Let them absorb the shock. It's coming."

"We can't," the President almost groaned. "Business details—I needn't bother you. But we can't." He tried to believe that Crane was merely letting his imagination run wild, but he could not. Innumerable slight inconsistencies of word and action on De Soto's part loomed up now with a sinister significance. For the first time the President suspected that De Soto's perpetual good humor and high spirits were the rather cheap disguise assumed by a man who had much to conceal. "I'm glad you have warned us," he admitted unhappily. "If you learn anything you will let us know? You won't find us ungrateful. Business is business, you know," he concluded with a rueful attempt at jocularity.

"I know," Crane retorted grimly. "So does Kent. That's why I came to tell you what I did first. I had no idea it would end this way. Thanks for the check; I'll need it. And please remember that if I get into hot water, it will pay the Foundation handsomely to fish me out. We are working on the same job, but for different reasons. Good morning, and thanks again."

They parted almost on good terms, but not quite. Crane still despised the Foundation's business methods; the President resented Crane's greater penetration in seeing a practical danger which he himself should have noticed months ago.

Crane's guess as to De Soto's probable financial tactics was shrewd but wrong. De Soto had no intention of using any of the obvious devices imagined by Crane. They lacked humor, and De Soto enjoyed nothing so much as a good laugh.

The next, and last, person to be warned was Alice. She, presumably, would still be living at the Director's residence; De Soto could not have turned the Kents into the street already. Hailing a cab, Crane directed the driver to take him to a locksmith's on the other side of the city. In the dingy little shop he asked the dried-up old tinker to duplicate the keys impressed in the wax, and to have them finished by five o'clock. "A rush order," he explained. "My partner lost his office keys, and I lent him mine." Crane then drove to the Director's residence and asked for Mr. Kent. The man who answered replied that Mr. Kent was out.

"Is Miss Kent at home?"

"I will inquire."

Before surrendering his card, Crane scribbled on it, "May I see you for a few minutes? Important."

ALTHOUGH he had not seen Alice since the night when she passed him in her car with the newly hired De Soto, he felt reasonably certain of her state of mind. Indeed Kent had spared no hint to make it plain that Alice, once fond of Crane, had now no further use for him, and that he need not trouble to call. While waiting for her to come down, Crane briefly reviewed his own feelings toward her, in order to be sure of himself and not blunder in his delicate task. Had he ever loved her?

Looking back on their friendship he admitted that he might have loved her, if circumstances had permitted their bantering good-fellowship to ripen, but that he had not. Her sudden and complete discarding of his friendship argued that she also had never cared seriously for him. If her indifference had been a pose to quicken his love for her, she would not have let it drag on indefinitely as she had. Her infatuation for De Soto, like his for her—according to Kent's sly, optimistic hints dropped to exasperate Crane—was genuine. Finally, Crane admitted to himself, he was a bachelor by instinct, as he had told Bork that afternoon in the high tension laboratory. A family was, after all, to a man of his temperament, only a lot of grief, as he had declared. He much preferred to live his own life, with its long working hours, its snatches of sleep, irregular meals, and scientific fights with Brown, to all the comforts of any home.

Alice entered, pale and distraught. He saw that she was still beautiful. But she had aged ten years, and all her happy spontaneity was gone. Worry over her father's plight, he speculated, could not account for all of the sad change. And instantly his hatred against De Soto doubled. He himself had never loved her, he now realized fully. But she had been such a good fellow that he resented De Soto's malign influence over her as fiercely as if she were his wife.

"It must be months since I've seen you, Doctor Crane," she said, extending her hand.

"Several, Miss Kent," he replied, noticing the formality of her address. Well, he could dance to any tune she called.

"You wished to see me about something?"

"Yes." He went to the point at once. "About Mr. De Soto."

"I must refuse to discuss Mr. De Soto with you," she interrupted hastily, her cheeks flaming.

"I don't intend to discuss him. As one human being to another, I shall tell you a fact that you should know. I do not apologize for what I say. It is none of my business. That is true. And it violates every decency of good society. What of it?"

"I won't listen!" she cried, putting her hands over her ears, and starting for the door. "Please go."

In one stride he overtook her. Forcing her hands to her sides, he delivered his message.

"De Soto is rotten to the core. He is not fit for any decent human being to associate with. If you marry him, you will kill yourself to be rid of him. Use your eyes and your brains!"

He released her hands and she fled, sobbing.

"Well, I've done it," he muttered. "It will make her watch him anyway. But I'm too late. That fool Kent!"

From the Kent's home he hurried to call on Brown. The doctor was in his office busy with a patient. At last the sufferer left, and Crane was admitted.

"Hullo," Brown exclaimed, "Not working today? Don't say you're itching again," he cried, hopefully.

"No such luck," Crane grinned. "But I'm hot enough. De Soto fired me the first thing this morning."

In answer to the doctor's solicitous questions, Crane briefly told the whole story, including his interviews with the President and Alice. Brown was shocked. The thought that his half dozen eggs had brought his friend to grief filled him with remorse and dismay.

"What will you do now?" he asked.

"Take things easy for a time. Till five o'clock this afternoon, to be exact. I forgot to mention that I'm having duplicate keys made to all the laboratories and workshops of the Erickson. They'll be done at five."

"What! You don't mean to say you're going to burglarize the place? That is what it would amount to, now that you are discharged. Better not try anything so foolish."

"It may be foolish, but I'm set on it. And I'm going to make my first attempt about one o'clock tomorrow morning—jus when it's darkest. I know when the watchman makes his rounds to the various buildings. He and I will contrive not to meet. There's no danger worth mentioning. If they catch me at it, I shall appeal to the President and ask him to lie me out of the scrape. But I'm going to find out what De Soto is up to, no matter what it costs. The sooner the better."

"I agree to the last," Brown seconded. "The way he smashed those eggs when he found they were raw looks bad. I don't half like it. De Soto knows something he shouldn't. We've got to learn what it is."

"We?" Crane echoed.

"Yes. You and I. Now, don't argue. But for me, you never would have got into this mess. I'm going with you to stand guard and see that you don't go to the penitentiary. Don't put too much faith in your friend the President."

"I don't," Crane grinned. "If he saw a chance of making a dollar out of it, he would double-cross himself. Well, I shan't mind if you do come. Two will be safer than one. You can slip away if anything unpleasant happens. Shall I call for you about twelve tonight?"

"All right. It has just occurred to me that we shall have a glorious chance to perform a crucial experiment if we can get hold of De Soto's tube for a second or two. Can I bring Bertha? I'll drug her before we start so she won't squawk and give us away."

"Bring her along. She can stand the risk, if we can."

De Soto's morning, after he had discharged Crane, passed pleasantly enough. The lack of an assistant did not inconvenience him, as he was essentially a lonely worker. In fact he had retained Crane more as a blind to the trustees than as a help to himself. By acquiescing in what seemed to be their desires with regard to Crane, he not only proved himself a good co-operator, but also a decent, human fellow, whose work need not be carried out in secret. Actually he feared no ordinary physicist. To understand what De Soto was doing, a spy would require at least his own intelligence.

When Crane walked out, De Soto's first act was to lock the door and pull down all the window shades. He was now secure from uninvited observation. No ray could penetrate the insulated walls, floor, windows and ceiling to give workers in neighboring laboratories a clue to the nature of the radiations which De Soto hoped to generate.

He was about to set his tube in operation when he paused thoughtfully, as if in doubt. Going to the closet, where the suits of insulating fabric hung, he selected a second shroud, pair of gloves, hood and overshoes of the transparent material, and put on the whole outfit over those he already wore. This double protection might be unnecessary; he rather thought it was. But De Soto was a cautious worker, careful of his perfectly tuned body, and he took no chances.

Ready at last for his test, he carefully connected his eighteen-inch tube to the terminals of what Crane called the devil box—a black cubic yard of insulated steel, apparently, capable of delivering a steady current at anything from one volt pressure to twenty million. If necessary, he could pass the full twenty million through his tube for a week. Having made the requisite adjustments, he released the full twenty million volts at one turn of a thumb screw.

There was no hissing crackle, no sudden splash of blinding light from the tube, no fuss or fury of any sort whatever. For all that an unskilled observer could have told, the tube was dead. Whatever was taking place in it, if anything, was far beyond the spectrum of light. If waves were being generated under the terrific impact of the electrons in the tube, ripped from the cathode by the full bolt of twenty million volts, those waves were so short that they affected no eye. Anyone except its inventor might have casually picked up the tube with his bare hand.

De Soto seemed satisfied. He disconnected the tube and turned a small screw on its side. Gradually, a thin pencil of black metal advanced into the vacuum, directly into the path that the discharge from the cathode must follow. The tube was again connected and the full current turned on and quickly off. Again there was no flash or other obvious indication that anything had happened. By a simple device it was possible to remove the pencil of metal from the tube without admitting a single atom of gas into the tube. Having removed the pencil, De Soto walked to the farther end of the laboratory, adjusted the pencil between the terminals of a huge storage battery, and turned on half the current. The metal pencil glowed from dull red to scarlet, then to pale blue, and finally to a dazzling white as the current passed through it. De Soto reached for a pocket spectroscope and studied the light emitted by the incandescent metal. Evidently the result so far was satisfactory, for he smiled. Still keeping his eye on the spectrum, he reached out with one hand and switched on the full current. There was a flash, a sharp report, and darkness. He had seen all that was necessary. The pattern of brilliantly colored lines crossing the spectrum as the incandescent metal exploded to atoms told its own story. The metal had been transmuted into a different element from what it had been before the full discharge of the twenty million volt tube struck it.

ONE after another De Soto inserted pencils of the metallic elements into his tube, gave them the limit of what the devil box concealed, extracted them, and subjected them to the simple, conclusive tests of flash spectrum and spark spectrum. He was already bored; the outcome was known in advance. These verifications of what he knew must take place in his hardest of all rays were but the necessary tests to assure himself that the construction of his tube was not faulty. As a mere detail in his true project, he had accomplished, on a wholesale scale, the transmutation of the elements—the dream of the alchemists and one goal of modern technology. Others had knocked the electron shells off the atoms of the elements, and still more ingenious experimenters had even tampered with the all but inaccessible inner core, the nucleus. By controlling the whole scale of radiation, from the longest radio waves to the shortest cosmic rays, in one simple, comprehensive generator, De Soto could pass up or down the whole series of chemical elements at will, as an accomplished pianist strums over his octaves. All this, however, was but the first step toward his goal. The hard, invisible, new radiations released by the transmutation of one element into another were the tools he required for his untried project.

For the moment he was lazily satisfied. After all, it was no great feat. Had he not done it when he did, some routine worker in physics must have succeeded within ten years. Literally scores were racing against one another along parallel roads to the same end. Where he surpassed what the natural development of physics would have suggested, was in his absolute control of the mechanism of disintegration. No sudden outgush of energy destroyed his apparatus in uncontrollable fury. The perfection of his technique permitted him to stop instantly any explosion of matter that might start; in fact an automatic regulator of the simplest pattern—simple, that is, to anyone with the eye for seeing nature as it is—held the incipient whirlwinds of destruction in leash.

So far all was well. To proceed farther he needed new materials. No rudimentary metal would serve his purpose. He must have highly complex compounds of a score of elements, all delicately adjusted in perfect, natural balance. The man-made products of the chemical laboratory were too artificial. If one would question nature, he must use the living things that are nature's most perfect mode of expression.

As he raised the blinds, he pondered his next step, and he smiled. Nature, or chance, he thought, had been kind to him. It had given him a perfect body and an unparalleled mind. What more could he wish? A partner with whom to share these bounties of generous mother nature. The thought of what he was about to do suddenly doubled him up in a spasm of laughter.

"Millions and millions and millions like her," he gasped, "and they don't know what is going to happen. All like her, every last one of them. How long will it last? Another ten or twenty million years? Or perhaps thirty million?" For a moment his mirth overpowered him. He was helpless, till his bitter humor died of its own exhaustion. "Thirty years," he said slowly, coldly, in answer to his own sardonic questions. "Eighty years from now every living thing will be happy. This is the end we have striven for since the days when we lived with beasts, and like beasts, in mouldy caves. Who will ever guess? Frogs and guinea pigs, Alice and the millions like her, my own children, will never know what I have done for them. What a joke!"

He removed his protecting hoods, shrouds, gloves and overshoes, and strolled over to take a last look at his tube. An exclamation of dismay burst from his lips. The crystal window of the tube glowed with a faint green fluorescence. Leaping to the devil box, he searched frantically for the faulty connection which permitted the current to leak into the box. There was no means of "killing" the whole box; it was automatic and self-contained. Until he found the leak there was nothing to be done. Not succeeding in his first dozen frenzied trials of the screw switches, he raced to clothe himself again in his protective armor. Was he too late? The hardness of the rays emitted along with that pale fluorescence was an unknown quantity until he could determine the strength of the current leaking from the box. In his confusion he had not thought of the obvious way of disconnecting the tube from the box entirely, but had assumed that some switch was not fully open. Hence his first frantic attempts now rose up to reproach him with the stigma of stupidity.

"Am I like the rest?" he gasped, hurrying back to the box. "A blundering fool after all?"

This time he found the trouble at once. The one screw switch that he could have sworn he opened was still just barely closed. For anyone working around such deadly apparatus, the trivial oversight was a blunder of the first magnitude. Approximately two million volts were still streaming into the tube.

"I should have tested that switch first," he muttered. "Am I a common fool? Well, this is a warning to do everything hereafter in the stupid, routine way these cattle use about this stable."

Once more he removed his protective garments. This time he found everything 'dead,' as it should have been. For a moment he felt old and tired. Before he realized that he was speaking, his lips had propounded a strange question.

"Who am I?" The voice seemed to speak from a forgotten world. "And what am I doing here?" Again the words seemed uneasily familiar. "Didn't I make a mistake like that before?" he continued in his normal voice. "Where was it, and when? Strange that I can't remember. Yet I could swear that I once saw a green light like that, only more intense. It brightened, and grew white. Then a black piston destroyed it in total darkness. How could that be? Only the complete destruction of radiation could give such an effect. I never did this before. What is the matter with me?"

Unable to answer, he left the laboratory, carefully locking the door behind him. Once outside in the brilliant sunshine he recovered rapidly. The cloudiness of his mind quickly cleared, and he began visualizing his immediate purpose. It was a few minutes past twelve. He stepped into the business office and used the telephone.

"Is Miss Kent speaking?" he asked when he got his number. "This is Mr. De Soto. I've been working hard all the morning, and don't fancy going to a restaurant for lunch. Can you give me something if I come out to the house? Anything you have will do."

The happy girl's reply was scarcely coherent. Yet De Soto understood the sense behind the nonsense of her words.

"Thank you, Alice. I shall be right out."

As he got into a taxi the queer sensation again overcame him for a moment. "Am I going soft? Bah! All I need is food and exercise."

To Alice the luncheon was nectar and ambrosia; to De Soto it tasted like lobster and icewater, which is partly what it was. The food, however, was not his chief concern. As they passed into the conservatory, he came to the point.

"Alice," he began in his resonant voice, "what happened yesterday has made me think a great deal about your future and your father's. Who would take care of you if I were to go away? No; please don't interrupt. You do need looking after, and so do I. Why can't we compromise? I have loved you since the first night I saw you. Will you marry me—now, this afternoon?"

Her answer was a foregone conclusion, and De Soto knew it. Feeling her warm young body in his arms he almost got a thrill.

THEY were married at three o'clock by a justice of the peace. Kent was not present, as he had disappeared into the bowels of the city in search of a job and could not be reached by telephone, radio, or prayer.

It cannot truthfully be said that love transformed Miguel De Soto, however devoutly such a consummation was to be desired. His marriage was for a definite purpose. If, toward the end, he got more than he bargained for in the way of love, it was by accident and not design.

To prepare for what he hoped to do, he took Alice on a shopping expedition as soon as they were married. She ordered whatever took her fancy in the way of personal adornment, while De Soto, admitting a weakness which she had never suspected, won her bridal love completely by his own purchases. They were made in queer quarters of the city, near the market places, where live stock is offered for sale. Small animals, he declared, had been his boyhood friends, and now that he was a sedate married man he could afford to gratify the thwarted longings of years to possess a select menagerie of his own. Guinea pigs, white rats and robust frogs were his special pets, although he also betrayed a weakness for the common chicken. All this squeaking, croaking, crowing and cackling family was ordered to be delivered at once to the Foundation residence—Kent's former home—and to be installed in the appropriate pens, coops, runways, ponds and cages by nightfall. By liberal bonuses De Soto extracted a ready promise that his happy family would all be settled in the back garden by six o'clock that evening. It was a collection that would have made a geneticist's mouth water. Alice almost cried, so happy was she at the unsuspected tenderness of her husband and lover.

At six o'clock Kent returned, footsore, heavy of heart and weary after a fruitless search all day for employment, to be greeted by his new son-in-law. Alice at the moment was upstairs. With great tact and delicacy De Soto hinted that Kent had better find quarters elsewhere, for a few weeks at least. Kent was so overcome with joy to learn that Alice at last had captured the elusive, reserved young genius—and millionaire—that he fell in with the suggestion at once.

"I understand how it is, my boy," he assured De Soto, laying a fatherly hand on his shoulder. "Just let me run upstairs and tell Alice how happy I am, and I'll be off at once."

De Soto resented the "my boy" of his father-in-law, but did not show it on his smiling face.

"By the way," he said casually, "since I am now one of the family, I shall pay all bills." He unobtrusively slipped a handsome check into Kent's hands. "As you belong with us by rights, it is only fair that I should take care of your hotel expenses." De Soto was not mean. Money meant nothing to him, and he cared a little less than nothing for the things that can be bought by money or genius. Crane was right when he told the President that De Soto was too brainy to take pride in anything.

While Kent was upstairs bidding Alice adieu and almost crying with her over this happy issue out of all their afflictions, De Soto paced the dining room carpet like a trapped tiger. For the first time that he could remember he felt maddeningly, stupidly ill. A hot prickling tingled over every inch of his skin like needle points of fire. It had first come on, faintly, while he was buying guinea pigs with Alice. Although he gave her no hint of the distress, it had required all of his self-control to act as if he were in perfect health. To one who recalled only the easy sense of well being of a young and healthy animal, the first experience of illness was mental torture not to be endured. De Soto was out of his depth. What should he do? Consult a doctor? He would ask Kent the name of a reliable man the moment he came downstairs.

Taking a grip on himself as he heard Kent's step, De Soto stopped his feline pacing and stood rigidly still.

"Who is your family physician?" he asked in a level voice.

"Brown," Kent replied, somewhat surprised. "Most of your staff consult him. Not feeling unwell, I hope?"

"Oh, no. But I thought Alice may have been doctoring with the wrong man. She has looked rather pale the last few weeks."

"That will all mend itself now," Kent assured him. "You are the right doctor for her."

The moment he was gone, De Soto bounded upstairs and tapped on his wife's door. "It is Miguel."

"Come in," she cried in a low voice.

"Alice," he began, "can you ever forgive me for running away and leaving you to dine alone? I have just remembered that I left a switch closed in my laboratory. I must go back at once, or the whole place may be wrecked."

"Can't you telephone to someone?"

"No. It is too dangerous."

Her face went white. "Let me come too," she begged.

"That would be worse than ever. I know exactly what to do. There is not the slightest danger to me. Anyone else——" There was no need to finish the sentence; he had produced the intended effect. "Don't expect me till you see me—I may be hours."

She kissed him passionately.

"I won't be a drag on you," she declared, "even on our wedding day."

For reasons of his own, he went out by the back door. On his way through the service port, he hastily emptied half a sack of potatoes into a box and tucked the sack under his arm. In the patio he found that the assorted pets he had purchased were all comfortably housed in their respective quarters.

"I may as well do two things at once," he muttered, slipping two large frogs and a pair of guinea pigs into the sack. "She might ask questions if she saw me taking these away in the morning."

Unobserved by any of the servants he got the sack into Alice's car. His immediate destination was Doctor Brown's house. At a drug store he learned the doctor's address.

THE doctor was just sitting down to a bachelor's dinner when the housekeeper announced that Mr. De Soto wished to see him at once. Brown rose with alacrity. He and De Soto had not met. The doctor, however, felt that he knew De Soto better perhaps than the young man knew himself. He found his caller in the study.

De Soto went straight to the point.

"Mr. Kent recommended you to me. For the past three or four hours my whole skin has felt as if it were on fire. Will you examine me? I may tell you that Miss Kent and I were married this afternoon."

"No wonder you are over-anxious about yourself," the doctor laughed, concealing his shock at the news of Alice's marriage. If De Soto was the man Crane thought him, poor Alice had been undeservedly punished. Brown had always liked her. Single or married, he silently resolved, he would stick by her.

"Is my condition likely to be serious?" De Soto asked, his vibrant voice growing husky with repressed animal fear.

"Probably not. I treated a similar case successfully a short time ago."

A curious change came over De Soto's eyes. For a moment they might have been those of a wild beast trapped and about to be killed. Brown caught the flash. It convinced him that Crane was not far wrong in his estimate of this young man.

"What was the patient's name?" De Soto demanded. His question was harsh and hoarse with fear.

To Brown it was evident that De Soto suspected Crane of having used the forbidden tube secretly. The doctor rose to the occasion.

"Oh," he replied, "the case I speak of was six months ago. What was the man's name? Let me think. It was before you came here. He was an assistant at the Foundation and got into trouble. You may have heard of him committing suicide. I've got it. Bork. That was the man."

"Aren't you mistaken?" De Soto asked in a voice which he did not recognize as his own. The question came from his lips involuntarily, as if some personality deeper than his own were expressing a doubt.

"I think not. Why do you ask?"

"Ask what?" De Soto rubbed the back of his hand across his eyes.

"You've been working pretty hard of late, haven't you? Take my advice and lay off for a spell. You just had a slight lapse of memory then. Well, the first thing is to ease your skin. We can do that here, in my bathroom."

Brown himself gave De Soto his bath. The moment the patient was out of the tub, the doctor hustled him into the dressing room and rubbed him down thoroughly with disinfectants. He was not going to lose the priceless bathwater this time, or have any third party see it pass from pink to crimson.

"You will be comfortable for an hour or two anyway. I suppose you won't want to go home until you feel sure you're cured. Did you tell your wife anything?"

De Soto confided the fiction of the danger of the laboratory, but saw no necessity for mentioning the sack and what it contained.

"Fine. Go to a hotel and spend the night there. Repeat the treatment every three hours. I'll give you a prescription for some stronger stuff. Telephone to your wife that the job at the laboratory will keep you there till ten or eleven tomorrow morning. Come and see me again at eight."

Promising to carry out the doctor's instructions to the letter, De Soto left. The desk clerk at the hotel addressed him by name, feeling highly honored to have as a guest the young inventor whose picture was always appearing in the papers. De Soto got the best room and bath in the hotel. Morbidly concerned about his health, he did not wait three hours to repeat Brown's treatment, but did it at once with drastic thoroughness. Then, cold with fear, he lay down to torture himself for two hours with unreasonable fancies. Brown had assured him the other man recovered quickly and easily. Would he? His fear of bodily discomfort was not cowardice, but simply the natural reaction of an animal experiencing its first pain.

The two hours passed without the slightest recurrence of the symptoms. Encouraged, De Soto repeated the bath and disinfection, and lay down again, this time with dawning hope. Luck stayed with him. And so it went, with complete success, till two in the morning. Feeling that he was free of his trouble for good, De Soto dressed and left the hotel. The numerous bathings and rubbings had made him feel like his old self, full of energy and eager for work. He got his car and drove to the laboratory. The sack had not been molested during his stay in the hotel.

VIII. TRAPPED

SHORTLY before midnight, while De Soto in his hotel room was busy with his prophylaxis, Crane descended upon the doctor to prepare for the proposed raid on the forbidden laboratory. Brown knew that he was taking his reputation, if not his life, in his hands by sharing Crane's somewhat foolhardy enterprise. Nevertheless he was determined to go through with it for scientific reasons as well as for the sake of friendship.

Crane found the doctor peering through his binocular microscope.

"Anything new?" he asked.

"Not exactly. The same protozoa that you contributed to the

cause of science. This really is most extraordinary. Old Wilkes would give his right eye for one look at these. They mustn't be exposed to the light too long, or they'll vanish into nothing."

In answer to Crane's rapid fire of questions, the doctor explained how he had secured his fresh supply of protozoa. The announcement that De Soto and Alice were married was received in cold silence. What could be said? The time for talk was past.

"De Soto has blundered," Crane hazarded finally. "What it took thirty hours for the two million volt tube to develop on my skin has shown up on his in half a day. This must have happened after I left this morning. My hunch is that he doesn't know what he is doing. Well, shall we be going?"

"If you insist, we may as well," The doctor pocketed his flashlight and a small medicine case. "I'll go and give Bertha her sleeping potion and join you in front."

Forty minutes later the two rash men were outside the door of De Soto's laboratory. Brown carried a large paper market bag in which the drugged brown hen reposed limply and silently. There was some slight difficulty at first in forcing the new key into the lock. Crane began to swear softly.

"Hadn't we better give it up?" Brown suggested. "A superstitious man would say our trouble in forcing an entrance is a sign from Heaven to quit."

For a moment Crane was inclined to agree. His square-jawed obstinacy, however, persisted.

"There," he whispered at last, as the key turned in the lock. "In with you!"

Before turning on the lights, Crane cautiously felt his way from one window to the next, making sure that the iron shutters had been closed as usual for the night.

"All safe," he announced, rejoining Brown by the door, and turning on the lights. "Now to find out what friend De Soto thinks he is doing."

"Your key?" Brown suggested. "Hadn't you better leave it in the lock?"

"No. The watchman is not due this way for nearly two hours yet. But suppose he were to come round out of his regular beat. If he found the door locked from the inside he would ring till he was let in. Otherwise he would just open the door, turn on the lights, look around from here and lock up again. You must stand here and switch off the lights if you hear anyone coming. I shall duck into that closet—where the insulating togs are hung—and wait till he goes away again. After turning off the lights, you sneak round behind that steel cabinet and stand as close as you can to the window.

The watchman won't see you from where he stands. Take the hen with you, of course."

To forestall the unexpected, as all trained scientists do, the conspirators rehearsed their parts six times before attempting any experiment. While Brown switched the lights on and off, Crane practised his disappearing act between the devil box and the closet. The doctor for his part managed to turn off the lights and vanish behind the steel cabinet almost in the same moment.

"Safety first," Crane grinned when the rehearsal ended. "The unforeseen always happens. Turn off the lights till I give the word."

As a last precaution, he unbolted the iron shutters of the window by which Brown was to stand in case of danger, unlocked and raised the window, and finally closed the shutters without rebolting them.

"If we're caught, you fling open the shutters and step out of the window. Then beat it."

"And leave you to face the music? What do you take me for?"

"A man of common sense. Don't argue. It is as much to my advantage as it is to yours not to be caught four-handed, as it were. The President will take care of me. Your reputation would be gone forever. Now, do as I say. I'm the captain here; you're a buck private in the rear rank."

After much further argument Brown consented. The point that finally won him over was quite unanswerable. Crane refused to start the experiment unless the doctor first gave his word as a gentleman to obey orders to the letter.

"We don't know what sort of rays De Soto's tube generates," Crane remarked, reaching into the closet for a protective suit. "Let us take no chances. Put on double armor."

Their preparations at last complete, they hopefully set about the experiment for which they had come. Bertha, still soundly drugged, was left in her sack by Brown's emergency window. If the tube generated nothing more penetrating than even hard X-ray, the unsuspecting hen would be amply dosed where she lay. But Crane, examining the curiously compact mechanism of De Soto's little masterpiece, had an uneasy feeling that the tube could emit radiations infinitely more dangerous than the most penetrating rays known to human science. Trusting that their double protection was sufficient, they tried to connect the stocky little tube to the black devil box.

For five minutes Crane fumed and fussed at the ridiculously simple terminals.

"Better take up your station by the lights," he snapped irritably to the helpless doctor. "I can't seem to make it work. We may be fooling here till daybreak."

Brown humbly retired to the door and, to reassure his exasperated collaborator, lightly laid his fingers on the buttons controlling the lights. Crane had not the least idea of what he was doing. Accustomed to the usual sputtering of ordinary tubes he naturally imagined that nothing was taking place in the silent, dead-looking apparatus before him. The transparent gloves, thinner than silk, seemd to interfere with his manipulations. With a gesture of irritation, he started pulling them off, when Brown sharply stopped him.

"Don't do that! How do you know that box is safe?"

"The box can't do any harm. It's the tube that counts. Why doesn't it glow?"

"Don't take off your gloves! It may be—."

The doctor's expostulation was cut short by a drowsy voice from the window that seemed to ask "What?"

"The lights!" Crane muttered tensely.

Instantly the laboratory was plunged in total darkness.

Brown recovered his nerve first.

"That was only Bertha coming to," he laughed. "Shall I switch on the lights?"

Crane assented, and once more began tinkering desperately with the connections. Barely had he started when the lights went off again. For the moment he forgot his own instructions to Brown.

"What's up now?" he fretted.

"Steps! Duck!"

As he shut the closet door noiselessly after him, Crane heard a key being inserted into the lock of the laboratory door. Brown was already in his station by the window, praying that Bertha would not continue talking in her sleep. The door opened, and the lights were turned on. It was De Soto, carrying his sack. Neither Crane from his coal-black closet, nor Brown from his station by the window could see who the intruder was. The doctor wondered why the supposed watchman did not turn off the lights and go away. To their horror both men heard the door being closed, the key turned in the lock, and the sound of confident footfalls advancing into the laboratory. Brown had the additional discomfort of knowing that the lights were still on.

WHAT followed was like a hideous nightmare to the three participants. In four minutes history was made on a scale that would have paralyzed the minds of at least two of the protagonists had they but dreamed what their foolhardy tampering with forces beyond their childish understanding would precipitate. Neither Crane nor the doctor saw in De Soto's outburst of fury anything more significant than the ungovernable rage of an overwrought man magnifying a real, but not very important wrong, into a cosmic disaster. Their crass bungling had unchained the devil. If any justification for De Soto's career be possible, it resides in the history of those four epoch-making minutes. According to his own account, he intended something quite different for the world, and for Alice in particular, from his actual campaign. We have only his word for all of this. But, in the absence of conclusive evidence to the contrary, it is simplest to assume that De Soto was not a liar.

The historic episode began with a hoarse, despairing cry from De Soto. In one amazed glance, as he walked toward the black devil box, he had noticed that the tube was fully connected as efficiently as if he himself had linked up the twenty million volts to the evil fiend of his own devising.

"I'm a fool like the rest," he wailed, dropping the sack with the frogs and the guinea pigs. "I left it on!"

He darted for the closet to fetch himself a suit of the transparent armor. Crane heard him coming, and squeezed himself into the farthest corner behind three of the dangling shrouds. De Soto groped for a shroud, gloves and overshoes without looking at what his hands grasped. Shouting incoherent nothings he got himself into a single suit, and darted for the devil box to disconnect the tube.

"I should have done this first," he raved, realizing his blunder too late. "Fool, fool, fool! What am I?"

Bertha brought the tragedy to its climax. As De Soto's lightning fingers disconnected the tube, a final surge of energy ripped the innermost cells of her body apart. Although she was only a brown hen, that exquisite pain gave her for a fraction of a second a voice that was three parts human. Her croaking shriek rose shrilly above the unnatural cries of the outraged guinea pigs and frogs in the sack, whose innermost sanctity of life had also been violated in that abrupt surge, and froze the fingers of the man blundering at the tube.

"What was that?" he yelled, his voice the cry of a lost animal facing death.

As if in answer to his question an iron shutter seemed to open of itself; a black mass hurled itself into the blacker night, and the wailing shriek of the outraged hen receded into silence, and died. Brown had escaped with his booty.

De Soto found himself staring in a dream at the fatal work of his too penetrating intelligence. That it had ruined him was sufficient for the moment. That his own imperfect mind, as he thought, had delivered him up to failure in its worst form, was an ironic jest that cut deeper than mere failure. His memory began to reassert itself. Surely he had disconnected the tube before quitting the laboratory? A clear visual image of the tube as he had left it, flashed on his retina. He rushed to the open window and stared into the darkness. Who had robbed and betrayed him? Crane? De Soto began shouting hoarsely for the watchman who, having seen the light streaming from the window, was already running down the walk to the laboratory.

The watchman as a matter of course began a systematic search. Within a minute he had found Crane.

"All right," the latter remarked dryly, stepping into the light and confronting De Soto. "I guess you've got me. What are you going to do about it?"

His story was already made up, such as it was. In preparation for it he had stripped himself of his protecting gloves, shrouds, hoods and overshoes, and hung them up in the closet before the watchman opened the door. De Soto regarded the suspect somberly before replying.

"How did you get in?" he demanded.

"I was passing here—having a look at things from the outside for old times' sake," Crane grinned, "when I noticed the open window and came in to investigate."

"You came in alone?"

"Presumably. The man who vanished in such a hurry when you unlocked the door must have left the window open. I judge he must be pretty well acquainted with the general layout of this laboratory. Otherwise he couldn't have found his way about in the dark."

De Soto affected to credit this theory.

"You had better tell the proper authorities in the morning," he said, watching Crane's face narrowly.

"Of course, if you think it necessary. I will tell the President of the Board, if you like, as soon as I can get hold of him."

"And you will agree to abide by his decision as to what is to be done?" De Soto suggested with a malicious smile. Crane nodded. "Then," De Soto continued, "I shall have to ask the watchman to search you. A mere formality," he smiled, "so that I may be able to assure the President that you were only safeguarding the interests of the Foundation like a loyal alumnus."

"Rather rough on me, isn't it? What if I object to being searched without a proper warrant?"

"None is necessary. You were trespassing. Search him."

The key was found at once. Although pretty far gone, the game was not yet lost. Crane pretended to take the damning discovery as a matter of course.

"Yours?" De Soto asked.

"Of course."

"Then you had a duplicate?" Receiving no reply, De Soto explained.

"To make sure that you would attempt nothing rash after your dismissal yesterday morning, I asked at the office before going home whether you had turned in your keys. They told me you had. This insanity on your part confirms my suspicions. You were discharged, as you doubtless guessed, because I had a strong feeling that you were spying on me. Now, if you will tell me who your confederate is, I shall take no action against you. Who is he?"

"I don't know what you are talking about. That duplicate key must have been in my pockets for weeks."

"It is too new," De Soto pointed out coldly, holding it up for the watchman's inspection. "For the last time, will you tell me who was in here with you?" Crane's obstinate silence seemed to infuriate his inquisitor. "You refuse? Then I shall turn you over to the police."

"What good will that do you? The trustees will believe my story—to avoid a scandal, if for no other reason."

"You think so? Possibly you know them better than I do. Let me think a moment." As if trying to make up his mind, De Soto began pacing back and forth in front of his devil box. At last he appeared to reach a decision. "Close that window, fasten the shutters, and go about your rounds," he directed the watchman. "Lock the door after you. I will be responsible for this man till you look in again."

"Now," he began when they were left alone, "there are no witnesses. We can speak the truth without fear of the consequences. How long had the tube been connected to the box when I came in?"

This tempting invitation to give himself away completely did not appeal to Crane.

"How should I know? Whoever was in here may have been tinkering with your apparatus for three minutes or three hours."

"So you refuse to talk? Very well; I shan't press you. Amuse yourself till the watchman comes round again. I must see what damage has been done."

TURNING his back on his prey, De Soto strode toward the evil black box. For half a minute Crane did not foresee his intention. Only when De Soto began rapidly making the connections necessary to operate the tube did the truth flash upon him. He was absolutely without protection against whatever fiend De Soto, himself sheathed from head to foot against the rays, might release. The memory of the unnatural cry which Bertha had emitted when Brown—also protected as Crane was at the critical moment—snatched her with him in his flight, roused every instinct of self-preservation in the doomed man. One terminal was already connected. De Soto's nervous fingers were about to close the circuit by connecting the second, when Crane hurled himself upon his inhuman enemy.

The unexpected impact catapulted De Soto against the black box and flung him violently to the concrete floor. Before Crane could fall on him, he had rebounded like an enraged tarantula and leapt to the farther side of the box. Vaulting the box, Crane tried to seize the desperately cool devil sneering into his face. De Soto kept him off easily with one hand, while with the other he felt for the second wire dangling above its binding screw. Crane's wiry strength was no match for the perfect machine of bone, muscle and brain opposing him. The free hand made the connection and began groping for the small button switch that would release twenty million volts to surge into the tube. The operator knew what the consequences to the other must be; the intended victim could not even guess, except that they would be evil. The all but human cries of the hen, and frogs and the guinea pigs seemed to echo again through the laboratory. What would his own cry be like?

Instinct saved him. Powerless to prevent the groping fingers from finding their mark, Crane ripped the hood from De Soto's head in one convulsive movement with all his strength.

"You know, then!" De Soto shouted, making a leap to recover the hood.

"I know you're crazy," Crane jeered, eluding him. He saw his chance and took it. Before De Soto could pounce upon him, he had seized the tube and hurled it to the floor. If not utterly ruined it was out of commission for at least the remainder of that night. Panting from rage, De Soto stood staring in speechless hate at Crane. At last he got his breath.

"You fool," he gasped. "The next ten years in the penitentiary."

"Not if I know it," Crane retorted. "Any jury would let me off, if I told them what you were trying to do to me."

"What was I trying to do?" De Soto demanded with deadly calm.

"Nothing for the good of my health. That's all I know, and it is enough."

"You're insane. I try to find out what damage has been done to my apparatus and you attack me like a madman. Explain that to your jury. Also tell them that you deliberately wrecked my tube. Remember that you were discharged on the suspicion of having tampered with it already. Will you wait for the watchman, or will you come with me to the police station and surrender yourself?"

"Why not compromise? Suppose we talk these things over with the trustees in the morning. After all, you are only the Director, you know. This laboratory isn't your private property. That tube I have just smashed and everything else in here belongs to the Foundation. I'll meet you in the president's office at nine o'clock."

"So the trustees hired you to spy on me?"

"I'd be likely to tell you if they had, wouldn't I? Look at the common sense of our row for a change, and give your imagination a rest. You lost your temper and went clean crazy. Then you tried to give me a dose of something you don't like yourself. It probably wouldn't have killed me. You're not so crazy as that. But it might have done something worse. You know best. I'm willing to go before the trustees or the police, because I shall suggest that they find out exactly what you are trying to do with your short waves."

To Crane's astonishment, De Soto began to rock with laughter.

"I will tell you," he confessed. "The trustees are good business men, but they need educating. I planned to educate them. Now I have changed my mind. They were too fond of money, I thought, and they used my brains to flood the world with trash that only fools would want and only imbeciles pay for. Without me they would still be poor. Now they dream of owning the world. And but for my silly inventions the public would never have dreamed that it could want the stuff it buys. They asked me for rubbish because they could imagine nothing better to want, and I gave it to them with both hands as I would shower idiotic toys on a half-witted child. Like a fool myself I thought it would be a great thing to show all of them the one thing that every rational animal should crave."

"Which is?" Crane interrupted.

"Why should I tell you? Your prying incompetence may have wrecked my work. And you, like all of the bunglers earning their livings here, pass for a man of more than high average intelligence. Could you be educated to want what I planned to give the trustees and all their dupes? No. Nor can any living man or woman. So I shall change my plan and glut you all with what you crave. You deserve nothing better. Tell the president whatever you like. You can go."

"Before I do," Crane replied grimly, "let me tell you something for yourself. I don't understand what you are trying to do, and your high theories pass clean over my head. But I am sure of one thing. You are lying. By dropping your charges against me, you hope to pull the wool over my eyes. Well, you won't. I shall tell the trustees nothing."

De Soto laughed indifferently.

"Here's your key," he said, restoring Crane's duplicate. "Let yourself out. But don't try to come back, ever again. The next time I may have changed my mind."

When Crane was gone, De Soto picked up the tube and examined it critically. The damage could be repaired in two or three days or, if necessary, a new tube might be constructed in five weeks.

"I shall need batteries of these all over the civilized world," he mused. "Then the golden age will dawn."

HE locked up and walked slowly through the cheerless mists of the early morning, thinking gloomily of his bride. She would have waited up all night for him, he guessed, in spite of her assurance that she would not be a drag on him in his work. All of his grandiose projects for the human race had gone glimmering through no direct fault of his own. Any ordinary man would have said "a good job too"; for no such man could have foreseen as clearly as did De Soto the inevitable end of the race from its present state.

Passing a dingy restaurant, he suddenly realized that he was faint from hunger. Not until he had taken a seat at a slovenly table did the full depth of the profound change which had overtaken him in the past three hours register on his consciousness. An untidy waiter in a soiled white apron came to take his order.

"A ham sandwich and a cup of black coffee," he said, without looking up.

"I don't need to ask Crane or anyone else how long that tube was connected," he thought bitterly as he sat sipping his coffee. "Six hours ago this stuff would have stuck in my throat. Now I need it. I'm not well."

Indeed he was not. Idly picking up the greasy menu, he began listlessly reading through the list an item at a time. It did not even occur to him at the moment that this was not his "natural" way of getting the sense out of print. Exasperated by this unaccustomed difficulty in following the meaning of what he read, he finished his coffee, flung down a dollar, and left the place. The cool air refreshed him.

"How stupid," he muttered. "I forgot to bring the frogs and the guinea pigs." His "natural" mentality began to reassert itself. He hurried back to the laboratory and got his sack with the four animals. Outwardly they seemed normal. What were they like inside? Only time would show. The prospect of an interesting experiment cheered him up, and he went straight home, to find Alice anxiously waiting for him in the breakfast room. Again a slight lapse of memory warned him that he was unwell.

"What have you in the sack?" she asked, when their greetings were finally concluded.

"Oh," he lied readily, "some new pets. I saw them in the window of a Mexican restaurant and bought them. Two guinea pigs and a pair of frogs."

Alice was enchanted and De Soto, with a curious twinge as of some forgotten instinct stirring within him, noticed that she was charming. When had he been charmed by a girl before? He could not remember. His impersonal mind was, however, still uppermost. Before sitting down to a light breakfast with his bride, he carefully housed his "new" pets, each pair in a separate pen away from all others of the same kind.

"Alice," he began after breakfast, "I have a queer sort of honeymoon to propose. At first I had hoped that we might get away for a week or two, but an awkward turn in my work has put a trip out of the question. Suppose you come down to the laboratory when you have nothing better to do and watch the work? You can bring a book to pass the time when I'm too busy to talk."

She was more pleased than if he had suggested a six months' pleasure trip to the most frivolous playgrounds of Europe. As her husband looked tired, however, after his strenuous night in the laboratory—as she supposed—Alice insisted that he spend at least the morning in bed before they began this most delightful of all honeymoons.

When Crane left the laboratory a free man owing to De Soto's generosity, he went to the nearest telephone booth, learned that Brown had arrived home safely with Bertha, and made a dinner engagement at the doctor's house to talk things over the following evening. Both men were too fagged to think clearly until they had enjoyed a long sleep. Brown made arrangements with a friend to handle his practice and went to bed, determined to sleep ten hours at least. Before turning in, however, he took a pint sample of the bath water which De Soto had left in the tub, wrapped the bottle in several thicknesses of black paper, and left the package with a note for his housekeeper, requesting her to send it, with his card, to Professor Wilkes by special messenger the first thing in the morning. On his card he wrote: "Professor Wilkes. Please examine this sample microscopically at once. The trick to keep it from decomposing is to exclude all light. I will be at home after seven tonight." This time he felt sure of himself.

The professor, duly instructed by Hayashi's microphotographs of the protozoan fish parasites, would not pour the interesting sample down the sink. Brown's forecast proved right. At four o'clock that afternoon the housekeeper had almost to use force to turn Wilkes away. The doctor, she asserted, had given the strictest orders that he was not to be awakened till five o'clock. The professor left, lugging his heavy brief case, which the housekeeper erroneously mistook for a bootlegger's portmanteau. At six he was back, this time not to be denied admittance. While Brown was shaving and dressing, and apparently taking his own time about both, Wilkes dumped the contents of his bulging brief case on the hastily cleared study table and displayed his astounding evidence—to him it was no less—like an elaborate variety of solitaires played with a dozen packs of cards.

At last Brown entered.

The professor, he decided, had suffered in silence long enough.

"Look at that!" Wilkes exclaimed with a dramatic gesture toward his massive game.

"I don't have to," the doctor retorted. "I saw all that through the microscope before you threw away my first sample."

"But they form a perfect series," Wilkes expostulated, "from the lower species to the highest possible, and only the first half dozen of them recorded. Over a hundred and eighty types of protozoa new to science at one swoop! Where did you get them?"

"Where did Hayashi get his?"

"Diseased fish. But that all cleared up months ago. There has never been anything like this in the history of biology. Where did you find these?"

"I made them," Brown replied coolly, not expecting to be believed.

He wasn't.

It developed that Wilkes had spent the day making crude sketches, as fast as his fingers would work, of the curious life—or rather death—in the pint sample which Brown had sent him that morning. Most of the sketches were mere rough outlines. Some, however, exhibited considerable detail. These marked every fifteenth or twentieth place in the long series into which Wilkes had arranged Hayashi's photographs, a few of Brown's sketches, and his own. The effect, as the eye ran rapidly down the entire series, was roughly like that of a motion picture of a rosebud opening out in full bloom. Development of some sort, not mere growth, was evident. The sizes of the creatures depicted remained approximately constant; their complexity, however, increased with beautiful regularity to its climax, reaching a maximum at about two-thirds the total distance from the beginning of the series, and falling steeply down the decline to degenerated simplicity of structure at the end. It was as if a whole race of living things were maturing to its peak before their very eyes, and toppling to its inevitable extinction even as they watched.

"Well," said Brown. "Do you believe now?"

"I will, when you tell me what to believe. I can't doubt my own eyes."

"Nor your own common sense?"

"What has common sense to do with it? We are face to face with a new fact of nature."

"That's what I thought the first night I saw all this happening in a drop of mist. But there is an explanation. It is so simple as to be almost shocking. Haven't you guessed it?"

"More or less hazily. The time scale is all wrong. Impossible, I should say, if—"

"If you hadn't seen it yourself. Excuse me a minute; that must be my friend for dinner. You'll join us, won't you? It's Crane, the X-ray man."

"Does he know anything about all this?" the cautious Wilkes demanded, making a move to secrete his drawings.

"He should, as it was off his skin that I collected my first specimens."

"Introduce me at once!"

On being presented to the excited professor, Crane modestly denied any design in his startling contribution to biology.

"Doctor Brown," he concluded, "will probably have something more exciting to show you soon. By the way, doctor, did you give Bertha a bath after you got her home?"

"Great Scott! I clean forgot the possibility of her being infected as you were. Excuse me a moment. Dinner won't be ready for twenty minutes yet anyway." He dashed out to bathe the unsuspecting Bertha.

LEFT alone with the professor, Crane submitted resignedly to a barrage of questions. How had he ever suspected the existence of these teeming protozoa on his skin? Easily enough, Crane explained, adding that the professor himself would have been in no doubt under the circumstances. Venturing no theory, he went on to state briefly the beginning of the whole story—his thirty hours' exposure, spread over several weeks, to the hard X-rays generated by his two million volt tube, the suddenness with which the intolerable itching began, and the immediate relief when the superficial cause was removed.

"You are positive that your tube generated nothing but hard X-rays? Well," the professor admitted on receiving Crane's fairly confident assurance, "it must have been the prolonged exposure that started the explosion—on your skin, I mean. None of the other biological workers with mere X-rays ever produced such results. Not that they tried, however; although now I fail to see why it never occurred to some of them to do just what you did accidentally. Of course, there would be a delayed, cumulative action under proper doses of the rays spread over a long interval. The sum of all the doses applied in one shot might well be fatal; it certainly would have a different effect from repeated applications of small amounts. Isn't that so, Brown?" he appealed to the doctor who had just reëntered the study.

"Probably not," Brown laughed. "But I confess I did not hear your argument."

Over the dinner table, Wilkes elaborated his not unreasonable theory, letting his soup cool until the diplomatic maid removed it untasted.

Brown did not disagree. In fact he pointed out a similarity between Wilkes' theory and the standard treatment by X-rays, whereby a strong beam that by itself would seriously injure healthy tissue, is split up into ten or more parts all focused on the desired inaccessible spot. However, he was less interested in Wilkes' guess as to what he termed the "explosion" of the protozoa than in what the nature of that explosion itself might be.

The professor was game.

"Don't laugh at me," he began, "and for Heaven's sake never tell any of my colleagues that I ever talked such fantastic nonsense. Well, here goes. It's an old story now how Miller, Dieffenbach and others first managed to produce permanent modifications in certain living flies, that were transmitted for generation after generation to the remote descendants of the original flies. You recall how it was done; the perfectly normal flies were exposed to X-rays, and then carefully segregated and watched while nature took its usual course with flies. They increased and multiplied. But some of the sons and daughters had curious defects of the eyes and other peculiarities from which their parents did not suffer. The sons and daughters were encouraged to mate without having been treated by the rays, as their parents had been. Their offspring inherited all the acquired characteristics. Thus it went for generation after generation; the artificial modifications initially produced by the rays were passed on from father and mother fly to son and daughter fly, precisely as if the first freaks were the natural offspring of their parents—which they were not. It was as remarkable, in its own way, as if a war veteran with only one arm should have a son with only one arm—and the same arm, right or left, and the son in his turn should have a son or daughter with the same defect, and so on for hundreds of generations."

"Don't you want any dinner tonight?" Brown interrupted, as the maid was about to make off with the professor's unviolated chop.

"There's only a salad and cheese with black coffee and crackers after this."

"Dinner? What's dinner in a crisis like this? Evolution has gone mad before my very eyes. Here," he called after the maid, "please bring back my plate. One must eat, even in a lunatic asylum. Now," he continued, firmly spearing his chop, "consider what all this means. Take the human race, for instance. We're mammals; you admit that. And what are mammals, ultimately, but an offshoot of the reptiles? How did they shoot off in the first place?"

"Don't ask me," Crane muttered guiltily, as the professor fixed him with a flashing eye. "Brown ought to know."

"He ought to. But does he? No? Well neither do I," Wilkes exclaimed, evidently well satisfied with himself. "But I have a theory —no, not now. Later, when we get to the bottom of your new protozoa. What do the biologists tell us?"

"You ought to know," Brown suggested. "Don't you make your living at biology?"

"I do know!"

"The mammals sprang from the reptiles by a mutation—a sudden change of species."

"Rot," Crane commented tersely and incisively, with the superior wisdom of the physicist accustomed to manufacturing theories in the evening to be thrown overboard in the morning.

To his great disgust, Wilkes unexpectedly agreed with him.

"Of course it is rot," Wilkes assented. "I know even better than you that mutations explain nothing; they merely give a fancy name to the fact we are trying to understand. Evolution by jumps, instead of slow, continuous growth—there's another statement of the same thing. What I want to know," he exclaimed, bringing his fist down on the table, "is what causes these jumps. The physical reason—not a restatement of the problem. Something suddenly took place in the germ cells of the reptiles, and they brought forth strange creatures—no stranger than those artificial flies with the queer eyes—that later evolved into your ancestors and mine. Tell me that, and I'll rule the world!"

"Shall we tell him?" Crane asked with a dry smile.

"I haven't the heart," Brown replied in the same vein.

"He might pour us all down his kitchen sink."

The debate lasted well into the night, and, like most battles with words, settled nothing. The real debate had not yet begun. Things, tangible and real, were presently to play their part in the argument. Nevertheless, the trio did succeed in forming a not unreasonable guess as to what the professor's interesting series of drawings signified. At two o'clock in the morning, when the little party broke up, they agreed to stick to the problem until they could control the protozoa at will. The professor's parting cry of triumph was to the effect that he now held the key to evolution in his hand.

"Better throw it away, then," Crane remarked. "I got caught this morning with a key that I had no business having, and I'm afraid I'm in for a peck of trouble."

On the way out, after Wilkes had gone, he briefly told the doctor of De Soto's truce.

"I don't like it," Brown remarked. "Especially his attempt to force you to tell him how long his tube had been running when he came in. De Soto has been fooling with something he only half understands. I guess that we caught him in his own trap."

"If so, we had better shoot him before he breaks out again. He's a bad egg. Good night; see you tomorrow."

IX. BERTHA'S BROOD

SOME three weeks after Brown's dinner party, a puzzled electrical engineer in New York sat reading and re-reading the most extraordinary letter that any human being ever received. The engineer was the once celebrated Andrew Williams whose early patents on high-power transmission remade the wholesale electrical industry and founded the colossal fortune of the now defunct Power Transmission Corporation—P.T.C. as it was known in its prime.

Vice-President Williams' brain had made P.T.C. both possible and prosperous; Miguel De Soto's better brain had made it both impossible and bankrupt. The decline of P.T.C. began when the Erickson crowd captured all long distance, high tension power projects with their new principle of electrical insulation. From decline to ruin was little more than one stride, and P.T.C. took it. Overnight, when the first great advertising campaign of the Erickson began to bear plums for its sponsors, and thistles for its competitors, the stock of P.T.C. fell from 180 dollars a share to 14 dollars and 50 cents. It was a washout, and the unfortunate corporation was drowned. All that remained was to wind up the affairs of the corporation—with the help of the somewhat unsympathetic courts—and start all over again. The first would take from six months to a year. What the reorganized P.T.C. should manufacture was a mystery. Williams rather favored radio sets, but the rapidity with which the Erickson Foundation relegated successive improvements in that field to the National Museum of Arts and Sciences, made the Vice-President's associates pessimistic and chary. They for the most part advised a complete clean-up of the business and a general retirement on the wreckage for all its officers.

The letter which caused Williams such bewildered astonishment was thirty pages long, typed in single space, and anonymous. No water-mark or other identification betrayed where the paper might have been purchased. The paper itself was rather peculiar for a business letter. It was thin, light brown wrapping paper, such as is commonly used in department stores for doing up parcels, cut to the standard typewriter size. The cutting apparently had been done with a sharp penknife. Although the typescript was plainly legible, the marks of numerous erasures on every page indicated that whoever had operated the machine was no skilled typist. The general appearance suggested that the entire thirty pages had been painfully pecked out a letter at a time. As a last, significant detail the type had all the earmarks of that from a practically new typewriter.

Most sensible persons consign anonymous letters to the fire, if one is handy; if not, they tear the letter into small pieces and entrust it to the wastebasket. Williams, on looking for the signature and finding none, was tempted to be sensible. The opening sentence of the letter arrested his attention, however, and he read it breathlessly to the end.

"Sir," the letter began, "I herewith present you with the infallible means for recovering all of your recent losses and regaining your monopoly over the power transmission industry at no cost to yourself."

The letter concluded with the suggestion that Vice-President Williams at once patent everything of value in the detailed specifications.

"My purposes," the anonymous writer asserted in a postscript, "are purely humanitarian and educational."

For the twentieth time Williams scrutinized the large Manila envelope in which the letter had come—unfolded. Only his own name, with the words "Personal and Important" added, all in the same kind of typing as that of the letter, offered any clue to the sender. Obviously no detective could hope to trace the letter from these data alone. Williams rang for his secretary.

"When was this envelope delivered?"

"I couldn't say. The office boy laid it on my desk at eight o'clock this morning with the rest of the mail from our own box."

The office boy remembered taking the large envelope from the mailbox with the rest. There the clues ended. The Vice President again summoned his secretary.

"If anyone asks for me, tell him I have gone to Washington, D. C. I'll leave my hotel address at the information desk in the U. S. Patent Office in case of an emergency. Don't expect me back for a week."

Williams had been a great inventor in his younger days, and he knew that noble game from alpha to omega. Unless some crank were hoaxing him by passing off as a free gift the work of another man already ready to be patented, but not yet divulged to the general public, Williams felt confident that he now held the world's tail in his right hand and a sharp ox-goad in his left. And how he would make the brute sweat and plod for him when once he started cultivating his rich opportunities! Provided the genius who had invented this irresistible goad had not yet filed the necessary papers, Williams cared not a damn for any moral rights the man might have in his masterpiece; the legal technicalities alone troubled him. Could he beat the cracked genius to the patent office before the idiot repented of his insane generosity for "purposes purely humanitarian and educational"? What wouldn't the rejuvenated P.T.C. do to the blustering, overbearing Erickson with this pointed stick in its capable hand?

From gloating over his anticipated revenge on his unscrupulous rivals, Williams, gazing absently over the fleeting housetops from his seat in the passenger plane, soon fell to speculating on his faithful associates and superiors at the flattened P.T.C. Who among them all had greatly concerned himself with the Vice President's comparative ruin? Not one; their only concern was to salvage at least the rind of their own bacon from the general mess. He, they intimated, was no longer useful to them. Therefore he might go to the devil as fast as he liked. Williams began to smile. His friends were no longer of interest to him. Could they raise capital to finance the goad? They could not. He, on the other hand, with an argument like this patent—which he now felt sure of obtaining—could persuade all the bulls and bears in Wall Street to dance jigs on their heads for his pleasure.

Williams, in short, was not one of those rare souls whom prosperity does not corrode. Had he but guessed that his anonymous benefactor intended by his gift that the recipient *should* go to the devil, as the P.T.C. had already hinted, his smile might have been less confident. The joke after all might turn out to be on him, as a mere pawn in the humanitarian and educational purpose of the donor.

It must have been the very morning that Williams rushed off to the U. S. Patent Office that De Soto rose much earlier than usual and, while Alice still slept, stole out to the back garden to inspect his menagerie of pets. For the past three or four days one of the guinea pigs and both of the frogs which he had taken to the laboratory had been acting strangely. In no case were their actions those of animals in normal distress. Each seemed to sense in some mysterious way the nature of the unseemly jest which chance—or design—had played upon it, and each of the hapless creatures appeared to be anticipating with an unnatural dread the miracle which was almost upon it. The natural rhythm of its vital functions had been violated.

Walking slowly over to the cage where the ailing guinea pig lay, De Soto took a firm grip on himself.

"In five seconds now," he thought, with a rueful laugh, "I shall know how long that blundering fool Crane had left the tube running."

A sack had been laid over the top slats of the cage, as the light seemed to irritate the prospective mother. With a firm hand De Soto raised the sack and peered down into the cage. The miracle had happened in the night. In one corner of the cage the wretched mother cowered in unnatural fright, panting with terror. The eyes of the stricken animal, already clouding at the approach of death, were fixed on the farther corner, opposite her own, where lay the four things to which she had given life against her will. De Soto had half expected a shock. But even he was unprepared for what he saw. He replaced the sack, strode to the garage, and fetched a shovel and a bottle of chloroform which he had concealed in the tool cabinet a week before—when the guinea pig first showed signs of distress. In ten minutes he had done what was necessary.

"Now for the other," he muttered, going toward the pen where the suspected frogs lived. Again the miracle had happened. In this instance there were no unnatural young. Frogs propagate from eggs. Therein this pair had an advantage over the guinea pig. What their offspring might be was yet undetermined. De Soto decided not to wait for outraged nature to reveal the unknown. The two repulsive monsters, whose grotesquely budded bodies made his blood run cold, were sufficient. Once more he used the chloroform and the shovel.

"I know now how long the tube was running," he thought. Involuntarily he began feeling his muscles and running his fingers lightly over his skin to detect the incipient nodules. "Am I to go like the frogs," he muttered; "or are only my germ cells affected? One or the other; but which? Perhaps both."

He walked slowly back to the garage to put away the shovel. The half bottle of chloroform being of no further use, he intended emptying it and throwing the empty bottle into the rubbish can. Drawing the cork from the bottle he started to pour out the remaining chloroform, and paused irresolutely.

"I wish I knew," he muttered, staring moodily up at the window of his bedroom. His bride of three weeks was still asleep in that room.

Whatever may be a man's abstract theories about humanity as a whole, three weeks of marriage, and especially the first three, will modify them in detail. Moreover, De Soto had undergone a profound physical change the first night of his married life; he was no longer, mentally at any rate, the man whom Alice had married that happy afternoon. Among other discoveries of those three weeks, De Soto learned that he was beginning to love his bride in the human and humane way of ordinary men whom, three weeks before, he had despised. "I wish I knew," he repeated, still undecided. A vivid image of what he had seen in the cage with the dying guinea pig flashed into his mind. Hesitating no longer, he recorked the bottle, slipped it under his coat, and stole into the house. In the kitchen he selected a clean dish towel and stuffed it into a coat pocket. Then he crept upstairs.

Alice was still sleeping, her bare arms gracefully disposed on the silken sheet, and her ruddy lips slightly parted like a child's. She was smiling in her sleep as De Soto stealthily extracted the cork from the chloroform bottle and drew the dish towel from his pocket. For perhaps five seconds De Soto stood motionless, staring at her beautiful face with something like dawning compassion in his eyes. Then he began pouring the chloroform, a few drops at a time, upon the towel. As the sweet, sickly odor flowed slowly down on the rosy face, the sleeper stirred slightly and murmured a word that sounded like her husband's name. Although his hand shook, De Soto did not desist.

At last the towel was saturated, and De Soto laid the bottle noiselessly on the floor. He straightened up, his muscles stiffened for the inevitable struggle.

"Where are those flowers?" the sleeper murmured, now half awake. "Miguel!" Her eyes opened fully, if drowsily. Instantly he thrust the towel under his coat. "What is it?" she asked, staring up. "You got up early?"

"Yes," he replied slowly. "I thought I smelt gas escaping from the refrigerating plant. Do you get it?"

"I thought I was dreaming of acres of red roses. Now that you mention it, I do notice a sweetish smell. Have you been downstairs to look?"

"No, I was just going when you woke up. Don't worry; I'm sure it's nothing serious. I'll open the dressing-room doors and let it blow out. Where are my slippers? Oh, here they are."

Bending down quickly he managed to secrete the bottle under his coat while pretending to put on his slippers.

"Hadn't you better call the servants?" she suggested as he flung open the doors of the dressing rooms.

"No," he laughed. "It's still nearly three quarters of an hour ahead of their usual time. You forget that I'm a sort of glorified tinker myself. I'll soon fix whatever is wrong. Now you take another nap; I may as well stay up now that I'm dressed."

"If she hadn't opened her eyes," he muttered as he descended the back stairs to the kitchen, "I could have done it. Now I never can. There must be some other way of neutralizing it in her—if it has happened. Why can't I think clearly as I used to think? Well, I can only try. This blind fighting in the dark——"

Although De Soto did not know it, and indeed was incapable of realizing the fact, he not only was changed but was also in the merciless grip of a slow but incessant transformation. He was like a robust man of splendid intellect suddenly assailed by an insidious and incurable disease of the bodily functions and mental faculties. Such a man, in the first, gradual stages of his decay, perceives nothing wrong with himself, and attributes his slackening grip to an inexplicable conspiracy of outward circumstances. The problems he could have attacked and solved in his prime baffle him in his decline because—according to his rationalization of his disease—they are more abstruse than any to which he is accustomed. His friends, pitying him in his decay, do not disillusion him, and he goes to his grave believing that the world has passed him in its ceaseless progress, whereas it is his own rapid retrogression that has shot the world ahead beyond his ken.

THE first three weeks of Alice's honeymoon had passed in a happy dream, at least for her. Every morning she accompanied her husband to his laboratory and passed the day pretending to read but actually following his every movement with devoted eyes. She proved herself an ideal companion for a desperately busy man, talking only when he showed an inclination for talk. When lunch time passed unobserved by her husband, she would slip out to the nearest restaurant, to return presently with an appetizing meal, which she spread out unobtrusively where he might notice it.

Even in the first week Alice observed a curious change in the man she worshiped. Mistakenly, she imagined that he was working too hard. All the staff had told her such wonderful tales of the lightning sureness of his mind, that it puzzled her to see him frequently baffled. Unaware that she was watching his slightest movement, De Soto would often sit for minutes at a time, turning some piece of apparatus over and over in his hands, as if in doubt concerning its use, although he had made it himself. These lapses became more frequent as the construction of the new tube progressed, until by the end of the third week practically half a day would be wasted in futile scribbling or blundersome manipulations. Alice became alarmed, and begged him to take a rest, if only for a week.

His reply was a stare of unfeigned surprise. Wasn't he getting along famously? Why interrupt the work with the end in sight? With a chill feeling about her heart, Alice realized that her husband was headed straight for a nervous breakdown, and was so far gone that he failed to appreciate his illness.

At length Alice could stand the suspense no longer. On the morning of the day when De Soto had been tempted to destroy her, she asked his permission to invite an old friend to dinner that evening.

"Of course," he agreed readily. "Who is it?"

"Doctor Brown. I haven't seen him since I was married, and he was so good to father and me."

"Why not invite your father, too? It must be pretty lonely living at a hotel."

She hugged him in an ecstasy of happiness. De Soto, for his part, felt an unaccustomed uneasiness at the prospect of a meeting with Brown. Would the doctor inadvertently refer to the strange disorder of which De Soto had never told his wife? He must see Brown first and warn him to be silent. Then a disturbing question echoed through his mind: Why must Brown be warned? Surely there was nothing disgraceful in a man keeping a passing sickness from his wife? Ah; De Soto remembered—but not clearly. It mattered nothing whether Alice learned of his itching skin, now permanently cured. No; but she must never hear of what happened in the laboratory that night when he caught Crane trying to work his tube. A worried frown darkened his face. Exactly what had happened that night? The main events stood out fairly clearly, but the details were blurred almost beyond recall.

"Alice," he said, "I guess I'll take a layoff next week, after I finish my tube. It will be done this morning, I hope."

"Oh, how jolly! That's just what I've wanted you to do ever since we were married. Only," she added in a low voice, her eyes shining with unshed tears, "you seemed to think so much of your work that I never dared to hint."

For some minutes he remained coldly silent. Had she displeased him by her outburst of affection? Alice glanced shyly at his face. Why was he so withdrawn into himself, so far away, in seeming, from her and the world she knew? At length he spoke, more to himself than to her.

"Something happened a long time ago, when, I can't recall. But it was so far away in time that it seems like a dream from another life. What was it? Why can't I remember? And why should I always seem to be on the point of meeting someone whose existence I have forgotten?"

"Never mind," she said soothingly; "if it is anything that you should remember, it will all come back after you have had a real rest."

As De Soto had prophesied, the new tube was finished and ready for operation that morning. Shortly before noon it was connected to the twenty million volt box, all but the last terminal which would close the circuit and start the generation of the rays. Alice at the time was pretending to read. Apparently she was absorbed in her story. De Soto furtively studied her profile a full minute and then went to the closet where the insulating suits were stored. Presently he emerged, clad from head to foot in a double sheath of the transparent armor. Alice put aside her book and laughed.

"How funny you look in those things! I never saw you dressed up that way before. What's it for?"

"Oh, just for a fussy precaution," he replied lightly. "You see, there might be a faulty connection that would cause a spark. This makes everything perfectly safe, no matter if the whole box blows up. But it won't, so you needn't worry. You stay over there."

He did not act in haste. As dispassionately as he could he weighed the probable consequences of what he was about to do. His penetrating insight into the laws of nature was already clouding. Like the ordinary man of genius he was now reduced to weighing probabilities and selecting what appeared the least undesirable. Involuntarily shutting his eyes he quickly turned on the full twenty million volts for an instant, and then off again, by two quick twists of the screw switch.

The shriek that Alice emitted sounded scarcely human. Although De Soto had expected it, his blood froze. Tearing off his hood he ran to her. She had not fainted, but stood staring at him like a shadow in a dream, her eyes dark with terror.

"What was it?" he cried, as if he did not know.

"Are you hurt?" she gasped.

"No. Don't you see? Why did you scream like that?"

"I don't know. For a second I thought you were killed. Then something seemed to tear me to pieces—inside, here."

"Imagination," he boldly reassured her. "You feel all right now?"

"I suppose so," she admitted doubtfully. "But I feel—oh, how can I express it? Changed." Then, after a pause she added in a voice which he scarcely heard,

"Defiled and degraded."

"Nerves, Alice. You imagined that what I was doing was terribly dangerous. Sorry I stirred you up by putting on all this ridiculous fancy dress. When I turned on the current you thought I was killed. Come on, let's go out to lunch and get some fresh air."

Still dazed, she sat down and waited until he removed his protective armor and put on his coat. What had happened to her? Merely an attack of nerves, probably, as he asserted. Yet she felt inhumanly unclean. By a curious coincidence the warning which Crane had thrust upon her recurred now with startling clarity. As if her old friend were standing before her, she saw his face with her mind's eye and heard his disturbing prophecy: "If you marry him you will kill yourself to be rid of him." What did Crane know of her husband that she did not? Surely nothing, she concluded reassuringly as her common sense regained the control of her subconscious mind. Then, from her deepest nature, just as her husband reappeared, a despairing instinct whispered, "Destroy yourself before it is too late." But this warning, like Crane's, yielded to gross common sense, and she joined her husband with a smile.

"I'm all right now," she said, and believed it.

On the way to lunch she telephoned to her father and Doctor Brown, inviting them to dinner that evening. Both accepted eagerly, especially Kent, who was longing for a sight of his daughter. Brown looked forward to the evening with mixed feelings. To sit down at the dinner table with a man whom you distrust and whom you have wronged is likely to be rather trying.

THAT evening Kent arrived first, three-quarters of an hour ahead of time. After a decently cordial greeting, De Soto retired to inspect his pets, leaving father and daughter together to discuss him to their hearts' content. To the happy father's uncritical eyes Alice seemed the picture of health and youthful happiness. Kent himself was in high spirits. For a week he had been employed as booster-in-chief for a go-getter real estate firm, and was enjoying his work tremendously. As the time for Brown's arrival drew near, Alice hinted that she would like to see the doctor alone for a few minutes. "About Miguel," she explained. "He has been overworking. Suppose you go out and ask him to show you his pets? He's crazy over them, and will let no one else have any of the care of them." The bell rang just as Kent made his escape.

"Well, Alice," the doctor greeted her, "this is just like old times. How is everything with you?"

"I'm ridiculously happy," she laughed, "except for one thing. Won't you drop Miguel a hint that he must take a long rest?"

"From what the men in the laboratory tell me, your husband

isn't given to long rests. Still, I shall do my best, if you wish it. What seems to be the trouble?"

"First, let me tell you that I spend my days in his laboratory, reading and watching him work. He is usually so absorbed that he doesn't know I'm there. So I can't help seeing him as he really is. And I have noticed that he is dreadfully tired, although he does not know it. For one thing, he has long lapses of memory."

"I'll speak to him," Brown replied decisively. "We can't afford to have him unwell or you unhappy. What about yourself? Feeling pretty fine?"

The doctor, eyeing her keenly, noted the slight hesitation and the flush before she replied.

"Never felt better in my life," she began. An overpowering wish to confide in her friend suddenly stopped her. Almost before she realized what she was doing, she had told him of the excruciating momentary agony she had experienced that morning in the laboratory. "It was probably just an attack of nerves, wasn't it?"

"Tell me exactly what happened."

She went into detail, describing the whole incident and De Soto's explanation. Brown, of course, noticed the flaming fact that Alice was unprotected while her husband neglected no precaution to shield himself against possible danger. Like a good doctor, Brown's face betrayed no concern. Nevertheless he was revolving in his mind a black question that chilled him to the bone. Had De Soto merely blundered, or had he intentionally left Alice unprotected? And if the latter, what could be his object? For Brown vividly remembered certain cries which he and Crane had heard—those of a helpless animal. What would a human being suffer in similar circumstances? Had Alice indeed been subjected to the same treatment as Bertha?

"Miguel was right, wasn't he?" she concluded. "There couldn't have been a leaky connection, or we should both have been killed. It was just my nerves."

"Not a doubt of it. You take my advice and keep out of the laboratory after this. The next time something real might happen. By the way, you have no tingling or itching of the skin?"

"Not a trace."

"Then that settles it," the doctor assured her. From his tone she inferred that he dismissed the flash of pain as a fiction of her imagination. That of course was precisely what Brown meant her to believe. The point, however, which her healthy skin settled in the doctor's mind was more important. She had taken the full bolt of the rays generated by twenty million volts, if indeed she had been exposed to any, and not the greatly softer rays given off at two million volts' pressure. Kent and De Soto joined them just as dinner was announced.

During the meal Brown concentrated his attention on De Soto, leaving Kent and Alice to gossip of old times at the Foundation. Poor Kent, in spite of his pride in his new job, longed for the fleshpots of his lost dictatorship. A jealous note crept into his voice, and the doctor overheard him surreptitiously expressing a hopeful belief that the Erickson would come to a bad end. They were too grasping, he declared, caring nothing for the common decencies of reputable business competition. De Soto overheard the remark.

"I agree," he said quietly. "The trustees need educating."

"In what?" Brown asked.

"Human decency, if there is such a thing."

"Miguel!" Alice murmured reproachfully. "You know you don't mean that."

"No, I meant more." His voice rose. "The whole human race needs educating—in the same way. Why, I remember when I was a young man—."

"You can't be so very ancient now," Brown interrupted, with a curious glance at his host's excited face.

It was an unfortunate remark. Something snapped in De Soto's brain. Flinging down his napkin, he pushed back his chair and leapt to his feet, his black eyes blazing. Luckily no servant was present at the moment. Speaking with great rapidity and in a low voice vibrant with passion he delivered a flaming tirade against everything human. Alice watched his face with something akin to terror in her eyes; Kent sat open-mouthed and blank; Brown followed every word with rigid attention. An alienist, knowing nothing of the facts, would have pronounced De Soto incurably insane. The very logic of his fantastic indictment was its most damning feature. Brown was not an alienist. But he had the average high grade physician's knowledge of the earmarks of insanity.

Silently admitting to himself that any specialist on mental disorders would be fully justified in declaring De Soto insane, he nevertheless felt confident that the raving man was sane with a terrible sanity denied most human beings. The outburst lasted but a brief two minutes. It was like a terrific stab of lightning on a sultry midsummer night. Breathing heavily, De Soto resumed his seat and began crumbling a piece of bread.

Brown broke the sulphurous silence. With a significant glance at Alice, which she interpreted correctly by kicking her father under the table, the doctor began a cool cross-examination of De Soto.

"Your theories of human society are interesting but academic. How can you put them into action?"

"Oh," De Soto laughed, apparently himself once more, "I can't. My theories are just theories, nothing more. I thought they might amuse you."

"They did. You seriously think it would be possible to educate human beings out of their greed for what you call trash by stuffing them with so much of it that they would rebel?"

"Not exactly. That would be merely the first step."

"And the second?"

"Give them different tastes. Even that cook and waiter had rudimentary minds that the right process could work on."

"What cook and waiter?" Brown demanded quietly.

"I just told you."

Before continuing his examination, Brown shot Alice a warning glance.

"Of course," he said. "I forgot. Let us suppose you have made the rest of us disgusted with the things we like. Would you give us something better?"

"I was going to. But——"

"But what?"

"Oh, what's the use of theorizing? Leave it to history."

BROWN changed his tactics. One or two statements of fact which De Soto had let fall in his tirade needed attention.

"As you say, history will attend to our descendants—unless we find some way of doing it ourselves. Another thing you said is more interesting, I imagine, to all of us. You have always been rather a mystery man to most of us, Mr. De Soto. We never knew that you spent some of your earlier years in the United States."

"Neither did I," De Soto retorted with an amazed stare. "Who said I did?"

"My mistake," Brown apologized. "But it seemed to me that the conditions you mentioned could exist only in the United States."

"They exist everywhere."

"In the Argentine, for instance?"

"The Argentine?" the puzzled bewilderment on De Soto's face showed plainly that he did not perceive the drift of Brown's question.

"I just used it as an example of 'everywhere'," Brown explained.

It was clear that De Soto either was lying or that he was so ill that he remembered nothing of his early life. Kent was about to break in when Alice silenced him with a warning look. She, too, had believed that De Soto spent his youth in Buenos Aires. Poor

Miguel was indeed unwell. She hurriedly turned the conversation into less personal channels.

The distressing party broke up early. At a hint from Alice, Kent left immediately after dinner, saying he had to be up very early to keep a distant engagement. Alice followed him to the door, leaving Brown alone with her husband. She did not hurry back. The doctor caught her expressive glance as she went out.

"Mr. De Soto," he began as soon as they were alone, "you are too valuable to society to overtax your strength the way you do. If you are not to squander all your talents in a silly nervous breakdown, you had better take a long rest."

"I am planning to," he replied. "My work is practically done."

"Not all of it, surely?" the doctor suggested. "That's no state of mind for a young fellow like you."

De Soto flared up again.

"What do you know of my age?"

"Keep cool. Don't fly into rages over trifles. As a matter of fact I don't know your age, but I should guess it to be about thirty."

"Thirty?" De Soto echoed in astonishment. "Why I was born—."

"When?" the doctor prompted. Receiving only a puzzled look, he continued. "You have forgotten that, too. Your wife is right. Take a lay-off."

Alice reëntered, and Brown took his departure. She saw him into the hall.

"Your husband will be all right," he reassured her, "if he lets up a bit. If there is anything I can do for you at any time, please let me know."

The doctor walked thoughtfully home, wondering what sort of a man De Soto was at bottom. Was Crane right in his estimate, and if so, in what particular way was De Soto a thoroughly bad egg? Brown half doubted his friend's opinion after seeing the suspect in action. More likely the brilliant young inventor was merely eccentric. But was he also a bungler in practical details? That was the hard question. Its answer would decide whether De Soto was guilty or not guilty in regard to the mishap to Alice.

As he passed along the south wall of his garden, Brown heard a prodigious fuss from the hens in the patio. At this hour of the evening they should all have been roosting and silent. That they were active and excited in the dark, in flagrant contradiction of the normal habits of the fowls, presaged some event of unnatural significance.

"Bertha's laid another," he exclaimed, hurrying into the house to fetch his flashlight.

Since her involuntary adventure in the laboratory, Bertha had set out to beat the world's record in laying eggs. She had already broken the record in the matter of numbers. The size, however, of her efforts disqualified her. None of her numerous eggs had been over a fifth the size of a normal hen's egg. The shells, too, of these "pigeon eggs," as Brown called them, were remarkably deficient in lime. Some were little more than sacs of flexible white skin, like the inner sheath of an ordinary egg. Naturally the doctor had watched his phenomenal hen as closely as if she were his wealthiest patient. She had laid no fewer than sixty-three of the dwarf eggs. She, herself, seemed quite satisfied, as she sat almost constantly on the whole nestful.

The henyard was in a wild commotion. The doctor's flashlight revealed an excited dozen or so hens pecking viciously at some dark red object. This proved to be Bertha, her feathers drenched in her own blood. She was dead, but still warm. Brown shooed the enraged hens away from the body and placed it under an empty coop. Then he investigated.

From the evidence it appeared that Bertha had died defending her brood. Eighteen of the eggs had hatched. Thinking for a moment that he had gone insane, the doctor stared down at the dead hen's living offspring writhing over the unhatched eggs. Then he scooped the lot, eggs and offspring, into his hat, hurried back to the house and telephoned to Wilkes and Crane.

"Come over at once. I have some things millions of years old to show you, and they're alive."

He turned one of the crawlers over on its back with a pencil.

"No wonder the other hens pecked her to death. I would have done the same in their case."

X. CAT AND MOUSE

In scientific circles there are several semi-human periodicals which contain, in addition to technical papers, brief personal notes concerning the scientists themselves. For example, if Professor X. is appointed to the vacancy created by the death or resignation of Doctor Y., the fact is stated, so that the scientific friends of Professor X. may know where to address him.

Crane, of course, took advantage of these free employment agencies when De Soto discharged him, and sent in a note to each, saying that he was no longer connected with the Erickson Foundation. He hoped to receive at least one tempting offer before his bonus ran out. The hope was not extravagant. Before De Soto's brilliance had eclipsed that of all inventors in his own many fields combined, Crane was justly rated as the best ray expert in the country. Hence, should some desperate firm attempt to hold its own small corner of the field against the Erickson, Crane was their most promising prospect, as De Soto seemed satisfied where he was. In fact several firms were already considering Crane when the official news of his "resignation" was published. They knew that his nose was out of joint at the Erickson and hoped to get him cheap. In this they were disappointed. Other attractions held Crane jobless to his post.

At last, five weeks after the evening when Wilkes and he responded to Brown's excited telephone call, Crane received a three hundred word telegram, signed Andrew Williams, President Universal Power Transmission Company, offering him a royal salary as chief consulting physicist. The telegram, while avoiding all details of technical value, stated that the new company had been formed to exploit a revolutionary invention for the transmission of electric energy. This much occupied less than twenty words. The remainder of the telegram was chiefly a roll call of the wealthiest business men in America. These, Williams stated, were floating the company on their own money. That list of names would have impressed the Sphynx.

"Hang it," Crane muttered, "I can't turn down an offer like this and keep my self-respect. I shall have to accept, just as Wilkes and Brown are getting to the most exciting point."

Before telegraphing his acceptance, he called on the president of the Erickson trustees. This time the president bustled out in person to greet his caller.

"Come into my office," he begged. "Well," he asked when they were alone, "you have found something about the subject which we talked of two months ago?"

"Nothing of commercial value," Crane admitted.

"Your opinion of Mr. De Soto is the same?"

"Yes. Only more so. I can't tell you why. But I am beginning to get a definite line on him. By the way, did he ever tell you that I spent an hour in his laboratory without his consent?" The president shook his head: "I thought he wouldn't. Well, what I came about is this." He handed the president the telegram from Williams. "It does not say confidential," he remarked; "so there is no harm in your seeing it."

The president read it through slowly twice. Its commercial implications for the Erickson were obvious.

"You will accept, of course?" said the president. Crane pointed out that he would be a fool to refuse. "I agree," said the president.

"You will not forget us, I hope? We were not ungenerous to you."

"What can I do that your own staff can't? This invention must have been patented before the company was formed. So anyone can find out by going to the Patent Office exactly what it is. Why not send De Soto to Washington at once? Even if the patents are ironclad to the ordinary man, he will find a way through them."

"Do you mind if I show him this telegram?"

"I guess it's ethical enough. Go ahead."

De Soto was not in his laboratory. On telephoning to his house, the president learned from Alice that her husband was not at home.

"Can you tell me where I could get in touch with him, Mrs. De Soto? This is a most urgent matter; otherwise I should not dream of troubling you."

"He had an appointment with Doctor Brown this morning at eleven. Probably he is at the doctor's office now."

"Not unwell, I trust?"

"Oh, no. It was just about a personal matter."

De Soto was located at Brown's office. He promised to be at the Foundation within half an hour. While waiting for him to appear, the president kept delicately reminding Crane of the great debt of gratitude, which he, Crane, as an altruistic scientist, must feel that he owed the Erickson Foundation. Crane had difficulty in smothering his grins. The game was too obvious.

When De Soto entered, he nodded curtly to Crane, and proceeded to business.

"What is it?" he demanded.

"Doctor Crane advises that I show you this telegram, Mr. De Soto."

De Soto was almost his "old" self for a few seconds. He took in the sense of the long telegram at a glance.

"Electrical energy?" he questioned with a short, contemptuous laugh. "So that's the sort of thing these great financiers gamble on, is it? Serve them right if they get cleaned out. I have neither sympathy nor patience with them."

"But," the president expostulated, "all of our own business is built up on electrical energy in some form or another. What is to become of our insulation if these people have something that beats it? And our radio valves—everything we manufacture. Don't you see how serious this may be for us?"

"No. It doesn't matter what they do."

"You know what they have?"

"I do not," De Soto snapped. "And what is more, I don't care. If I did wish to learn, I should telegraph at once to Washington for a copy of the patents."

"Hadn't I better do so?"

"Why? I can beat anything they do."

"Really, Mr. De Soto," the president demurred, "although we all have the utmost confidence in your genius, I must say that your attitude strikes me as a little too—how shall I say it?"

"Call it cocksure, if you like. I shan't mind, because I do know what I am talking about."

"But consider this list of names for a minute. Would men of such standing in the business world put their own money into a scheme that wasn't gilt-edged?"

"They would, and they have, because they are one and all uneducated fools."

"I must protest! These men——"

"Do so. And so shall I. In fact I have already protested in the only way that counts. I call a financier uneducated when he puts a lot of his money into a scheme that he does not *know* will win. As I said, I can beat anything they do, and I don't mind if Crane tells them so. They won't believe it."

"BUT what are we to do?"

"Nothing, for the present. Wait until they are in up to their necks. Then I will finish their education by shoving their heads under. It is either this or nothing. If they are right, we are ruined; if I am right, they are ruined. We can't compete with them on their terms—if they have what they think they have. And neither can they compete with me, if I have what I think I have. Our policy is plain—wait."

"May I suggest a third possibility?" Crane interjected, as the president was about to reply. "Mr. De Soto says either they or we shall be ruined. We might properly consider the case in which neither is ruined."

"Impossible," De Soto snapped.

"All right," Crane retorted. "There is only the fourth thing possible."

"There is no fourth," the president objected.

"Oh, yes, there is. There are four possibilities, and only four. We've discussed three. The fourth is the least pleasant of the lot. Both we and the other crowd might be ruined."

"But how?" the president demanded, missing the ominous flash of De Soto's eyes which Crane observed. "Industry must have electrical energy. How can they lose, provided we also lose?"

"I'm sure I don't know," Crane admitted. "I'm not a great inventor."

And there the matter rested. Forced to accede to De Soto's policy of inaction because he could devise no better, the president delivered the fortunes of the Foundation into its director's capable hands. Crane left them arguing and went out to wire his acceptance. His sympathies were with the president; De Soto seemed entirely too sure of himself for comfort.

Before taking the train that night, Crane went to bid the doctor goodbye.

"I hate to rush off and leave you and Wilkes just as things promise to get exciting. But what can I do? Offers like this don't come in every mail."

"It's the only sensible thing to do," Brown agreed heartily. "I'm glad you had time to drop in. There is a new development." His face darkened. "Professionally, I have no right to tell you. But in this case we are beyond ethics. I shall also tell Wilkes. We three are the doctors in this case. What I tell you must go no farther."

"I promise."

"Alice called me in this morning. She is to have a child."

"Good God! What will you do?"

"Take care of her, of course. She asked me to."

"But——"

"I know. Or at least I don't know. Neither does her husband. He came to see me this morning, after I got back from visiting her. I believe he has blundered and tried to correct his mistake. But he is not sure of anything."

"Did he tell you?"

"No. It would be impossible for him to commit himself beyond the vaguest suggestion."

"Of course. What did he say?"

"Nothing true or of any unmistakable consequence to us. He merely insinuated that Alice's health is not good enough to stand the strain. Having just examined her, I knew that he was lying, and I suspected him of wishing me to know that he was lying in what he considered a good cause. You see, of course, he could give no hint of what may be in his mind. As I said, I feel that he himself is not sure of his ground. Still he does seem to suspect that he may have failed. What could I do? I was bound, professionally if for no other reason, to ignore his suggestion."

"What if he consults some other physician?"

"How can he? Any physician who would do what he hints—and there are plenty, I admit—would not be safe. A reputable man is the only one who can be trusted in a case like this."

"But there hasn't been another case like it, if——"

"Not exactly; that is true. But there have been several on the same level ethically. You see what I mean."

Crane brooded miserably in silence for some moments.

"I wish she would die," he said at length.

"So do I," Brown rejoined. "But there's no hope. She's too healthy."

Six days later, in New York, Crane and his new employers held their first conference over the epoch-making invention which, according to President Williams, was to revolutionize all industry. From the moment he set eyes on Williams, Crane disliked him. The suave president of the new Universal Power Transmission Company was inclined to be fleshy, although still in his forties, with a perpetual and exasperating smile of self-satisfaction greasing his smug features. His assumed joviality and mock goodfellowship made Crane long to smash him in the face.

"What do you think of it, Doctor Crane?" Williams beamed. The patent papers and a rough, small scale model lay before them.

"It's a washout," Crane admitted. "By the way, you haven't told me the inventor's name."

Williams laughed obesely. "I thought you physicists were keen observers. The name is plastered all over the 'Evidence of Conception' alone, to say nothing of the final patents."

"So I observed," Crane remarked dryly. "But you haven't answered my question. Who invented the thing?"

There was an ominous silence. Williams' face lost its oily joviality as he glared at Crane, and the consultants of the staff fixed their chief with doubtful, questioning eyes.

"Do you mean to insinuate," Williams demanded in a voice that cut like steel, "that I did not invent this method of power transmission?"

"Not at all," Crane responded promptly. His tone was conciliatory. Instantly it changed. "What I mean is this. You are a . . . . . . liar and a thief."

Williams leapt to his feet, trembling with rage.

"What do you mean?"

"Exactly what I said. You did not invent this. I have known of your work for years—ever since I was a sophomore at the University. It was good stuff—no doubt of it. But the best you ever did was not within a million miles of this." He paused, to emphasize his point. "Gentlemen," he said, addressing the staff, "it is as impossible for President Williams to have made this invention as it would have been for the village idiot of Stratford-on-Avon to write 'Hamlet.' You see the point? President Williams' own stuff is several thousand levels lower. Therefore, I say, he stole this invention."

The silence grew oppressive. Williams broke it.

"You may leave me to settle with Doctor Crane," he said to the silent group. "This is a personal matter. Unless," he added, addressing Crane, "you prefer to apologize publicly?"

Crane shook his head and the staff filed out.

"Now," Williams began when they were alone. "You will withdraw what you said."

"How do you know? As a matter of fact I shan't. I don't want your job."

"You have no job, Doctor Crane. I was not offering you a chance to retract and be taken on again. It is now merely a question of whether you wish to stand suit for libel. The staff heard what you said."

"I'll say it again, if you'll call them in. And I'll tell them who made that invention, if they care to know."

In spite of an effort to control himself, Williams went the color of a dead cod.

"Who do you think made it, if I did not?"

"Miguel De Soto. It has all the earmarks of some work he has been busy on since he joined the Erickson. I would recognize it in my sleep. How did you get hold of it?"

Without a word, Williams rose and opened his private safe.

"You know too damned much," he admitted with a cynical laugh, thrusting the thirty-page anonymous letter into Crane's hands. "What do I care who knows where I got the stuff? It's mine, and I have the patents."

Crane read the letter through. The only point of interest to him was the postscript: "P.S. *My purposes are purely humanitarian and educational.*"

"Well?" Williams demanded as Crane handed back the letter.

"I knew it. De Soto invented your wireless power transmission. The postscript would give him away at once to the President of our Board of Trustees. De Soto is a bigger fool than I thought he was. He has blundered again."

"How?"

"By mentioning education. It's too long a story to hash over again. Besides, what is there in it for me?"

"If you know any facts of value, I could see that you are well paid."

"All right, I know one fact that will save you hundreds of millions —possibly a billion or two."

"Does it concern the invention?"

"Vitally."

"How much do you want for it?"

"One hundred thousand dollars, paid in advance, in thousand dollar bills—common currency. No stopped checks for me."

"You can be insulting when you're in the mood, can't you?"

"I haven't tried yet, so I don't know. Take my offer?"

"I'll consider it if you tell me why De Soto sent me that letter."

"Because he knew you would bite."

"Then you consider the invention deficient in some detail we have overlooked?"

"Not at all. It will work."

"Where is the catch, then?" Williams demanded.

"I don't know."

"Yet you have a suspicion?" Crane nodded. "Very well," Williams concluded, "I'll give you a hundred thousand for your fact. What is it?"

"Easy. Write out this: 'I hereby pay to Doctor Andrew Crane, for technical services rendered, one hundred thousand dollars in U.S. currency, thousand dollar denomination, numbers'—leave space to write in a hundred long numbers. Then you come down to your bank with me and get the bills. We'll have your signature witnessed by the cashier and a couple of clerks, and the numbers of the bills written in. Then you can't stop anything on me—unless you hire a gunman."

"You must think we're crooks," Williams retorted coldly. Nevertheless he wrote. "My backers have billions," he added with a touch of snobbery. "A hundred thousand for vital information is not an unreasonable fee."

"You bet it isn't. Ready?"

At the bank Crane refused to divulge his 'fact' until the bills were safely in his pocket with the duly witnessed statement.

"Now," Williams demanded when they reached the street, "what's your tip? You have your money."

"Just this. Throw away the invention and dissolve your company."

WILLIAMS glared at the lanky young man before him in speechless rage.

"You—" he sputtered.

"Keep cool. That tip is worth all the money your crowd has. If you touch the invention, De Soto will break you."

"How do you know?"

"Because he told our president so just before I left. I heard him. Of course he did not tell us that he had made a free gift of this invention to you. Some things are better left to the imagination."

"But why——"

"Because he hates your methods of doing business."

"What about your own?" Williams flashed.

"The same there. He doesn't like any of us. My idea is that he plans to break all of your crowd first and attend to us later. What he doesn't know about the business mind isn't worth knowing. He knows that all the big money in America would fall for a sure thing —it certainly looks sure enough—like the wireless transmission of all electrical energy at a tenth of a per cent of what transmission costs now. Who wouldn't? I'd have fallen for it myself, if I hadn't known De Soto. Can't you see? It's all so simple. Your crowd puts all its cash into a sure bet and finds out the day after tomorrow that there is no market for what it sells. Where are you? In the soup. It will cost money—lots of it—to manufacture this device on a world-beating scale, as you intend. Go to it; De Soto will bankrupt you the day you begin to market."

"If I thought you knew what you were talking about," Williams muttered, "I would call it off now. We've already spent four hundred and fifty million in buying up strategic locations for our plants."

"Better swallow your loss and back out. You'll be smashed. Call it off. De Soto is a hardboiled Tomcat and you're an innocent little mouse."

Williams was one of those high-powered Captains of Finance who made lightning decisions in a bold, impressive way, and frequently kicked himself afterward for the heady, natural fool he was. His square, beefy jaw set.

"I'll see it through," he decided, as if he were Napoleon at Waterloo. "This can't be beaten. You're welcome to your fee."

"Thanks. And you are more than welcome to my tip. If I can be of further service, here's my address. I'm going back tonight."

The game was now becoming fairly clear, especially to Crane, who knew certain facts not yet divulged to the commercial world. Feeling that his loyalty—if he had any—was still to the Erickson, Crane did not wait for the slow transcontinental railway service to get him home, but engaged passage on the combined rail express and passenger plane routes. Forty hours later he was in Seattle, telephoning to the president of the Erickson Trustees.

"I'll be at your room in fifteen minutes," the president promised. And he was.

Crane's report was disturbing enough. What could be De Soto's object?

"I can't understand him," the president admitted after a two-hour session during which every aspect of the singular situation was minutely examined. "Well, I can soon put him to a test. If he is on the square, and really has our interests at heart, he will tell us at once how we can beat the Williams crowd."

"He hasn't your interests at heart," Crane remarked quietly. "As I told you the morning he fired me, he hates your guts."

"I'm not so sure," the president demurred. "De Soto is a genius, in business as well as in invention. How do you know but that this scheme of his to trap all the big fellows isn't just a fine evidence of his loyalty to us? After all we have treated him handsomely. What more could he ask? We've deferred to his slightest suggestions. Who made him rich? We did. No; I believe De Soto will make good and show us how to break the Williams crowd flat."

"The biggest smash in the history of American big business," Crane mused. "When it comes, let me know. I'm putting my pennies in a safety deposit vault till De Soto is shot. Now," he continued with his slow grin, "if I really loved humanity I would go out and shoot De Soto now, instead of waiting six months or a year for some busted banker to finish the job as it should be finished. I know a lot about our friend that you don't."

"What?" the president demanded, going white in a vague panic.

"I can't say yet. The information isn't mine to give out."

"Then who can say?"

"That would be telling. I've had my say. My advice to you is the same as that I gave Williams. Fire De Soto, shoot him, have him locked up—anything you like—but get from under him at once. Otherwise he will explode and blow you and all your crowd into little bits. Do I get anything out of this?"

The president reached for his cheque book.

"If Williams could afford to fee you, I guess we can. We're not paupers yet. I shall watch De Soto."

Crane nonchalantly glanced at the cheque.

"Thanks," he said, concealing his elation. "Take my advice and get out. Let the Williams crowd swallow the loss."

The president decided to take the devil by the horns immediately.

"Would you care to come with me and repeat your story before De Soto?"

"Not in the least. Where is he?"

"At home, resting. Mrs. De Soto is not very well, and neither is he, I imagine."

"All right, I'm game, provided we don't run into Mrs. De Soto," Crane agreed. "The last time I called on her she was Alice Kent. She showed me the door. So make this strictly a business call."

THEY drove to the house and were admitted at once. Alice did not appear to greet them. It was a full ten minutes before De Soto entered the reception room. When he did, a strong odor of chloroform accompanied him.

"One of my pets was suffering," he explained, seeing that they noticed the smell. "Excuse me for having kept you waiting. Mercy first," he concluded with a strange smile.

"Pardon me for coming to your house on a business matter," the president began, "especially as you are not feeling very well. But I thought you would be interested in hearing Doctor Crane's report of what happened in New York."

"I can guess it," De Soto replied indifferently. "You remember that I gave him my permission to tell Williams that I can beat anything his firm does. Crane told him; Williams didn't believe him. Is that how it stands?"

"Exactly," the president nodded.

"And you wish me to make good on my brag—as you thought it was?"

"It seems to me, Mr. De Soto, that we have no time to lose."

"I agree. Shall I come to your office at three o'clock this afternoon? Very well. Please ask the technical staff to be present. I shall explain to you and the other trustees exactly what I propose to do. To the staff I shall give only the necessary instructions for making full-size instruments for demonstration purposes. The finishing touches must be done by me when the technicians have completed their part—say about eight or nine months from now. Then, with the perfected apparatus in our hands we can get our patents in short order, just as the Williams crowd is beginning to sell. We shall scrap all of their plants and the rest of their investment overnight. To manufacture their device on a world scale—which is what they will do—will take practically all of their capital. They won't be content with the American demand, but will strike from the first for the world market. Let them; so much the better for us. In half an hour, or in one hour at most, I will destroy their world market before they have delivered a single transmitter."

"But how?" the president doubted, his eyes rounding with cupidity.

"Later—eight or nine months from now. Let me have a little fun and I'll give you the world to play with. All I ask is the opportunity, when the time comes, to wreck them utterly in half an hour. I'll make it spectacular," he laughed. "No one shall get hurt—except Williams' hand-picked mob of moneyed easy-marks. They'll be flattened. Financially, only, of course. Then you can step in and take the world market they have paid for with their millions of dollars' worth of bribed publicity. If I can't convince you this afternoon you may forget the second."

The president was almost convinced. Still, the fact which Crane had uncovered regarding the origin of the "Williams power transmitter," caused him a twinge of uneasiness. If De Soto could go out of his way to injure men whom he had never seen, what would he do to his daily associates when their backs were turned?

"Is Doctor Crane right," he asked, "in thinking that you sent

Williams a thirty-page letter containing the invention they are exploiting?"

De Soto flung back his head and laughed as he had not laughed for months.

"Of course he is right," he chuckled. "But did either of you know that I guessed Crane would see that letter and report what he did? The moment he told me he was going to join Williams' firm, I foresaw everything that has happened—even to this talk and your last question. Aren't you all normal human beings? And don't all such react in the same way to given stimuli? I couldn't help seeing what has come days before it happened."

"But you wouldn't play a trick like that on us? We gave you your opportunity, remember."

"I shan't forget. Haven't I made good use of your generosity? Here I am offering you the world—that is what your monopoly will amount to—and you look for the trademark to see if it is bogus. Of course it isn't! Wait till I have told you my answer to Williams this afternoon. Then you will see the truth."

"I can't see," the president objected, "why you have gone to all this trouble to deceive Williams if you have something that beats his scheme—your other one, by the way—out of sight. Wouldn't it have been simpler to have started with the winner? Think of the time we shall lose—nine months, you say."

"And you a business man!" De Soto said reproachfully. "With all your possible competitors eliminated before you start, you can gobble up all the markets they might have controlled—wheat, cotton, oil, everything—if you had left them any capital to gamble with. But they will be bankrupt, all their wealth squandered on the one key monopoly they thought they were going to get, but which actually you will have. It is the world I am offering you, I tell you! And you begin to cry because you can't get it for a short eight or nine months. I'm almost disgusted with you," he exclaimed with sudden petulance, which was not all in jest.

"Don't think me ungrateful or over-suspicious," the president begged. "But as a business man I perhaps see some things more clearly than you, a scientist, possibly can. You say these men will be ruined overnight. Capital can't be destroyed that suddenly. These men are solid—the soundest in America. Their money is not paper. Steamship lines, great banks, whole cities of office buildings, farm lands, timber, and a dozen other tangible things are their actual fortunes. This is no fight on the stock market. We are attacking real assets. Have you thought of that?"

"Yes," De Soto replied wearily. "I know my economics. Also I know my human nature. To build plants, to manufacture the new transmitters on a smashing scale, to advertise wherever power is sold or used, to get the sales force into the world field, all of this will require real money by the shipload. And where will our competitors get it? From loans or bonds on all those tangible things you catalogued. Who will lend the money or buy the bonds? Not the big men, as usual, because they are borrowers this time. They will get it from smaller men, little banks, conservative investors, and the great public at large. All these will inherit the big men's office buildings, farm lands, timber and the rest. Then we shall step in and take it all away from them again, for we shall control each and every industry from raw material to ultimate consumer. So much for economics. The human nature of it is even simpler. I needn't explain."

"Perhaps not," Crane agreed. "But would you mind telling us how you got that letter delivered to Williams?"

"Ah," De Soto replied sarcastically, "*there* is a real problem. How would you have solved it?"

"Private messenger, provided I could find one I could trust."

"Good. Just what I did."

From the tone in which he said it, Crane inferred the contempt in De Soto's answer. It seemed to say, "Here I am offering you the world and you turn aside to fiddle over a trivial problem that an idiot could solve.' The talk was suddenly interrupted by the sound of firm steps descending the stairs. Through the arched doorway Crane saw Brown coming down with his black bag. Excusing himself, De Soto hurried out to intercept the doctor.

"Mrs. De Soto is quite ill, I understand," the president confided in a low voice. "Did you notice how nervous and worried De Soto looks? His color is bad, and he has aged ten years in the past week."

"I have noticed the change in color for some time," Crane replied. "When he first came to us he was the color of mahogany, like a full-blooded Mexican. Now he's a sort of lemon yellow, as if he had been living like a beetle under a board for weeks."

"We have tried to make him let up on his work," the president sighed, "but he won't. Some research of his own, he says, has reached the critical stage, and he must carry it through now or lose everything."

"Did he tell you what its nature is?" Crane asked, thinking of the smell of chloroform which followed De Soto wherever he went.

"Something to do with the cosmic rays, I believe, but I'm not sure."

Crane wondered whether the research had anything to do with animals. If so, the strong odor of chloroform would be explained. But he did not share his speculations with the president.

"If you have finished with me," he remarked, "I may as well go. Probably you and De Soto will have private matters to discuss."

"Aren't you coming to the conference this afternoon?"

"I had better not. You see I am no longer officially connected with the Foundation. De Soto might resent my 'spying,' especially as he suspects my feelings toward him. If anything important happens, you can let me know, if you think it wise."

In the hallway De Soto and Brown were conversing in a low tone. Seeing Crane, the doctor stopped short with an exclamation of surprise.

"You back? What happened?"

"Fired, as usual," Crane grinned. "Only I fired myself this time. I'll wait for you outside."

When Brown joined him on the sidewalk, Crane briefly summarized his adventures in New York and his conference with De Soto and the president.

"The hundred thousand," he concluded, "with what the president gave me as a tip are enough to make me independent for life. My tastes are rudimentary. Now I can get to the bottom of what friend De Soto has started." He hesitated. "If it isn't a breach of professional etiquette you might tell me how Alice is."

"Everything is apparently normal. If it were an ordinary case I shouldn't have bothered to call. Young husbands are always so fussy in these circumstances that we usually pay no attention to their worries—they mean nothing. But with Alice, of course, I can't afford to take any chances. The thought of what might happen if De Soto called in another physician is appalling."

"You say she is quite normal?"

"Yes," the doctor admitted hesitantly, "except that she is too anxious. There is something not quite natural about her worries."

"I shouldn't wonder," Crane muttered, and changed the subject. "Wilkes is still determined to present his paper at the meeting of the Biological Society?"

"You know how he is. I've been trying to talk him out of it ever since you left, but he insists. Do you want to come along and see the fun? I shall go, of course, if I can get away."

"Sure," Crane exclaimed. "That's why I made Williams fire me. I wouldn't miss that meeting for a million dollars—and I've only got two hundred thousand. It's tomorrow at ten, as scheduled?"

"Ten o'clock, in the university auditorium. Wilkes' paper is first on the program. Well, I must run along to see an old lady with gas. See you tomorrow at the meeting."

"How are your pets coming on?" Crane called after him.

"Too well," the doctor replied grimly. "I've had to build a high concrete wall round my patio."

XI. THE TOAD

"The man is here about the chickens," the housekeeper announced the following morning just as Brown was about to begin breakfast.

"What does he want now? I paid him for grain yesterday."

Nevertheless the doctor went out to see what the male harpy sought. Since Bertha's death the doctor had given up keeping chickens on his own premises. Not having the heart to sell his feathered family to the poulterers, he had pensioned them with a farmer in the country. This genius knew a soft thing when he saw it. According to the bills he presented for chicken feed, Brown's pets must have quadrupled their appetites since moving to the country.

The pest extracted a dollar from the doctor—"for grain," he said—but showed no disposition to leave.

"What are you raising now?" he demanded inquisitively, pointing to the twelve-foot concrete wall with the heavy, solid wooden gate, which had been erected all around the former chicken yard.

"Skunks," Brown briefly informed him.

"For their fur?" the pest persisted.

"No, for their perfume. The Chinese say it is good for rheumatism. I'm going to try it out on some of my patients."

And with that the doctor left the skeptical farmer scratching his head and returned to his breakfast. The housekeeper had been told a similar yarn, so that she should not feel tempted to feed the new pets in the doctor's absence. She was a kind-hearted soul, but prudence puts limits to charity. Brown felt secure in his innocent deceit.

After breakfast he drove over to the university. Being on the program committee of the Biological Society, he wished to be at the auditorium well in advance of the meeting to round up the speakers.

"What's this stuff old Wilkes is springing this morning?" a somewhat flippant young man in rimless glasses demanded. "He's down on the program for a paper on 'New Light on Evolution.' Where did he get it? Wilkes hasn't had a new light on anything for the past twenty years. Do you think it will be worth hearing?"

" 'He that hath ears to hear, let him hear,' " Brown quoted with an enigmatic smile and passed on.

"Now what did he mean by that?" the cocksure young man muttered, unconsciously scratching his left ear. Wilkes' paper had been accorded the place of honor on the program, also the unusual time allowance of forty-five minutes. This was solely due to Brown's earnest persuasions with the committee. The other members took the doctor's word for it that he had carefully gone over the paper and that it was of the first importance. As ten o'clock drew near Brown began to show traces of nervousness. What if Wilkes overdid things and made it too sensational? The society would jump all over him. To ease his feelings, he fussed about the lantern and the motion-picture machine, heckling the operator with unnecessary directions.

"Run it through in slow motion first," the doctor emphasized for about the twentieth time. "Then give it to them as fast as you can without blurring."

"Sure, I understand," the operator replied gruffly. "You told me that before."

"If you foozle it—" The doctor hurried for the platform. It was time to open the meeting, and the chairman was still smoking in the lobby. Just as Brown reached the door De Soto sauntered in and took a front seat.

"Hullo," Brown exclaimed under his breath. "He suspects someone. I hope it isn't me." Going over to De Soto, he gave him a hurried greeting. "Mixing a little biology with your physics?"

"Only a little," De Soto smiled. "I saw the title of Wilkes' address in the paper and thought it might be amusing."

"It will. The old chap has something brand new." He lowered his voice. "How is Mrs. De Soto this morning?"

De Soto's face clouded. "Nervous again. I made her take some of what you prescribed. Could you drop 'round to see her some time today?"

"Certainly. I'll go as soon as Wilkes has read his paper. Excuse me now; I've got to start things going."

The chairman regretfully flung away his half-smoked cigar, mounted the platform and called the meeting to order. As the business meeting had already been attended to by the council, he proceeded at once with the scientific program.

"The first paper is entitled 'New Light on Evolution,' by Professor Wilkes." He turned and nodded to Wilkes, who sat in the front row not far from De Soto. "Professor Wilkes."

Wilkes gravely mounted the platform. The curious audience of some three hundred expert biologists and intelligent amateurs with an interest in evolution noted that the professor had no manuscript in his hand. The experts sat back with a sigh of disappointment. After all it was to be a popular address, ninety-nine per cent hot air and inspiration, one per cent scientific fact. It was just what they would have expected from Wilkes, who had been scientifically dead for years. Wilkes gave them a surprise.

"Mr. Chairman, ladies and gentlemen," he began and proceeded at once to scientific business. "The first slide, please."

The hall was darkened and a beautifully executed micro-photograph was projected on the screen.

"Old stuff," one skeptical expert whispered to his neighbor. "He got that out of Blair on the protozoa."

"Next," Wilkes requested.

"Blair's again," the skeptic whispered.

"Next."

"If he's going to show us all the protozoa in Blair, he won't get through till this time next year."

"Next."

"Hullo! Where did he get that one?"

"Next, please."

"Another, by Jove! Caught in the very act of dividing."

"Next."

"Fake," more than one expert whispered.

"Run them through more rapidly, please," Wilkes directed the operator, "one at a time."

As fast as he could change the slides the man at the lantern flashed on approximately a hundred photographs of the simplest animals known to science, the living things which consist of but a single cell. The exhibition was received in uncanny silence. Experts held their breath, amazed at the magnitude of what they were seeing—provided it was all genuine—or grimly waiting their chance to pounce on the audacious Wilkes should he prove to be hoaxing them. Laymen who had strayed into the meeting in the hope of witnessing a battle royal between monkeys and men felt vaguely disappointed. Why didn't the professor say something? The answer was simple. Words were superfluous to those who could read the pictures, and he was talking only to them.

The long series of individual slides came to an end.

"The motion pictures now, please," Wilkes requested. "Slow motion first."

THE fruit of laborious weeks of toil by Wilkes and Brown was now slowly unrolled in a coherent sequence on the screen. The spectators saw a different succession of protozoa gradually evolving before their eyes. Types of the utmost simplicity survived through their transient generations, passed out of recognition as individual species and bloomed into new life, more complex and more highly specialized than their ancestors, and those again gave place to higher forms. The history of a million years flashed by every five seconds, and still the general trend was upward toward diversified perfection and increased richness of life. Gradually the rate of ascent slackened. The millions of years represented by sixty seconds of the moving film revealed no discernible variation in the structure of the minute, perfected creatures; they seemed to have passed forever into their perennial Golden Age. Then, in five seconds, first one splendidly developed organ degenerated, atrophied, and passed out of living history, then another, until within thirty seconds the descent was accomplished, and the countless millions of years of the slow, upward climb were undone. The whole cycle of evolution had swept round its circle, and the last generation, the end product of it all, was a degraded thing fit only to fasten as an inert parasite on the first creatures that had risen. Wilkes added a footnote.

"About one-third of the pictures from which that film was made are photographs, the rest are sketches by myself, Professor Hayashi of Tokyo, and a third man who wishes to remain anonymous. Please run it through fast now."

"One-third fake, two-thirds humbug," the skeptics whispered. "Wait till he gets through. He's the Charlie Chaplin of biology.'"

The fast motion pictures were even more impressive. A whole race of animals seemed suddenly to open out like a rose in the sunshine, bloom gloriously in perfection for a few seconds and fade in a flash. The struggle of millions upon millions of years justified itself in those few seconds of beauty; the complete and final futility of the end mocked the struggle and made its justification a bitter nothing.

"Lights, please," Wilkes requested. "Thank you." He bowed, left the platform and resumed his seat. He had used but thirty-five of his allotted forty-five minutes.

"Is there any discussion?" the chairman asked.

A dozen men were on their feet instantly, but De Soto was first.

"Mr. De Soto," the chairman nodded. The others sat down on the edges of their seats.

"Mr. Chairman," De Soto began, "I must apologize for speaking in a biological meeting. But I should like to ask Professor Wilkes whether he has prepared a similar motion picture of the evolution of man."

"No," Wilkes replied, rising. "The data are not available."

"Do you think they could be obtained?"

"It is not impossible," Wilkes admitted quietly.

This was the last straw to the outraged experts. The chairman was forced to use his gavel.

"Professor Barnes," he announced when the commotion subsided.

Barnes was an unimaginative, middle-aged man who had made a very considerable reputation by contradicting his superiors on details of no importance and proving them in error on things which they had never said. If any disagreeable job was to be done,

Barnes was the man to do it. The experts leaned back, satisfied that their case was now in competent hands.

"I fail to see," Barnes began in an injured tone, "why a meeting of the Biological Society should be turned into a vaudeville for the entertainment of amateurs. No competent biologist would give Professor Wilkes' fantastic reconstruction of what he imagines to be the past and future history of the evolution of the protozoa a moment's consideration. I move that Professor Wilkes be requested to withdraw his paper."

"Second the motion!" came from a dozen scattered points, like the cracking of snipers from an ambush.

"It has been moved and seconded that Professor Wilkes be requested to withdraw his paper. Is there any discussion? Professor Wilkes?"

"I have nothing more to say at present."

"Any further discussion?"

"Before we vote," the chief skeptic, Barnes, volunteered, "I should like to know what Professor Wilkes meant by his last remark. It sounded to me like a threat."

"Professor Wilkes?"

"Mr. Chairman, it is only fair to answer the gentleman's question. The society holds its next meeting three months hence in San Francisco. Six months from now we meet here again. At that time, if the gentleman still wishes further evidence, I will present him with an argument that would silence Balaam's ass."

All but two of the audience laughed. Brown noted that one of the exceptions was De Soto. The motion was carried.

"Professor Wilkes is requested to withdraw his paper," the chairman announced. "Professor Wilkes."

Wilkes rose up, lean, angular, self-possessed and obstinate.

"I'll be damned if I do." he said simply and sat down.

In the ensuing debate it developed that parliamentary law had no statute adequate to deal with Wilkes' offense and his unrepentant contumacy. To the chagrin of the conservatives, the paper had to stand as delivered. It would be duly printed, slides and all, in the society's sober proceedings. Several left the auditorium. Wilkes stuck to his seat like a barnacle, saying nothing, his jaw set and the light of battle in his eyes. He was not without sympathizers. Already the astute reporters were composing their sensational stories in which the name "Balaam Barnes" figured with undue frequency.

Brown nodded to De Soto and they left the meeting together.

"A great paper," De Soto remarked as they stepped into the doctor's car. "Where did Wilkes get his material?"

"Do you really want to know?" Brown asked seriously.

"I may as well," De Soto replied.

"Wilkes and I got most of it from the water in which you bathed that evening you came to my house."

To the doctor's surprise, De Soto showed no astonishment.

"I suspected it," he admitted finally. "Do you and Crane know what you are doing?"

"Not exactly. Nor," he added after a pause, "do you know what you are doing. Otherwise how do you explain obvious ignorance when you came to consult me? You did not know the cause of the itching of your skin."

"I admit it. But you forget that nature is like an open book to me—when I am feeling well. Something is happening to my brain," he continued after a long pause. "Thinking tires me. I never used to think, but saw the inevitable consequences of any pattern of circumstances—no matter how complicated—immediately, like a photograph of the future. The tingling of my skin did not puzzle me. I knew the cause."

"Then why did you consult me? You were pretty badly upset."

"I was and I still am. Through a stupid blunder I exposed myself to rays of an unknown hardness. If only two million volts or less, say, than five million, were being fed into my tube when I forgot to open the switches, I should not worry. In that case only the lowest forms of life would be affected."

"The protozoa on your skin?"

"Exactly. Have you any idea where those initial forms originate?"

"That is the one thing that puzzles me," Brown admitted. "The average human skin is alive with bacteria and other low forms of life, but not with the sort of thing we have just seen."

"Not even with lower forms that might evolve into the types in Wilkes' pictures?"

"No. I am certain of it. The whole trend is different. Do you know what I suspect?"

"I can guess. You think that you and Crane have stumbled upon the secret of creating life. You haven't."

"Then what have we done? Where do those types originate?"

"In star dust. They are not those that have survived in the course of terrestrial evolution. But let that pass. What can theories do for me, with Alice on my hands?"

"You suspect something?"

"I do. And so do you. You have guessed by now, of course, that I know who Crane's confederate was in my laboratory that night?"

The doctor went cold.

"Who?" he asked in a level voice.

"You, of course. Couldn't you guess that human motives and commonplace human deceit would be childish games to a man who reads all nature as you read your newspaper? Or rather," he added in a low voice, "a man who once had that capacity."

"You are losing it?" Brown demanded quietly. "I thought I had noticed a dulling of your faculties. Why don't you rest? Your color is not good."

"I can't. But let that go; it is of no importance. To go back to the other for a moment. You men are all so trivial, so unambitious for anything that will count a million years from now. Laugh if you like. What good are the futile things you do for yourselves and your children? Think of the race—the human race! As individuals we are like those parasites on my body that Wilkes and you have taken all this labor to elaborate. The race is on my body; men, the protozoa swarming over it and breeding aimlessly. If we cannot preserve and mature the whole race and make one intelligent, purposeful being out of it, we are no better than an irritating itch on the skin of eternity. I could have done so much for it—once. They asked me for trash that would delight an idiot child for half a minute. They still ask it and I shall give it to them—till I get tired."

"Let me repeat," Brown persisted, "that you are ill and must rest."

"Don't I know it? Then why can't I rest? Just because I *am* unwell. When I first thought of marrying her, Alice was no more to me than you are or even Crane. She was just another human being. Some day I may tell you why I married her. Then a stupid accident began my degeneration. In another six months I shall be as foolishly humane as you are—curing the sick and helping the defective who should be mercifully exterminated or at least sterilized. I have grown to love my wife, even as you might yours, if you were married. That is why I have let you believe that you and Crane had deceived me. When you know everything, you will see that I am degenerated and done. Four months ago I could have solved my own problem. Now I can't. I have to rely on you."

"In what way?"

"Need she go through with what is before her?"

"I am afraid she must, even if I could throw my professional ethics overboard—which I can't. She is too far along. Why can't you speak out? Has the worst happened?"

"I don't know. I have degenerated, I tell you!"

"Well," the doctor muttered, "here we are. It can't be undone now. I'll go up and see her. She eats well and sleeps normally?"

"Yes, but she is afraid. Even I can see that she is not natural."

"It is only your morbid fancy, man. Cheer up. She will come out of this with flying colors, and you'll be the happiest man on earth."

The doctor found Alice happy and cheerful. The usual sickness had left her and she was busily fussing with the plants in the conservatory off her bedroom.

"Tell Miguel I'm all right now," she begged. "I can't bear being marooned here all night while he is off working at the laboratory."

"But I thought he was taking a layoff, Alice?"

"Oh, I know he is supposed to be having a vacation. But he spends practically the whole night at the laboratory and often most of the morning. Then, when he comes home all tired out in the afternoon, he is so cross I hardly dare speak to him." She smiled ruefully. "He seems to prefer the company of his pets to mine."

"You just imagine it. Don't you know that a woman in your condition always sees thousands of things that aren't so? Why, I was just talking with Miguel about you when we drove up. He's positively silly about you."

"Do you think he would let me watch him working in the laboratory again as he used to do?" she asked, brightening. "He loved it."

"Why not ask him?" the doctor suggested, eyeing her narrowly.

"Oh, he always puts me off. I sometimes wonder whether there isn't another—" She stopped, embarrassed by the accusation she could not frame.

"Woman?" Brown finished for her, laughing. "My dear Alice, you are like all the rest at this time. Tell your husband what you fear, and he won't let you out of his sight."

THAT evening at dinner De Soto, acting on a hint from Brown, went out of his way to keep Alice amused and interested. She had a natural taste for science and was fairly well informed on all that went on at the Foundation. Biology, however, was an unexplored romance to her, as it is to most young women who should know it —if they should know any science. At school and college she had been fed the traditional slops of literature, economics, art and domestic science, with not one significant word of the one body of knowledge which women, above all others, should know. The vital functions of her own being were *terra incognita* to her, and the simple facts of the great miracle now transforming her whole life were as unknown to her as they might have been—and were—to an educated woman of the middle ages.

Her husband sought to enlighten her. He began with an amusing account of Wilkes' paper and its reception by the hopeless conservatives. Thence he launched out on a flaming prophecy of what mankind might do, were it so minded, with its own destiny.

"But," Alice objected, "fate or destiny is something that cannot be altered."

"In the past, yes. We have blindly let nature lead us. A century from now, if we wished, we might be leading nature."

"Is that what you are working on?"

"I was," he admitted in a strange voice. He rubbed the back of his hand across his eyes. "But I am forgetting how."

"Perhaps if I were to be your mascot again your luck would return," she suggested gaily. "Can't I come and watch you tonight?"

De Soto started to raise some pertinent objections, saw the hurt look in her eyes and yielded.

"Come along," he said cordially. "On one condition, however. You must take a nap whenever you feel sleepy. I shall probably be working all night. There is a comfortable cot in the closet there. I'll drag it out when you begin to nod."

She was absurdly happy. "Miguel," she confessed, "do you know what I was imagining in my morbid condition? Other men run about with women, and I feared you might get that way, too."

He laughed boisterously. "Women? I haven't thought of another woman since—" The puzzled frown that was becoming habitual with him suddenly darkened his laughing face. "Since when?" he muttered, scarcely aware of her presence. "I seem to remember a dirty suitcase full of letters. From girls. Where was it?"

"Buenos Aires?" she suggested softly.

"How could it be? I was never in South America."

"Oh, Miguel! Can't you remember anything? Where did you study? You knew all about physics when you first came to the Foundation. At least that is what my father told me."

"Did he? Then he must be right. I have forgotten. Never mind now. It really doesn't matter." He paused irresolutely before putting the question he vaguely feared to ask. "Did your father ever speak of anyone by the name of Wilson?"

"Not that I remember. Why do you ask?"

"Just a fancy. I seem to recall a man of that name who had a great deal to do with my education. Have you ever heard of amnesia—loss of memory? Well, I often think that is what is the matter with me. Some day my whole past life will come back. Honestly, Alice, it is all as black to me as it is to you. That is why I work incessantly—so that I shall never remember."

"You are afraid of what you have forgotten?" she asked quietly. She spoke to him as one might to an ailing child. He, not she, was the one in need of care.

"Desperately," he admitted. "Work is the only relief. Sometimes, do you know," he continued gravely, "I am so disturbed that I am tempted to try drink. Yet I have never touched the stuff."

"Don't," she counseled. "That would only make it worse. Can't you remember anything of your father and mother?"

"It is all so impossible," he replied with a short laugh. "Did you ever hear how Leonardo da Vinci is said to have remembered, when he was a grown man, the days when his mother nursed him? You have read that? I go farther back in my memories. I remember the dark place where I lived before I was born. There was an intolerable flash of light, a terrible conflict in the darkness, and I found myself in a world that seemed strangely familiar yet utterly new. My very life contradicted itself; I had no right to live, and yet I lived. Gradually the dark place of my prenatal memory faded and I found myself a man. The same thing is happening again. It is just like those slides that Wilkes showed this morning and his great moving pictures. Those protozoa I told you of slowly climbed to the very peak of their perfection, only to shoot to ruin in what, comparatively, was a second. The flower of my manhood has closed. Old age is upon me and beyond it the darkness of oblivion."

"Oh, Miguel! Can't you see that you are still a young man? Isn't your mind as fresh as it ever was—since you began your true life work?"

"My true life work? I have forgotten what it is. Only an aimless conflict of cross purposes remains. No sooner is a project started than I tire of it. There was one thing—or were there two?—that I hoped to do for the whole race. Did I ever start them? If so, I have forgotten. For all I know, both of them may now be working out for the good or evil of us all."

"Don't you have some definite aim in the work you are doing now?"

"Apparently not. I work by instinct and by habit to drug my mind. Without incessant work I should be forced to deaden my brain with drugs or drink. The most terrible part of it all is that one dead purpose after another speaks unexpectedly from its grave when I am alone and thinking of nothing. Then I try to put it into action, only to lose interest before I have completed a definite piece of work."

"Can't you find some one thing that will interest you and make you happy for its own sake?"

"There is one," he said slowly, fixing her with his sombre eyes.

"And it is at the root of all the others, if only I could remember why it is."

"What is it?" she whispered. The look on his face made her feel old and ill.

"Life and what it may become," he answered. "The creation of life and the remaking of it to my will, in spite of chance and blundering evolution. This was my dream." He absently reached for her cigarettes, took one, put it between his lips, lit it and inhaled deeply like an inveterate smoker. "I have not yet told you the worst that rides me like a nightmare and makes me afraid to lie down at night." She was staring at him, round-eyed. "The worst is this. I know that I shall return to the black place where I lived before I had a mind, and I know that I shall remember everything when it is too late. One hideous thing that I cannot explain always comes out of the darkness when I close my eyes."

"What?" she asked, cold with fear.

"A black spider. This is the key to my lost memory."

She tried to hide the terrible shock his confession had given her.

"Miguel," she said, "I never knew you smoked."

"Am I smoking?" he exclaimed, staring at the cigarette as if it were a deadly viper. "When did I light this?"

"A minute or two ago. Don't you remember?"

"No! I have never smoked." He wiped his mouth distastefully. "The smell of tobacco nauseates me. That settles it. Time I was at work, instead of sitting here talking nonsense."

"I'm coming," she insisted firmly. "You said I might."

"Did I? Well, come along. Brown was right," he laughed. "He told me not to let you out of my sight or you'll be getting foolish notions into your head. We'll have a good time; I'll work while you read and sleep. Come on; there's nothing like work."

THEY reached the laboratory shortly after nine o'clock. It was quite like old times. Work, after all, Alice thought with secret joy, was the one solvent for her husband's moodiness. Like many who tax their minds incessantly, Miguel was inclined to be neurotic. Creation was the only relief for him—self-forgetfulness. "Who would find his life must lose it." So she thought, poor girl, little dreaming that the self-torturing man at the dinner table was her true husband, and the brilliant inventor absorbed in his work the artificial shadow.

"I'm working at the two million volt level tonight," he informed her, "so I must be careful."

"But I thought you handled twenty million volts without worrying much," she objected with mild surprise.

"I do. The two million volt is the critical point. The slightest slip, and I pass from the gamma rays to the cosmic—the softer, of course. Once they start generating in the tube, they may go on indefinitely and rip through the whole scale, beyond the very hardest rays that come to us from interstellar space. Then there is likely to be the devil to pay unless we are adequately protected. So I shall make you wear a triple outfit of the screening material. It won't interfere with your movements. The stuff is as light as a cobweb."

"Are you sure you won't be in danger?"

"Positive," he laughed. "I've been working at this for two days now."

Going to the closet, he clothed himself in three suits of insulation and selected the same for Alice. Before taking the garments to her, he glanced furtively toward the chair where she sat reading, noticed that she was apparently absorbed in her book, and softly closed the door of the closet. Then, from a shelf beneath the electric light, he picked up a small flat dish the size of a silver dollar, and held it up to the light. The dish was full of water. In the water a single transparent globule, as big as a small pea, just floated. The globule might have been an oil drop or a fish egg for all that the uninstructed observer could see without close inspection. A slightly darker nucleus, however, precluded the oil drop hypothesis. De Soto seemed satisfied. He deposited the tiny dish on the floor, picked up the three suits for Alice, turned off the light, and opened the closet door.

"Here are your togs," he called, carefully closing the door of the closet. "Come over here and I'll help you on with them."

They were as happy as a pair of children. All the gloomy talk of the dinner table was forgotten in the simple adventure of dressing Alice up to look like a strayed aviator from another planet.

At last she was dressed in her triple armor and went back to her station. De Soto walked over to the black devil box and began making the connections with the new tube. This was not a replica of the one which Crane had smashed, but an improved design. It was indeed the very model which he had exhibited the previous afternoon to the desperate trustees as his answer—when fully developed—to the bid of Williams and Company for the power markets of the world. This, he had emphasized, was merely the key idea; the commercial development of it would be a work of months for the whole staff. But it would be ready when Williams shot his bolt. Experiments for the good of commerce and the salvation of the trustees, however, were not De Soto's object for the moment. His purpose was more abstract. One cannot always be thinking of money, especially when one has more than is necessary. The evening's work was to be devoted to pure curiosity.

It started tamely enough. The easy connections were made almost automatically, and De Soto threw in the first two hundred and fifty thousand volts. Unlike Crane's unwieldy tube, De Soto's kicked up no spectacular display. There was no fluorescence. Alice followed his movements surreptitiously, saw that he was absorbed and happy in his work, and dipped into her book. By carefully timed steps he worked the voltage up to the two million mark and stopped. Alice glanced up.

"I must say your experiment isn't very exciting," she called across the laboratory.

He had completely forgotten her presence. At the moment she spoke, his back was toward her. Hearing a voice, he started violently. Then he remembered, and laughed. His wife was there. But in wheeling round he brushed against two of the screw switches with the sleeve of his transparent armor. The tube was set to receive and withstand only two million volts. Instantly, an unpredictable mishap, twenty million surged against the cathode with an irresistible impact.

It was too late to rectify the error by "killing" the whole apparatus. De Soto did this automatically when he realized what had happened, as he did immediately. Alice saw his face freeze in horror, why, she could not understand.

"Is anything wrong?" she cried, starting up and running toward him.

"Stay there!" he shouted. "Don't touch your clothes!"

"Come away!" she cried, dreading she knew not what. "Oh why don't you come?"

"I can't," he groaned, frozen where he stood. "I begin to remember. Watch!"

In the lower half of the tube a blinding blue light suddenly flashed up, flooding the laboratory with a ghastly, lurid brilliance.

"It should be white!" he croaked. "This is wrong!"

The blue light contracted, as if compressed by an invisible piston, and increased intolerably in intensity. Narrowing rapidly to a mere plane of blue fire as the piston descended, it became extinct.

"Look out!" he shouted. "It is going to explode!"

The concussion never came. Staring at the sheer black of the vacuum, De Soto saw the tiny vortices which he anticipated like a man in a dream, spinning from the outside of the crystal window and expanding as they spun. One broke against his protected hand, another struck the transparent insulation before his lips, and still he could not remember.

"I have done this before," he groaned. "Where? When?"

"Come away!" Alice entreated, seizing his arm. "This must be dangerous—oh! what is that?"

His eyes followed hers to the door of the closet. Something was moving about angrily in the darkness and blundering against the loosely fastened door in its efforts to escape.

"What is it?" she choked, clutching his arm in terror.

"I can't remember. There was a spider in a box——"

He never finished the sentence. The flimsy catch suddenly gave way, and the incredible monster lurched into the laboratory. Believing she had gone mad, Alice fled shrieking for the exit. De Soto froze where he stood, fascinated by the enormous creature hopping toward him. It was a toad, the size of a full grown man, hideously deformed, without eyes, its gelatinous skin pitted and pocked with holes the size of a human fist from which dripped and trickled a constant shower of young. As they rolled helplessly over the concrete floor the lumps of spawn began to develop, to thrust out feeble legs, and to increase in bulk like the arithmetic of a nightmare. The huge mishapen brute collapsed and became a swarming lump of fecundity.

Before he realized what he held in his hands, De Soto found himself playing the withering flame of the oxy-acetylene torch over the hissing mass and its multiplying offspring. As they puffed up and burst under the fierce heat, to disappear in wisps of vapor, he had a vision of thousands of black spiders boiling from a small box. It happened once, but where?

Sick with loathing when his task ended, he rushed from the laboratory to overtake his wife. She had collapsed outside the door.

"I must make her believe it never happened," he groaned, lifting her in his arms. "Taxi," he shouted, hailing a passing driver. "My wife is unwell. Hurry!" He gave the address and tumbled in with her. "I am a fool," he muttered. "Like all of them I can only blunder."

On reaching home he put her to bed and telephoned for Brown.

"She had a fright in the laboratory," he explained. "Tell her it was nothing."

"Was it nothing?"

"Yes, if she is to keep her mind."

Alice lay critically ill for two weeks. During her waking moments she was barely rational. Whether she believed the assurance of De Soto and the doctor that she had imagined the horror, neither ever learned. When at last she recovered, pale and shaky, she never referred to the incidents of that terrible evening. They thought she had forgotten.

XII. HIS SON

One morning six months later, a puzzled oculist sat staring into the right eye of a tired-looking young man of sallow complexion.

"It is the most extraordinary thing I ever saw," the oculist exclaimed. "You say your vision is still perfect?"

"As good as it ever was," the oldish-looking young man responded wearily.

"When did you first notice this?"

"About five months ago, one morning while I was shaving. I saw a small blue speck on the top rim of the iris—at the base of the blue wedge now. At first I thought it might be the beginning of a cataract. As I never read now, I didn't worry much."

"It is not a cataract," the oculist asserted. "There is simply a thin blue wedge in the general black of the iris. Your eyes are changing color, that's all. Nothing to be alarmed about. Would you mind my reporting the case to the Medical Society? Of course I shall not give your name, Mr. De Soto."

"Not at all. So there is nothing to worry about?"

"Nothing that I can see. You are just reversing the usual order. Babies born with blue eyes often turn brown-eyed or black-eyed after a few months. I hope you're not going back to the nursing bottle," he concluded with a laugh.

"No fear," De Soto responded gloomily. "But I should like a good jolt of whiskey."

"Perhaps I can oblige you," the oculist smiled. "I keep this for my patients when they must hear bad news." He poured a stiff drink for De Soto and half a dozen drops for himself. "Here's luck."

"Luck," De Soto responded, and tossed the drink down his throat. "That was what I needed."

Outside in the cool morning sunshine, he had a sudden revulsion of distaste. "What ever made me drink that rotten stuff? It tasted like varnish. Ugh! Never again."

He hailed a cab and drove to the Foundation. There was to be a full meeting of the Board of Trustees to discuss the offensive of the Erickson against the Universal Power Transmission Company. Disregarding Crane's hundred thousand dollar tip, Williams had gone ahead at top speed for the past six months developing "his" invention on a world-wide commercial basis. For the past month he and his associates had been deluging America, Europe, Africa and Asia with their propaganda, broadcasting the glad tidings that the wireless transmission of electrical energy—high power or low power—was no longer a dream of the theoretical engineers, but an accomplished fact that would shortly be on the market. This, as they justly claimed, was an industrial advance comparable in importance with the invention of the steam engine. Just as the steam engine with its railways and steamships killed the stage-lines and the windjammers at one swipe and brought about the industrial revolution, so this new method, as simple as A, B, C, of transmitting electricity without wires from producer to consumer, would stand the industrial world once more on its head and shake the last nickel out of its pockets. The nickels, the dimes and the dollars were already beginning to rain down in a jingling shower that threatened to drown the new company in a deluge of prosperity. Many a solid concern rated in the billion or half billion class had already thrown up its hands. Why fight? Their flanks were turned and their retreat cut off. Better to make peace while they might by selling out to the junk dealers and passing on the loss to their stockholders and bondholders.

Through all this furious publicity the Erickson crowd remained strangely silent. Was it the silence of defeat or the prelude to a stealthy, wholesale throat-cutting that wouldn't leave the foolish Universal a larynx to crow with? There was no doubt that Universal actually could transmit electricity without wires at a negligible cost and that it was prepared to do so throughout the civilized world. Then why was the Erickson so quiet about it all? Surely it must be ruined with the rest? Only the trustees and the technical staff knew the answer. Patents had been applied for but not yet granted. And the applications were so ingeniously framed that not one expert in a million would guess their particular value. Even the technical staff as a whole did not fully grasp what they were doing; De Soto so apportioned the details that no one man could possibly get a glimpse of the whole. The preliminaries were ended; he himself would put the finishing touches.

The president opened the meeting with a glowing tribute to the genius of their Director, who, he declared, had given them the world to play with. They must not, he concluded in tones of lofty solemnity, abuse the great privilege which their own business enterprise and the great skill of their Director had given them. Far from it. Greed and unscrupulous monopoly might actuate their competitors—witness the ruthless manner in which the Universal was crowding less lucky corporations into the ditch—but such base motives never had been those of Erickson and never would be. A world monopoly not only of power transmission but of the means of generating power would put the Erickson beyond competition. Be theirs the mission to bring industry and the public—the ultimate consumer—into closer harmony and a deeper appreciation of the inestimable benefits which a wise business foresight confers upon groping humanity. All this for a reasonable and legitimate profit of a thousand per cent on their investment. Would Mr. De Soto care to make a few remarks?

Mr. De Soto would. He swayed slightly as he rose to reply—for to him it was a reply, and not a mere footnote.

"GENTLEMEN," he began, "you must pardon me for being just a little drunk."

"Mr. De Soto!" the president soothed in an audible undertone. "We know you are joking."

"I am not joking. I'm drunk. Fifteen minutes ago I had a damned good stiff jolt of real whiskey. Otherwise I shouldn't be talking now. I had intended saying it sometime later. Please don't make the mistake of thinking I'm so drunk that I can't see straight. It was the first drink I've taken since—God knows when, I don't. And it has gone to my head. It gives me a warm, human glow."

They stared at him in astonishment. Was this their usually polite —if sometimes brusque—severely scientific and eminently practical Director? The man who had given them the world to play with? Surely not. And yet—*could* he be telling the truth? But then, he never drank. At their hospitable homes he had always waved the cocktails and the gin, the sherry and the wine aside with an air of sincere indifference that no amount of art could hope to simulate.

"A warm, human glow, gentlemen," he repeated with emphasis. "Do you know what that means? You don't. Right now you are thinking of ways to quarter Universal after it is dead. You don't like its presumption in daring to invade your territory. Will you stop when you have broken them? You will not. As long as one of its backers, or its bondholders, or its stockholders has a dollar in his pocket, you are going after it till you get it. Pardon me, gentlemen, if I cannot restrain my feelings."

He turned aside and spat out of the window. Continuing, he made his plea.

"You make me sick. Sicker than that rotten whiskey made me. All my life I have been looking for a human being, and I haven't found one." His tone changed. "For humanity's sake," he said in a low voice, "I implore you to drop this before it is too late."

A trustee rose. De Soto's words had impressed him.

"Are we to understand that your answer to Universal is not what you thought it was?"

De Soto burst into a roar of laughter.

"Incorrigible," he shouted. "Absolutely incorrigible. Take what is coming to you."

The president took up the parable. Numerous disquieting hints released by Crane came home to roost. In particular he recalled Crane's disquieting theory that De Soto might ruin both the Universal and the Erickson, not merely one or the other.

"You feel confident that our demonstration will convince the experts?"

This time De Soto did not even smile. His plea, he realized, would fall on stones.

"It would convince anyone," he said. "Send out your invitations for four weeks from today—cable, telegraph, write. That will give the Europeans ample time to get here. Don't forget to include liberal travelling expenses and expert fees. You will get it all back. But, for the last time, I ask you to call off the whole thing. There is one humane thing to do now, and only one. Lay your whole project before the Universal. They will see that they are hopelessly beaten. Then agree to withdraw your scheme, scrap the invention, and forget it completely, if they will do the same with theirs. They can lose no more that way than if they stick to the last. If they ever attempt to market their device or to transmit power themselves you can stop them instantly by threatening to compete."

"But what is the point?" a trustee objected.

"I can't tell you."

"Why didn't you warn us—as you seem to be doing now—six months ago?"

"Because then I had not gone soft. My plans were different, although even then I was beginning to doubt and to weaken."

"Weaken on what, Mr. De Soto?" the president demanded curiously.

"My purpose when I first sought employment at this Foundation."

"And what was that?"

"I will not tell you."

"Why not, Mr. De Soto? It cannot have been dishonorable, surely?"

"Dishonorable?" De Soto laughed. "What is honor to a fool? I do not choose to tell you because I have changed my mind. Or rather," he added, "my mind has changed me."

They scrutinized him shrewdly. Was he trying to betray them to Universal? At length one trustee expressed the common sentiment.

"If, as Mr. De Soto assures us, we can't lose out, I don't see why we should discuss the matter further. I move that the Director be instructed to carry out his program, four weeks from today, as already arranged."

"Second the motion."

"Moved and seconded—."

The vote was carried unanimously.

"This is your final action?" De Soto asked quietly. The president nodded. "Then I shall make my last appeal. You will smash Universal, as I have promised. But in doing so you will not benefit your customers. Have you their interests in mind, or your own? I can convince Universal that it also will not make its customers any happier. If you abandon this now, I will make them give up theirs tomorrow. Which is it to be? Your own gain, or that of the people you serve?"

There was a dead silence.

"Very well," De Soto continued. "That is your answer. I understand. Please accept my resignation, to take effect immediately. After all, I shall have accomplished my initial purpose in joining your staff. Perhaps it is the best. I tried to nullify it only because I have gone soft. You yourselves are the best judges of what is best for you."

"Don't act in haste," the president begged as De Soto walked from the room. "We shan't accept your resignation until you have had four weeks to think things over.

"Take a rest and you'll feel better."

"Four weeks?" he echoed with a bitter smile, his hand on the door knob. "Why keep me? The full intructions for capturing the world markets in everything, not only power, which is at the bottom of it all—are already in your hands. Your Board has the detailed plan before you, and your very competent engineers can execute it. Put it into action four weeks from today. You will not need me. I shall move out of the Foundation residence tomorrow."

"Mr. De Soto!" the president protested in a shocked voice. "The residence is yours indefinitely, whether you stay with us or not. Surely you do not think us——"

"I think nothing whatever about you," De Soto retorted, opening the door, "except that you are hanging yourself, your sons and your daughters, and saving me the trouble. I would tell you to go to hell, if I did not know that the next thirty years on this earth are going to beat any hell ever imagined by the worst diseased imagination of the middle ages—Dante's." Closing the door behind him he left the outraged trustees to their thoughts.

"Drunk?" one hazarded.

"Or crazy. It will be a good thing if he does resign. We don't need him any longer, with this in our hands. I vote we make no advances to him to reconsider. What can he do for us? Nothing."

And that seemed to be the general opinion. The meeting dissolved without formal action on the resignation of the Director. Watch and pray, wait and watch, are good slogans, in business as elsewhere. They decided to watch. For the moment they would take a firmer grip on the world's tail and flex their flabby muscles for the luscious twist.

On reaching home, De Soto at once told his wife of his resignation. Alice was pale and ill. She listlessly acquiesced.

"You know best," she said.

"I plan to move out of this house tomorrow. It would be impossible to continue living here practically on the Foundation's charity. Let us move out to the country—I'll find a nice place."

"Can't we wait till—?" She did not complete the sentence. "It won't be long now."

He glanced at her, something like fear struggling with pity in his eyes.

"Certainly. We can stay here at least four weeks, if you really wish it. What does Brown say?"

"He hasn't called today. Doubtless he is busy."

"Yes, I remember. The Biological Society is meeting today and he is on the committee. Don't you worry. Everything will come out in fine shape. We can stay here indefinitely if you like—it was your home for years. Perhaps we had better."

"But your resignation?"

"Oh, that. I can do what I please with the trustees. If the worst comes to the worst, I'll buy the place. We're almost indecently rich, you know," he laughed, trying to cheer her. "That's why I resigned."

All her sparkle was dead. "I wish it were over," she sighed.

"There, there! You'll soon be as happy as a queen."

"Tell me, Miguel," she said slowly, "has my mind been right since that evening in the laboratory? Sometimes I seem to be living in a horrible dream. I fainted, didn't I? Do I seem rational to you?"

"Why shouldn't you?" he asked with assumed astonishment. "You are. These fancies are natural to you at this time. They mean nothing. Ask Brown when he comes, if you think I'm just talking to disguise the truth. What I tell you is cold, scientific fact, and he will back me up."

"I wish he would come."

"If that's all you're worrying about, it's soon cured. He will be here in fifteen minutes if he's still alive."

He left her to telephone to Brown's office. The doctor was at the Biological Society but was quickly reached and promised to come at once.

"She's imagining things," De Soto informed him in the hall. "Cheer her up."

"I'll do my best. They often get like that at this stage. It means nothing."

Thirty minutes elapsed before Brown rejoined the anxious husband.

"Well?" De Soto inquired.

"She is normal, except in one thing. Her mind seems to be straying."

"In what respect?" De Soto paled beneath his fast-fading tan.

"Sit down. I want to tell you something that I have never had the courage to confide to another living man—except Crane. He and I saw it together. If Alice is losing her mind, her delusions have a peculiar quality of truth. At least that is how I feel. Perhaps you will agree, when you have heard what I have to say. Ready?"

"I'm ready. You have seen the effect of the hardest rays on living tissue?"

"Yes. Crane and I together." In five minutes the doctor gave De Soto a sufficient account of what he and Crane had witnessed in the twenty million volt laboratory. "Those spiders," he concluded, "had evolved, bred and multiplied at a terrific rate in less than twenty-four hours. What accelerated their rate of evolution beyond all reason? Millions of years were compressed into those twenty-four hours. Where did those swarms of voracious brutes obtain their food? These are some of the questions that Crane and I think you can answer."

"Why do you think I should know? I wasn't connected with the Foundation when this happened. Although," he added with a bitter smile, "the solution of your problem is no more difficult than Crane's. He could not see how an anonymous letter might be delivered so as to arouse no suspicions among a pack of dull-witted drudges—cooks and waiters of the business world. Yours, I admit is a less trivial problem. Suppose things happened as you say they did. Where did those spiders obtain their food to make possible their greatly accelerated rates of evolution and development? They sanded the floor, you say, with millions of unhatched eggs. The mothers, at least, must have been well nourished. Did it never strike you that the same short wave rays which started the surge through all evolution for your spiders could also provide them with the necessary food? The nitrogen of the air, the carbon dioxide, the oxygen and the traces of noble gases were instantly aggregated into complicated organic compounds, based on the electrons positive and negative, under the influence of those rays. If matter can be utterly annihilated, or as 'miraculously' created out of the wandering protons and electrons by the hardest cosmic rays, might not the softer induce chemical changes, making food from the air? It is done even in our stupid laboratories. But it may all be a dream—I don't know."

"You admit that it is not unreasonable or absurd?"

"You wouldn't after seeing Wilkes' demonstration on the protozoa! A different set of cells were affected in your spiders; that's the only distinction. The hardness of the rays—or, if you prefer, the shortness of the waves in the radiation emitted, determines what cells will be stimulated or destroyed. You have guessed that much?"

"More, as you may see tonight, if you care to come to the public lecture. Wilkes is to talk again."

"And silence Balaam's ass?" De Soto suggested with a sardonic smile. "It can't be done. I tried this morning to answer several, and left them still braying. Still, if Alice is well enough and won't miss me, I'll be there to see the fun. She suspects that what came out of the closet was real, and not the creation of a sudden nervous breakdown?"

"Suspects? Alice knows that it was real. And what is darkening her mind is your silence. Why did you do it?"

"A pure blunder. I'm always blundering. Alice spoke and startled me. My sleeve did the rest. What happened was as much of a discovery to me as it was to her. Since that evening I have studied the effect exhaustively. If you care to inspect my menagerie, you will see that the last cage is empty. I'm done—beaten. I'll never use the chloroform bottle or the oxy-acetylene torch again. Nature has got the better of me at last."

"But what on earth did you think you were trying to do when you blundered?"

"As you refused to help me," De Soto replied grimly, "I tried to help myself. If I could control evolution in one direction, why not in the opposite? Then I could undo what you, as well as I, believe may have happened."

"And you found you could not pass up or down the scale at will?"

"No longer. Ten months ago I could have played on it like a flute—and I did. Now I have lost my capacity. Can't you see that I am degenerating? Look at my right eye. Is that blue wedge a normal change in a healthy man?"

Brown peered into the affected eye.

"When did this begin?"

"Nearly five months ago—more or less. Can you explain it? No? Neither can I. Nor can I account for my washed-out feeling. Do you notice my color? And the deadness of my hair?"

"All that is merely lack of tone due to overwork and worry. As soon as Alice is safely through you will be as good as ever."

"Better," he said bitterly. "That night when she saw the thing,

I told her that I was going back to the dark place where I was born. Your account of what you did with those spiders is like a hand pushing me into the darkness. Something will rush out of it presently and destroy me. But before it does, I shall see the light I have been groping after for months." He brooded in gloomy thought for some moments without speaking. "Promise me," he said, looking straight into the doctor's eyes with a flash of his old dominance, "that you will take care of Alice whatever happens to me. I have loved her, and that has been my ruination. All of my business affairs are in good order. She will be wealthy. See that she is not fleeced and keep her from marrying some scum who wants only her money."

"Look here, De Soto," the Doctor retorted quietly, "you mustn't think of anything like that. In spite of all that she half suspects, you are still her one reason for living."

"But if I die—naturally?"

"You won't, for years yet. However, I'll face it. If anything happens to you, I will see that your wife gets a square deal. Now let us talk of something more cheerful. Coming with me tonight to hear Wilkes' paper? There has been nothing like it in the history of science. Not a soul but Crane, Wilkes and me, and possibly you, has any idea of what the old chap is going to spring on the skeptics. We have played at least one bar on your magic flute."

De Soto brightened. "I'll be there," he laughed. "But wait till you hear the full orchestra."

"When?" Brown demanded.

"Thirty years from now. It will begin four weeks from today."

"What do you mean? Have you—."

"Wait and see. I may be dreaming."

"Then Crane and I must awaken you," the doctor retorted. "Don't fail to come tonight."

"I won't. *Au revoir.*"

THE auditorium for the evening lecture was crowded. De Soto found a seat in the rear. Brown presided, to introduce the speaker. News had leaked out through the committee that the address of the evening, "New Light on Evolution" was likely to prove exciting. The newspapers had spared neither conjecture nor innuendo to advertise the meeting. Some even hinted that the long-missing link was at last to be exhibited to shut up the Fundamentalists. Others recalled the incident of Balaam's ass and wondered whether he would be present in person.

At eight fifteen exactly, Brown briefly introduced the speaker. This time Wilkes had a manuscript in his hand. He began by dryly reviewing the theory of evolution. Sensation hunters yawned and shuffled their feet. Wilkes paid not the slightest attention, but continued to bore through his dry-as-dust argument like a beetle on a board. At last—after forty minutes—he had finished his preliminaries. Tossing the manuscript aside, he squared his shoulders, adjusted his cuffs, and let loose without notes.

"All that, ladies and gentlemen, is old stuff. You learned it in the grammar school—or if you didn't you should have. Evolution is less a theory than a description. Does it assign any *physical cause* for the origin of species? It does not. The facts which it is alleged to coordinate are almost as complicated as the theory which strings them together. Compared to any of the greater mathematical or physical theories, it is rather a childish effort. It does not go to the root of the matter."

The papers reported the next morning that there was considerable disorder at this point of the professor's address. Undismayed by the boos and jeers of the scientific fundamentalists, Wilkes raised his voice and kept on, disregarding Chairman Brown's frantic appeals for order.

"Old stuff!" he shouted. "As old as Democritus and as dead as Lucretius. Metaphysics, ladies and gentlemen, metaphysics! Until we can control the course of evolution in our laboratories we are no better than Aristotle with his cock and bull."

"Can you control it?" a ribald voice from the back of the hall demanded.

"Order!" Brown snapped. "There will be an opportunity to ask questions after the lecture."

"Since the disorderly gentleman in the rear has asked a pertinent question, I will make an exception, and answer him. No. I can not control evolution."

"Then what do you think you are talking about?" an infinitely dismal, sepulchral croak from the gallery inquired.

"Listen, and you will find out. Another interruption and I leave the platform."

There was a dead silence. A man in the front row, showing a disposition to chatter, was promptly squelched by his wife. Wilkes continued his extempore discourse.

"Facts first, fun later. Before you will be in a fit state of mind to appreciate my clinching argument and enjoy the fun—such as it is—I must get some hard dry facts into your heads. It may hurt those unaccustomed to using their brains, but nobody will be seriously injured.

"First, there is the cause, the physical reason for evolution. What is it? I don't know, and neither do you. Like Newton, 'hypotheses non fingo'—I don't indulge in wild guesses. But, like all scientists, I guess as Newton did. Then I check up my guesses against the facts, or against the experiments predicted by the guess.

"In this instance," the professor continued with evident relish, ignoring the drowsy blonde at his right in the third row, "in this instance the ascertained facts of paleontology are indisputable to all but Fundamentalists. We human beings are mammals—the female suckles her young, and our young are born alive. Reptiles are not mammals. For one thing their young are born only half alive, as eggs. Nor are birds mammals. Yet birds and mammals both sprang from the reptiles. That is the incontrovertible record of paleontology.

"Circle squarers, believers that the earth is flat and that the moon has no rotation, swarm in our midst, as the late Professor Tait observed on an occasion similar to the present. Modern statisticians have found that one person in five thousand believes he can square the circle, one in five hundred that the earth is flat, and one in five that the moon has no rotation. Therefore, I conclude, what I am about to say will be distasteful to my present highly cultured and intelligent audience. After all, science *may* be wrong, and the moon *may* be made of green cheese.

"Any human being who cares to go back far enough will find his family tree to be a mere twig on the greatest tree of life this earth has ever known, that of the reptiles. In short, the reptiles were our ancestors."

A prolonged hiss from the third row broke the thread of the professor's discourse. Wilkes paused appreciatively until the objector ran himself out of steam.

"Ah," he resumed, "I perceive that evolution has still a long way to go for some of us. To continue what I was saying before the gentleman in the third row obliged me with a practical demonstration. Suppose we *could* control evolution, both backwards and forwards. Imagine first that we can reverse the natural progress of man, and that we can do it at a greatly accelerated pace. In half an hour we should see ourselves chattering in the trees with our cousin apes; an hour would find both us and our cousins on familiar terms with queer little mammals that none of us would recognize as our great, great grandfathers; and finally, after about two hours of this prodigiously fast sweep into the 'backward abysm of time,' you and I would behold a strange and pathetic sight. We should see a bewildered colony of reptiles, their short, feeble arms clutched about their narrow bosoms, contemplating in horror and awe their unnatural broods—the first mammals. Could these unhappy parents look far enough into their misty future, they would see the last of their kind being mercilessly exterminated by the lusty descendants of these first, puny mammals.

"Before turning to a brighter picture, let us glance at another, more flattering to our human conceit. Suppose a common hen, or any other bird, could be sent back along the path which it had taken from the beginning of time. It would reach the reptiles much faster than we. Almost in a quarter of an hour—at the same relative speed as our own trip to our family tree—the hen would perceive that its feathers had given place to scales, and its toothless bill to a vicious, horny mouth crammed with long, sharp teeth.

"Now for the brighter picture. Accelerate the rate of evolution forward. What becomes of us? Ultimately, of course, we shall probably become as extinct as the great reptiles from which all our kind originally sprang. But, on the way to extinction there is one not wholly unpleasant prospect. We shall subdue the physical forces of nature almost completely, and the entire race of mankind will become incomparably more intelligent than it now is, with a greatly heightened joy in living. The discontented will have perished. That they may be noble in their discontent does not concern us. They will have gone the way of the dodo long before the race begins to live, for the simple reason that discontent is a destroying influence. It is nature's anaesthetic to drug the misfits into a readier acceptance of the death which is their one answer to a world with which they are unfitted to struggle. Many of them may be remembered for great work, for a little time, but they themselves, and in the end their work also, will perish.

"That is at least a not improbable conjecture. A second possibility that the future holds for us is equally obvious. Just as the mammals sprang from the reptiles, so from the mammals in turn, man included, may spring a totally new race of creatures. It is even possible, from minute examination of the germ cells of our own bodies. to predict in its broadest outlines what the race of our successors may look like. I shall not bore you with these speculations now, as facts that can be seen, heard and handled are more convincing to those who have eyes to see, ears to hear, and fingers to touch.

"Six months ago, I showed before this Society a series of drawings and photographs from life, in which it was proved that my associates and I had succeeded in compressing the whole evolution—millions and millions of years—of certain species of the lowest type of animal into a few hours. Those protozoa, beginning with the humblest, passing to the highest, and again sinking to the very lowest through innumerable generations, all within the short span of less than twenty-four hours' actual experiment, should have convinced those capable of human reason that my claims are valid. Was anyone convinced? No. 'Though one rose from the dead,' they would not believe. Hence I have prepared a more convincing demonstration, this time in the opposite direction. Rather, my friend has prepared such a proof; I am merely the showman. He has a professional reputation to lose; I never had one worth considering.

"Ladies and gentlemen, I now present you with a proof that we have succeeded in reversing evolution. What I am about to show you illustrates our process as applied to birds. If we are able, as we claim, to reverse evolution for the birds, we should be able to produce the prehistoric reptiles from which the birds sprang.

"Our starting point was a common brown hen of the Buff Orpington variety. Until she was subjected to the proper influences, she laid excellent eggs, many of which were eaten and enjoyed by my collaborators. They were normal hens' eggs. After our experiment, she began laying very small eggs. They were not shelled, but encased in a porous membrane like tough skin. Eighteen of these abnormal eggs hatched. I now show the reptile which hatched out of one of those eighteen eggs. It was a few days over four months of age when it died. Mr. Chairman, if you will have the alcohol tank wheeled onto the stage we can proceed with the demonstration."

As one the audience rose to its feet. Those in the rear stood on the seats; those in the very front were restrained by guards from climbing to the platform.

"Everyone will have an opportunity to see the reptile," Wilkes shouted. "Please do not come up to the platform until the guards permit you to file past."

An oblong box like a coffin, draped in gray tarpaulins, was now wheeled onto the stage beside the speaker's stand.

"A little to the right, so that the whole house can see without interference," Wilkes directed. "That's it."

With a pardonably dramatic gesture, the professor unveiled his masterpiece by flapping off the tarpaulins.

"There!"

Submerged in the glass tank of alcohol a long, lemon-yellow monstrosity, like a huge lizard with an over-developed head, lay supine on its spiny back. The enormous head rested with its flat occiput on the bottom of the tank, its long, gaping jaws almost projecting above the level of the alcohol. From tail tip to head the reptile measured between eight and nine feet; its evil jaws could have crushed a young pig at one snap. The teeth, in double rows on both upper and lower jaws, might easily have crunched to fragments the bones of a large dog. The hind legs, like a crocodile's, were muscular and well developed; the front, mere fins with claws, were clasped pathetically over the narrow chest in the eternal resignation of death. The skin could hardly be called scaly. Rather it was a compact weave of triangular warts, each about the size of half a postage stamp. About the rigid jaws of the dead reptile lingered the frozen remains of a sardonic smile, as if the creature had looked both before and after, and was now as wise as a god.

Seeing is said to be believing. Those who assert that it is do not know either the scientific mind or the fundamentalist. The pickled reptile was received first with the silence of incredulity. Then, in ludicrous unison, a rhythmic chant of "Fake! Fake! Fake!" shook the auditorium. The crowd filed up to the platform, hustled by the guards, passed before the glass tank, saw with their own eyes the yellow monstrosity in the alcohol, and doubted. This is not set down in any critical spirit; it is merely recorded here—as it was in the late extras that night—to show that the average human being is not the sort of fool who believes that seeing is believing. The skepticism of the crowd did it enormous credit. Through all that unsympathetic hour, while the irreverent humans filed past, the prehistoric reptile smiled his enigmatic smile like a cynical Pharaoh lying in state. He knew all evolution now, both forward and backward; his belated descendants some day, would be as omniscient as he.

At a gesture from the chairman, the crowd at last resumed their seats. Brown made a brief address.

"In conclusion, I may say," he remarked, "that Professor Wilkes is not surprised by your reception of his evidence. May I ask for a show of hands? Those who consider this thing in the tank as substantiating, in some slight degree, Professor Wilkes' contention that evolution may be reversed by man, will please raise the right hand."

Several hands—at least a dozen—shot up. Before the meagre count could be taken, an indignant voice claimed the privilege of the floor.

"Mr. Chairman!"

"Mr. Barnes?"

I must protest against a meeting of the Biological Society being turned into a revivalist experience orgy. Professor Wilkes has tried to foist upon the lay public a gross imposture. His so-called reptile is dead. I deny that any such reptile ever lived. The majority of those professional biologists now present—whose spokesman I have the honor to be—pronounce the yellow thing in that tank to be an extremely able fraud. Whoever has spent weeks, possibly months, in manufacturing that fake, might well have employed his talents to better advantage. That it is an almost perfect restoration of an extinct reptile of the middle period of the great reptilian race, which flourished on the earth ages ago, we do not deny. We merely assert that it is a forgery."

When the applause, foot-stamping and shouting, which greeted this fearless indictment of the exhibit in question as a bold fraud, had subsided, a resonant voice was heard claiming the chair's attention.

"Mr. De Soto?" Brown invited.

The whole audience turned to stare at the world-famous inventor standing up at the back of the hall. Until now he had passed unnoticed, save by those in his near neighborhood. What would he say? Light into the audacious Wilkes as Barnes had done?

"May I ask how Professor Wilkes induced the change in the germ cells of his hen to obtain this result?"

"As Professor Wilkes' paper has been received unfavorably," Brown replied, after a consultation in an undertone with the professor, "he prefers not to state for the present."

"In that case, Mr. Chairman," De Soto replied, "may I have the floor for five minutes?"

Brown's decision was drowned in an uproar. "De Soto! De Soto!" the crowd chanted. Brown at last got order.

"Mr. De Soto will take the platform in a few minutes, if he will be so kind. In the meantime, Professor Wilkes wishes to add a few remarks. May I ask you to keep your seats while he is speaking? Professor Wilkes."

The professor began in his driest voice.

"Any good scientist enjoys being called a liar by his brother scientists. It puts him on his mettle. I have to thank Professor Barnes for having performed that service for me. You will recall that I said eighteen of the reptile eggs produced by that brown hen hatched. One of the reptiles died at few days over four months of age. From the beginning he was the puniest, and we despaired of keeping him alive for a week. In spite of all we could do for the poor creature, he died. I, myself sat up with him anxious nights, trying to nurse him back to health. Had Professor Barnes lavished his own maternal care as I did mine on that unhappy child of the prehistoric past, he would not scoff at its pitiful inadequacy now. That reptile, ladies and gentlemen, was kindly and affectionate—provided you kept out of reach of his teeth. I grew to love him more and fear him more than I love or fear Professor Barnes.

"'Eyes have they and see not; ears, and hear not.' Of such are Professor Barnes and all his followers, the fundamentalists of biology. They call my poor dead friend a fake. I wish they were right, for then I might, as an artist, rival nature herself."

"You haven't answered him," a hollow voice from the second row suggested.

"You are right," Wilkes admitted. "I cannot answer him. His kind is unanswerable. For the rest, however, I have a little surprise, as a reward for their patient faith. Remember, eighteen eggs were hatched. One of the reptiles died; you see him here. What of the remaining seventeen?"

"Yes!" Barnes shouted, leaping to his feet. "What of them?"

"Kindly address your remarks to the Chair," Brown suggested acidly. "Professor Wilkes, what of the remaining seventeen?"

"They are alive and well," Wilkes replied simply.

"Show them to us!"—This from the audience at large.

"Unfortunately I cannot do so," Wilkes admitted regretfully.

Shouts of "Fake!" all but drowned the disappointed. "Why?" Ignoring the former, Wilkes satisfied the latter.

"Because this stage would not hold all seventeen of them, or even six. They are not pleasant to handle outside of a steel cage. So I have brought only one, which my friend, Doctor Crane, will now show you. Doctor Crane."

Oh's and ah's bathed the professor like incense. He had scored his point, and Balaam Barnes was about to be silenced—at least they hoped so. For the average audience, scientific or other, is about as fickle as a flame.

The gorgeous purple velvet curtains parted at the back of the stage, revealing Crane in the act of bossing eight brawny workmen who tugged and hauled at an enormous cage of steel bars mounted on two low trucks. The cage was wheeled into the center of the stage; Crane withdrew his workmen; the purple curtains closed; Wilkes followed Brown from the platform, and the guards braced themselves for the onset.

At first there was silence. Then fear. Then astonishment. Then a foolish, fluttering applause, that died instantly. Again silence, tense and heavy with fear. The sluggish reptile in the cage raised its enormous head, stared for an uncomprehending five seconds at the pink and gray sea before it, regurgitated, and unconcernedly turned away. As the horny lips snarled back, the breathless spectators saw two double rows of cruel teeth, sharper than a shark's and as long as a sabre-toothed tiger's, bared for the attack.

"About six and a half months old," Wilkes remarked dryly. "Has Professor Barnes any comments?" The deathly silence remained unbroken. "If not," Wilkes continued, "you will presently notice a characteristic odor. Those of you who have ever smelt a large living snake, say a boa constrictor, will recognize the odor in a general way. This, you will admit, is similar, but much more intense, with qualities of its own. You are smelling, ladies and gentlemen, the same smell that paralyzed our mammalian ancestors with fright when they tried to hide from their reptilian parents in the reeds. Familiar, isn't it?"

There was no reply. The indifferent brute with a brain no bigger, perhaps, than a baby sparrow's, raised his head and preened its scales. Along its spiny backbone, and over its massive flanks, a riffle of triangular flecks of bright green passed lightly, like the sudden rubbing of an armor of artichokes the wrong way by an invisible hand. The crowd shuddered. They had seen birds do that. With a sudden movement of its sinewy neck that was almost graceful, the squatting brute ruffled the upstanding scales under its armpits, rapidly combed its backbone with its chattering teeth, shook its whole body luxuriously, and settled down to indolent ease. A cold, foul odor wafted over the audience.

"I refer you," Wilkes remarked from his station by the stage steps, "to any competent treatise on paleontology for the original of this reptile. It is well known. At least we think it is. When full grown, it will be as tall as a giraffe and as bulky as an elephant. This is one of the later species of reptile. The great ones had already begun to fade from the screen of evolution when this one thrived. Notice the degeneration of the thorax. It has an obviously inadequate lung capacity. The hind legs also show weakness. On the flanks—not where one would naturally expect to find such things—you will see two serrated excrescences. These are the rudimentary wings trying to break through the tough armor of scales. The wings, of course, did not originate in this way. What you see is merely one of nature's innumerable hit and miss, blunder and succeed methods of evolving a new species. The wings that finally came in were of deeper origin—in the mutated chromosomes of our friend here. Her—this reptile is a female—her germ cells contained the irresistible mutation that finally gave us the birds, including the brown hen from which this terrific beast was born.

"I call her terrific," he continued, "because I personally am very much afraid of her. You observe that she is just like her dead brother in the glass tank here, except that she is five times his size in linear dimensions, and therefore one hundred and twenty-five times his bulk. Before I state why I am afraid of her, let me assure everyone in this audience that neither I nor any of my associates has ever fed her a living animal. The pigs and calves which so far have kept her alive were duly slaughtered and butchered before being introduced into the cage. A pet cat belonging to one of my collaborators chanced to stray within reach of the cage one day when this reptile was much smaller and could get her head through between the bars. The cat was nipped. It died in four seconds. Now, for all that paleontology can tell us, we do not know whether or not this prehistoric reptile was venomous. From what happened to the cat, I suspect that it was. We shall have to wait until one of the seventeen dies. For sentimental reasons I do not care to dissect my dead friend in the tank. I shall ask you not to attempt to inspect the reptile on the stage. She may be dangerous."

As if to underline the professor's remarks, the huge mass in the cage suddenly became a spitting fury. Hurling herself against the bars of the cage, she slavered and screamed at the audience in an access of reptilian fury. Women fainted and were carried out; men stood their ground and tried not to show the white feather under the intolerable, nauseating stench which filled the auditorium as the raging half-snake, half-bird, lashed herself with her muscular tail and clawed at the steel bars with five-fingered hands that were strangely human.

"Take her out!" Brown shouted from the floor. Crane rallied his crew. Three minutes later the hissing screams were suddenly cut off by the closing of steel doors behind the purple curtains. Brown remounted the platform.

"Mr. De Soto wishes to say something," he announced.

The crowd sat down in dead silence, and De Soto walked to the front of the hall. Refusing Brown's invitation to mount the steps, he began speaking in a low voice, which carried to the farthest corners of the galleries.

"I state facts," he began, by way of introduction. "Several months ago I began to experiment on living tissue with high-frequency, short-wavelength X-rays. The results were encouraging. I used what knowledge I had gained from these preliminary experiments to predict what must happen under the influence of cosmic rays—the rays of shortest wavelength known to science. These rays will penetrate forty feet of solid lead. With this penetration they should be capable of affecting the smallest cells in all animals—insects, mammals, protozoa, man. By properly modulating the wavelengths of the rays sprayed upon the chromosomes, I found it possible to accelerate normal evolution or to retard it; to produce mutations—the creation of new species, such as mammals from reptiles—or to inhibit them. Perhaps here I overstate; my completed experiments do not fully justify my last assertion. I undertook, many months ago, to put my theories to a crucial test. Unfortunately certain accidents, due entirely to my own carelessness, make the outcome doubtful. I can only await the decisive answer which, I anticipate, will be given within the month. You agree, Doctor Brown?"

"I think so," Brown assented in a voice that was scarcely audible. De Soto nodded and went on.

"It is possible, I assert, to control evolution in both the forward direction and the backward. Professor Wilkes' two exhibits—that of six months ago with the protozoa, and that of tonight with the hen-reptile—put this beyond dispute. You have seen it with your own eyes. Even Professor Barnes, legitmately skeptical, has no further objection to offer.

"All this, ladies and gentlemen, is purely academic. It is of interest only to professional biologists. Of what application can it possibly be to you?

"Let me tell you. If we can control evolution; if we can hasten nature forward at the rate of a million years in one of our human years; if we can perfect our race as Professor Wilkes has predicted, who will profit? Who? Is it worth perfecting? I confess that I do not know.

"Suppose you were given the chance to perfect yourselves. Would you take it? I think not; for no one of us knows what our perfection is.

"Suppose again that you were offered the opportunity of settling all of your problems, once and for all, within one generation—thirty years. Would you take it? No. Why? Because you are human and blunderers, of which I am one.

"Suppose, lastly, that the decision was made for you. Would you be happy? I doubt it. Stupidity, or human kindness, if you like, is the one thing that distinguishes us from that brainless reptile which Dr. Crane just showed us. For to be stupid is to be kind, and to be kind is to be stupid. Do not think I am bandying epigrams. I am not. Reflect. Is it not true—humanly true—that every time any one of you has given way to a decent, 'human' impulse, he has kicked himself later for having been a fool? Think of it: kindness equals stupidity; stupidity equals kindness. If you doubt it, what keeps your hospitals for paupers full, your homes for the aged prosperous, and your institutes for incurables jammed to the doors? Reflect, I say; if you wish individuals to persist, when they should have perished; if you wish the race to perish, when it might persist, be kind, scorn intelligence, and choose an evolution which will send you back to the reptiles. I personally have no choice. Either alternative is 'a tale told by an idiot, full of sound and fury, signifying nothing.'

"But, ladies and gentlemen, your decision has already been made. Four weeks from today you will know what has been decided for you. It is neither reptile nor superman, neither back to the brutes nor on to the gods. In the meantime——"

Certain light-witted members of the audience whose attention was already wandering, noticed Doctor Brown hurriedly follow a page off the platform and disappear behind the purple curtains.

Joyously anticipating that the she-reptile had bitten and killed one of her keepers, they sat back, waiting for the chairman to reappear and announce the welcome tragedy. They were disappointed. Within a minute Brown was back, but on the floor of the auditorium. They saw him pluck the ranting speaker by the sleeve. But they did not hear what the Doctor whispered in De Soto's ear.

"Come with me at once. Alice—"

THEY were in a taxi before the audience realized that it was deserted. The second extras speculated on the significance of a scientific meeting—especially one of this importance—being abandoned without ceremony by speaker and chairman, but they drew no rational conclusions.

By noon the next day a verbatim account of that historic meeting, with the word for word reproduction of De Soto's speech, was printed in heavy type on the front page of every important newspaper or journal of the civilized world.

De Soto's son was born an hour after the meeting broke up. An hour later Alice was dead. Thirty minutes after Alice died, Brown reeled into Crane's apartment.

"She is dead, thank God! It was born alive."

"What is it?"

"I don't know. It is not a mammal. It is still alive. De Soto has it!"

XIII. HIS LAST WILL AND TESTAMENT

POOR old Wilson had not prospered since his lodger deserted him. The all but deaf, half blind old man had puttered about for months in his inefficient endeavors to find a successor for the departed Bork, but without any luck. Finally he abandoned the effort to rent his shabby room, and resigned himself to fare a little more Spartan than what he had been accustomed to, in the days of his poor luxury. Bacon no longer was a possibility. Flapjacks, potatoes and the scanty greens from his own garden kept his sleeping old soul in his lethargic body. The neighbors became alarmed lest the old man die alone and thus smirch their shabby, decent street with the scandal of man's inhumanity to man.

One morning, long after his needy friends had given up all hope that old Wilson would ever again be on speaking terms with bacon and prosperity, he ambled proudly over to his nearest neighbor's with the glad tidings that the room was at last rented.

"Who to?" the gossip bawled in Wilson's better ear.

"Eh? I'm hard of hearing."

"Who did you rent the room to?"

"Durned if I know. Some fool. He paid in advance. Say, is that a ten-dollar bill? My eyes ain't what they was."

Being assured that it was, old Wilson doddered off to the corner grocery and purchased a whole side of bacon. For four weeks the neighbors saw nothing of old Wilson or of his new lodger, although they kept a sharp watch for the latter. Finally the theory that the new lodger was a night worker, leaving the house after dark and returning before dawn, was generally accepted. Substantially it was true. The lodger left his room only between the hours of midnight and three in the morning, to purchase at cheap lunch counters and bootlegging joints the necessities of life. Not only was the shabby neighborhood totally unprepared for the tragedy which suddenly burst upon it, but also the whole world. At the end of the fourth week, when old Wilson began fretting lest his invisible lodger overlook the vital matter of the rent, the horror happened, without the slightest warning, at midnight of the last day of the fourth week. Fifteen minutes after it happened the tragedy was broadcast by telegraph, cable and radio to the farthest corners of the civilized world. And it was broadcast barely in time to save the human race from a similar fate.

The police were on the spot five minutes after the first inhuman scream shattered the dog-tired silence of the mean neighborhood's midnight. Even old Wilson heard that cry from hell. The siren of the police car shrieking through the night was not more shrill. The officers battered down the door of the lodger's room just as the last sounds of agony expired in a dying groan. Entering with drawn revolvers, they stumbled over a litter of empty bottles, dirty papers and fragments of half-eaten meals. The man had died defending himself against terrible odds. When they saw what had destroyed the victim, they froze where they stood. One officer recovered his senses and raised his arm to take aim. The captain knocked the automatic aside and the volley of shots went wild.

"Don't shoot! Get the envelope in his hand."

At the risk of his life the officer darted forward, snatched the envelope from the dead hand, and followed his shaking companion from the room.

"Get all the furniture in the house and block up the doorway!'" the captain shouted. "Rip off the doors downstairs and bring them up. I'll stand guard."

While his men tumbled downstairs to fetch everything heavy that the shack contained, the captain glanced at the letter. It was stamped and addressed to Dr. Andrew Crane at the Erickson Foundation. Across the envelope "Private and Personal" was scrawled in red ink.

"Get this man on the telephone and tell him to come here at once," the captain ordered the first man who staggered up under a load of furniture.

Crane was located at his own address. The officer repeated the street and number. "Come at once."

"I'll be there in three minutes." Crane was as good as his promise. "Bork's old place," he muttered as he gave his machine the gas and shot into the street. "What now?"

He soon learned. The captain handed him the envelope and ordered him to read it. The meat of the letter was on the first page. Crane read it at a glance. Not bothering to look at the rest of the bulky manuscript or to inquire what had brought the police to Bork's old lodging, he stuffed the letter into his pocket and bolted for the stairs.

"Come back!" the captain shouted.

"Can't. This must be broadcast at once."

"Halt!"

The front door slammed after Crane just as a bullet flattened itself on the brass doorknob. He was roaring up the street before the second shot overtook him, missed him by an inch, and shattered the windshield of his low, open car. Shooting round a corner he put his pursuers hopelessly out of the running. Four minutes later he was seated before the broadcasting keyboard which the experts of the Erickson Foundation had especially designed at De Soto's suggestion for a purpose totally different from that for which Crane now used it.

WITHIN half an hour his short, insistent message had girdled the globe. Newspaper broadcasting stations in those countries where it was still daylight or early evening took up the desperate message and drowned out all programs and other unnecessary interference. Where the radio failed, cables and wireless got drowsy engineers, sleeping editors and snoring politicians out of bed at unearthly hours, from Senegal to Capetown, from Shanghai to Valparaiso.

In the less sophisticated countries fire sirens shrieked through the streets in the dead of night; criers followed them up, yelling to the startled people to rise at once and destroy the plants, root and branch, of the newly constructed stations of the Universal Power Transmission corporation. They needed no urging. De Soto's wild speech four weeks previously had been translated into every living language, popularized, and made accessible to the people of all countries. The telephotographs of Bertha's brood were in every newspaper office of the world two days after Wilkes had exhibited one of the seventeen living monsters that were now world-famous. Crane's selling campaign had been ably engineered for him before he ever sat down at the Erickson keyboard. The human race, or at least the civilized part of it, was already prepared for the hell about to burst upon it, which one man, who might easily have been shot by a stupid police officer, averted. Eight hours later the damage would have been beyond human repair.

Martial law in the more civilized countries made a feeble, ineffectual attempt to hold the raging mobs in control. Many were shot down in cold blood by the rifles and machine guns of the militias that vainly struggled to protect the property of an alien corporation. Property, to the custodians of human life, is more sacred than human life itself. Capital had been heavily invested in their bailiwicks. What did it matter what the scientists said? Money is money; business is business; and a fool is a fool the wide world over. Therefore the devoted members of the militia were butchered by sheer weight of numbers before humanity prevailed. For the argument of the people in this instance was beyond political or international palliatives. The deepest, fiercest instinct of the human race was about to be violated.

Instinct fought; civilization for the moment went under. From Senegal to Capetown, from London to Leningrad, from Shanghai to Valparaiso, from New York to San Francisco, and in every corrugated iron settlement of the earth's wilderness, a sombre torch of destruction flared up against the midnight skies or darkened the silver glare of the age-weary, tolerant sun. The vast plants of the Universal Power Transmission Company were destroyed the world over by flames and bombs four hours after Crane broadcast the first call to arms. Universal and all of its backers were ruined.

Thus far had the Erickson triumphed, but not in the way De Soto had predicted. What of the counterattack De Soto prepared for the trustees? Crane destroyed that also. Before daybreak both the Erickson and the Universal were a total loss. One was destroyed outright with all of its equipment and all of its expensively captured markets; the other receded at one step to its comparatively harmless monoplies which it had held before De Soto tempted it with a vision of all the kingdoms of the earth. And what, through all this, of De Soto, the unprecedented world genius who had precipitated it all?

To appreciate De Soto's motives, historians must take account of his own tragedy. Brown would have delivered him from the worst at the last moment—when it was too late. Alice should never have been permitted to bear a son to the husband she loved. This Brown admitted—when the son was born. There is a simple surgical trick, a quick snip of a pair of scissors, which is permitted in such circumstances to even the most conservative obstetrician. Brown would have used this, but the father forbade.

"Will she live?" he asked, referring to Alice.

"Only a few hours, at most."

"Then I refuse to have this thing put out of the world. It is mine. My first intention was right. So as far as I am concerned, Alice is already dead. This episode in my life is ended."

De Soto was not with his wife when she died. He had already fled the house, taking with him his newborn son wrapped in a quilt.

For four weeks the world speculated on the fate of its greatest inventor, Miguel De Soto. Gradually the theory was accepted that he had destroyed himself in the sudden madness of grief when his beautiful young wife died. Brown did this much for the principals in the tragedy which he might have aborted: he signed a death certificate for both the mother and the child, stating that the latter had been stillborn. The remains were cremated within thirty hours. Only Kent and the doctor witnessed the last. Brown of course told the heartbroken father that Alice had died naturally—as, indeed, she had. Nature, however, is hell.

The trustees of the Erickson Foundation mourned their brilliant director for two days. Then, convinced like the rest that De Soto had committed suicide, they reverently forgot him in a bronze tablet in the president's office, inscribed to "Miguel De Soto, Benefactor of Humanity and Founder of Our Fortunes." Finally, they decided not to canonize their Aladdin for twenty-six days, until the second phrase of their inscription would be an overwhelming fact.

As the days passed and no trace of De Soto was discovered by the police, Crane and Wilkes agreed with Brown that the unhappy father had indeed destroyed not only himself but also his offspring. Had he been alive, they argued, he must certainly have given some sign before his wife, whom he had loved, became an urnful of ashes. The three friends attended to the immediate present, and let the future go for the moment. De Soto's threat, that the world within four weeks would begin to solve its greatest problem, might be only the defiant gesture of a defeated maniac. They set about consolidating their definite scientific gains, writing up the voluminous report on the protozoa, giving the full history of Bertha and her reptilian brood, and finally putting forth the bold hypothesis that all of these apparent miracles were nothing more than the orderly progress of nature, hastened or retarded several billion-fold by the control of radiation in relation to the germ cells of living animals.

Requests from every scientific center of the world for one of the artificially evolved—or rather, devolved, reptiles poured in by the bushelful, and less presumptuous academies begged for at least one microphotograph of the perfected protozoa. The latter were easily satisfied. For months Wilkes had been preparing a new treatise, which was now published and sold as fast as the presses could print it off. The more convincing proof, the seventeen living reptiles and their pickled baby brother, were started on a world tour two days after Alice died and De Soto disappeared. It is well that they did, for when it became necessary to destroy billions of dollars' worth of property, the public of at least one continent was thoroughly educated visually—and the world at large had seen hundreds of photographs of its grandparents.

THE world was educated in one detail. When Crane began broadcasting the warning that unless the people of all countries at once destroyed the plants of the Universal Power Transmission Company, their own *children,* not possibly their great, great grandchildren, would be very similar to those reptilian grandparents now touring the civilized world, the warning struck home at once. Half an hour of wireless transmission by means of the new devices, Crane asserted, would suffice to change the germ cells of every living human being permanently. Thirty minutes, no more, he declared from the Erickson keyboard, would hurl every child born of parents then living back to the reptiles. Mothers would bear, not snakes, but things with legs and gigantic heads like those which the hen had brought forth. These, however, unlike the hen's would be born alive and not from the egg. At one stride the race would retrogress hundreds of millions of years to its pre-mammalian ancestors. This, it was broadcast, would be the inevitable outcome of the first use of the new "Universal" system for the wireless transmission of electrical energy. The unborn would be born reptiles; the fruit of every union not yet consummated, for as long as the present generation lived, would be a race of carnivorous reptiles, possibly venomous.

The preservation of the species is a deeper instinct, even with the individual, than is the preservation of self. Bertha's fellow hens pecked her to death when their instincts taught them that she had betrayed the birds to the reptiles. Likewise when Crane, desperately transmitting De Soto's unintended warning from the Erickson keyboard, spelled out the impending degeneration of the human race, instinct prevailed. Machine guns, gas and tear bombs, flame-projectors and human militia melted like smoke before a hurricane, when a race about to be outraged surged over the merely human defenses created by unlimited wealth. In four hours Universal was wiped out; the race was saved.

Money dies hard—if it ever dies. Crane, still sweating over the switchboards at nine in the morning, suddenly had a vision. Business, he saw in one transcendent flash of revelation, is immortal. Man may have a soul, the race a purposeful mind, but lucre has a belly and it has all-consuming powers of digestion and assimilation.

For seven hours the night and early morning had been turned into clanging day. Extra after extra headlined the progress of the world riots to excited householders as Universal's gigantic plants went their predestined way by bombs and flames. One shrewd go-getter after another hugged himself in the chilly dawn. These keen men of affairs had backed De Soto and the Erickson. Their money was safe. Had the Erickson been bombed? Not on your life! Were its trustees panicky? Again, not on your life. They knew what they were talking about when they cautiously released a "preliminary announcement" two days before the present fiasco of Universal. The canny trustees had presaged the collapse of the Universal. They themselves, they hinted, would broadcast the story of an invention which would scrap Universal in half an hour. Was this the prophesied revelation?

It was not. For two hours the perspiring president of the Erickson had been trying to distract Crane's attention. Crane stuck to his job, methodically transmitting the whole of De Soto's last will and testament. Universal was already destroyed; what Crane now did was a labor of hate. He broadcast the truth as De Soto's twisted, infinitely clear mind had conceived it, in the vain hope that common sense might at last prevail. He was deceived.

Unable to restrain himself any longer, the president roughly brushed Crane's hands off the keyboard.

"What do you think you are doing?" he demanded, red in the face, the veins on his neck and temples swollen to the bursting point.

"Putting a crimp in you, if you want to know," Crane grinned. "Get out of my way; I've got to finish this."

Appeals to gratitude for past benefits received, threats of arrest, promises of any reasonable sum up to fifty million, tears—almost all of these were offered and rejected in the brief space of ten minutes while Crane rested and the president wallowed.

"The man was crazy," the president all but sobbed as his final argument. "You know as well as I do that he had been out of his head for months. We've bluffed off the Universal. The world is ours! Fifty million if you stop broadcasting. You shan't——."

"Steady!" Crane ordered. "Hinder me now and I'll—. Sit down! Wait there till I'm through." He reached for a heavy steel spanner which some careless workman had left near the keyboard. "They can hang me if they like, but I'll smash your skull like an egg with this if you interfere."

As De Soto's last will and testament filtered into space, the whole purpose of his insane life became brutally evident and coldly clear. According to his own account he had fully intended helping the race a hundred million years in its struggle toward perfection, when he first realized his own incomparable powers. Then, as the strange decay which was ultimately to undo him began to steal through his cells, he foresaw the futility of any help; for in the end the whole race must perish or be mutated to another, not human. Why strive for its perfection? What are a billion years in the life of the universe, where galaxies measure their moments by the pulse beats that are the birth and the lingering extinction of a noble race, like that of the kingly reptiles? On such a scale the chronology of the mammals, and their puny human offshoot, are less than the tenth of a second. The reptiles vanished, leaving only the comparatively indestructible accidents of their bony frames in the hardened sands; the mammals must follow their predecessors into oblivion; the very stars of heaven crumble to dust or dissipate in futile heat, and the records of all life's struggle must in the end be smoothed out in eternal cold. Why strive? To what end? Only an idiot would say "for the greater glory of the human mind." The reptile mind forgot its glory before the first mammal gave milk to its feeble young.

PESSIMISM, black, irrefutable, and absolute, seems to have been De Soto's creed at this transient stage of his own evolution. The next stage—induced, as he declared, by a blunder on his own part, which initiated the degeneration of his clear seeing mind—began when an accident in his laboratory started his descent. At first his purpose was clear and rational. A race that must perish, or at best lose its individuality beyond all hope of past memory, was not worth any rational being's efforts toward perfection. The longer it struggled to attain the unattainable, the longer would be its agony of frustration. Therefore, in mercy, it should be destroyed. This was De Soto's first purpose before he degenerated.

He was not brutal; destruction should come in thirty years, swiftly, painlessly, mercifullly, like the dawn. How? By universal sterilization of the human race. The physical means were simple; he had grasped them in the first hour of his study after leaving the library. Not X-rays, but shorter radiations, capable of affecting the most intimately complex cells of the human body, could easily be broadcast over the entire earth in a short morning. He would save humanity from itself by wiping it out, painlessly, in an hour. Scientists would speculate for thirty years on the cause of the universal sterility. Their speculations would end in death, complete, quiet and peaceful for the whole human race; and no last handful of sages, hundreds of millions years hence, would be condemned to see their dwindling star die and their leprous planet freeze. Sterilization, complete and universal for the race of men—that was the one sane answer to the riddle of the ages. When he joined the Erickson Foundation, this great dream was De Soto's purpose.

To accomplish it, he declared in his will, he needed technical assistance—broadcasting stations over the whole world. These he could not command without financial aid. Seeking that assistance, he met with his first doubt and his first check. Was he wrong after all? Is there something in mankind of a different order from anything that the splendid, perfect, all-conquering reptiles possessed? There was. Man, he learned to his astonishment, had a soul. Who knows, he sneered in his last will and testament, but that the carnivorous reptiles, who had two more or less centered nervous systems, had not a pair of souls? The human soul, De Soto declared in his will, shows itself in art.

To his perfectly adjusted nervous system, all human art appeared as a blundering attempt to harmonize what cannot be harmonized, and to seek proportion where none is possible. A certain restaurant inspired him to these reflections, and later, a cook and waiter induced him to apply similar principles to the human body and to its concomitant, the human mind. The soul of man, if it exists is, he concluded, an abortion that should be chloroformed at birth. The reptiles, he asserted, had a better substitute.

De Soto was scientific. Although he scoffed at the existence of a human soul, he decided to experiment before declaring that it did not exist. Should such a thing be found, he would throw his unbound talent aside and aid the race to develop this mysterious spark into a flame that would consume the universe. His will here becomes somewhat incoherent. In substance he seems to be saying that he offered mankind the stars and it asked for a better radio. Some who heard Crane's broadcasting of the original, interpret the obscure passage as meaning that De Soto offered all men everlasting oblivion, and they demanded eternal life. Whatever may be the correct interpretation, the objective facts are plain. De Soto was disgusted. In a last desperate battle he tried to educate a handful up to a taste for black pearls. His attempt failed, and he set out to make his friends kings and rulers of the world.

About this time, he asserts, he wavered. Might it not be possible, after all, to breed a race that would see nature eye to eye? How decide? Experiment answers all. He experimented, blundered, proved himself to be a human fool like all his kind, fell in love with his wife, tried to undo his blunder, failed, and, like the fool he admitted he was, doomed the whole race to follow in his own footsteps. He had hoped to show to all mankind, in his own son, an example of the transcendent genius that human nature, aided by human skill, may produce.

While experimenting he blundered—humanly, irrevocably. He grew to love his wife and longed for her death. Like the degenerated wretch he was, he could not kill her. He had failed. Was there still hope for the race? On a last appeal to the men whom he had made rich, he tried to make them see as he saw. The Universal, broadcasting its only half-understood wireless transmission of power, would avenge his own misfortune.

He knew that no living physicist or engineer could penetrate the subtle complexity of his mechanism. The best of them would see in it only a marvelously ingenious device for transmitting electrical energy without wires and without costly power stations. None would analyze the inevitable consequences of the profitable transmission, for none had the inventor's all but superhuman genius. They could not calculate, as he did, from the subtle equations, the accompanying radiations that would spray the chromosomes of every human being with hard radiation. Before the keenest living physicist or biologist could suspect the danger, the damage would be done, and the whole race, profoundly changed in its most intimate germ cells, would be irrevocably reversed toward its reptilian ancestors. Like an explosion, the whole course of human, mammalian and later reptilian evolution would be undone in a single generation.

De Soto was not without mercy. Feeling that many might have at least the beginnings of a soul in their minds, he provided for them. An entire generation must bring forth only reptiles. This he had already ordained, in putting into Williams' hands the dangerous key to a financial fool's paradise. The wireless transmission of *electrical* energy, and with it the instantaneous pulse of *dysgenic* energy, degrading the unborn offspring of all then living to the outward shape and the inner bi-souled status of prehistoric reptiles, was a certainty. Williams and his crowd, human as fish, had swallowed hook, bait and sinker. They, not De Soto, should have the honor of hurling humanity backward hundreds of millions of years in one generation. So much for justice; mercy must be heard. De Soto's mercy was this, and it was adequate.

ACCORDING to his last will, he baited Williams with the wireless transmission of *electrical* energy, and this is a fact. The counterblast with which he planned to destroy Williams was not electrical. At one stride De Soto put electrical energy forever on the shelf. It became as obsolete as the fly-coach—or it would have so become, had not Crane threatened the president with that hefty steel spanner. Atomic energy was the bait dangled by De Soto before the trustees' bulging eyes. At will he could pass up or down the atomic scale, transmitting any element into any other, as a skilled harmonist modulates his compositions, and in the passage from one element to its neighbors he released and controlled hells of energy that made the lightnings of heaven or the millions of volts dispensed by Universal as obsolete as the thin, steam whistle of a peanut stand. Many had released atomic energy; none had controlled it. De Soto did both and he gave the great secret into the hands of Erickson trustees as a free gift. They grasped it greedily. The moment Universal began marketing, the Erickson was to broadcast the full account of its own wireless "power"—controlled atomic energy—which would forever banish all electricity and all its devices, as steam and gasoline had banished the plodding horse.

Included in that hard scale of cosmic rays, with which De Soto tempted and won the Erickson trustees, was another, a high harmonic of the first, tuned to disintegrate the procreative germ cells of all living things—plant, protozoon, animal, man. Thus would he show mercy. Universal's product would be on the air before the Erickson replied. For one generation the females of the human race would bring forth their reptilian young alive. Then, forever, the pulse of cosmic rays, generated from the disintegration of matter—universal matter, the stuff of which galaxies are made—disintegrated to swell the bellies of half a dozen human beings, would sterilize human and reptile alike. "Curtain," De Soto adds in his manuscript, "Humanity; Reptiles; Sterilization. The Great Comedy; Reptiles, Humanity, Extinction."

The last phrases of De Soto's great message to humanity flickered into space. The story of his own redemption by love, as his superb intellect rotted, is now a classic. Those who know it by heart may wonder why Alice was not redeemed by love, as De Soto was.

De Soto was not redeemed. He died as he lived. The letter which Crane broadcast was his last, futile gesture of triumph. The world was his, he said; the letter would lead the world through the hell it deserved for at least thirty years.

"You can broadcast this," the letter concluded, "as soon as you receive it, for then the Universal will have generated its reptiles in the bodies of your young women and in the cells of your young men. Nothing can ever again start evolution forward. We are reptiles, and as reptiles we shall live, propagate, and die, unless you accept my mercy. The Foundation which has taught me all that I know of humanity as it now is, may save at least the gray hairs of those now living from utter disgrace. Lest those whom I have served see their grandchildren—not merely their children—snapping at their prey, with reptilian bodies, I prescribe and offer you the solace of extinction. This, as I saw clearly at first, is the one hope of the human race. Use my device for the generation and transmission of atomic energy, and within a century the human race will have perished. For your offspring now will be reptiles; thereafter you and they will be sterilized—if you use my device. It will give you world supremacy in finance for so long as the human race endures.

"I mail you this when it is too late to avert the disaster which Universal will precipitate tomorrow. May the whole race taste the bitterness which I have drained. Once I had a vision, I blundered, I loved. I blundered again and again. I had a vision only to blunder irrevocably. The one that I loved is dead—dead as the whole futile human race will some day be, and she has left me a son, the sum and substance of all my blunders. Like you that I despised and would once have helped, I am a failure, undone by my own humanity. I cannot hate you, for you are reptiles, even as I am. Your intellect, like mine, at its best, is no better than the blundering instincts of a thing that perished before the first of our kind was conceived. Why prolong the farce? For thirty years you will see yourselves as you were, are, and shall be. Then the curtain will drop forever on this silly interlude of eternity. You will find my body with my son's. His mother would love neither of us, could she see us now. 'As I am, you shall be.' "

"I guess you're wrecked too," Crane remarked to the president as he finished broadcasting De Soto's testament. "We all are. Shut up! Get out."

The president left hurriedly, and Crane called up the doctor.

"Come around to Bork's place with me, will you? I haven't the nerve to go alone."

Fifteen minutes later they were cautiously admitted by the police. Crane was now responsible—the extras had restored his good name. The captain volunteered to lead an expedition into the barricaded den.

"Let me go first," he advised. "It has been moving about and whistling birdlike for the last two hours."

The barricade was cautiously removed. Not a sound issued from the room. The living thing within had taken its brainless revenge on the author of its unnatural life. With steady hand the captain aimed for the reptile's rudimentary upper brain and pulled the trigger. Three short convulsive jerks, and the monstrous son expired in shambles which had been his father.

WHITE LILY

JOHN TAINE
(ERIC TEMPLE BELL)

DOVER PUBLICATIONS, INC.
NEW YORK

CONTENTS

Part I—BUNGLERS

I. FOUNDERED

SOMETHING was moving about the house. It was not alive, nor was it being propelled. Yet it moved. Such was the flesh-raising impression Mrs. Lane got first as she started up in bed and groped for the electric lamp. Her fingers moved without feeling over the small table by the head of the bed, upset a tumbler of water, and found nothing. The house was as still as the crypt of an unviolated pyramid, and as dark.

Failing to find the lamp, Mrs. Lane remembered with ghastly exactness where she had left it. Too tired to read that night before going to sleep, as was her custom during her husband's numerous absences on duty, she had left the lamp on the dressing table by the door, a good ten feet from the bed.

Should she prove that she was a soldier's wife by getting out of bed and turning on the light, or would it be more prudent to acknowledge that she was just an extremely frightened young woman, and bury her head under the pillow? Instinctively she breathed her husband's name, "Bob!" as if her extreme terror could pierce a hundred miles of darkness and recall instantly her natural protector.

Captain Robert Lane, asleep on the U. S. transport *Sheridan* rushing him and his marines to China, dreamed neither of his wife nor of his four-year-old son, but of legions of revolutionary Chinese bent on making Shanghai interesting for tourists. His wife and son were safe in Los Angeles. Why should they visit him in sleep? He and his machine guns, his leathernecks and their ugly steel tanks, had a stiff enough job ahead of them to keep the international peace, without worrying about any trivial domestic explosions that might brew in their absence. A cruel Chinese face without head or body behind it swam like a saffron bladder toward the Captain's; a pair of dead eyes fastened with cold hatred upon his own; the slit that was a mouth in the yellow, floating thing opened as if to spit a curse, and Bob Lane turned over with a groan, his nightmare broken, but not by his young wife's horror of the clammy darkness that clung to her like a shroud.

Why had the black silence of her bedroom suddenly taken on an unearthly chill? Surely the air was drifting slowly over the bed, and flowing silently into the other room where her son slept in his cot.

"I must see! I must see!" Mrs. Lane muttered to herself, not daring to put her foot to the floor and slip out of bed. "I'm not a coward." She spoke the words aloud, as if challenging the sooty cold to deny an obvious truth. Then an impersonal being, a passionless embodiment of the primitive, unaging logic of things material, spoke with the terrified woman's voice. "There is something in that room," it whispered, "that is neither dead nor living. It is not a spirit, for it never breathed. I know this is true, because I feel it. Whatever is in that room is trying to live, but does not yet know how." Mrs. Lane recovered her mental balance. "Nonsense!" she commented tersely, but without conviction.

The voice that had spoken was the forgotten danger signal of an all but eradicated instinct, so early rooted in the very tissues of life that its existence has passed unsuspected for ages. When the first uncouth parodies of living things took shape in the primeval slime, that same voice uttered its already ancient warning to the crystals and colloids that blundered their slow way toward life and evolution. Age after age that secular fear had whispered, to remind the nascent races of plants and animals how precarious was their grasp upon the fleeting dream called life, and how insecure their temporary dominion over death.

"It is an accident, no more, that you, not I, have life," the nameless instinct seemed to whisper, speaking for the uncreated lives behind the fear; "yet, in the end, my kind shall destroy your kind."

Mrs. Lane had at last recovered her courage. "I shall find my slippers and see what it is," she declared, making no move to carry out her intention.

"Mother! Mother!"

The terrified scream of young Tom cut through her indecision like a razor. Instinct shot Mrs. Lane out of bed, through the icy darkness, into her small son's room. Isabel Lane was twenty-five, healthy and supple. She had not tarried over her slippers. Whatever might be in her boy's room, inhuman monster or mere burglar, might expect no more than swift and painful justice from her tense fingers.

"What is it? Oh——!"

Before she could switch on the electric light, it—whatever it may have been—had happened, appallingly, horribly. There was a crash, a multiplied, incredible crash, of falling, splintering glass, as if a massive old-fashioned ballroom chandelier had shattered itself on the floor. That was all. Not even a subsiding tinkle of fragment on broken fragment lent coherence to the insane dream. There was no chandelier or gaudier hanging abomination of glass in the house, much less in the boy's bedroom.

She snapped on the light. Was it all a nightmare? Then why had her son screamed, in the utter extremity of unnatural terror, and why was he now crying so lustily? She would not believe her dazed eyes. On the smooth oak floor she saw absolutely nothing, not even a trace of impalpable dust. And yet, with her own ears, she had heard the thing—whatever it may have been—fall. Not only had she heard it crash to destruction; the sound of its sudden dissolution was but the momentary echo of a definite, prolonged and terrible death. The thing, now dead and invisible, had gone out in agony. Only its pain lingered.

The boy, crying in her arms, could tell her nothing. "I'm afwaid, I'm afwaid," was all he could say to express an emotion which it might have baffled the most subtle of psychologists to analyze. The fear, which chilled him no less than his mother, was older than instinct, more ancient than the human race. The insentient cells of his young body, the inert minerals of his bones and the traces of iron in his blood had answered to the immemorial fear which all living beings experienced when first they gained, by a hazardous survival, the right to live. That right was now, after unnumbered millions of years, being challenged by a forgotten enemy, whose defeat in the beginning of creative time made the miracle of life an unexplained reality.

Still but half awake, in spite of the sudden shock to her nerves, Mrs. Lane had a cold, clear knowledge that the vanished anomaly—she did not call it this, because she was too dazed, nor did she account for her crystal intuition—had perished in its first, infantile attempt to walk. A subdued, all but inaudible sound of stealthy motion stole back through the silence of her memory, and she seemed to recall that the darkness before the crash had not been a dead nothing, but a stifled clamor of pain and abortive movements. The tentative, almost forgotten sounds of the motion of the thing, before it crashed and dissolved into nothing, were strangely like those of a baby venturing its first steps.

All of these impressions were on a deeper level than that of memory or intuition. They were immediate knowledge, such as mystics claim to experience, conveyed directly from one material thing to another. Mind did not speak to mind, but matter to matter. That silent message of fear in the night was more ancient than any mind. What misshapen mistake of time had found its way up through the darkness of forgotten ages, only to blunder in its first crude movements to an agonized death, in search of the light it could not reach? For the thing suffered an equivalent of pain, although it had no mind; the intensity of its agony still congealed the silent air and froze in the memory of its end. That also was immediate experience, a thing not known or sensed, but lived, from one dead atom to another. Whose careless head had flung back the bolts shutting off this half-created thing from the life it dumbly coveted?

Mrs. Lane, deciding to consider the incident a nightmare, although fast within her bones she felt that it had been singularly real, carried the boy back to her own bed and soon had him asleep. She herself could not sleep. To establish her courage she switched off the lamp, now restored to its usual place on the table by her bed, and debated whether she should get out in the dark to put the lamp back upon the dresser, just to prove conclusively that she was not afraid. Prudence conquered, and she cuddled up to her son. There might be another nightmare—she carefully avoided giving the disturber of her sleep any more tangible designation—in the house, and she did not wish to be unprepared for emergencies. The sense of a nameless fear, and with it the unaccountable chill, had definitely departed, as if the cause of the "nightmare" were indeed dead and less than dust.

Shortly before daybreak she began to doze off. How long she lost touch with the world of living things, Mrs. Lane cannot guess, but she imagines it was less than three-quarters of an hour. She awoke with a start, feeling that she was about to be strangled. A faint but unmistakable odor of corruption tainted the air. A brilliant oblong of sunlight on the floor of her boy's room at once caught her eye through the door which she had left wide open. Tom was fast asleep at her side, apparently in perfect health, although he breathed somewhat loudly. Instantly alert, his mother noticed in almost the same glance that the patch of sunlight shone with a peculiar brilliance, and that her boy's upper lip, where the breath from his nostrils played over it, was discolored a distinct yellow. Her first thought, although she could give no logical reason for it, was that the kitchen gas range was aleak and filling the house with deadly carbon monoxide.

Not stopping to verify any leaks, she rushed out of doors with Tom. Then she returned to fling open all the doors and windows of the bungalow. Everywhere that faint breath of decay poisoned the air, most noticeably in those rooms brightened by the early morning sun, barely perceptible in those where the sun had not yet penetrated, and just distinguishable in the dark closets.

It was still but a few minutes after sunrise. Moreover, it was a Sunday morning—Easter Sunday at that. It was out of the question to call a plumber or a man from the gas company to examine the range. Mrs. Lane, resourceful as are most women whose husbands must be away from home half of their lives, took the Fire Department into her confidence and appealed for help. The man on duty yawning at the other end of the wire promised to send two men immediately. While help was on its way, Mrs. Lane had time to get Tom and herself partially but presentably dressed.

The two firemen who came to render first aid were skeptical, not to say cynical. They nosed about with a sophisticated air, found nothing wrong, and said so plainly.

"Last night the first your husband was away?" one of them asked to corroborate Mrs. Lane's story as she had told it.

She acknowledged that it was, but added that being alone was nothing unusual in the life of an army officer's wife.

"You've got a fit of nerves, that's all," the fireman assured her. "Get one of the neighbor women to stay with you tomorrow night. There's no gas leaking here."

"Very well," she replied, feeling a little foolish. Then suddenly she experienced a sharp sense of danger, and decided to tell the men all about the "nightmare," which till now she had not mentioned. The firemen listened respectfully, with not more grinning than might pass unrebuked. But when the agitated young mother concluded her recital with a frankly feminine appeal that one of the men look under the cot in her boy's room, they burst into a guffaw.

"All right, lady," they agreed, "we're game."

When they saw the cot, standing about three feet high, with a rare Mexican valance of woven horsehair concealing its legs, they roared. The thought that any burglar or other beast of prey could secrete himself successfully under a baby's bed proved too much for their sense of humor. Nevertheless they had promised to rescue a distressed mother, and they now stuck like firemen to their word. One on either side they got down on all fours and poked their heads under the hanging valance, still gurgling like young bulls with repressed mirth. Then suddenly they collapsed and stiffened. Mrs. Lane dragged their unconscious bodies out to the veranda and telephoned for a doctor.

The men recovered before the doctor arrived.

"What hit me, Joe?"

"What hit *me?*" his companion countered. "Did you get it, too?"

"I sure did. Say, lady, I guess you were right about the gas. It must still be hanging about the floor."

"But you said all the fixtures are in perfect shape," Mrs. Lane demurred. "It can't be the gas."

"What was there under that kid's bed, then?" one of the men demanded suspiciously. "I ain't knocked clean out by nothing."

"There was nothing under the cot that I know of. Unless," she added as an afterthought, "you count an egg."

"An egg? What kind of an egg?"

"Just an egg—an Easter egg. I hid one of the dozen we colored yesterday under my boy's cot, for him to find this morning."

"Oh, so it's just an Easter egg breakfast you've invited us to?" the fireman queried sarcastically. "It struck Joe and me like a bootlegger's picnic. What brand of eggs do you use in your business, anyway?"

"Hens' eggs, of course. Did you notice if the green one was under the cot?"

"The green one!" Joe echoed disgustedly. "Say, what are you handing us? I've a good notion to call a cop."

Joe was interrupted by the arrival of the doctor.

"You are too late, fortunately," Mrs. Lane explained. "The men are better."

In answer to the doctor's queries, Mrs. Lane and the firemen succeeded in giving him a confused impression of a wild Saturday night party unduly prolonged into Easter Sunday. Although too suave a gentleman to express his suspicions openly on so delicate a matter, the doctor privately diagnosed the trouble as a mild case of alcoholism. Still, he admitted to himself, Mrs. Lane looked all right; and the firemen exhaled no tell-tale odor.

"Perhaps I had better see for myself what is under your boy's bed," he suggested, with just the right inflection to indicate that he suspected Mrs. Lane of hysteria.

"Watch him get his," Joe whispered.

"Is the green egg there?" Mrs. Lane inquired expectantly, as the doctor lifted the horsehair valance to peer under the cot. "Why," she exclaimed to herself, "what's become of the floor mat?"

"Green egg?" the doctor echoed incredulously in a dazed voice. "You——."

Then he too collapsed. When he revived in the cool air of the veranda, he was somewhat dazed and quite crestfallen.

"There must be gas on the floor," he declared. "Is there a connection for a heater in that room?"

The firemen assured him that there was not. As experts, they agreed that escaping gas had nothing to do with the case.

"Did you see the green egg?" Mrs. Lane persisted. She had an obscure, half-formed intuition, which she would not have trusted to words for any bribe, that some evil thing had hatched out of that innocent looking Easter egg in the night, and was now polluting the clean morning air with its unholy, nocturnal exhalations.

"What green egg?" the doctor demanded, consciously hearing of its existence for the first time.

Mrs. Lane explained in detail. Intuition, mother instinct, or whatever we may choose to call supersense, prompted her to be explicit. The egg, she felt, was not so innocent as most eggs usually are. But she did not confide her suspicions to the three men. As yet her doubts were too nebulous to be taken seriously.

"Just an ordinary hen egg?" the doctor quizzed with a disappointed air when she finished her story. "Sure it wasn't a bad one?"

"It may have been," she admitted. "You see, it was a storage egg. The other eleven that we dyed were guaranteed fresh laid."

"Ah!" the doctor exclaimed, brightening. "That explains this mysterious odor that you say you noticed."

"Odor nothing," Joe interjected decisively. "Did you ever see three healthy men knocked out by one bad egg?"

"But you say it isn't gas," the doctor agreed. "Suppose we have a look at that egg—if there is one." He rose, deliberately cut off a long pole of green bamboo from the clump by the steps, and proceeded to Tom's bedroom. Half ashamed of their expectant curiosity, the three watched the doctor fish under the cot for the guilty egg. Standing bolt upright as he cautiously explored the floor with the pole, the doctor took no chances of encountering a second gas attack. Presently his persistence was rewarded. Out trundled a beautiful, grass-green Easter egg.

"Don't touch it!" he ordered. "The thing may be poisoned. I don't half like its color. Is there a shovel about the place?"

Mrs. Lane fetched the garden shovel, and the doctor, accompanied by the gaping firemen, gingerly bore the suspected egg out of doors.

As he tipped the egg off the shovel, a fourth spectator joined the charmed circle. This was Hoot, the Lanes' enormous yellow family cat. From what region of space he now materialized himself is not known; he just appeared, as he always did, when interesting events were about to happen.

"Don't let him sniff it!" Mrs. Lane implored.

But the doctor, acting in the interests of impartial science, gently restrained her and let curiosity earn its reward. His own curiosity was piqued. The firemen were content to permit the doctor to handle the case. Like Hoot and the doctor they too were now imbued with the scientific spirit.

Hoot's elaborate caution in attacking the problem availed him nothing. First one testing paw patted the egg and found it docile, then the other. It was safe, according to the cat's expert judgment, and would not bite him. Very delicately he elongated his neck and sniffed the virulent looking green shell. He received worse than a bite. With a dismal, croaking howl, as if he were about to be deathly sick, he staggered groggily away, to sink down in a heap at his mistress' feet.

"Poor Hoot," Mrs. Lane exclaimed, picking up the limp form. "Never mind; you'll soon recover—the doctor and the firemen did. Tom! Keep away from that egg."

She rescued her son just as his four-year-old curiosity was about to overmaster him. One of the practical firemen seized the shovel.

"Don't smash it!" the doctor snapped, knocking the poised shovel aside. "That's the most interesting egg in California. Poisoned, beyond a doubt." A wavering blotch of sunlight played over the villainous egg as the leaves of the walnut danced in the morning breeze, and the doctor continued his theorizing. "Look at that vile color. Did you ever see so hideous a green? Something new in the way of poisonous dyes, I'll wager. It isn't a copper green, nor yet an arsenic. I'm going to have it analyzed by the city chemist."

"Yeh," Joe agreed, "it's sure poisoned. Well, we've got to be getting back to the station. Good morning, everybody."

The doctor stood doubtfully regarding the egg. How to pick it up safely?

"Of course you will destroy the rest of the eggs you dyed?" he suggested.

Mrs. Lane nodded. "Have you any idea what kind of poison it is?"

"It acts like concentrated carbon monoxide *plus* hydrocyanic acid, but I doubt whether it is. Otherwise that cat would probably be dead. And he's not."

As if to confirm the doctor's verdict, the supine Hoot made a heroic effort to throw off his stupor. The huge cat rolled over in his mistress' arms and deftly wriggled his way to freedom.

"Keep away from that egg!" the doctor warned, as Hoot made a beeline for the enemy. "Isn't once enough?"

Before they could catch him, Hoot was gratifying his instinct for scientific research. The full, strong sunlight had now been bathing the bright green egg for several minutes. The cat sniffed once, tentatively, then again, thoroughly. Nothing happened. With an air of intense disappointment the enormous Hoot turned his back on the contemptible enemy that he was too proud to fight, and stalked away on his morning business.

For a moment the poison hypothesis seemed to have exploded. Then the doctor hit upon the obvious explanation. His simple theory was in perfect accord with sound common sense. Its one defect, not revealed until some weeks later, was that it was quite wrong. This, however, is nothing against it. A physical theory that is not smashed nowadays within ninety days survives merely because it is not worth smashing. The egg, he declared, had obviously lost its evil cunning because the poisonous principle of the green dye, being exceedingly volatile at blood heat, had all evaporated in the full sunlight. It was as incorrect as it was plausible. Before carrying off the egg to be analyzed for traces of poison, the doctor obtained its full history, so far as known, from Mrs. Lane.

The essential facts are these. Captain Lane and his wife spent their last morning together doing odd jobs about the house and dyeing their son Tom's Easter eggs. As Tom insisted that he could dispose of a full twelve, Captain Lane went out and bought a dozen fresh eggs from a neighbor, instead of using those already in the house. Those which they had on hand were preserved in water glass —the liquid silicate commonly used by housewives for the purpose. Although these might be considered fresh, at least theoretically, the Lanes decided to play no pranks on a baby's stomach, and got an honest dozen. The Easter dyes they bought at the corner grocery store. There was no reason to suspect anything wrong with the colors, as they were a standard brand, guaranteed harmless to man or animal.

All went well till they came to the eleventh egg. Captain Lane, who was doing the dyeing, not being very skillful in handling such fragile things as eggs, tried to be too delicate with his technique. As a result there was a casualty. The eleventh egg eluded his grasp and committed suicide on the tiles of the kitchen floor. Young Tom began to howl. To a child's discerning ear there is a golden magic in the words "a dozen Easter eggs," which is hopelessly tarnished if eleven, or even twelve, be substituted for the mysterious dozen. Argument, reason, exhortation to be a man and not a crybaby, all failed. There must be one dozen, no more, no less. To pacify their clamorous son the Lanes replaced the ruined egg by one "just as good"—although it wasn't—from the crock of waterglass, with the compromise that this egg, the eleventh, was not to be devoured like the rest, but merely admired. So that there should be no mistake about the identity of the sophisticated egg, Captain Lane mixed a special dye for its identification. From equal parts of sky blue and sunflower yellow he brewed a dazzling, virulent golden green that shrieked. Tom prized this egg above all the others, and insisted that his mother "hide" it under his cot, so that he could be sure to find it before she got up.

During all these ceremonies the captain of course got himself rather messy. By the time the job was finished he was more gorgeous than a rainbow. In fishing the substitute egg out of the waterglass he managed to splash his army shoes, his tunic, his face, and his arms up to the elbows with the slithering mess. It took his wife the best part of an hour to get him and his uniform clean enough to pass inspection.

If the doctor's theory of poison had any truth in it, Captain Lane was a pretty dangerous enemy by the time his wife was through with sponging him and his clothes, and she herself was not entirely innocuous. But, as appeared later, the doctor's theory was too simple to be quite right. Nevertheless, a truly cautious health officer from a wiser planet might reasonably have quarantined the whole family for at least five years. And the same experienced officer, knowing more about life in general than do we earth dwellers in our own narrow range, would undoubtedly have forbidden Captain Lane to change his shirt at the last moment, because one of the spots on the left sleeve persistently defied soap and water, hastily cram the discarded shirt into his kit, and jump into a taxi on the first lap of the long journey to Shanghai.

Having satisfied himself that he had all the facts in the case, the doctor left, carrying with him the guilty egg. Only by promising to send young Tom a bigger and greener one within an hour was the doctor permitted to bear off his booty. He felt confident that the chemist's analysis would disclose traces of some complicated poison in the dye which would demote the guilty egg from its interesting status as an inexplicable mystery, and reveal it as nothing more than a rather common accident.

It may be recorded here that the good doctor was bitterly disappointed. The following afternoon he received the chemist's report. The green dye was quite harmless; a child might swallow a quart of it and ask for more, if he happened to like the stuff. Rather ashamed of his part in the affair he tried to doubt that he and the two firemen had suffered more than an attack of nerves in sympathy with Mrs. Lane. Although he never quite succeeded, he wisely decided to forget the incident for the sake of his professional reputation.

After church on that fateful Easter morning, Mrs. Lane and Tom left Los Angeles with some friends for a three days' auto trip to the desert to see the wild flowers. The winter had been warm and wet, so the display promised to be more than usually splendid.

As there are neither telephones nor telegraph stations in the desert, Mrs. Lane missed the first report of the tragedy that made America wish it had kept out of China's private affairs. It is perhaps just as well that she did not hear the first and worst report. Later news made the tragedy more bearable—for a few.

At eleven o'clock in the evening of Easter Sunday, Pacific time, the country received its first shock.

"Extra! Extra! All about the disaster at sea," the newsboys piped from San Francisco to Boston. "Transport *Sheridan* founders at sea. Read all about it! Great loss of life; read all about it; extra, extra!"

It was true. The *Sheridan* had foundered less than three hundred miles from Los Angeles, with nearly all hands, before her sister ship, the *Sherman,* could come to her aid. The one fact that seemed clear was that the tragedy had actually happened. In its details the disaster stood out alone, without precedent or parallel, one of the mysterious riddles of the sea. And this was but the first of a rapid sequence of apparently inexplicable mysteries that puzzled certain curious persons for weeks, until an unpractical dreamer verified his guess at the truth.

At first certain of the reports were received with open ridicule, as the too ambitious efforts of publicity seekers. This was true, in particular, of the strange tale told by the two "desert rats" who drifted into Los Angeles, half insane from what they had seen in the desert, two days after the *Sheridan* went down. It seems strange now that no one had sufficient imagination to link up these true but incredible reports into one simple chain of cause and effect. The fact is, however, that it required extraordinary penetration on the part of one keen-eyed old man to see what was as glaring as the sun.

II. WHAT THE RATS SAW

OF the entire human cargo of the *Sheridan* but sixteen men were saved. These included Captain Lane and three other commissioned officers whose quarters were far forward on the upper deck. At the time of the "wreck"—about nine p.m.—Captain Lane, fully dressed, and three lieutenants were playing bridge in his quarters. The transport sank stern first. The sixteen who escaped managed to launch one of the life rafts just as the ship foundered. In all, twenty men tugged at the raft to get it free of the plunging vessel before they all were hurled into the black water. Four perished in the desperate struggle to reach the raft before the suction of the sinking ship spun it like a chip in a millrace, making a boarding impossible. The wireless operator went down with his ship, after having summoned the *Sherman,* steaming through the night on her course, less than five miles to the east.

When the *Sherman* reached the scene of the wreck she found nothing but the raft with sixteen dazed men, drifting helplessly in a calm as placid as that of a mountain lake on a warm summer day. Among the survivors were two noncoms, who had been standing watch when the *Sheridan* foundered. Their depositions are the only account of what happened.

The story is told in three words. "The ship burst."

That was all that cross-examination and a bluffing threat of court-martial could get out of them. Elaboration was not forthcoming. They stuck obstinately to their simple assertion of fact: without warning the *Sheridan* simply burst. Steel rivets in her plates cracked by thousands like the rattle of a battery of machine guns; the whole ship seemed suddenly to sit down in the water; she sank. There was no explosion, no smoke, no smell of burning. In fact, there was nothing beyond the indisputable fact that the *Sheridan,* steaming on her way as peacefully as a ferryboat, plunged to the bottom of the Pacific less than four minutes after the first rip of the rivets gave warning that the plates had burst asunder. Thirteen of the men who escaped were jolted from their bunks by the first wild plunge, picked themselves up, and scrambled for the clear deck, to fall over the first life raft. They launched it automatically, somehow, not knowing what they were doing or what was happening, except that the ship was going down in record time.

In response to a wirelessed request for orders, the *Sherman* absorbed the sixteen survivors into her own companies of marines and proceeded on her course to China, as if nothing had happened. Such is life in the army.

The families of the survivors were of course notified; the rest it was unnecessary to notify, except such as were entitled to widows' pensions. Captain Lane resumed his duties within eight hours, too dazed to be thankful for his escape or to make guesses concerning what had caused the inexplicable disaster. He had lost his kit, and had now only the uniform in which he stood. Not until he reached China did he fully recover his senses. What happened to him in China, with him an unwilling and unsuspecting spectator of the drama, all but made him lose his senses for good and all. But it happened with such devilish casualness at first, and with such an illusory appearance of being merely an unexpectedly interesting detail of his duty, that he completely missed the sinister point of the play until it was almost too late to divert its climax. In the meantime, while he and his men marched resolutely and unwittingly to meet their destiny, Mrs. Lane and Tom enjoyed the excitement nearer home, and old Jonathan Saxby, retired geologist, found much to interest him in the eccentric antics of the desert.

Just as the sun set on Easter Sunday, Mrs. Lane, Tom and their friends found the ideal camping place in the desert at which to spend the night. They had driven hard all the afternoon, and had now penetrated to the very heart of the desert. A sharp outcrop of limestone provided adequate shelter from the strong east winds which freshened as the sun dipped swiftly to the horizon, and several acres of flat slabs suggested the ready means of improvising a camp kitchen. A thorough search of the chosen site confirmed the general opinion that it was still too early in the season for rattlesnakes, so the party set about preparing supper. Dead sage brush gave all the fuel necessary, and in half an hour Mrs. Lane had a hot meal ready. They dined by firelight before the moon rose, cleaned up, thrust the refuse into a cleft between two limestone slabs, made up their beds, and in ten minutes were fast asleep. The following morning, half an hour before sunrise, they were on their way farther into the desert to see the best of the early flowering cacti.

The California deserts are more than alluring mysteries to tempt holiday makers. They are heavily mineralized wastes that have trapped scores of prospectors for life. Before Mr. Ford put padded leather cushions and twenty miles an hour within reach of anyone with fifty dollars to spend for a second-hand car, the old-timer used to tramp the desert for weeks, from one spring or water hole to the next, leading by its halter his sole companion, the patient, long-eared burro. Occasionally two or three of these inveterate prospectors would travel together, sharing the hardships and playing poker for the winnings—if any; but the majority pegged along alone. Conversation, human companionship, having to think at every step what the other fellow wants, become intolerable bores when civilization is left behind. A couple of sides of bacon, enough flapjack flour, coffee, beans and salt to last a month or six weeks, a burro to pack the outfit, and the ideal prospector was complete. Most of them were sinewy, grizzled men, long past middle age, with stubby white beards stained by tobacco juice, their skins the rich brown of old mahogany. Many had tramped the desert for fifty years, and all believed that they should find King Solomon's mines before they dropped in their tracks, to become russet husks like dried frogs.

Not one in twenty ever found anything of value in the desert. In the credulous cities, however, even the poorest prospector could always unearth at least one flush sucker—usually a stock broker or bond salesman, eager to put up two hundred dollars to grubstake the next jaunt in search of the mystical mines. As a rule the real old-timer was shrewd, sanguine, and superstitious beyond belief. When the Ford cars began skipping like sandfleas all over the desert, the genuine prospector passed them up with silent scorn, and stuck like a brother to his faithful, plodding burro that never ran out of gas or water, or got itself punctured on the cactus thorns.

Shortly after Mrs. Lane's friends had left their limestone camp ground, old Dan O'Brien puffed up to it leading his burro. Dan had not yet breakfasted. The flat slabs offered a luxurious table. As he approached the outcrop—which he knew to its last chunk from innumerable previous visits, his expert eye automatically estimated the number and social status of the departed visitors. He read their standing from the signs of their visit as accurately as if he were silently criticising them in a hotel lobby. Although they had cleaned up before quitting the place, they had left tracks and crumbs enough to broadcast their entire life history to a seasoned prospector like old Dan.

"This durned place is gettin' worse'n a city park," the pessimistic "rat" grunted, as he mixed his batter for his morning flapjacks.

Not a soul was in sight in the dazzling dawn, and no flivver bounded over the vast beds of purple and crimson, of lavender and yellow, that were the desert's springtime. Yet the poor old rat, true lover of holy solitude, believed that the place was defiled and no more private than a brawling, smelly city street. He felt sad. Not that he saw the astounding beauty of the desert aflame with exotic flowers, for old Dan probably had never seen a flower of any kind in his fifty-five years in the desert. His beauty was elsewhere—in his soul, in his taciturnity, and in his passionate desire to be alone. Why the devil, he pondered, couldn't these damned tourists stick to the paved highways?

His flapjacks tasted sour. Probably they were. But this was a spiritual sourness, quite distinct from the wholesome acidity to which long years of inefficiency had accustomed him, and to which he unconsciously looked forward with an eager zest. As he scoured the frying pan with clean, gritting sand, he gazed disconsolately out over the rolling billows of blinding colors that flowed in diminishing brilliance to the far, azure horizon, and wondered if anywhere on this earth there is still a desert that does not charm the idle. A tiny cloud of white alkali dust, five miles to the west, shone mistily in the blue haze. But this, thank Heaven, was not the nimbus of a flivver.

"That must be Jake," he muttered. "Guess I'll be sociable-like and wait."

Old Dan waited, as motionless as a lizard basking on a hot rock, till his venerable friend Jake plodded up with his burro. The desert rats had known one another intimately for at least forty years. In all that time they had exchanged, perhaps, a thousand words, no more. They were, in fact, boon companions.

"Morning," said Dan.

"Morning," Jake responded and sat down. He had long since breakfasted. He just sat, enjoying that luxury as only a man, who sees a chair or a really comfortable rock but once or twice a year, knows how to enjoy sitting. Conversation languished. Presently Dan got up to go to work. His "work" consisted in exploring every crevice of the outcrop for evidence of ores.

Although it was a geological improbability that the weathered limestone could contain gold, and although Dan O'Brien knew this fact as well as any professor of geology, he never neglected an opportunity of thoroughly prospecting those barren rocks. He must have examined every slab at least a hundred times in the past fifty years. The task always gave him something to do, and it also proved an inexhaustible source of "reports" to the successive generations of credulous city folk, who grubstaked old Dan's innumerable expeditions to the desert. In this respect the limestone outcrop was incomparably more profitable to Dan O'Brien than any gold mine he could possibly have discovered. For if he had been so unfortunate as to locate a real gold mine, some slick promoter would instantly have skinned him out of it.

Jake spent an equally busy day prospecting the gritty sand that abounded in the vicinity of the outcrop. It might be monazite, rich in osmium, cerium, iridium, thorium and half a dozen other precious metals that come small and sell big, but Jake knew perfectly well that this plebeian trash was not worth two cents a ton. He also was expected to "report," and the old chap wished to be as honest as the proprieties demanded.

Sunset found them tired, taciturn and happy. Without a word they adjourned to the oozing spring that seeped out of the limestone at its highest point on the north side. There they watered and fed their burros, prepared their respective rations of beans and bacon in silence, ate their suppers without conversation, either necessary or unnecessary, cleaned up, and turned in for the night. It was still indecently early according to city standards—barely seven o'clock.

If there was anything in the adage about "early to bed," Dan and Jake should have been practically immortal, richer than Rockefeller and wiser than Solomon, for they never stayed up later than seven, and were always out of their blankets before three forty-five. On the whole, considering their almost perfect lives, one might say that the proverb is more true than false.

The moon was full that night. Through its soft radiance the subdued hues of the desert flowers shone mistily in vast beds, like the gardens of a dream, but the tired men were too old to care. Had they been awake to see, they would have noticed nothing but the promise of another scorching day in the serenity of that unearthly landscape. Old Dan stirred uneasily in his blankets, turned over with a muttered sigh, and sank into a deeper sleep. He was used to complete silence and absolute stillness at night. His rest had been disturbed, but as yet not sufficiently to break his iron slumber. Presently he lashed out pettishly with one leg, toward what he imagined was the general direction of Jake.

"Quit movin' around, will ye?" he quarreled in his sleep. But Jake was snoring softly, almost inaudibly, like an old and comfortable cat. He lay like a log, too tired to toss. Dan forgot his unrest, except subconsciously. The two slept on, weary to the bone.

The hobbled burros began to snort. Something that they did not like was moving in the desert, where it had no business to move. Keener of muscular sense than the men, they apprehended the unnatural movements long before the sleepers began to dream uneasily of charging cavalry and regiments of braying mules. As daintily as geisha girls the two burros teetered off in the moonlight, to seek safety at the south end of the outcrop. The men slept on.

Jake woke first. His wild yell brought Dan shaking to his feet.

"Earthquake!"

A steady, creeping noise, as of millions of growing things sending out their brittle tendrils over the desert floor, rustled through the night from the farther side of the limestone ridge, and the rock slabs vibrated rapidly in unison. The air was as cold as midwinter; a slow, icy breeze drifted past the terrified men toward the source of the sound. Then in rapid succession a series of appalling noises shattered the silence of the desert for a radius of twenty miles. First a terrific report, sharp as a pistol shot, whanged through the air. Instinctively the two men dropped flat on their faces to miss the imagined shell. Then two almost human screams from the strayed burros, the unmistakable sounds of terror from animals about to be done to death, froze the blood in the old men's hearts. Their beasts were being killed, inhumanly, unnaturally, and they were powerless to help. A terrified crashing drowned the last screams like the instant collapse of a cathedral of brittle glass on a pavement of steel. The inexplicable clamor ceased instantly, like a summer thunderclap, and only the steady, horrible creeping noise made the ghastly moonlight hideous.

Half paralyzed with fright the two desert rats reeled away to what they imagined was safety. Glancing back involuntarily Dan saw the pursuing "thing" almost upon him. For perhaps two seconds he halted in his tracks, stiff with fear, staring up at a shape which no man could name. It glistened in the moonlight like a colossal octopus fresh from the sea, its uncouth tentacles angular and jagged, shooting erratically in every direction, as if the thing were feeling its way into space. Unlike a living creature, this monster was all but transparent. Strange purples and greens pulsed and flickered through its inchoate mass like a subdued play of phosphorescent flames; a hundred dazzling pinnacles glittered like gigantic broken diamonds on the advancing crest, and from each of these points of light a score of zigzag, angular tentacles flashed into instant existence. The thing seemed not to move but to grow toward its prey. The main mass did not advance, but planted itself more firmly on the desert floor and conquered distance by lateral growth.

At the risk of his own sanity Jake turned back and dragged Dan away. Then they fled panting into the silence of the desert, blundering into cacti and stumbling over rattlesnake holes till they sank from utter exhaustion. They lay where they fell, huddled together in stupor till the endless night ended and the dawn broke.

THEY agreed that it was not a dream. But what of it? They were old, incurious men, used all their lives to nature at first hand, and not easily moved by the wonders that take the tourist's breath away. This, however, was new, beyond even their experience of earthquakes and the vagaries of desert storms. The thwarted curiosity of two long repressed lives suddenly burgeoned in those withered old hearts, and they became inquisitive to the point of sheer foolhardiness.

"Guess I'll go take a look," Dan remarked, picking himself up.

"Me, too," Jake seconded.

Without further parley they made their way back to the limestone ridge.

"Smell something?" Jake inquired as they drew near the first outcrop.

"It's the burros," Dan theorized.

"Couldn't smell like that after just a few hours. The sun's only been up a short spell." This was probably the longest speech Jake had ever made. Dan reproved him by reiterating his terse theory.

"See anything?" the loquacious Jake demanded as they drew near the exact spot of their mutual vision. Dan deemed a reply unnecessary. There was nothing to be seen.

They stood staring incredulously at the slabs of rock.

"There's no smell now," Dan ventured. Jake took his revenge by ignoring this superfluous remark. Unabashed, Dan chattered on like a vivacious flapper.

"Them scratches warn't there yesterday."

He indicated several fresh, deep grooves in the soft limestone. Jake nodded.

"The sage brush is all tramped down over yonder, too," he observed. "Let's find the burros."

Exploring the environs of the ledge they found abundant but inexplicable evidence of unaccountable doings in the night. In some places for a distance of fully a hundred yards from the ridge, the sage brush was flattened and broken as if a fleet of battle tanks had passed over it, and the alkali was pitted with huge pockets or scarred by short, deep furrows where some heavy object had apparently dragged itself forward a foot at a time. The furrows were comparatively rare, the pockets much more numerous. Although it was difficult to decipher this strange evidence, the old-timers silently agreed that some massive body had rested on the dirt, and by its sheer weight sank the impress of its irregularities deep into the dust and conglomerate.

At the inner edge of one of these devastated bays in the sagebrush they came upon the carcasses of the burros, or rather upon what was left of them. Two sickening smears of crimson, an indescribable tangle of lacerated flesh, as if the wretched animals had been cut to ribbons in a slicing machine, propounded their tragic riddle to the silent sky. The poor old desert rats almost wept. They had loved their burros. Their aged eyes stared pityingly at the shocking spectacle.

"There are no bones," Dan remarked, a note of superstitious terror creeping into his voice for the first time.

"They were crushed," Jake hazarded.

"Where are the pieces?" Dan demanded.

"Don't know. Let's see."

Cold with a morbid fear, they set about their gruesome search. It was thorough. Not a splinter of bone and not a single tooth was found. The horny husks of eight hoofs, all but crushed out of recognition, lay in approximately the positions that might have been expected from the general appearance of the remains.

When the fact that the bones had vanished was finally established beyond any reasonable doubt, the shaken old men stood silently staring into one another's eyes. Neither dared to speak for fear of giving himself away. Their superstition was like the ordinary decent man's religion—an experience not to be mentioned in public. Each knew what the other was thinking, and each considered the other rather a fool for his thoughts. In silence they made their way back to the outcrop, to the spot where they had met the previous morning.

Here another freak of the night's orgies greeted their bewildered eyes. A gaping fissure five feet broad and about three hundred long parted the main body of the limestone into two irregular masses by a jagged chasm. It appeared as if the solid rock had been suddenly burst asunder by a deep-seated and violent explosion. The snap of the parting rock undoubtedly was the "pistol shot" they heard before the obliterating crash sent them fleeing into the desert. Of what had caused that crash, like the smashing of a million bottles, they found not a trace. Yet it had seemed as real and vivid as the screams of the slaughtered burros.

Not being used to expressing themselves in speech, they acted. It was tacitly agreed that they should return at once to civilization and "report." As fast as their old legs could carry them they made for the desert highway, confident of hitching a lift from sightseers returning in their flivvers to Los Angeles.

Just before they flagged their chosen victim, Dan spoke, breaking the charmed silence of a six hours' strenuous hike through the broiling heat.

"We'll get our pictures in the paper," he prophesied with lickerish glee.

"Both of us," Dan agreed.

They did.

III. SAXBY'S EXPERIMENT

DAN and Jake had no difficulty in getting a sympathetic specialist from a Los Angeles paper to listen to their story. They made all the usual mistakes of the beginner in journalistic adventures and told the polite young fellow a great deal they did not know they had said. He promised to give them a good write-up. Technically he kept his word. The "story" was genuinely funny. The poor old desert rats did not know that the professional humorist of the United Press had been turned loose on them. With such a start as Jake and Dan gave him, the humorist romped his easy way to a classic of slapstick wit. The town roared; the rats cursed. So good was the story that it was syndicated. Within a week it had been read and enjoyed by twenty million intelligent human beings, not one of whom saw the point. It was not the laughing matter those twenty million readers thought it.

The disillusioned prospectors became notorious overnight in Los Angeles and its environs. An ambitious gentleman from Hollywood offered them a fabulous sum for a three months' tour in vaudeville. Dan and Jake were now thoroughly enraged. Their exact account had been laughed out of court. Now they burned with a righteous anger to vindicate themselves. They signed the contract. Being familiar from long experience with business methods of a certain kind, they insisted upon a fifty per cent cash payment in advance. It was well that they did. Their "act" was a complete flop. At the end of the week the gentleman from Hollywood was glad to send them back to the desert with his blessing and the fifty per cent.

It is rather remarkable that of all those who became familiar with the story, not one thought of verifying the details of the scratches on the limestone and the deaths of the burros. In preferring talk to the simple act of seeing, the twenty million only repeated on a small scale the dreary annals of the human race.

When Mrs. Lane returned to Los Angeles on the Thursday following Easter Sunday, she glanced over the headlines of one of the accumulated papers to see what had happened during her holiday in the desert. She did this hastily on the veranda, before she and Tom entered the cottage. The funny story of the two desert rats and their novel spree caught her eye—it was heavily featured. Skimming the lively skit she failed to catch its sinister meaning. It was too funny. She bundled up the papers and looked in the mail box.

"Well, Tom," she remarked, "we can't expect a letter from him yet, but let's see if there is one, just to be sure. Why! Here's a telegram."

She tore it open and took in the curt message at a glance, without comprehension.

"Captain Lane proceeding safely to China on U.S. transport Sherman."

This consoling but mysterious message was dated at San Diego and signed by a staff officer of the U. S. Army. What could it mean? Mrs. Lane hastily entered the house, sent Tom away to bring back Hoot from a neighbor's, and began a systematic search of the newspapers. She soon found all she wanted.

"He's safe," she sighed. "That's all that matters."

She sat thinking in silence, wishing Bob were out of the army. As her mind roamed half dreaming over their happy past together and the doubtful months ahead, the subconscious part of her went busily to work on the rich, curious feast which she, unknowingly, had spread before it. The Easter Sunday "nightmare," the "bursting" of the *Sheridan,* the ludicrous yarn told by those imaginative old prospectors, all seemed curiously interlined, although strangely unfamiliar and individually incomprehensible. What was the silly phrase that humorous newspaper man had used in repeating Dan's story? "Bombarded by billions of beer bottles." The asinine alliteration almost analyzed the astonishing antics of the anomalies—this absurd rejoinder flashed through her mind. She came out of her daydream.

"That's curious," she said, not knowing exactly to what she referred. "I must read that bit about those prospectors again."

On this reading the badly distorted account cleared up with startling lucidity. Even that humorous genius had not succeeded in disguising the eerie truth beyond recognition. The crash which Jake and Dan had attempted in their halting way to describe must have been very similar, although on a much larger scale, to that which she and Tom had heard in his bedroom. Like her, the desert rats had failed to find any traces of broken glass. Yet, if the "bombardment" were not a bad dream but something more substantial, the old men should have found tons of shattered glass on the limestone. The strange coincidence between her dream and theirs took on an oppressive, evil significance. Mrs. Lane suddenly felt an overpowering desire for fresh air. She went out to the back garden to wait for Tom and Hoot. The old men, she recalled uneasily, had also reported a smell of decay that dissipated as the morning advanced. What could it all mean? The rock, they declared, had "burst." Suddenly, too, like the *Sheridan*. Again a coincidence, or was it more?

The injustice of the ridicule accorded those poor old men, who had done their humble best to tell the truth, however strange, made her pulse beat faster. Isabel Lane, like her husband, was a born fighter when the cause was a just one. Her indignation rose.

"I shall write to the editor," she declared, "and tell him exactly what I think of his lying paper."

She darted into the living room and dashed off a red hot protest to the editor. Unfortunately Isabel was so angry when she wrote the letter that she made it excruciatingly and unintentionally funny. It beat the professional's effort on behalf of Dan and Jake.

"There!" she said, slapping down the inoffensive two-cent stamp, "that will let him see he isn't as smart as he thinks he is." In the rash heat of her wrath she had given a short but complete account of her own experience of a "noise" on Easter Sunday, to prove that the desert rats were not suffering from delirium tremens as was hinted by the funny man. "I myself," she added, "never touch alcoholic beverages, and I am sure that my four-year-old son is not a drunkard. He heard it, too."

When the editor read Isabel's letter he sat speechless in an enchanted ecstasy. Finally he found words.

"Call up this woman," he directed his stenographer, "and offer her fifty a week for half a column a day. She's a pippin, a red-hot mama. Oh, boy!"

Isabel's response was an indignant No. She could spark for principle but not for lucre.

"May we print your letter, Mrs. Lane?"

"If you don't, you're cowards."

"Thank you, Mrs. Lane. You will find your letter on the front page tomorrow morning. Goodbye."

THE letter duly appeared, and the country enjoyed another laugh. This time, however, journalism did accomplish something useful. Isabel's letter was the essential link in a strong chain of evidence which, without it, might never have been closed. Undoubtedly old Jonathan Saxby could have got on without the letter, but its singular significance gave him a flying start of at least a week. This early start was extremely important; with it, he almost succeeded in wrecking Asia; without it, he might have stayed at home and wrecked the United States.

Jonathan Saxby, formerly professor of geology at the leading university in America, was now in his sixtieth year and at the apex of his keen, analytical powers. Although he was commonly known as "old" Saxby, he was elderly only in appearance—resembling Mr. Pickwick as that sage is usually portrayed in his later years. In mental agility he was about twenty-five. In physical endurance, according to his easily exhausted young colleagues, old Saxby beat the devil. He did not know what it was to feel tired, either in his laboratory study or on his summer rambles up precipices and over all but infinite wastes of drifting sand. He ate but once a day, but when he did dine, he depleted the commissary. In the matter of drink he was equally abstemious. Three bottles of wine, not too light, taken with his dinner, satisfied him for twenty-four hours.

When he retired from teaching, Saxby hesitated long between Italy and California as the perfect haven for old age. He could afford either, as he had made a huge pot of money as geological consultant for three of the luckiest oil corporations. These rewarded him amply. Old Saxby was no fool at business. At fifty-five he found himself with "all the world before him where to choose," and he chose California.

It was not without regret that Saxby abandoned the rosy dream of Italy. His strange hobby cast the deciding vote. Saxby was an inveterate and passionate collector. His collection was probably the weirdest that acquisitive man has ever made. It consisted of thousands of earthquakes, all neatly tabulated, classified, cross-indexed and resolved into their simplest harmonic components. To such a collector California offered obvious advantages over Italy—although California's notorious modesty might restrain her from bragging about it. Outside of Japan, possibly, California does afford the collector of earthquakes the most efficient and best organized seismological service in the world. When old Saxby learned also that the California vineyardists retail a delicious, virginal blend of three grape juices at the price of one good song per forty-gallon cask, and that nature will do what is necessary for nothing if you merely pull the bung out of the cask and let it stand for three weeks, he hesitated no longer. He settled down in Los Angeles to spend the next sixty years of his life collecting earthquakes and eating one meal a day.

Old Saxby was a confirmed bachelor, in both theory and practice. He tolerated the presence of an old cook only because he almost never saw her. If Jemima had been so rash as to venture out of her own quarters into the master's presence, she would have been fired on the spot. His more intellectual wants were ministered by a so-called secretary, usually a young Japanese, Chinese, or Filipino. The secretary's formal duties consisted in keeping the thousands of earthquakes straight in the filing cabinet, and in improving old Saxby's mind with quaintly frank and heathenish views on all Christian customs.

Saxby had hired Buddhists, Confucians, Taoists and plain infidels in his time, and once he had tried a Moslem. The last nearly proved his undoing. This swarthy young man was a brilliant geological chemist, an International Research Fellow, and just the collaborator Saxby needed at the time in his classic investigation of the basalts. He was obliged reluctantly to discharge this paragon of secretaries because the fiery zealot preached incessantly against the Christian vice of wine-bibbing, which to a Moslem is the filthiest of all habits. Old Saxby felt that if he kept the pest he must inevitably be reformed.

The present incumbent of this most desirable secretaryship in the word was young Mr. Yang, a Chinese Government student with his Ph.D. from Columbia. Yang also was a hybrid between geology and chemistry, but unlike the eloquent Moslem, he was the soul of circumspect discretion. Yang had but one fault; he obstinately maintained that old Saxby's topaz wine was not fit to drink when one could get the crystal clear volatile Chinese gin. Saxby could not convert him.

It was but natural that old Saxby's dragnet method of fishing for earthquakes should haul up the Dan–Jake episode. In addition to receiving weekly reports from all the seismological stations of the world, Saxby subscribed to at least two clipping bureaus in each civilized country. These were instructed to comb the daily press for the slightest mention of anything even remotely resembling an earthquake. The clippers had their lists of key words, such as temblor, tremor, shake, quake, landslide, and a hundred others, by means of which they sifted the daily tons of facts and misinformation dumped upon a suffocating and helpless world.

Occasionally their gleanings drove old Saxby to profanity. Thus, at election time, he received under the caption of "landslide" several tons of clippings celebrating the latest victory of the invincible grand old party. Again, under "shakes" he was wont to be deluged with advertisements for ague cures, and once under "temblor," the bureau in Mexico City sent him minute instructions for the self treatment of an unmentionable weakness to which he had never been a slave. The Dan–Jake account was gathered in under the captions "shake," "tremble" and "crash." This wild yarn, Saxby decided, would bear further inspection. He instructed Yang to file it away in the incubator—the technical term for the cabinet containing reports of embryo earthquakes that might hatch out into vigorous, adult shakes. Yang was also to inspect the local press daily for further details.

THE extraordinary disturbance in the desert, if an earthquake at all, was of a new species. Old Saxby almost prayed that Dan and Jake might prove as truthful in the end as they now seemed not to be. The one piece of evidence in their account which might be of scientific value was the splitting of the limestone rock. That sounded like science, although it probably was only another lie. Before taking a jaunt out to the desert to see for himself, Saxby decided to wait for further details. There was one particularly suspicious circumstance about the whole alleged miracle. The extremely delicate Anderson–Smith seismographs at the Pasadena observatory had failed to record any trace of a disturbance on the night of the supposed event. Therefore, Saxby concluded, it was probably no more than an unusually interesting fake.

When the efficient Yang duly laid the clipping containing Isabel Lane's indignant letter before his employer, old Saxby rubbed his eyes and grunted.

"There's something in it. I'm going to call on this lady. You may dine without waiting for me this evening, Yang. I shall lock up the gin before I leave. And I shall take the key with me. So don't waste time hunting for it. Goodbye."

WHEN Mrs. Lane answered the door bell, she looked straight into the shrewd, questioning blue eyes of an elderly, carelessly dressed man, whose loose alpaca suit bagged in every conceivable way in which clothes can, and whose hatless bald head blushed with a charming pink like a newly bathed baby's back. The rather rotund figure concealed the stocky, well-knit frame of a powerfully built man. In his thirties old Saxby was as strong as a draft horse; in his first sixties, although somewhat shrunk, he gave the impression of great muscular power and inexhaustible endurance. His bland, childlike smile as he gazed up into Isabel's eyes was wholly disarming. She took him for an itinerant mender of umbrellas.

"Thank you," she said, hoping to get rid of him as quickly as possible, "I have nothing today."

"Not even an earthquake, by any chance?" old Saxby suggested innocently.

"An earthquake? What on earth do you mean?"

"Why—ah—an earthquake, of course," Saxby replied as if it were the most natural thing in the world to ask for one. "You see, ah—you see," he continued, laboring to explain his mission, "I collect them. And I read your most interesting letter in the paper. So I thought—naturally I thought—that you might still have some interesting details which you did not tell the paper. You see I am—ah—I'm Jonathan Saxby."

Isabel scanned the childlike face doubtfully. The old chap seemed sane enough. Should she invite him in? Hoot, materializing noiselessly from nowhere, brushed confidently against old Saxby's baggy trousers and stalked majestically into the house. It was clearly an invitation.

"Won't you come in, Mr. Saxby?" Mrs. Lane suggested.

"Thanks, I think I will. I think I will. Now, about your earthquake," he began when he was comfortably seated; "you are sure it happened?"

"But there was no earthquake," Isabel protested. "I very carefully avoided giving any suggestion of a shake in my letter to the paper. What Tom and I heard was quite different. It was like a shower of broken glass."

"'Bombarded by billions of beer bottles,'" old Saxby quoted softly. Yang had underlined that poetic phrase in the clipping which he laid before his master, and it had captivated old Saxby's sense of beauty.

"What do you mean?" Isabel demanded sharply. "If you are going to insinuate anything about me, as that smart Alec did about those prospectors, you may leave now."

"Not at all, not at all," he murmured deprecatingly. "I just thought what a beautiful phrase it is. Now this earthquake—or shall we say bombardment?—really was an earthquake. Those old men felt the rock shake."

"I don't believe it. Nothing in this house moved, although something *tried* to move."

"Really!" Saxby exclaimed, leaning forward. "How extraordinary. You are a human seismograph, Mrs. Lane. You see you felt the earthquake before it happened——no, that's not quite it. You felt the tension of the rocks that almost gave way to cause an earthquake. You must be singularly sensitive."

"For a sane man you talk the most extraordinary nonsense I ever heard."

"I know I do," he admitted blandly. "I always have, you know. That's why I am who I am and not, for instance, the poor old peddler you thought I was when you opened the door. But, to come back to your earthquake, or whatever you like to call it. Please tell me everything that happened. You corroborated the prospectors in their account of a tremendous smash and a bad smell. But I feel ah—I feel that you are concealing something, Mrs. Lane."

"I am. An egg."

"An egg? How extraordinary. And why didn't you tell the paper about the interesting egg?"

"Well," Isabel admitted, "I didn't wish to appear ridiculous, for one thing. For another, I thought my husband—he's a captain in the Marines—might be court-martialed if I did."

"Court-martialed?" old Saxby echoed in bewilderment. "For an egg? It isn't done, Mrs. Lane, I assure you."

"It *hasn't* been done," Isabel corrected. "But it might be if the staff officers knew enough to put two and two together."

"Have you been doing arithmetic, Mrs. Lane?"

"I have. A lot."

"And what answer do you get?"

"None. I'm not good at figures. But I know enough to hold my tongue."

"Oh, come now. You can trust me. I don't know any army men—I don't even know a policeman. And if I did I shouldn't tell him anything, even my own name. What about this egg?"

"It was just a green Easter egg."

"Do you still have it?"

"No. The city chemist destroyed it after analyzing the green dye. It was quite harmless."

"It would be," old Saxby commented drily. "I don't see what your green egg has to do with any of this, but let me tell you a little story. It is quite true. About forty years ago some very great professors of chemistry in Germany made a beautiful theory to account for all sorts of chemical reactions. They could explain almost everything. When an experiment came out wrong, and instead of getting a nice, clear liquid or a respectable precipitate, they got a slimy mess that was neither liquid nor solid, they put the beaker up on the top shelf behind the door, because it contradicted their theory. There had been a stupid 'experimental error,' they declared. Soon the top shelf was all cluttered up with glass jars of blue and green and brown slime—experimental errors. Then they used the next lower shelf, and so on. Finally they had to use other shelves not hidden by the door, and at last, after twenty years, they had to move out of the big laboratory to a smaller one. Then a young fellow. who had no beautiful theory, was assigned to the dirty old laboratory as his workshop. The messes in those jars interested him, and he began pottering with them. When he finished, there was nothing left of the theory, and he had made slime fashionable. It is quite all the rage now in chemistry. Need I point the moral? When the city chemist finds your green egg harmless and wholesome, don't believe him. He has probably made an experimental error."

"I am glad you think so. Although I know nothing of science, I feel with my common sense that there was something radically wrong with that egg. The cat—you saw him, the big yellow—sniffed at it and became unconscious. A similar thing happened to three men, one of them a physician."

"This sounds interesting," Saxby commented. "Won't you tell me the whole story?" he begged. "I give you my word I shall not tell anyone if you would rather I didn't. I hate publicity, anyway."

"Very well," she agreed. "You may be able to see the connection between all these freaks of nature. I can't. First, my husband was one of the sixteen men saved from the wreck of the *Sheridan*. Have you read about it?"

"I can't say that I have. You see, earthquakes are my hobby, and I have no time for newspapers. The clippers send me all I read. I never see a whole paper."

"Well," Isabel continued, "the ship simply burst. Suddenly. Those two prospectors say the rock in the desert burst with a sound like a cannon going off. They also smelt the same kind of odor that Tom—my boy—and I did. That is one pair of coincidences. The sound of breaking glass is another. There are several more if you will follow everything."

She gave him an accurate account of all the facts from the dyeing of the Easter eggs to her letter to the paper.

"Now," she concluded, "if you can make anything of it, you are a lot smarter than I am. What became of that floor mat by Tom's cot? Who would steal a dollar's worth of cotton?"

Old Saxby's eyes glistened.

"I wonder," he muttered.

"What about?"

"Everything. I make no theories. You say you replaced the broken egg by one that was preserved in waterglass?"

"Yes. My husband and I used them. They were all right, but we always got new-laid ones for Tom. Some doctors think the preserved eggs lack vitamins."

"I see. May I take a look at that crock of waterglass?"

"I'm very sorry. I threw it out."

"Why?"

"Because it had gone bad."

"How 'bad,' Mrs. Lane?"

"It was all stringy and full of milky bluish spots."

"And you threw it away?" Saxby cried, a note of anguish in his voice. "Oh, what a pity! Another of those priceless 'experimental errors,' I'm afraid. Where did you put it?"

"In the can with the wet garbage. The men collected the stuff this morning."

Old Saxby groaned. "What a pity! An irreparable loss. Unless," he exclaimed, brightening, "we can find it. Where do they dump the garbage?"

"It is burned."

"Oh, dear! Hopeless. You should have been a professor in a German university—Berlin or Leipzig. I have daydreamed of this very thing for years. And now, when it happens, a German professor throws all my experiments into the garbage can. Thank Heaven I never married."

Although Saxby's devout gratitude was not very complimentary to Isabel, she accepted it with a smile.

"If the city chemist could analyze an egg, you should be able to get along with the crock."

"Oh, you blessed woman. You did not throw away the crock?"

"Of course not. We aren't millionaires."

"Then it will still be dirty—chemically I mean. May I borrow it?"

"Certainly. Are you going to check up the prospectors' story?"

"I am. Tonight. If newspapers are good for anything, someone at the office should know the exact location of that limestone outcrop and how to reach it by automobile. May I use your telephone?"

"It is in the dining room—there. I have been thinking," she continued slowly, "that I should see that place, too."

"Perhaps you should, although I see no earthly reason why. Still, I never professed to understand women. Come with me, if you like."

"Thanks, I shall. While you are telephoning I'll hunt up Tom and leave him at a neighbor's."

When Isabel returned, she found that Saxby had obtained all the information necessary from the efficient newspaper office. He had also telephoned for a good car and a driver.

"We shall be there before midnight," he announced. "You are sure Captain Lane will not object when he hears of our trip?"

"Why should he?" Isabel retorted casually, much as she might have alluded to Hoot.

Old Saxby muttered something about "modern women" and suggested that they snatch a dinner at a lunch counter on the way. Isabel agreed.

"Do you want that crock now?"

"I shall leave it with my Chinese secretary. He is a chemist, you know. It won't be much off our road."

The crock was duly left with Yang to be examined chemically, and the machine sped away toward the desert highway. At first Isabel did not recognize the road in the declining light as they entered the desert; but presently one landmark and then another made it certain that the car was taking the same route as that which she and her friends had followed. The man drove straight ahead, sure of his way, for five hours. When the moon rose he slackened the pace.

"It must be over there to the east about five miles," he said. "Shall I let you out here, or will you risk a puncture? I have four spares."

"Chance it," Saxby ordered. "I'll pay."

The car left the road and cautiously picked its way around the cacti. Within half an hour they made out the dim blue mass of a low ridge directly ahead of them in the moonlight.

"That's it," Saxby exclaimed. "We can walk the rest of the way. Wait here for us," he directed the driver.

On reaching the outcrop they found the jagged fissure immediately. The desert moonlight etched every detail in glaring relief.

"This is the first check," Saxby remarked.

Isabel did not reply. She was staring at her surroundings, strangely unfamiliar in that light, not yet certain of her surmise. She walked over to a cleft in the rock and pushed aside the small flat slab covering it. The desiccated refuse of the meals she had cooked was still there.

"This is the place," she said slowly, cold with a strange fear, "where we ate our supper and breakfast. I must have sat directly over that fissure. And I remember now," she continued, "there was a long crack in the limestone just where we sat. Tom called our attention to it when he saw a small lizard run out of it in the morning. I did not recognize it fully in the moonlight. We went to sleep before the moon rose."

Saxby said nothing immediately. He was thinking and using his eyes.

"Two and two," he commented. "And here is the four. Do you notice these fresh scratches in the limestone?"

He got down to examine them.

"Most interesting," he commented. "You can find any combination of minerals you like to name in this desert. This rock is sandstone speckled with particles of coarse quartz sand. Calcium carbonate and silicon dioxide. Common enough, both of them. But most interesting."

"Is there anything unusual?"

"Not a thing. Let us see what the curious fissure looks like. It may give us an idea for an experiment that should have been tried a century ago. But we were all professors together, and we put away the really interesting things out of sight on the top shelf—where they couldn't make us think."

"What sort of an experiment will you try?" Isabel asked as they reached the lip of the fissure.

"Hard to say. I shall know better when Yang finishes analyzing the inside glaze of that crock. But I shall begin it tomorrow morning in any event."

"We sha'n't be home till morning," Isabel reminded him. "And you will be all tired out."

"I never sleep when I'm working. Well, this crack is the most interesting thing yet," he continued from his knees.

"Why?" Isabel demanded, again going cold with that unaccountable fear.

"Because it is just like the rest of the rock except for one detail. All the particles of quartz have disappeared." He struck a match. "See for yourself. The limestone is peppered with little holes—all empty. There's not a particle of quartz sand visible."

"Promise," Isabel said suddenly, "never to tell a soul that I know of this place, or that I was ever here."

"Very well," Saxby agreed. "On account of your husband, I suppose?"

She nodded. "There may be no connection between the wreck of the *Sheridan* and what those prospectors saw. But it is safer to say nothing."

"Undoubtedly. There may be no connection. More likely there is. I shall know definitely after I finish my experiment. Never mind; Captain Lane sha'n't be court-martialed. Now let us check up on the rest of the story. I want to see exactly how those burros were killed."

They soon located what they sought. The weather had been hot. Saxby was about to go on alone when he stopped suddenly. The faint rumor of an all but inaudible sound had almost crept over the threshold of his hearing. Listening consciously he heard nothing. He went on in the glaring moonlight, hurrying to get his unpleasant task done. He had gone perhaps twenty yards when he stopped instantly, half paralyzed by an instinctive fear.

"Good God!" he ejaculated. "What's that?"

ALTHOUGH he was in no position to realize the truth in that awful moment, his intended experiment had already started and was now progressing at a terrific rate. A dry, creeping rustle, like the gentle friction of innumerable withered snake skins being slowly rasped over one another, whispered aridly through the moonlight. It was the same sound as that which the prospectors had heard and which they had vainly striven to describe to the humorous reporter. To Saxby it was an unexpected horror; the prospectors had succeeded only in describing the shattering crash which ended their vision.

Slowly turning his head he stared back toward the ridge and saw Isabel transfixed by fear before something that seemed to move. It was dimly self-luminous with a milky, palpitating radiance that rhythmically oscillated between purple and green, and the whole mass was utterly shapeless. Its form, if it had any, was beyond analysis. But even as he watched the flickering phosphorescence, the dim bulk began to assume definite shape and became angular at a thousand glittering points. Whatever the thing might be, it was striving to come to life. Sensing the intensity of that dumb struggle to live, Saxby came to his senses. He darted forward toward the almost living mass and dragged Isabel away. She was full conscious, and she knew now what had frightened her four-year-old son half out of his mind.

Expecting at every instant to hear the annihilating crash of the thing's destruction they raced for the car. The crash never came, at least in their hearing. Their failure to hear the thing's end filled them with a new fear. Was it alive? And if so, how long would it live? Could it move? If it did not overtake the car before its exit from the desert, in what shape would it appear in some city or village? And what was its food, if indeed food was necessary to its continued existence? They remembered the burros. But these had been merely slashed to ribbons, not devoured, unless the failure of the prospectors to find a trace of the animals' bones accounted for some unnatural manner of feeding.

They stumbled into the car exhausted.

"Home, as fast as you can go!"

They sat tense and silent, waiting for the echo of a crash which never came. As they shot out to the highway, Saxby recovered his curiosity.

"I wonder," he muttered, "whether I carried that crock into my house with both hands or only one?"

"You carried it in one hand. I remember because you had to open the door with your key."

"Then my fingers must have come in contact with the glaze on the inside. That explains a lot. Gad! I hope nothing has happened to Yang. Can't we go a little faster?"

Saxby's fears were unfounded. Nothing had happened to Yang.

IV. YANG'S DINNER

"Yang," old Saxby inquired, one morning about two weeks after his return from the desert, "do you think I could learn Chinese at my age?"

Yang, who spoke an almost faultless English after his exhaustive linguistic purging in both Canton and New York, considered the problem dispassionately. His delicate, intellectual features bore a slightly pained expression.

"No," he answered simply.

"Why the devil not?"

"Because," the truthful Yang replied, giving his answer an unintended twist, "I do not know how stupid you are, Mr. Saxby."

"You don't, eh?" old Saxby snorted. "Well, I can't say the same for you. Here you've been messing about for a fortnight with that analysis, and you haven't found a thing."

"There are heavy traces of silicon," Yang reminded him reproachfully.

"Naturally. There would be. Especially after I told you there was waterglass in that crock before Mrs. Lane scoured it out with boiling water. What would you have found if I had told you she used the crock for making home brew?"

"Traces of alcohol," Yang replied promptly. "I am one expert chemist."

"You seem to be one expert diplomat, too," Saxby remarked.

"Oh, no, Mr. Saxby. I should find whatever you told me Mrs. Lane kept in the crock because you are like the great George Washington. You never lie. May I inquire why you wish to learn Chinese at your age, Mr. Saxby?"

"Because I want to study the geology of China at first hand."

Yang received this information with a dead silence that was eloquent. To Saxby's ears that respectful silence announced that George Washington had stepped off his monument.

"As you don't believe me," he continued, "I may as well tell you the truth. You would find out sooner or later anyhow. I must overtake Captain Lane and induce him to spend a few months in China. There is no telling how long your fellow countrymen may be fighting among themselves. That isn't our affair. But I have a strong suspicion that our men will be withdrawn as soon as all American citizens are safely out of the danger zone. Lane may be on his way home in one month, or two, or three. I must get to him before he starts back to the United States. His wife and I agree that he had better not come home just yet."

"Mrs. Lane would like a divorce?" Yang inquired blandly.

"You unscientific idiot! Why must you always jump to the most ridiculous conclusion?"

"Because I have lived in America six years. I know the customs of the country," he added proudly. "And you call on Mrs. Lane every day."

"Well, you've slipped up this time. You have an oriental mind. Mrs. Lane is twenty-five. I'm sixty and no fool. I am more interested in Captain Lane's clothes than I am in his wife. Do you know anything of the province of Kansu in China?"

"I know everything about it," Yang admitted modestly. "I was born there."

"That's good. We shall probably be leaving for Kansu some time next week, if I can get passports for one of the English concessions on the coast."

"Captain Lane is going to Kansu?"

"Of course. I expected you to draw that conclusion. It's obvious. Mrs. Lane had a cablegram from the Chief of Staff in Hong Kong saying that her husband had been ordered to lead an expedition into Kansu to rescue a nest of British and American missionaries at Teng-shan. He is on his way there now. I've got to follow at once."

"I think it will be very dangerous," Yang remarked with an engaging smile. "Probably you will be killed."

"I doubt it. How am I to get permission to start for the interior? The military authorities will coop me up on some stuffy battleship. I can't even begin to get killed, as I see it. That's the crux of the problem. Now, if I could learn enough Chinese to ask my way intelligibly, I could go alone after your friends do for you. If only I can get past the busybodies at the seaports I shall find my way somehow to Kansu and join Lane there. You will have to think of some way of getting me in and well started. After that I can shift for myself. I've been in worse places than China, and I'm not dead yet. And I'll wager the Chinese in Kansu, or anywhere in the interior, won't hear a word of all this revolutionary fuss till five years after the row is peaceably settled. You are still as primitive as the early Israelites once you get away from your westernized coast cities. Now, Yang, I put myself unreservedly in your hands. Get me safely started for Kansu and I'll remember you handsomely in my will. If I return to Los Angeles with my own head on my shoulders, I'll give you a cash bonus of exactly double what you would get otherwise. So it will pay you to treat me tenderly. Do you accept?"

Yang made a formal bow.

"I accept, Mr. Saxby," he said. "My father is a very old man. I have not seen him since I left Kansu to enter the Christian College in Canton."

"All right, Yang. It's a go. How will you get me through the lines?"

"We shall walk through. I think you overestimate the difficulties, Mr. Saxby. Am I to know why you wish to catch Captain Lane in Kansu?"

"Eventually you will have to know. So shall I. But as I am not exactly clear yet in my own mind, I can't very well enlighten yours."

"It may be what you call a wild goose chase?" Yang delicately suggested.

"Possibly. In a way I hope it does turn out so. Then again I pray that it may not. Curiosity is the one vice that I have not yet overcome. I never cared much for the others—eating, reforming people, and so on." Old Saxby sighed. "I wish I were a cat or something of the sort with nine lives. There's so much to be pried into."

Saxby sat dreaming for a few moments while Yang busied himself with the daily crop of earthquakes. Suddenly he started up as if stung.

"Why didn't I think of that before?" he exclaimed, seizing the telephone. "Taxi at once," he ordered when he got his number, and gave the address. "Of course," he continued to Yang, "you found nothing but traces of silicon in your analysis. I see it all now. Clear this mess out of the way as fast as you can. I'll be back in an hour with work enough to keep you busy till we leave for China."

When Saxby returned, he presented Yang with two cartons full of neat little packages of dyes for Easter eggs. He had bought out the entire stock of the neighborhood grocery where the Lanes had obtained their half dozen packages. The man assured him that this stock was that from which he had sold for the past season. It had been put away in the storeroom to wait for the next Easter week.

"There's your work," Saxby announced. "Analyze the lot. Don't overlook anything. Get the results accurate to a tenth of a per cent."

Yang groaned, but dutifully set to work. It was a routine job such as any competent senior in college could have done easily, and Yang hated routine.

"Oh, I almost forgot the most important thing," Saxby continued lightly. "Mix this blue with an equal amount of yellow in tap water and analyze the mixture."

Yang sighed and set out his apparatus on the laboratory table by the west window of the room.

WHILE Yang toiled twelve hours a day at the multitude of little packets, old Saxby used all his diplomacy to obtain passports for himself and his secretary. On the third day he succeeded. Within a week they would be on their way to China. In the meantime, while Yang slaved, he could run out to the desert for a farewell inspection. He invited Isabel to accompany him, but she was forced to decline, as Tom was suffering from the effects of a surfeit of watermelon. Saxby set out alone, this time early in the morning, with a competent driver, on a small truck. He chose this unusual and jolty conveyance because its solid tires eliminated the danger of punctures. He wished to drive right up to the limestone outcrop and be able to leave in a hurry if necessary.

They reached the ridge shortly before noon. A shimmering heat haze hovered over the slabs of rock, and regiments of lizards scurried over the scorching surfaces with their tails up and heads erect. From the carefree manner in which they pursued their avocations it was evident that no ponderous enemy had recently marched over their barren territory. Bidding the driver wait with the truck at a convenient spot, old Saxby began a systematic exploration of the whole vicinity.

The fissure was apparently unchanged since it had first opened nearly three weeks previously. Saxby confirmed his discovery that all the quartz particles in the limestone walls of the fissure had disappeared. Searching the surface of the slabs in the neighborhood of the deep, fresh grooves, he noted a similar peppering of small cavities that must have contained silicates.

The important point was, when were these pockets emptied? Before or after the prospectors heard the "shot" that announced the fracture of the limestone? And if the former, precisely how long before? Although he all but went into a trance thinking of possible ways and means, Saxby could devise no experiment to fix the age of those holes. There must be some simple method, he reasoned, of deciding to within one per cent of the exact age the length of time that a rock surface has been exposed to the air and sunlight. Pondering this simple riddle, he almost broiled himself before reluctantly abandoning the outcrop to the lizards, who seemed to enjoy being fried.

His next task was to examine the spot where the burros had perished. Sun and the desert air had removed practically the last trace of the animals. The eight shells of the hoofs alone remained. Saxby raked every foot of the dust in the vicinity with a stick of dead sagebrush, but found nothing more. There was not a trace of the animals' bones. If the bones were indeed in that dust they must have been pulverized to the fineness of flour.

Trained by long years of scientific work to exact observation and the cool sifting of evidence, old Saxby sat down in the dust to recall every detail of the prospectors' story before leaving the spot. Had he checked every point? What else, besides the animals' bones, should he naturally expect to find in the place where they had been killed? What were they doing when they met their deaths? An obvious but singular fact, whose significance had escaped the shrewd, practical intelligence of Dan and Jake, leaped into old Saxby's mind.

The prospectors related as a matter of course that their burros were hobbled for the night. They had strayed at the first hint of danger. Dan and Jake even theorized a bit. They remarked that, had the poor beasts been free to run, they could easily have escaped. With their front fetlocks tied together, so that they could move forward only six inches at each step, the animals were helpless before their enemy. What, Saxby asked himself, had become of the ropes that hobbled the burros? They were not where they should have been. To eliminate guesswork as far as possible, Saxby searched every yard of the terrain from the spot where the hoofs lay to the oozing spring on the north side whence the burros had strayed. At the end of a four-hour search he concluded that the ropes had gone the same way as the bones—whatever that might be.

"This," he remarked with a smile of satisfaction, "probably explains why the *Sheridan* burst. Still I mustn't jump to conclusions. Yang hasn't found anything, and I half hoped he would."

He next made a careful inspection of the spot where Isabel and he thought they saw the luminous apparition. He found nothing suspicious except two slight depressions in the alkali dust. These, however, might have been mere natural accidents or rabbits' sleeping places. Whatever they might be, Saxby judged that they were too doubtful to have any value as evidence.

"If I could only put together the pieces I have," he pondered,

"I could probably solve the whole puzzle now. Unfortunately I don't quite see how all the pieces fit together. I hadn't allowed for the missing ropes last week, and I thought then I saw a probable way through. It follows that what I think I know now is probably not so."

As he strolled back to the truck he toyed with a possible explanation which Isabel had shown him, with some indignation, the previous day. One of the leading psychologists of America had sent her a marked copy of the *Weekly Psychological Bulletin,* current issue, with a learned article by himself adorning the place of honor. The title of this metaphysical attempt to be scientific was *Collective Hallucinations.* In it the eminent author proved (or said he proved) that two or more persons in the same place at the same time can, and should, see the same thing when it isn't there. He cited the recent story of Dan and Jake, also Isabel's and Tom's similar experience in confirmation. Carried to its limit, this theory would prove that life is a morbid succession of multiple nightmares. Saxby weighed it and found it wanting. The ingenious author of course did not know that the hallucination was triple, not merely double; Saxby had not advertised his adventure with Isabel in the desert. Therefore the psychologist may be pardoned for rushing into print with a half-baked theory.

Even the most careful observers will sometimes overlook a significant detail in the investigation of a brand new problem. In summing up his day's work Saxby thought that he had accounted for all the vital possibilities. He climbed up with the driver, and the truck started home, jolting over the stunted cacti and smoke trees just as the sun set. Saxby had overlooked the most obvious of all the facts in the prospectors' experience, in his own and Isabel's, and in the wreck of the *Sheridan.* What is even more remarkable, when we consider the singular sagacity which Saxby exhibited in this strange investigation, is that he completely missed the same obvious fact in Yang's "hallucination"—for Yang also was to bear out the psychologist's fantastic speculation.

The morning of Saxby's second expedition to the desert, Yang set to work at seven and slaved through the day till seven at night. He was determined to get the last of those exasperating little packets of gaudy colors analyzed before his master's return. There remained only the blues and the yellows and the bright green dye made by mixing the two. As he expected, and as was but natural, several rather delicate complications arose when the blue and yellow were mixed in ordinary tap water. Of course the specific chemicals responsible for the respective colors reacted to form new and more difficult compounds than either presented individually. In spite of himself Yang began to become interested in his analysis.

The problem before him was a good example of an extremely difficult type of manipulation. The numerous compounds formed by the union of the blue and yellow dyes were extremely unstable. A difference of a tenth of a degree Centigrade in the temperature of the mixture permuted these unstable compounds through long series of allied substances. It was an exceedingly ticklish job at any stage of the game to isolate a particular one of these compounds, and it required even more delicate skill to keep the initial substance constant throughout the analysis and prevent it from slithering into one of the others. Yang almost began to enjoy himself.

NOON came and passed, but he never thought of lunch. At three o'clock Jemima stuck her head cautiously into the laboratory to ask if he were going to eat. Her best corn fritters had twice been thrown out, but she would make a fresh batter if Yang so desired. Yang said something snappy in Chinese. Then, repenting of his profanity, he instructed the humble Jemima to prepare him a real Chinese dinner for seven o'clock—soup, pork, fish, rice and six hard-boiled eggs. He continued his pursuit of the elusive twentieth compound.

At seven-fifteen, while his master was still jolting homeward on the truck, Yang sighed, washed his hands, and took a last look around the laboratory before going to dinner. He had not succeeded in capturing his prey. The twentieth of those subtle compounds still reposed undisturbed in its beaker. The table by the window was in a rare mess. By habit a tidy technician, Yang as a rule left everything in apple-pie order. This evening, however, exhausted by twelve incessant hours of the most exacting work, he knocked off without setting everything to rights, planning to return after dinner and clean up. The soiled towel on which he had dried his hands he carelessly tossed into the glazed earthenware crock, which Mrs. Lane had used for preserving eggs, and on which he had wasted nearly two weeks in a futile attempt to discover something of chemical interest. Dog-tired he locked the door of the laboratory after him as a matter of habit and went to dinner.

The first course, a really excellent subgum soup, somewhat revived him. He began to long for more stimulating conquests. The wistful quart of old Saxby's topaz wine did not attract him. He wondered whether Saxby, in the excitement of an early start, had forgotten to lock the sideboard. In the true scientific spirit he left the table to investigate. Old Saxby had forgotten. With a short exclamation of triumph, Yang extracted a full wicker quart of his favorite Chinese gin, and removed Saxby's offensive grape juice from his range of vision.

The first moderate cocktail acted merely as an inspiration to

Yang's appetite for roast pork. The second and third spurred him to great deeds on the fried fish. By the time he had downed the thirteenth he was calling shrilly for another half dozen hard-boiled eggs. Thereafter he became somewhat confused and upbraided the perspiring Jemima for the bushels of rice which she insisted he had ordered.

By nine o'clock he was very serious. A high sense of duty impelled him to set the laboratory to rights before his master's return. Saxby might be expected now at any minute. Before leaving the table he peeled another egg, ate it, and stuffed four into the pocket of his coat to sustain him in the laboratory.

After considerable experimenting he managed to unlock the laboratory door. His logic now became somewhat erratic. It seemed to Yang that the most important thing to be done first on entering the laboratory was to lock the door after him. Otherwise old Saxby might come and catch him. Not that Yang felt guilty or intoxicated; he merely had a strong intuition that Saxby would jump to an unjust conclusion and give him the devil for nothing. The locking of the door in the dark was a long and complicated operation. It never occurred to Yang that it would have been much simpler to have turned on the lights before attempting to find the keyhole. Having succeeded at last he groped for the light switch. It was on the wall to the west of the door. Yang was now in that sublime state when "east is west and west is east and never the twain shall meet." He began swearing volubly in his native tongue as he sawed blindly for the switch. After five minutes of knocking over stools and smashing glassware that had no business being where it was, Yang lapsed into cold English.

"Oh hell," he muttered, on the verge of tears, "what's the use? All damned things are against me."

He tumbled over to the one fairly bright spot in all that hostile darkness, the dimly outlined rectangle of the west window by his work bench. The slim sickle of the setting moon and the blaze of icy stars shed a doubtful half light on the clatter of beakers and ring stands on the table, rendering their barely visible outlines mistily unreal. Yang lurched for the stool which was not where it should have been, missed it, tipped over a full beaker of bright green dye, and came down heavily on his side. A crunching in his pocket announced the tragedy. His four priceless hard-boiled eggs were ruined. To Yang in his fuddled condition this loss took on the vast proportions of a cosmic injustice. The stars, that wisp of a moon, the darkness and the treacherous stool on which he had jarred his jawbone in falling, were all against him. He was too deeply hurt for tears. Pulling himself up to the edge of the work-bench, he covered the stool and slumped down on it.

To console himself he fished the ruined eggs out of his pocket and tried in that feeble light to salvage some of the yolks at least. For his pains he got a gritty mouthful of egg and broken shells. With a pettish gesture of impotence he hurled what was left of the eggs into the one receptacle that loomed huge in the semi-light above all its lesser neighbors—Mrs. Lane's glazed crock into which, three hours previously, he had tossed the soiled towel. Then, baffled and defeated by the brutal injustice of the universe, he sank his weary head on his arms and sought solace in oblivion.

Only the faint radiance of the stars comforted him, and only the cold light of the sickly moon gleamed uncertainly on his glossy black hair, but he dreamed with agonizing intensity of blinding suns that pulsed with a baleful green, or glowed evilly with a ruddy purple like the living hue of some unnatural blood.

About half past ten Saxby returned. Jemima did not dash out to greet him and trumpet the disgraceful tidings of Yang's orgy. She knew better. Like the essentially catty female that she was, in spite of her two hundred and fifty pounds of shoggling, good-natured flesh, she had left the empty gin bottle in a conspicuous place on the dining-room table. It could not fail to catch old Saxby's eye where it stood, directly under a sixty-watt electric light going at full blast.

"That damned Yang is drunk again," Saxby exploded when he beheld the mute betrayal. "Why can't he learn to drink good wine like a Christian?"

Believing that the dissolute Yang had gone to bed to sleep off his indiscretion, Saxby prepared to do likewise. There would be time enough in the morning to attend to Yang. For once in his life, Saxby looked forward to going to bed. His tramping in the desert and the jolting ride had left him rather tired.

Saxby's bedroom was on the second floor, directly over the laboratory. As he turned off the light before getting into bed, he glanced out of the open window, over the low, distant hills behind which the sharp horns of the setting moon were just dipping. The unearthly beauty of the night landscape gripped him for a moment, as he stood motionless, trying to fix permanently on his consciousness its elusive appeal. His whole body, not merely his reasoning memory, seemed to sense a new quality in this sudden strangeness of a familiar, commonplace world. He experienced a feeling of intimacy, not with the spirit of the night, but with the solid bulk of those massive hills behind which the moon was fast setting.

"What a beastly sensation," he exclaimed aloud, turning his

back on the window. "Nerves, that's all. I felt as if the earth of my grave were feeling through my flesh to get at my bones."

Going to bed with such a thought as that would be sufficient to give almost any man a nightmare. Old Saxby was no exception. For ten feverish hours he tossed in a torment that his drugged will strove vainly to end. Part of the time he was half awake and conscious that he was dreaming, yet he could not shake off the lethal stupor poisoning his mind. The dreams were strangely unnatural and yet more strangely real. There was a curious, insanely illogical but yet inevitable sequence in the meaningless panoramas that rolled past his vision like an infinite succession of thunder clouds, each of them instinct with some forgotten significance which he struggled to recall.

THE isolated fragments were the least endurable. A small, shapeless thing would materialize out of an infinite void, seem to expand and yet not to expand, till finally, in some appalling sense, it reconciled its own self-contradiction by ceasing to exist. Again and again this motif recurred and each time that the void prepared to give it birth, the helpless spectator rehearsed the sight he dreaded a million times before it happened. A second recurrence of a different kind was almost as bad. Like the pulsations of a vast aurora a slow rhythm of dull purple and green throbbed maddeningly through the whole of infinite space, coming and going with discordant regularity. This also was self-contradictory; yet it existed and was real. Through all that horrible dream a voice kept chanting monotonously. "This is not a dream; this is not a dream; these things have happened; you felt these older things before you had a mind."

When he finally threw off the incubus that oppressed him, Saxby felt like a wet towel.

"What a night," he groaned, feeling under the pillow for his watch. "Great Scott! No wonder I had a nightmare. Serves me right for lying in bed ten hours."

But, as he began to dress, he felt with every bone of his body that he was unwell and that his awful dream was not merely the result of over-exhaustion. It had been too real. Some definite, physical thing must have caused it. A faint odor caught his attention. He sniffed the air critically.

"That infernal woman has been putting the garbage can right under my window," he snorted. "If she wasn't such an artist at cooking I'd fire her before dinner tonight. Hang it! I'll have to speak to her." He shaved and hurried downstairs to do his disagreeable duty by Yang and Jemima.

On reaching the dining-room he relented so far as Yang was

concerned. The empty gin bottle still squatted blatantly in the exact center of the table. The table was set as usual for breakfast for one, although it was long past Yang's customary hour. Old Saxby concluded that the wretched Yang had taken one look at the table and bolted back to bed to sleep off his headache. At any rate the fellow was honest, he reflected; he had not tried to hide the empty bottle and lay his indisposition to the weather or overwork. Saxby forgave him and rang for Jemima. She came, waddling, expecting a crown of gold for her perfidy in the matter of the gin bottle.

"Jemima," Saxby exploded without any priming, "I want you to stop putting the garbage can under my window. It is one of your most disgusting customs."

Jemima called upon her Lord to bear witness that she was innocent. Saxby, invoking his own gods, declared that he had smelt Jemima's offense with his own nose. The debate degenerated into a shouting match, wailing and tearful on Jemima's part, vigorous and vociferous on Saxby's. At last, getting nowhere by such means with the obstinate woman, Saxby assented to her plea that he look for himself.

The can was in its usual place on the north side of the house.

"Uh," Saxby grunted as the victorious Jemima waddled back in triumph to her kitchen. "There must be something dead under my window." He walked round to the west side of the house to inspect.

The windows of Yang's laboratory were directly under those of Saxby's bedroom. At first glance Saxby thought the laboratory windows were open. At the second he stopped short. The morning breeze was blowing into the laboratory, but the windows were down and locked. The panes of glass had vanished. Not a splinter remained in the putty, and there was no mark of any implement, either on the putty or the surrounding frames, to give a clue to the manner in which the panes had been lifted clean out of their beds.

"What the devil?" he muttered, going up to examine the window frames. Then he staggered back as if shot, suddenly sick and faint. He had seen what, less than ten hours before, was Yang. Now it was only a shapeless lump of flesh draped over a work-table and flowing down over a four-legged stool. It looked more like a squid than a man.

Saxby's first thought when he recovered his senses was of the coroner. There would have to be an inquest. He had seen enough to know that half an hour after any inquest that might be held the whole country would be paralyzed with fear. All the facts would have to come out, and the public was not yet prepared to receive them intelligently. Saxby himself did not understand the half of them. What good could come of throwing the country into a panic? To warn the people would be futile. They had no means of protecting themselves. Until he or someone else succeeded in tracing the evil to its source, it would be sheer insanity to advertise its existence.

Looking round to make sure that Jemima was not where she had no business to be, Saxby returned to the window of the laboratory. The high tile wall, the shrubs and trees of the garden, secured him from the curious eyes of passers-by on the street. He climbed in at the window. It was essential to his plan that Jemima, the only possible human witness, should believe that he had not entered the house.

As he had half anticipated, he found the laboratory door locked on the inside. He did not unlock it. Poor Yang had apparently shut himself in for fear of being caught by his employer in his usual evening haunts about the house. The old-fashioned wooden shutters were still intact. Saxby set about his task. The odor of decay was still strong but bearable.

There was no time to examine all the inexplicable havoc in the laboratory. One detail, however, was obvious on the most casual inspection. Every particle of glass had disappeared. Multicolored messes still dripped from the shelves as the chemicals from the vanished bottles mingled, and neat little piles of rainbow-hued salts marked the places of innumerable glass containers that had simply ceased to exist. All metallic objects were apparently normal.

Going over to the work-bench Saxby picked up Yang's laboratory notebook and glanced rapidly through the pencilled entries of the preceding day. Although much was half obliterated by the bright green dye which had drenched the open book and soaked into the porous paper when Yang in his fall upset the beaker, short jottings and long chemical equations told the brief story of the nineteen successful analyses. Then followed a disjointed sequence of tentative guesses and abandoned trials on the twentieth compound generated by the reactions of the blue and yellow dyes upon one another.

Saxby slipped the notebook into his pocket and explored the work-table in detail. From the tangible evidence before him it was not difficult to reconstruct Yang's last day on earth. The soiled towel in Mrs. Lane's crock and the crushed fragments of the four hard-boiled eggs, one partly eaten, told their own story. Yang had wiped the composite green dye off his hands on the towel, and he had brought back the eggs for a late supper after returning intoxicated from dinner. By some drunken mishap he had smashed them, tried to eat one, and thrown them away. The smears on the black surface of the work-table marked the places where the test tubes and beakers had disintegrated like the rest of the glass in the laboratory.

Struck by the singular fact that the glazed crock seemed to have survived intact, Saxby reached for it to examine it carefully. It fell to powder in his grasp. The towel also, still discolored by the stains of the dyes, became a pinch of white dust as he tried to pick it up.

It was necessary to examine Yang. At the first touch his clothing fell apart like the towel. The whole of it now weighed perhaps as much as an open handful of uncrushed thistle-down, and it crumbled to dust at the lightest touch. On the body itself there was not a scratch. Thus far it seemed perfectly normal. But its solidity was gone. In a horrible manner it was shapeless and without resistance, like a lump of melting jelly, held together only by its skin like water in a thin rubber bag. So far as Saxby could force himself to explore, he found no trace of a bone in all that shapeless lump. Yang's bones had vanished as completely as had the glass. His hanging lips disclosed gums that were toothless.

Saxby executed his gruesome task as quickly as possible and set about his more practical work of preventing the inquest. Cautiously opening one shutter, he slipped out of the window, closed the shutter after him and walked round to the kitchen door.

"Where is Mr. Yang?" he asked.

"He done been sleeping off his gin in the laboratory," Jemima replied promptly, glad of the chance to unbosom herself at last. Saxby laughed.

"All right," he said. "Don't disturb him till seven o'clock. He should be pretty hungry by that time. By the way," he added as an afterthought, "I want some fresh crabs for dinner. Go down to the fish market and pick out a dozen big ones. They must be fresh. If they're not, I'll fire you."

Jemima began to grumble. It was a good hour's ride on the street car to the fish market, and Jemima was too fat to get into a taxi.

"Get along with you," Saxby ordered. "What do you think I'm paying you for? I want those crabs. I'm going out myself in a minute or two, but I shan't leave till I see you on your way with a basket."

When Jemima was safely round the corner, Saxby dived into the cellar and brought up a five-gallon can of gasoline which Jemima kept for cleaning and other household purposes. This he hurriedly transported to the laboratory, entering by the window as before. With the chairs, tables, the wooden shelves and two cabinets, it was easy to arrange the materials for a very hot and quick fire. The large metal cans of highly inflammable mineral oils, which

Yang had kept on hand as a matter of course for use in his work, also about fifty pounds of the proper chemicals scooped off the shelves, and four large cans of thermite, added greatly to the potential heat. Saxby then drenched the body in gasoline and sprinkled what was left over the highly inflammable stuff piled around and over the body. Finally he tore several pages out of a book and placed them on the floor about a foot away from the pile. The laboratory supply of white phosphorous—two dozen long, cheesy sticks—was then taken out of its can, where it had been submerged in water, and carefully disposed on the paper. Before Saxby was through the window the phosphorus was already fuming.

"I could get life for this, I suppose," he remarked as he darted into the kitchen. "Well, I can't help it. This is the lesser of two evils."

The house was at least two hundred feet from its nearest neighbor. The smoke and flames issuing from the shuttered window of the laboratory should be seen by the neighbors five minutes after the fire started, and the firemen would be on the spot in another five minutes. There was no danger to the neighboring houses, but Saxby's rambling frame structure would probably burn to the ground. One thing was certain; the firemen would not succeed in extinguishing the furnace in the laboratory until what was left of poor Yang had evaporated in smoke. The heat of the thermite fire would preclude any immediate attempt to recover the body—provided its presence were suspected. When Jemima returned, she of course would tell the neighbors that Yang had been burned to death in the laboratory. His intoxication would account for the fire and his being overcome before he could escape or call for help. They would search the ruins for his calcined bones and find nothing, not even his teeth. Saxby considered his alibi perfect. Yang's disappearance would merely become a newspaper mystery for a month. Well, let them theorize. They could say he had gone back to China or Mexico, while under the influence of liquor.

With a last look of regret at his beloved earthquakes in their stacked filing cases, Saxby slipped his passport into his pocket, opened the front door, and walked out. At the corner he glanced back to ease his conscience with regard to the neighbors' houses. There was no danger. If the worst came to the worst, and his own house was burned to the ground, the firemen could easily play on the others, the nearest of which was in but slight danger of falling sparks. Old Saxby sighed. He hoped the firemen would save the front room and his earthquakes. The filing cabinets were steel, but that wouldn't help much in a really hot fire.

He hailed a taxi and gave the driver Mrs. Lane's address. Easy lies the head that has a perfect alibi.

He first heard that his house had been burned to the ground as he sat sipping tea with Isabel. The afternoon paper featured the spectacular blaze. None of the neighboring houses were harmed. The hectic neighbors had broken into the front room when they first saw the flames shooting up from the laboratory and they had saved all of Saxby's earthquakes.

"God bless them!" he ejaculated as Isabel read him that bit.

"Oh, I'm so sorry," she consoled. "Were you insured?"

"Heavily. But it doesn't matter. I'll be in China in four weeks from today."

Part II—AMATEURS

V. WHITE LILY

EINSTEIN has remarked that any blockhead can draw correct conclusions from a consistent theory, but that it requires genius to deduce the truth from one that is full of contradictions. On such authority we cannot deny that old Saxby had genius. Although his theory was not utterly wrong when he left Los Angeles for China, it was a tissue of holes and glaring inconsistencies. Nevertheless, as events proved, he drew the right conclusions.

His hypothesis was what the mathematicians call necessary but not sufficient. Quite logically, and equally inadequately, he reasoned as follows: Tom's Easter egg started everything. Yang, apparently, had been so unfortunate as to reproduce the exact circumstances which had initiated all the trouble. These included Mrs. Lane's glazed crock. Since all of those necessary—as he thought—conditions now no longer coexisted, having been destroyed together by fire and otherwise, it was extremely improbable that anything further of interest could happen in or near Los Angeles. Captain Lane, however, was still open to grave suspicion. He, no doubt, was still "infected"—Saxby used the word for want of better, although it failed to express his thought. Therefore China called him, not Los Angeles or the desert.

Old Saxby should have remembered that as in love, so in science. Unless the time, the place and the girl, or their equivalents, get together somehow there is nothing doing. He had neglected, among other things, the essential element of time. But he was so eager now to seize the likeliest opportunity of verifying his hypothesis and seeing it work before his very eyes, that he hastened to overtake Lane before the latter should lose all his fascinating dangerous qualities.

With a parting assurance to Isabel that nothing much was likely to happen to California in his absence, and a promise that he would never give her husband's unconscious secret away, he packed his grip and caught his steamer. The earthquakes were loaned to the Southwestern Museum until his return. His bank undertook to look after his affairs while he was in China.

"If I don't come back within ten years, the Society of Earthquake Lovers of California is to get everything. You will find the details in my will. Goodbye."

On his way across the Pacific, Old Saxby had ample time to ponder his sins of omission and commission. Yang's laboratory notebook was the first cause of Saxby's qualms. Although by no means the chemist that Yang had been, Saxby was quite respectable and indeed an expert in all the chemistry that pertained to geology. His chemical classification of the basalts, for example, marked an epoch in the science, and his bold theory concerning the origin of the silicates, although openly scoffed at by jealous or less imaginative rivals, at least arrested the attention of chemists. Saxby was nothing if not daring, in thought as well as action. Yang, on the other hand, was a more conservative type of genius, in spite of his weakness for gin. When he theorized—which he rarely did—his speculations had an awkward trick of turning out right. The last, in modern physical science, is almost a miracle. So when Saxby at last thought he understood the pencilings which Yang had scratched on the last page of his notebook, he began to doubt his own wisdom because it contradicted Yang's.

"I wish I had locked up the gin that morning," he sighed. "Poor Yang might have solved the whole problem if he had stayed sober enough to keep out of the laboratory after dark. If there is anything at all in these guesses of his—well, it is too late to turn back now. What a pity Yang died without knowing what he was looking for, or what he found. I wish I had given him a hint. Another of those infernal experimental errors. Confound my luck. I'm always making them."

While Saxby stewed and fumed, another great man of about his own age was also doing his unconscious bit toward the making of history. The venerable Hu—"Hu the Good" as he was called by his followers, was within a year or two of sixty. He looked eighty. For one thing he was pure Chinese; for another he was much too fat, and finally his kind old face was wrinkled like a wad of crumpled parchment. This was the prophet and uncrowned king whom Captain Lane had been ordered to interview.

Long before Lane and his escort of marines reached the Holy Caves where Hu the Good dispensed blessings and absorbed communist propaganda, the footsore men had nicknamed him Who the Devil. It was indeed but a poor play upon words, yet it eased the feelings of the men as they tramped endlessly over sand and rock, or sweated like cattle in unspeakably dirty river boats. Whom the devil they were to civilize, and exactly why they were to do so, were the questions they debated endlessly. Hu the Good had a bad reputation with the Marines weeks before his friends welcomed them to his sanctum.

Hu was truly a good soul. He was benevolence itself and one of the most temperate men that ever lived, even in a peace-loving, moderate China. By faith he was a Moslem, as his fathers before him had been for generations. Indeed his one vanity was the boast, probably just, that it was one of his direct lineal ancestors who first brought the true faith to China.

The children of Allah, as all the world knows, are a warlike pack, always spoiling for a fight in order to convert the unbelievers—to *their* faith. Hu the Good would have none of this muscular Mohametanism He detested it, declaring that it was his mission to bring peace, not a sword, to the farmers and bandits of sleepy old China. Yet, in spite of himself, as his powers waned and ever mounting billows of fat submerged his common sense, he began to waver as he approached old age. After all, he declared, there might be something good in this notion of a jehad—the technical term for a holy war (if such a thing is not a contradiction in terms) of the Mohametan brand. Were not the unbelievers, white, brown and yellow, tearing one another to pieces in an endeavor to prove that might is right? Why not give all of them a practical demonstration of their own doctrine? They were weary and ripe for instruction. It would be easy to teach them the truth in their present exhausted condition. Then there would be no more infidels. It almost seemed as if Allah himself had turned schoolmaster. And Hu the Good would be Allah's first assistant to teach all Asia, and possibly the whole world, the letters of the Mohametan alphabet. It was at least as worthy an object as the promotion of free trade. If successful it would open the door, not to China, but to Heaven.

By himself, even in his premature old age, Hu was incapable of hatching so venomous a reptile out of an innocent egg. It is a pity that he grew so fat after he passed fifty. Had he weighed only two hundred pounds it is likely that his mind would have remained as shrewd as ever when the agents from Moscow sought by flattery and sham respect to seduce it. But all his vitality was drawn off to keep the blood circulating through a quarter of a ton of solid flesh. Hu's bulk almost equalled his benevolence, and his senescent feeblemindedness surpassed the sum of both. It was but a sorry pair of rogues that succeeded in debauching what was left of the poor old man's intelligence, but they were the best that Moscow could spare. In his prime, when he weighed only a hundred and eighty, Hu could have swindled them out of their souls in his sleep.

THAT precious pair of rascals, Liapanouff and Markoff, were the two parasites from Moscow who battened upon poor old Hu. It names. Neither was a Russian.
will be observed that both of them had perfectly good Russian

Liapanouff was a fairly able, well-read man of about thirty. He was a dank-haired, pimply, unwholesome looking man, stoutish, with a flat, round face like an underdone pie. He habitually wore enormous, unrimmed glasses with thick lenses that made his humid dark-brown eyes glow like a myopic moth's.

Markoff was about forty. He had resided nine years in London, where his name was Marks, ostensibly as a waiter. His true profession is not mentioned in decent society. In personal appearance Markoff was not absolutely repulsive. His tan hair had not thinned, and his sparse mustache was as youthful as ever. Doubtless he wore it because he had sense enough to know that his mouth gave him away. It was as cruel as a rattlesnake's. His pinched nose recalled a vulture's beak, and his all but transparent ears, pointed like those of lynx, stuck close to his bulging, bony skull. Taken piecemeal, Markoff was an unattractive mongrel; in the *ensemble* he made quite a striking impression, especially upon women. Unlike Liapanouff, Markoff was an ill-informed, narrow-minded, bigoted ignoramus. Such were the vampires who hung like a pair of parched bats to the enormous Hu, draining him of his common sense.

The gist of Liapanouff and Markoff's mission to Kansu was childishly simple. The "Kansu mission" was delegated to them because they had half mastered spoken Chinese in the shortest time. They were, technically, "provocative agents" on a grand scale. The technique of such agents has seven main operations.

First, find a large class of human beings whom you hate and who are being oppressed by a more powerful class whom you envy. Second, ingratiate your way into the friendship and confidence of the oppressed. Third, incite the oppressed to attack the oppressors against whom they have not a worm's chance of victory. Fourth, betray all the secrets and plans of the oppressed to the oppressors, thereby winning the confidence of the latter. Fifth, join the oppressors in their overwhelming counter attack upon the oppressed, but be careful not to venture within a hundred miles of the actual fighting. Sixth, find a more powerful class than that with which you are now affiliated, and repeat the preceding program indefinitely. Seventh, if at any stage of the application of the rules a finite limit is reached, so that no further treachery is possible, swallow your capsule of cyanide of potassium, as the only logical conclusion.

Markoff and Liapanouff were as yet only at the second stage. They had convinced a large mass of the Christianized Chinese that their more numerous heathen brothers were walking all over them with wooden clogs. The Mohametan followers of Hu the Good outnumbered those of the Christian missionaries and their converts twenty to one. The Buddhists and Confucians in their turn were dozens to one against the Mohametans. After Hu had wiped out the Christians, he and his followers were to get their own medicine.

In all this the westerners would of course suffer heavily. Bourgeois Britain and capitalistic America would be drawn into the row on a huge scale. Asia would end by fighting the rest of the world. The Liapanouffs and the Markoffs would be on the winning side when the gas and flames cleared away, and the statesmen took out their jeweled fountain pens to autograph the treaties. Then the "provocation" would begin all over again, and the victors would find themselves going the way of King Herod. The grand objective for the present was the communization of Asia.

Throughout this vast game Hu the Good was merely a pawn, but the Moscow agents were unduly contemptuous of poor old Hu. They forgot that chess as played by masters often turns upon the gain or loss of one humble pawn. Hu had been a master in his day; old Saxby still played a pretty good game, while Liapanouff and Markoff were handicapped by Markoff's petty vices which somewhat dulled the expected brilliance of his moves.

The queen of the board was Hu's eighteen-year-old granddaughter, whose pretty Chinese name is equivalent in English to White Lily. She spoke only Chinese. Markoff was endeavoring to teach her enough Russian to make conversation salaciously interesting. As the instruction always took place under Hu's watchful eye, Markoff found his pupil rather dull. He did not get very far with her.

Hu the Good cherished White Lily more tenderly than anything else on earth. Even his religion took the second place when she was near. Small and well formed of body, White Lily was perfect of her kind. Her youthful grace was evident even under the flowered blue of her tunic, and her delicate, oval face was as quaintly piquant as a Chinese fairy's. Her father was Hu's son, her mother a commoner undistinguished for anything but good nature and the fading remains of a once great beauty. Hu's son was just a law-abiding, hardworking farmer on his own land. The shrewd, subtle mind which was Hu's in his prime had skipped a generation. White Lily inherited it. She had an added advantage, which Hu had never possessed. There was never any mistake about him—until he grew too fat. He always looked his proper part—wise, strong, calm and benevolent. White Lily was such a pretty girl that strangers—and many who had known her for years—mistook her for nothing more. Consequently she usually did what she liked with people, and did it charmingly. They frequently were too dazed to know what had happened until long after it was all over.

Under the pretense of seeing that she was becomingly educated—White Lily needed no education—Hu borrowed her from her parents and kept her by his side. As his powers waned, hers waxed. It solaced and yet saddened him to see himself rising from the grave in a beautiful reincarnation. For in his secret thoughts in the long, sleepless silence of the nights, he knew that the great man he had been was dead.

White Lily reciprocated her grandfather's affection. If she did not think much of his technical faith, and still less of his ability as a prophet, she kept her doubts to herself. She was content to let him enjoy his little foibles. They were an old man's weaknesses of no great moment. Provided no cloud rose between them to chill the warmth of their perfect understanding, Hu might start his precious jehad whenever he felt inclined. She herself did not greatly care for the cocksure coolies and beggars who bragged incessantly that they had been converted to a better faith than hers, and who missed no opportunity of telling her that she and the good old Hu must fry forever in Hell. If the jehad should succeed in letting the offensive conceit out of some of these boorish braggarts in this life, she and Hu would gladly take their chances in the next. The converts no doubt were oppressed. On the other hand they were not conspicuous for humility. Therefore White Lily remained, on the whole, neutral.

She knew exactly what the thin-lipped, persistent Markoff was trying to do to her. It rather amused her to think that he believed in his ability to succeed. But it grieved her that Markoff was not a Christian. There could be no equitable grounds for eliminating him in the jehad. Liapanouff she rather liked. He never talked to her of Russian love, which disgusted her, but conversed quite entertainingly of Western culture—its politics, its science and its literature. His Chinese, too, was much better than the intense Markoff's, although the latter's was not half bad. From Liapanouff she also learned—without his knowledge—enough Russian words to follow the general trend of the private conversations between the two agents, particularly when they concerned her. And yet Liapanouff, like Markoff, found her exasperatingly dull in her pitiful attempts to learn Russian. The pasty Liapanouff was more of a dilletante scholar than a diplomat, while Markoff knew too much about women ever to sense when one was making a fool of him.

White Lily turned the pair inside out and read their private weaknesses as readily as the old augurs used to decipher the entrails of an ox. Ostensibly she was on their side. She saw the spectacle they were making of poor Hu, but kept her knowledge to herself. If the playmate of her babyhood wanted his fun in his second childhood he should have it, for she loved him. So she thought while it was all only a nebulous theory.

Thus the jehad brewed while Lane and his men strove by forced marches to reach Kansu before it was too late, and Saxby fumed and fretted to overtake Lane on what, after all, might turn out to be a fool-hardy wild-goose chase. Revolution and counter-revolution made Lane's going delicate and difficult. Warring factions of inflamed patriots tore pacifist old China to pieces for their own gain, and religious hatreds smouldered like a chain of volcanoes about to erupt. Europe and America watched the trouble uneasily, but not altogether passively, while Great Britain tried not to see the end of white domination in Asia. All in all it was as busy and as black a day in human affairs as this troubled planet has suffered.

Yet all of this furious fuss was but the mere disorderly running to and fro of an excited community of ants beneath a gigantic foot about to descend and smash them flat. Like the voracious nations of insects, who lack the imagination to combine their armies against their common enemy, man, and who miss their easy victory by fighting among themselves, the swarming hordes of human beings were striving to exterminate one another, all unconscious that their desired ends could be more easily attained by a coalition against their universal enemy, brute nature.

Would the foot descend? Nature is impartial, or perhaps indifferent. A sudden impulse in another direction might urge her aside and let the busy ants live. But if not, and if she kept to her present blind way, the ants would be crushed. Saxby, if urged to bet, would have placed his money against the ants. Nevertheless he was on his way to do the best he could for them.

To a moderately critical mind, he was used to assert, when feeling blue, the whole sweep of organic evolution, human and otherwise, must appear as the aimless dream of an idiot realized in meaningless action. It remained in this instance to be seen whether nature and evolution can be directed by human intelligence. If not, the stupid game would come to an end forever; if so, it would be the beginning of an end of pessimism.

Such was the setting when Hu the Good brought ten thousand boils to a head by officially prophesying a jehad. The prophecy was equivalent to a command to all faithful followers of Mohamet to slaughter the infidel missionaries and all their converts. The blaze thus started in remote Kansu was—so Hu prophesied—to sweep all China like a grass fire. The holy heat of China was to kindle all

Asia, and Asia's conflagration in turn was to sweep the world and consume utterly the last unbeliever. Hu's fat had at last gone to his head.

The prophecy was vouchsafed from the innermost shrine of Hu's vast sanctum, near Teng-shan, in the once famous limestone caverns of Kansu. White Lily smiled fondly on the old man who took his self-imposed office so seriously. His artless importance and his sudden flash of belief in himself were cheap at the cost of a dozen jehads. He was happy. Liapanouff blinked his moth's eyes and moistened his slack lips. Markoff's fanatical face set like a rattlesnake's about to strike. The agents' first task was accomplished. In a few days they could safely start the second by betraying Hu.

At the very beginning of the holy war a slight difficulty arose that threatened to abort the whole jehad, until Markoff's masterly mind found a way out. A jehad is nothing if not swift and vigorous. It must go with a punch or it peters out. Now, unfortunately for Hu's prophecy, the Mohametans had no firearms and no swords. A few antiquated, inefficient pikes of the seventeenth century were all they could muster. The governor of Kansu had long since sent all the more modern weapons to a personal friend, at the time a general in the army of the revolution. How in the name of Allah were the infidels to be converted under these deplorable conditions? It would take forever, even if the Mohametans, unarmed, should be strong enough and sufficiently numerous to round up all the unbelievers and feed them a dozen at a time to the pikemen.

Markoff wriggled up to the enormous Hu and whispered a few short sentences, glancing behind him from time to time toward the far darkness of the eastern wall of the cavern. Hu nodded. He had prophesied. If the jehad should fall flat before it even started, Hu's authority as a prophet was over. With a guilty glance toward White Lily, who stood a few yards away demurely trying to overhear what Markoff was whispering, he assented. His reputation would be saved. Markoff slipped away like a snake, and began whispering to Liapanouff, who squatted yellow and damp on the floor of the cave like a diseased toadstool.

White Lily smilingly advanced to coax the truth out of her errant grandfather. She knew that he was feeling thoroughly ashamed of himself.

"Tell me what he said," she entreated, like a child begging for a toy.

Poor old Hu looked troubled, and a slight tremor agitated his vast bulk, to die out in broken ripples on his huge hands.

"It was just a political matter," he muttered in the folds of his chin.

"Was it about the jehad?"

Hu the Good tried to lie. But he could not. All her life White Lily had heard nothing but the truth from his lips. Habit now overmastered him.

"Yes," he admitted. Then, after a pause, "Would you be sorry if my prophecy should turn out to be false?"

"Of course I would. But you are always right, so the jehad must happen. Did Markoff tell you *how* to make it happen?"

Hu did not deny that the thin-lipped reptile had given him more than a hint toward making the prophecy a fact. But, having found his courage again, Hu thought it better to tell his granddaughter only the half of Markoff's brilliant scheme.

"These caverns have many chambers, and they are sacred," Hu rumbled as if he were prophesying again. "All the infidels of Kansu might gather in the least of these holy places that my fathers blessed, and be but a handful of sand on the floor. Here, in these hallowed caves, shall the unbelievers hear from my lips that Allah is God and Mohamet his prophet. Then, if they still hug their unbelief, I can do nothing more for them.

"You will not destroy them?"

"How can I? The governor of Kansu has robbed the faithful of their arms."

White Lily was but half convinced. Against reason she hoped that her good old grandfather had at last recovered his sane benevolence. She knew that he had hated bloodshed all his life. Was it too much to believe that the cataracts of old age had rolled back from his eyes for a moment, giving him a vision of his true self?

"There will be no jehad?" she questioned doubtfully.

"I did not say so. But this jehad will be bloodless."

"Even after all the shameful insults those arrogant beggars have flung at you—and at me?"

"Yes, even after all those, and after all their brawling self righteousness that has stirred up hatred and riot in Kansu."

She gave him a long look, but he did not wince. Then, wondering whether she had lost him at last, she turned away without a word.

Markoff and Liapanouff stopped whispering when they saw her coming toward them. She halted within a yard of the squatting pair. Like two whipped curs they furtively watched her face with their eyes, not daring to raise their heads. Liapanouff moistened his loose lips; Markoff's bony jaw set.

"Stand up," she commanded.

They shuffled to their feet, and stood slouching with their hands behind their backs.

"Is there to be a jehad?" she demanded.

The reptilian Markoff, after a swift glance at Liapanouff's mushroom face, took it upon himself to reply. "There will be a bloodless jehad," he answered.

White Lily saw that it would be merely wasting breath to question them further.

"Remember," she warned them, "that I am my grandfather's brain and I am his right hand. What his brain thinks of your jehad will determine what reward his right hand shall give you."

Turning her back abruptly on them she walked rapidly away toward the far crescent of bright yellow that was the sunshine on the hillside beyond the entrance to the cave. Sweating with a cowardly fear they watched her dwindle and pass under the vast arch, a toy figure no taller than a match. The very indefiniteness of her threat, and their uncertainty as to the exact meaning of the idiomatic Chinese in which she had uttered her warning, only multiplied their terror. A cold shiver ran up Markoff's back and his jaw set convulsively.

"Shall we go back to Moscow?" Liapanouff suggested.

"If we go back unsuccessful, we shall be shot." Markoff's snake mouth closed viciously. "We can get away at once after it is over. What can she do? She is a Moslem. The Buddhists and the rest won't listen to her—no! The governor has promised to help us. The Moslems will be wiped out, and she with them, a week after we finish. I shall ask the governor," he concluded with a bestial leer, "to spare her life for a day or two."

Liapanouff, the sedentary scholar and man of zero physical courage, began to suffocate.

"Let us get out of here now and go to the coast. Japan, anywhere——"

"Tch!" Markoff cut him off. "The governor is a fool and a friend of ours. Let us take a walk through the caves instead," he suggested with a cold, ophidian smile. "Over that way."

Linking his arm through the cheesy Liapanouff's, Markoff dragged the cowardly lump of flesh off toward the shadowy vastness of the cavern's eastern wall.

While the two agents flitted silently as bats from cave to darker cave, dispensing with the torches which long familiarity with their objective made superfluous, White Lily walked unhappily and alone through the afternoon sunshine.

FOR the first time in her eighteen years White Lily was crossing the great gulf between theory and practice. As long as her grandfather's jehad was only something to be talked about in a large, philosophical way, she had aided and abetted him in his harmless foolishness. Searching her mind now she realized that she had always hated the thing itself, and that she had never dreamed of it actually happening. Hu was after all only a benevolent dreamer, a prophet in the true sense, not a stupid firebrand. And now these vile agents, with their flattery and their incessant suggestions, preying upon the old man's senility, had debauched his intelligence. They had even so far degraded his high honesty that he was now not above putting her off with a half truth. The bloodlessness of the prophesied jehad did not for a moment deceive her. What devilish thing had that snake whispered in her grandfather's ear? All her young sagacity deserted her and she found herself as helpless as a baby before a mathematical equation. She could not solve it. Nevertheless she knew that it had a solution, and an evil one.

What should she do? The true spirit of her grandfather had indeed descended to her. Her hatred of salvation by force of arms was as fierce as ever old Hu's had been. To avert that "bloodless" jehad was her one passion. It should not happen. But how was she to prevent it, when its very nature was unknown to her? At least she could warn the white missionaries to leave Kansu with their converts while there was yet time. She approached the Christian school nestling in its grove of firs at the foot of a long slope, and entered the main room without knocking.

The missionary, a gray-bearded, dreamy-eyed Scotchman, was just about to dismiss the last batch of his young pupils for the day. Seeing the pretty Chinese girl hesitating by the door, he left his class for a moment to ask her what she wanted. He addressed her in Chinese, as White Lily knew no English, never having attended one of the Christian schools. To his inquiry she replied that the Moslems were about to start a crusade of extermination against all sects but their own.

"I have heard such rumors," the missionary replied. "They are just gossip."

"They are not. The jehad has been prophesied. Do you understand what that means to the Moslems of Kansu?"

The gray-bearded face set like the death-mask of a martyr.

" 'I fear no evil, for He is with me.' "

"But your women, and your children?"

"They will be true to Him."

White Lily shot him a brief, oblique glance of contempt.

"I tell you there is time to escape to the hills where you can hide till your friends come for you. You can bring them to you by the talking wire"—White Lily's description of the electric telegraph which still presumably connected the main towns of Kansu with the seaports. Unfortunately the revolutionists had destroyed the first three hundred miles from the coast inland, and Kansu was now completely isolated.

The missionary drew himself up.

"Shall I forsake my Christ and my God?"

White Lily turned her back on him and walked out.

VI. HU'S FOLLY

LANE's flying squadron did not fly very fast. Transport, never strikingly efficient in the interior of China, was almost hopelessly disorganized by the revolution. Pinched between two hostile armies the marines proceeded most of the way by sufferance only, and were glad to take at any price what the Chinese officers left. Lane's orders were to reach Kansu and rescue the missionaries without firing a shot unless driven to the extreme of self defense. Any other course would have been suicidal; either of the rival Chinese generals could have annihilated the intruders with a gesture. So long as the Americans minded their own business they were free to go as they pleased. Should some get plugged by stray bullets it was no more than they could expect, and the fault would not be China's. The column was armed only with rifles; tanks and machine guns were left behind, partly to humor the Chinese army officers, partly to make speed at least half way possible.

The telegraph service, like the transport, was practically nonexistent. Either the native operators had been shot by one faction or the other, or each side had tried to better its rival's record in pulling up poles and cutting wires. There was of course no wireless for the use of outsiders. Not till he was in far western Shen-si, within fifty miles of the border of Kansu, did Lane succeed in getting a message through to Teng-shan. The last fifty miles of the line were intact, as was also the Chinese boy tapping the key. Lane asked the operator to call the Protestant mission station at Teng-shan and ask how things were going. The day operator at the other end, evidently a Moslem, replied cheerfully that the province of Kansu as a whole was doing as well as could be expected, although perhaps a little too slowly.

"The jehad of Hu the Good," the operator concluded blithely, "will not leave one infidel's head upon his neck."

"All right," Lane remarked to his first lieutenant, "we shall have to hoof it. No stop till we get there—except for chow."

The men had done twenty-six miles on their feet that day over sand and gravel. Most of them were now dead to the world. On falling out they had dropped off to sleep without waiting for their rations. Before giving the order that set the column into motion like a well-oiled machine, Lane briefly explained the reason for the apparently absurd command. Military discipline did not require that the men know why they were being treated like machines, but common sense did. Lane knew from long experience that an occasional descent to the level of human decency will get the impossible out of a company that is just about done. The column moved briskly off, cursing Hu. The first twenty-five miles before them was a steady grind uphill from 1,500 feet to 6,000 over one of the poorest apologies for a road in all of western China.

At midnight the column halted for thirty minutes at the last telegraph station east of the Kansu boundary line. Lane, his first lieutenant and the interpreter went in search of the operator. They located him in the village gambling den betting on a cockfight.

"What news from Kansu?" Lane asked through his interpreter.

This boy was a Christian convert and knew a few words of English.

"Damn bad," he replied. "You going to Kansu?" he inquired of Lane through the interpreter.

Lane explained his mission and asked whether it would be possible to raise anyone at that hour in Teng-shan. The operator was greatly interested. As a sporting venture he offered to bet that Lane and all of his men would be killed the next day. The stakes could be left in the hands of the gambling den boss. Yes, he thought he could raise the night operator in Teng-shan, provided the Moslems had not yet martyred him. The night operator also was a Christian convert. When the cockfight ended suddenly in the deaths of both combatants, the telegrapher rose obligingly to see what he could do.

In ten minutes he was back, smiling, with a reply. It appeared that the Teng-shan night operator had been trying for four hours to communicate with the outside world. Hearing from his Christian brother over the border in Shen-si that an American column was on its way to rescue the missionaries, he sent them this simple greeting, "For God's sake hurry." The column fell in and proceeded immediately up the barren pass.

No matter what the prize, or what voice calls, there is a limit beyond which human endurance cannot pass. The column went to pieces all of a sudden at sunrise, just as it was about to descend the pass into the first long valley of Kansu. Its objective, Teng-shan, was still twenty miles distant. To preserve the proprieties and save at least the shell of military discipline, Lane ordered a four-hour halt. The men flung themselves upon the jagged rocks where they stood. They were asleep before they hit their stony bed. In those four hours, while the men slept, the prophecy of Hu the Good was in part fulfilled.

While the exhausted men slept on the mountain pass, old Saxby, more than a thousand miles away in Shanghai, began definitely to play his part in the drama which was now sweeping to its climax. For the moment he was being buffeted from one unsympathetic official to the next in an almost hopeless attempt to get started on his way after Lane.

"I've been in worse messes than this," he reiterated to keep up his courage. "I'll get there."

THE chilly welcome accorded him and his interpreter by the Chinese, American, French and British alike, had its inevitable effect. In spite of himself, Saxby fell a victim to the blackest pessimism. He began to doubt his theory and to suspect that his reward at the end of his intended journey—if he ever got there—would be a large and empty mare's nest. Why the dickens hadn't he stayed in Los Angeles? The desert, the Lanes' bungalow, the ashes of Yang's laboratory—any of these offered greater chances of success than anything he might get from Lane. Wishing himself anywhere rather than in China, he dropped into the Army and Navy Club and ordered a bottle of port. As he sat gloomily sipping his wine he went over every detail of his theory with critical disgust. One possible check that he had overlooked in his previous analyses emerged from this searching examination.

"It is probably as wide of the mark as the rest of my guesses," he muttered as he finished the bottle. "Still, I overlooked it. That's bad. If there's nothing in this hypothesis I may as well take the next boat home. Well, it's easily verified one way or the other."

He rose to go in search of the president of the club. It was the president who had introduced old Saxby to the club and got him a "distinguished visitor's" privileges for the length of his stay in Shanghai. When the president saw Saxby coming he tried to dodge. The eminent geologist had made rather a nuisance of himself with his persistent buttonholing of anyone who might possibly help him on his way. Failing to escape, the president made the best of it.

"Not off for Kansu yet, Mr. Saxby?"

"No. And I doubt whether I shall go."

The president brightened. Saxby explained his impending change of heart.

"It all depends on what the Nautical Almanac has to say about the moon for the third of last month. I know you and the rest of the men here think I'm a lunatic. I am. And to prove it I want to borrow a Nautical Almanac—you must have one. If the almanac says it was impossible for the moon to shine into the east windows of a house in Los Angeles on the third of last month at any time between the hours of ten at night and five the next morning, I take the next boat home and leave you in peace. But if the moon did shine into the windows between those hours, I shall be forced to pester you till you send me to Kansu or till I start walking there. You might ask one of the younger naval officers to give me a hand with the necessary calculations while you are about it. You know I'm crazy. Better humor me."

The president humored him. With the help of a dapper young ensign Saxby soon found what he wanted. The moon did shine into the east windows on the third till approximately two hours after midnight, when it passed the zenith and threw the east sides of the houses into shadow.

"That settles it," Saxby exclaimed to the apprehensive president. "I must go on now to Kansu even if I have to walk."

"What has the moon to do with it?" the president asked. Old Saxby did not look like a lunatic, and in ordinary affairs he seemed sharp enough.

"I'll tell you when you talk the Army or the Navy into giving me an escort and an interpreter who won't run home when he hears the bullets singing. How about it? Can't you see I'm no fool? I tell you, on my word of honor backed by the full force of my scientific reputation—you can check up on that much—that I know what I'm talking about. This potty little revolution that all you fellows are making such a fuss over is nothing to what *may* happen if I don't get to Kansu in pretty short order. Mind, I don't say that it *will* happen; I only say it *may*. And further, the moon may have nothing to do with the case. It is a mere hypothesis that I overlooked. Still, since the moon does not contradict me, I feel more confident that I'm on the right track. Half an hour ago I was clear down in the dumps. Now I feel that I'm right in the main, although possibly wrong on every detail."

The president and the ensign exchanged a furtive glance. The emphatic old chap was clearly daft. How could they rid the club of him without raising a scandal?

"I suppose you can't give us any hint why all this secrecy is necessary?" the president suggested.

"That much is easy. As you can verify by looking in *Who's Who,* I have been a bachelor all my life. I know nothing about women. Still, I believe it is not the thing to let a woman down when she honors you with her confidence. Anyhow, I'm an easy mark for any woman who asks me to do something for her. I promised one that I would never tell on her—"

"Ah," the ensign and the president commented in unison. Here was something they thought they could understand. "Husband," Saxby concluded.

"Oh," they remarked, somewhat crestfallen.

"Because," Saxby continued, "he would probably be shot if I did. There you have it all. If I tell all I know, an innocent man, technically guilty, may lose his life. That is one reason I hold my tongue. Another, more important, is this: If I go off half cocked, there will be a blue panic all over the United States and Asia. My objective is to destroy the very real grounds for such a panic—if they still exist—as quietly as possible. Any army or navy man knows what a panic among the civilian population will do to the forces at the front when the enemy is about to start his grand offensives. My situation is exactly similar. Now, when can I get away for Kansu?"

The president's efforts to "humor" his guest were only half-hearted. He was beginning to believe that this self-assertive man should be taken at his own valuation.

"I don't see what the moon has to do with your problem," he concluded, "unless it helps you in some way to fix the date of a crime—say the theft of an important document." He shot Saxby a keen glance. "The Moscow reds are not mixed up in all this by any chance?"

The activities of the communist agents in all departments of the Chinese armies during the revolution were common and disquieting knowledge not only to military men but to every civilian on the streets. Moscow was more feared than the whole of China, and for obvious reasons. Was Saxby hinting at some vast communist plot which he alone was in a position to nullify? If so, why had he not come with proper credentials from the United States Government? Was he perhaps a secret agent of the Government, on a mission so delicate and so dangerous that no Government department or cabinet officer could risk sponsoring him and being found out if Saxby should fall down on his job? Saxby was not blind before his ludicrous opportunity. The anti-red nervousness of all Americans, British and French in China had delivered the president and his military friends into Saxby's hands.

"I can say nothing as to that," he declared guiltily.

Old Saxby, of course, was speaking the literal truth. He could not say anything about the possibility of the Moscow communists being involved in his project because he knew nothing whatever about them and, until the president obligingly mentioned them, had never given them a thought. He now concentrated his whole mind on

Moscow, bolshevists, communist propaganda and the redder shades of anarchy, in order to look as guilty as possible. The ensign and the president were studying his face as attentively as if it were a map of the whole world's future history.

"You couldn't even drop a hint, I suppose?" the ensign suggested.

Saxby mumbled something indistinct in which the sacred phrase "word of honor" seemed to occur. He looked as if he were about to be hanged. In a burst of candor he glanced up suddenly and looked the president squarely and manfully in the eyes.

"You understand, however, that I must get to Kansu in the shortest time possible, don't you?"

The president would not admit in so many words that he did.

"I shall have a talk with General Maitland," he promised vaguely.

"May I urge," old Saxby begged, his face as solemn as an undertaker's, "that you do so without further delay? Although I can tell the general no more than what I have told you, I shall be glad to lay my case before him. You will find me in the lounge when the general wants me."

He marched off to the lounge before the president could say yea or nay. In half an hour he was paged, as he had expected to be. He was now thoroughly primed for his part.

Old Saxby knew "Hardboiled Maitland" well by reputation. Maitland was a queer mixture. When not actively fighting, but only planning to fight, he was a martyr to nerves. In these trying interludes he earned a fearsome reputation for drastic severity with his men. The least infraction of discipline meant courtmartial. So heavily addicted was he to this form of relief that his more levelheaded colleagues on the staff used to call him "Courtmartial Harry" behind his back. But, in spite of his faults, Maitland was a competent soldier, if not a brilliant general. Given a definite, hard task to perform, he snapped into action and forgot himself and his nerves. As it was Maitland's personal eccentricities that, in the last analysis, encouraged Nature's worst, and as the same idiosyncrasies helped in no small measure to undo the damage in the final phase, he may be given at least a positive mark of merit for his share in the crisis. Many a better known man came out of the World War with only a doubtful zero.

The interview was an extremely harassing experience for the general. At dropping nebulous, disquieting hints old Saxby proved himself a past-master. In all the six hours he spent that evening conferring with the general and his staff, Saxby said precisely nothing that meant anything definite. The very vagueness of his attitude was its most disturbing quality. More than once in that long grilling the general glanced uneasily round the room as if to detect Russian spies behind the Chinese silk hangings.

When the boy entered with a tray of highballs for which the general himself had rung, Maitland demanded in a loud, military tone why the devil the boy kept wandering in and out of the room without knocking. It was a hectic night for an overwrought man whose duty compelled him to sit on the safety valve of half a dozen anarchistic revolutions. To aid the general in acquiring a proper frame of mind, Saxby waited till his host's head was turned and then shot his glass to the tile floor. Applied psychology is a great force for good—if applied at the right time. The general jumped as if bombed from below. Thereafter he was old Saxby's meat.

LANE's footsore men, refreshed by their four hours' sleep and a full meal, were swinging down the pass toward Teng-shan, still fifteen miles distant, when Markoff, with a thin smile, turned to the pasty Liapanouff and gave him his parting instructions.

"Now for that fat fool Hu. Stay here and talk to him while I go to the governor. Don't let White Lily run away. She looks as if she needed attention," he concluded with a leer, nodding toward the girl. Her huddled body lay prostrate with grief and horror at her grandfather's feet.

Liapanouff blabbered some reply and moved off to do his dirty duty. He walked slowly, for his knees felt as weak as water. No mere remorse for what he and Markoff had done caused his debility. A lively apprehension of what might happen to his own flabby neck, should the fanatical Moslems take a fancy to him, made him the sweating pulp he was. For he too was an "infidel" to the Mohametans. The vast caverns of the outer caves were now packed with yelling mobs whose fanatical hatred Liapanouff himself had helped to fan into flame. Now he would have given ten minutes of his life—not the proverbial ten years, for Liapanouff was too great a coward ever to visualize himself voluntarily letting go of life—to put out that bloodthirsty, flesh-hungry fire of his own kindling. His greatest chance of safety was at the side of the prophet Hu.

The old man sat dazed and blind in the glare of a thousand torches, trying to recall what in God's name he had done, and wondering why in the name of God he had done it. Liapanouff approached like a bloated leper and laid one damp, white hand on Hu's vast forearm. The huge face turned and loomed before Liapanouff's. Through the Russian's clouded mind flashed a memory of a setting sun he had once seen when a boy on the wintry steppes. The prophet's face flickered in the torchlight as that watery sun had flickered before it abandoned the world to the iron grip of a merciless cold.

Brushing the memory aside he began to babble. Hu gave no sign that he comprehended either the agent's sickly flatteries or the fanatical shouts of his faithful followers. He turned away his face from the Russian's and stared stonily at the misty eastern wall of the cavern.

Liapanouff moistened his lips and swallowed nervously. He had had enough. The certainty that he would get more if Markoff's negotiations with the governor of Kansu should miscarry in a certain detail, impelled him to mercy. The chance of failure on Markoff's part was all but negligible. Still, Hu *might* escape with a body of followers sufficient to repay one debt before he died. Better risk Markoff's cold anger than face Hu's Chinese fury if the one chance in a million should mature. The Chinese mind has a natural genius for devising strange forms of death. Liapanouff did not wish to be Hu's inspiration in case the improbable happened and Hu escaped for a day or a week. He stirred White Lily fearfully with his foot.

Thinking it was her grandfather who had touched her, she looked up, her eyes dim with tears, and saw Liapanouff. With a shudder of disgust she buried her face in her arms. Liapanouff bent over her, shaking in the uncontrollable uprush of a dozen clutching fears.

"Leave the caves at once," he whispered in her ear. "Markoff—"

He could say no more, choked by his cowardice. After all, Hu could not escape. Markoff would succeed. If Liapanouff let White Lily go, his life would be at Markoff's mercy—and Markoff had none. Liapanouff had assisted at the jehad and he knew. White Lily did not stir. Liapanouff ventured no second effort to warn her. His own skin was too sensitive.

Hour after hour that strange trio, the broken girl, the stunned old man and the half-fainting agent of a new gospel, remained motionless, while the victorious hosannas of the faithful clanged and reverberated through the vast caverns like a dream of hell, and Markoff rallied his legions for the next betrayal. The "bloodless jehad of Kansu" was already history, and Markoff dwelt by preference in the present and the future. Already he was on the march.

THAT memorable jehad, now but a troubled memory that would not sleep, had been imagined, put into action, and finished in the short space of forty hours. It began with Markoff's whispered suggestions to Hu. While White Lily fared forth alone to warn the missionaries and earn her rebuke from the lips of one of them, Markoff explained the details of the bloodless jehad to Liapanouff. The two agents wandered far into the secret places of the mountains in complete darkness, footsore and unafraid, confident of every step of the black way they had traveled a hundred times.

For fifty black miles or more the vast caverns of Kansu honeycombed the limestone mountains with a chambered labyrinth of calcite corridors and pillared halls, each shadowy antrum loftier than the nave of a great cathedral, curiously carved and hollowed from the living rock by water seeping drop by drop down to the subterranean rivers for ages. A tattered tracery of stalactites depended from the arched ceilings of these silent halls like the bleached banners of long forgotten armies, and massive pillars of all but transparent whiteness soared from the undulating pavements to bell out and vanish in the banners. Through some of these halls the distant rumor of rushing water echoed drowsily, but most were as soundless as the midnight of a desert. In others the oppressive stillness palpitated with a deeper silence, as if the blackness fell away to a bottomless void. These were the "forbidden caves," where the faithful never wandered.

The wise decree that forbade the curious to explore the forbidden caves was an ancient tradition that needed no enforcement. The torches of the first explorers who discovered them revealed these silent caverns for what they were: unsounded wells of darkness. No echo rose when a stone was thrown into those black gulfs. The scream of the condemned criminal hurled down one of those wells thinned and dwindled to silence long before the wretch who emitted it died. Hu the Good abolished this form of capital punishment which his fathers had sanctioned for generations, and the forbidden caves were roped off in eternal darkness.

In preparation for the jehad that was to be bloodless, Markoff and Liapanouff, feeling along the pitchy corridors, found the copper pins driven fast into the rock walls. They undid the knotted ropes, pitched them into the blackness ahead, and laughed. No slap of rope on rock answered. Silently as bats the two agents turned carefully around where they stood and felt their cautious way along the wide corridor of death, back to the main gallery, and thence to the audience hall of the prophet. They had prepared the road; they must now guide the destined travelers.

Without venturing to inform Hu that all was in readiness, they hugged the eastern wall of the audience chamber and flitted out under the crescent of the exit just as the evening shadows fell athwart the eastern hills. Turning to the north, they followed the path that White Lily had taken less than two hours previously.

While the agents toiled that evening to bring about the jehad, Hu sat dreaming alone in the vast entrance hall. For generations the Moslems had dwelt in these sacred caves. Every foot of the very hall in which the old man dreamed was hallowed by the blood of martyrs who had died for their faith. At first a persecuted handful, the faithful had fled in seasons of massacre to these friendly caves till the blood madness of their enemies abated, when the starving remnant would emerge to cry once more that "There is but one God and Mohamet is his prophet."

The indifference that sooner or later breeds tolerance on all sectarian hatreds preserved the Moslems. They multiplied and prospered. But they never forgot the holy caves that had saved their faith when it scarcely breathed, and the entrance hall became their Mecca. As the decades passed the feeling of awe and reverence mellowed to affection. The faithful found in the caves a warm shelter from the bitter mountain storms, and a haven of peace and comfort for themselves and their beasts. They stabled their cattle and stored the harvest of their fields in the dry caverns, and gradually found themselves living in the caves. The whole vast honeycomb in the limestone mountains became their citadel and their populous metropolis. Mindful of their harried past, the faithful, with a new appreciation of the good things of this life, depreciated the itch for martyrdom, trusted nobody, and cultivated human prudence. The narrower entrances were walled up against possible enemies. Only two secret exits, opening miles away on the mountain side, were left unclosed for emergencies. All that entered the subterranean city of the Moslems must pass under the crescent of the audience chamber, where the uncrowned king of forty thousand faithful reigned.

THEY had prospered and multiplied. But they never forgot their martyrs, whose unavenged blood was still visible by torchlight on the rose quartz floor of their holiest place where, once a year, they celebrated the feast of the dead. Nor could they lightly forget that their first prophet, Mohamet the implacable, put infidels to the sword. A rival, gentler faith, proclaimed the way of peace. Its cocksure converts belied its humane teachings by prophesying eternal fire for those who rejected it, and by riotous brawls among themselves to settle minute differences of doctrine. These blustering braggarts were ripe for chastisement. Hu had prophesied. They should be chastised and corrected without the shedding of blood, in accordance with their own professed faith.

"It is good," Hu rumbled as he nodded drowsily, exhausted by the incessant labor of keeping the blood circulating through the mountainous billows of his flesh. " 'There is but one—' "

But he was fast asleep. The battle cry of Islam expired in a futile puff on his lips.

While Hu dreamed of a whole world purged of infidels, Markoff and Liapanouff extended the olive branch of mutual understanding and love to the missionaries and their converts. All that evening, and late into the following afternoon, they labored to spread the glad tidings that strife between Moslem and Christian was forever at an end in Kansu. They were spiritual ambassadors, the two agents declared, from Hu the Good, to announce a perpetual truce between the warring sects. More, they offered their late enemies the healing balm of brotherhood. Would not all come early on the morrow to the audience chamber of Hu the Good, to seal the bond of a new friendship and celebrate the same with a feast of love in the less stately caverns? Not only would love in abundance be provided for their refreshment, but succulent food without stint. For a busy week had the most skilful cooks among the followers of Hu the Good toiled to prepare a feast worthy of the occasion and of the hospitable traditions of old China.

This greeting, larded and made enticing to the ragged with liberal promises of bounties beyond belief, was carried joyously by the smiling ambassadors from school to school, from one missionary residence to the next, and from squalid hovels to squalider market places. By the invisible telegraph system of all primitive peoples, the invitation swept the villages for a radius of thirty miles before the ambassadors of a new era of love had lied eight hours.

By nightfall the mean roads and trackless hillsides were a-crawl with a moving multitude converging toward the crescent mouth of the sacred mountain. By dawn of the appointed feast day the caverns of Kansu were jammed by a milling mob that clamored for the feasting to begin. Markoff and Liapanouff had returned before dawn, but they were not in the yelling crowd.

Not all who were invited to the feast accepted. The Christian telegrapher was not credulous. He stuck to his post and tried to call the governor of Shen-si. Many who would have come gladly were bedridden. Many more were too young to toil up the steep mountainside for a feast of love they could not understand, and more were too heavy to be carried by their mothers. There also were some few cynics who stayed away. Others had plenty to eat at home and did not hunger for heathen love. Of the white missionaries more than one hesitated long before subduing their unworthy doubts of a fellowman's offer of love, and consented only with reluctance to shepherd the glad pilgrimage of their converts. Three refused outright to go. If Hu had repented it was his business to come to them for forgiveness. Two who got as far as the crescent entrance turned back, unable to force their way in. One dreamy-eyed man with a gray beard, who had entered early and who stood near the exit, fled when the killing began.

It was a bloodless jehad. Not a sword was drawn, not a shot fired. An authoritative shouting and concerted waving of flares from the eastern wall of the cavern gained the momentary attention of the clamoring mob in the reception hall. The Moslems were inviting their brothers-to-be to begin the feasting. The flares receded into the gloomy cavern behind the announcers and a river of humanity streamed into the darkness. Presently the flaring torches reappeared at the sides of the black entrance as if to mark the hospitable portal. The volume of the mob moving slowly but irresistibly forward urged those already in the corridor of death onward to their doom. To the very lip of the black well the broad sluiceway was lit up by flaring torches stuck securely into copper sockets on the white, glittering walls. Within a hundred feet of the fall the crest of the advancing mob damned up in sudden panic. Their shouts of terror were drowned in the clamor of the main torrent. All knew now that they were betrayed. A tempest of fanatics armed with staves and stones broke upon the rear and flanks of the packed mob in the audience hall, herding the unarmed multitude to their slaughter. The crescent exit was barred by a regiment of gigantic men yelling the battle cry of Islam. There was but one motion possible, forward. As the tide vanished into the insatiable maw, the cohorts of the prophet swept the adjacent caverns clear of the curious, the laggards and the timid who had come early to explore, and who had dispersed like fallen leaves before the wind down the vast galleries when the feasting began.

Once more the tide in the audience hall swelled to its full volume, and again dwindled to a feeble eddy. Again and again as the sweepers worked farther and farther into the labyrinth of caves the living tide rose and fell monotonously. Crest after crest of the human river leapt the lip of the bottomless well to flutter out on the void in tattered spray. Not one drop of blood was shed.

ONLY the memory of it remained. Drunk with victory, the faithful danced before their prophet who had purged Kansu of infidels. He did not hear their hosannas. A sharper clamor, now stilled forever, beat incessantly upon his tortured soul. When it was too late Hu had realized his folly. The sudden onslaught of his fanatical followers, when they burst like a whirlwind upon the flanks of the helpless mob, awoke him to the full horror of what he had done. His prophecy had engendered the slaughter. Rising to his feet he had lifted his mighty voice in all the strength and thunder which his older followers remembered from their youth, and which had not been heard in Kansu for forty years. For ten minutes Hu was young again, strong and dominant as he had ever been. But he could no more have quenched the mad fury of his followers than he could have put out the fires of all hell with his tears. He commanded, he besought, he prophesied, he wept; they were deaf. Not Mohamet himself could have stemmed that merciless slaughter. Exhausted by futile entreaties, Hu surrendered to his senility and sank back, an old and defeated man, staring blindly at the constant ebb and flow of the human tide. The rise and fall of that struggling mass no doubt had some significance, but what it might be Hu was too old to remember. At last the tide rose no more. The monotonous recurrence of ebb and flow gave way to an eternity of noise. He seemed to be alone in space, isolated in time. Once a white face seemed to be looking up in the extremity of fear into his own. It was a man's face, and familiar. But Hu could not recall whose it was. A huddled body lay at his feet; why did it not move? He knew that it was alive. The world had crashed and gone to pieces. Why did not the interminable echo of its ruin come to an end?

The celebrants petrified suddenly in their mad dance. Had they heard aright? Yes! The gigantic guards at the crescent entrance were shouting a warning that froze the blood in the hot veins of the dancers.

"The yellow banners!"

Markoff was returning with his new friend and dupe, the governor of Kansu. And after him marched a disciplined horde of armed men, who were neither Christian nor Mohametan, but merely Chinese. This was the fine flower of three months' masterly treachery. The Chinese Moslems had annihilated the Chinese Christians and their white friends; the Chinese of the older faiths would wipe out the victors. The yellow banner of the dragon in its turn should go down to defeat.

The advancing horde was well armed. In sending to his friend, the revolutionary general, the arms of the Moslems, the governor of Kansu had squeezed a tax of one rifle in every four. The arms of his own men were thus augmented by enough to swell his forces by two regiments. They advanced up the sunny mountainside singing.

The sudden cessation of the shouting in the audience chamber roused Hu to his senses. At his feet White Lily still lay like a crushed flower. She had heard the shout of the guards and she knew the meaning of the yellow banners. She did not stir. Why flee? By lying where she was she might drink deep of oblivion and win eternal peace before the hour was out. As Hu bent down to lift the wilted form the whole of what he had done flashed upon his mind. He straightened up lest his hand defile her.

Liapanouff, hearing the singing of the advancing Chinese, started to creep toward the crescent of yellow sunshine. Hu's huge bulk leaped after him. Again he was a young man. One enormous hand grasped the Russian's right arm and dragged the limp coward back to where White Lily lay. The audience hall was already deserted but for Hu, White Lily and Liapanouff. Like panic-stricken rabbits the Moslems had vanished to seek safety by hiding in the darkest caverns.

"White Lily," Hu said, "if you ever loved me, stand up!"

She stood, but avoided her grandfather's eyes.

"The yellow banners will be here in a few moments," Hu continued. His voice was that of a young man. "I know that you fear them no more than I, for sleep is sweet. If all your love for me is not dead, do what I ask. Take food and water for three days' journey and leave these caves by the hidden way that you know. Make your way to Shen-si and seek out the governor. Tell him all that has happened and ask him in my name to come here and make peace between my people and those who follow the yellow banner of Kansu. There must be no more killing. Blood cannot wipe out blood. I am guilty and I will pay. My people must be spared. Hasten, or you will perish."

She flung herself in his arms.

"I will not leave you. Your death shall be my death."

"Go, if you have ever loved me!"

"I cannot, unless you come with me."

"How can I? This great body of mine would stick in the narrow places. But I will follow by another way."

"You promise?"

"I promise. It is a longer way, but I will join you when I am free. Hurry! They are almost here. Remember my message. Good-bye, my White Lily."

She ran to one of the caves where food and water might be found. Hu watched her out of sight. Confident that she was safe and would bear his message of mercy to the governor of Shen-si, Hu turned to his immediate task. Disregarding the screams and frantic struggles of the thing in his grasp, he dragged it with him toward the eastern wall of the cavern. The first of the avengers leaped through the yellow crescent just as Hu strode like a colossus into the black corridor of death. He shook the breath out of the limp rag in his hand.

"Be quiet! You have earned the wages of folly. If I should kill you I should do no wrong, for you are neither beast nor human."

An occasional torch still glowed somberly in its socket. The pair marking the lip of the well were flickering out fitfully the last remnants of their life.

"Open your eyes and look down," Hu commanded. For perhaps ten seconds he held the white face over the black void. "Have you seen?"

Crazed with fear Liapanouff screamed incoherent prayers which he had not uttered since he was a boy.

"Whatever you say is a lie," Hu cut in coldly. "No man can see the bottom of this pit."

A patter of hurrying footsteps sounded along the corridor behind them.

"Your friends would save you," Hu remarked. He threw the struggling wretch face down on the stone floor and planted one enormous foot firmly on his back. "I am Chinese," he continued calmly, as he quickly divested himself of his prophet's robes and tossed them far back into the corridor. "My people say it is good for a man's soul that he should die slowly with his eyes open. It is a long way to the bottom of this pit."

He stiffened, listening intently. The rabble of pursuit, headed by the panting Markoff, burst out of the darkness into the dying glow of the torches. Just before he stumbled headlong over the prophet's robes, Markoff saw the naked form of Hu bend swiftly down and grasp Liapanouff by an ankle. For an instant the gigantic Hu dangled the screaming wretch over the abyss. Then he opened his hand. Liapanouff shot from sight and his screams dwindled to silence.

Stepping back five paces to gain momentum, Hu raised his arms high above his head like a swimmer about to dive. Leaping forward he plunged into the black well without uttering a sound.

VII. THE DRAGON

Two miles from Teng-shan, and about three-quarters of a mile from the entrance to the caves, Lane's men met the first survivor. A gray-bearded man, evidently a missionary judging from his clothes, marched along the road waving his arms and singing, in a high falsetto, shrill snatches of hymns. When he saw the column of marines swinging toward him he stopped and peered intently through the late afternoon sunshine as if to read fine script. Having deciphered the invisible words, he broke into a shout of laughter and yelled at the men, "Mahomet is God and Allah is his prophet!"

Lane halted the column and, with his first lieutenant, captured the man. They got nothing out of him beyond curious perversions of the battle cry of Islam, an incoherent torrent of words, and the remark, whispered with an air of great secrecy, that he had denied his master. They turned him loose to wander at will.

"There seems to have been a massacre or something," the lieutenant observed. "Crazy as a loon. Acts as if he were shell-shocked."

Lane agreed, and the column marched on to the cracked singing of "Onward Christian Soldiers" by the madman. He was still singing when they rounded a buttress of the foothills and swung into full view of Teng-shan and the entrance to the caves.

"It still seems to be going strong," the lieutenant remarked, referring to the jehad. A sharp order brought the men to the double, pounding over the rubble in an oblique ascent to the crescent entrance. The last regiment of the army with the yellow banners was just about to stream into the caves. That tail-end alone outnumbered the marines five to one.

Lane's orders were to provoke no bloodshed. They seemed ludicrously superfluous in the present circumstances. The Chinese were fully armed. One flick of the dragon's tail would wipe Lane's column off the hillside. The huge body of the brute, its real fighting strength, was of course out of sight in the caves. What remained visible was an ample warning to use common sense. Lane decided to halt.

Leaving the column in charge of his subordinate officers, he went forward alone with the interpreter to parley. A white flag, handkerchief or other mark of truce seemed unnecessary. If the Chinese wanted to fire, a piece of cloth wouldn't stop them. Why should it? Lane argued, mistakenly imagining that these men were butchering the missionaries and their converts.

The crawling dragon tail ceased moving. The Chinese officers had noticed the strange troops arriving on their private battlefield. They were too astonished to order a volley, even if such seemed the best policy. The interpreter showed signs of nervousness.

"They will shoot," he muttered, and bolted like a rabbit down the mountainside toward Teng-shan.

Lane paused long enough to speed the fugitive with a parting curse and proceeded toward his objective, wondering how the devil he was to make himself understood. As he was to learn in a moment he needed no interpreter.

A lean vulture of a man in European civilian clothes emerged from his station at the entrance to the caves and advanced to meet the captain.

"Looks like a Russian," Lane remarked to the hillside in general. "Probably a red at that. Well, I guess the boys are in for it."

Markoff opened hostilities at once. It was no accident that had posted him on sentry duty outside the caves while the Chinese marched in. Having witnessed the end of his fellow agent, and not being a man of outstanding courage, Markoff deemed it prudent to return to the exit and wait outside until the last of his new friends entered. He was off with the old love forever, but the old love had not yet been heard from. A sudden flurry of Moslems might well do to him what Hu had done to Liapanouff. Like all diabolically cruel men, Markoff was a physical coward from skin to marrow. He now studied Lane's uniform minutely.

"American?" he screeched.

"Can't hear. Come closer."

"Are you Americans?" Markoff demanded from the comparative safety of thirty feet.

"Marines. Looking for white missionaries. Know any?"

Markoff ignored the inquiry. His rattlesnake jaw set and a mask of fanatical hatred froze on his cruel face.

"The governor orders me to tell you that he will tolerate no capitalistic aggressions in the province of Kansu. Your presence under arms here is an act of war. Surrender unconditionally or be shot down."

A startingly vivid image of a bungalow in Los Angeles slowly crystalized on the air before Lane's eyes. He saw Isabel reading on the veranda. Four-year-old Tom was dangling a piece of paper at the end of a string before the indifferent nose of the lofty Hoot. Isabel laid her book aside and got up to shift the sprinkler from the lawn to the bed of marigolds. The colors dissolved and the curiously real mirage vanished.

The inconsequential interlude cleared the captain's mind. He could not afford to get killed. Nor could the boys behind him. They were worth more than their life insurance. He must use his head and bluff it out somehow.

"From Moscow, aren't you?" he asked casually, as if Markoff had not delivered his awkward ultimatum.

"Surrender or be shot!"

Lane appeared to consider. He realized that an appeal to the governor would be futile. Without his own interpreter he was helpless. This red fanatic would translate Lane's questions concerning the missionaries into a declaration of war upon China by the bankers of America. Surrender probably meant death by torture. He temporized.

"Not so fast. All we want is to get track of the white missionaries and escort them back to Shanghai. We met one about a mile back on the road. Where are the rest?"

"In there."

Markoff jerked his head in the direction of the cave. He could not restrain the smile that twisted his lips like a grinning snake's. Lane guessed, but guessed wrong.

"Being killed?"

"No. They're all dead."

"Then what's all this fuss about?"

"A punitive expedition. The Moslems massacred the Christians. These soldiers are Chinese—neither one sect nor the other. The governor is in command. He will stand no religious riots in his province."

"That's a sound policy. Where do you come in?"

"The Moslems murdered my fellow adviser to the governor of Kansu."

"And what was *he* doing?"

"What business is that of an American like you?" Markoff screamed. "Capitalist robbers and murderers! Surrender unconditionally, or I advise the governor to open fire at once."

"All right. I guess what you say goes with him. My orders are not to fire until we are deliberately fired upon. Now, just this for yourself. Those boys behind me will put up one hell of a scrap when you do give the signal. Don't bite off more than you can chew. The whole United States army and navy are behind us. You know what that means, I guess."

MARKOFF was listening. Encouraged by the beginning of success, Lane tried a little bluffing. Had the Russian been as sure of himself with the governor as his ultimatum seemed to imply, he would have ordered the firing to begin immediately, instead of listening to a speech.

"The rest of the marines are just a few miles east of us in Shen-si. They will be here tonight or early tomorrow morning. If they find us missing they will hang the governor and chase you as far as Moscow—if you're a good runner. Then one of them will stick a bayonet into you where it hurts most. Better reconsider your ultimatum. Tell the governor we only want to look for the missionaries. Give him my promise that we leave without firing a shot the minute our job is done."

Markoff leered in the captain's face.

"You tell him yourself."

"I would, like a shot," Lane replied indifferently, "if I knew any Chinese."

"Where's your interpreter?"

"Back there with the boys. He was too scared to talk, so I left him behind."

"Call him now."

"Too much bother. You speak English like an Englishman anyway, so what's the use?"

"None. I'll be your interpreter. Come with me."

"No, thanks. If those Chinese shoot me in the back before I reach my men—look out. They'll get you, too."

"I don't think so. Your men are good, but they can't shoot round a corner. I shall retire to the cave. Goodbye."

Lane turned and sauntered unconcernedly back toward the column. The game was up. Well, if he failed to reach his immediate objective the boys would give a good account of themselves. Too bad it had to end this way. If that damned interpreter hadn't bolted things might have gone differently. He glanced up at the blue sky, involuntarily, like a man about to be executed. The field of his vision included the dip in the mountains which marked the pass from Kansu into Shen-si. Could be believe his eyes? An exclamation burst from his lips. He turned in his tracks and shouted to the retreating Markoff.

"Look there! Coming down over the pass. That's ours!"

Already a faint hum droned on the evening air. The Chinese stood paralyzed with fright. The drone rapidly swelled to a whirring roar and the wings of the huge creature became visible to their staring eyes. With yells of terror their regiment broke and scattered in panic down the mountain side. Not one of those dwellers in primitive Kansu had even seen a flying dragon that roared and smoked as it outflew the wind. The huge bombing plane swooped directly toward them, circled thrice at full speed low above their fleeing rabble, and soared suddenly upward with a rush to spy out a safe landing place. The terrified Chinese, governor, officers and all, lay stiff with fear where they had fallen, or crawled mechanically over the rubble in search of safety.

"Into the cave!" Lane shouted, not waiting to see where the plane landed.

The marines rushed the entrance without opposition. Markoff, however, had preceded him. Lane caught a fleeting glimpse of him in the dim light trailing the Chinese who fled in all directions into the blacker shadows. They, too, had heard the awful roar of the dragon. In fact the cave acted as a resonator to intensify that terrible sound a hundredfold. In five minutes the marines had the audience hall to themselves. The governor of Kansu was among those who had retreated to Teng-shan.

Lane lost no time in digging in. Guards were posted at the entrance of all the caverns opening into the audience chamber and a double guard at the crescent entrance to the whole vast labyrinth. They located the stores of torches, flares and food. Comfortable beds were dragged out of side caves, and half the men at once turned in for a four-hour sleep while the others mounted guard. It was better than being in barracks at home.

The governor's soldiers were not the only victims of panic caused by the roaring, smoking dragon. A few minutes after sunset White Lily emerged from the inconspicuous secret exit. This was a black hole, no bigger than a large badger's burrow, in a desolate jumble of shattered rose quartz that had burst through the ancient limestone. Exhausted of body by her long crawl through the last miles of the narrow burrow, and still stunned by the memory of the jehad, she sank down on the rocks and fell fast asleep. Although she had planned to travel all night she could not go on. The natural reaction of her flesh after a day of horror overcame her spirit.

In that brief, deep slumber she lived again the whole eighteen years of her life, including the last day. The clamor of the victims in the cavern again rang in her ears. Then it became a strong, resonant voice prophesying doom for all whose bloodlust makes them lower than the brutes. The voice of her dream gathered volume and prophesied that the innocent brutes who slaughter one another for natural sustenance, and not for the sake of righteousness, shall also perish from the earth. The prophecy became a destroying roar that foretold the end of all plant and animal life. Suddenly she woke in terror, conscious that she was not merely dreaming.

The golden twilight still lingered on the evening air. She must have slept for a few moments. Gleaming like burnished copper in the yellow light the huge body of some strange flying creature cleft the air directly over her head, and straight as an arrow shot with the speed of a dream down the pass toward the entrance to the caves.

She had no conception what it was, or what might be its purpose. A false instinct, bred by her vivid dream on the black memory of the morning, whispered that this monster had left its lair beyond the mountains to avenge the slaughter of the Christians. Did not their teachers prophesy that the angels would descend with flame and sword and judge and damn all unbelievers? She had heard this from the very beggars who threatened her with everlasting fire. Her grandfather was guilty. With his own lips he had sworn to pay the price of his guilt. This fiend of the air had come to collect that price.

"I will pay," she cried. Filled with a new strength she raced down the mountain side and ran as she had never run in her life toward the crescent entrance. "Wait, wait! I am coming."

ABOUT half an hour after Lane had posted his sentries, the man on outpost duty in front of the entrance heard resolute footsteps crunching up the mountain side in the dark. At his peremptory challenge the footsteps halted instantly.

"Take me to Captain Lane," a voice shouted through the darkness. "I'm sent here by General Maitland. From my voice I guess you know I'm white. As I know nothing of military etiquette you'll have to use your common sense and pass me. My business is urgent."

After the usual formalities Maitland's messenger was brought before the captain, who stared in astonishment at the hatless, bald-headed elderly man in a baggy alpaca suit.

"My I ask who you are, sir?"

"Jonathan Saxby. Personal messenger from General Maitland. I must deliver my message in private."

"Very well. Come this way."

When they had withdrawn out of earshot of the men, Saxby plunged into the middle of things.

"General Maitland instructed me to convey this verbal order to you: 'If Russian agents cause you any trouble, eliminate them, but use discretion and employ all means in your power to avert a clash between Russia and the United States.' Now," Saxby continued, "I suppose it is clear why General Maitland chose to transmit that order by word of mouth rather than on paper. Code is too easily deciphered. And if you are the man he takes you for, you won't go shooting reds in broad daylight on the village streets."

"All that is obvious enough," Lane remarked. "But what I can't see is this. How did General Maitland know there was a Moscow agent within a thousand miles of here? The Chinese prohibit the use of wireless by foreigners, and the telegraph lines are out for three hundred miles."

"General Maitland didn't know," Saxby replied, "until I told him."

"And how did you find out?"

"Intuition," old Saxby chuckled. "By the way, *are* there any Russians in the neighborhood?"

"One that I know of. There seems to have been another, but the Moslems eliminated him."

Old Saxby burst into a roar of laughter.

"Well, I'm hanged," he choked in his spasm. "There is something in what I made Maitland believe after all. When you get back to Shanghai tell him from me always to act on his nerves."

"Didn't you know of these agents?"

"I? How could I? Moscow means nothing to me. Anyway, I'm here." He stopped suddenly and stood staring at the floor of the cave. All his mirth had evaporated. "This is bad," he said. "The ideal conditions again—limestone and quartz. How long have you been walking about in here?"

"Since your plane landed," Lane replied, thinking he had to deal with a lunatic. "You got us in for the first time."

"Is that the uniform you had on when you left Los Angeles?"

"No." The captain was too dazed to resist answering.

"What did you do with the other one?"

"As the salt water had ruined it—I was pitched into the sea, I suppose you know, when the *Sheridan* sank—I borrowed some clothes from one of the officers on the *Sherman* and chucked my own overboard. Then in Shanghai I got a complete new outfit."

"Shirt, shoes and all?" old Saxby demanded tensely.

"Yes. But what is all this about, anyway?"

"Another experimental error!" Saxby groaned. "I might have known. Of course the immersion in salt water would ruin your clothes. I'm as blind as a bat. Why in thunder didn't I see that before I left Los Angeles? Here endeth my wild-goose chase. Thank Heaven the Russian agents didn't turn out to be a myth, I'll have something to tell Maitland. Well, I had better be going."

He started toward the exit of the cave. In one stride Lane overtook him.

"You might tell me what it's all about before you leave. I'm curious. You don't look cracked."

"I'm not. Merely a bungler, that's all. Oh, by the way, I almost forgot. Your wife asked me to give you her love and tell you to take care of yourself."

"Thanks. But you didn't fly over a thousand miles from Shanghai just to tell me that, did you? According to your own account you went to a lot of trouble to fool the general in order to get here. Again, my wife knew you were coming. There's a big rat under all this. Sergeant!"

The sergeant stepped briskly forward and saluted.

"Put this man under arrest."

"What the devil do you mean?" old Saxby shouted. "I'm not in the army."

"From now on you are. And until you find your tongue you clean the cave—or boil rice."

"I *can't* talk."

"All right. Shut up."

Bedding was found for the prisoner and, while Saxby protested vociferously, a bed was made up on the floor. The guard was no amateur at swearing, but old Saxby almost made him blush. Finally the guard had to silence him forcibly as he was disturbing the men asleep. Saxby neither slumbered nor slept.

Barely had Lane disposed of this problem when another was presented to him. Two of the sentries half led, half carried an exhausted young Chinese girl before him. Her blue tunic was torn and her shoes were mere tatters of rags. One of the men held up his torch so that the captain might see her plainly. He looked into a pair of eyes that had seen death and a face of great beauty that would never lose its fixed tragedy.

"What's the trouble," he asked gently.

In reply she wailed over and over again some phrase in Chinese.

"She evidently knows no English. Damn that interpreter! Bring the prisoner here."

Old Saxby was walked up under guard.

"Know any Chinese?" Lane demanded.

"Not a word."

"Did you bring an interpreter with you?"

Saxby shook his head.

"The pilot and the mechanician are both young fellows in the navy. But, if I may offer a suggestion—"

"Go ahead."

"The telegraph night operator says he is a Christian. He seems to know some English. I left him trying to talk to my boys. They stayed with the plane of course." He scanned While Lily from head to foot. "This girl seems about all in. If I weren't under arrest I would suggest that you give her my bed. Her feet are nothing but bleeding pulp."

Lane looked down.

"Put her in the prisoner's bed and get hot water to wash her feet. The prisoner will attend to her."

OLD Saxby fished into his capacious coat pocket and drew out Yang's notebook and two clean handkerchiefs.

"I've had enough arrest," he remarked, opening the green stained notebook and extracting a small folded paper. "I know when I'm licked, and I'll talk any time you care to listen. This may help you to believe me." He handed Lane the slip of paper. "Is this your wife's handwriting?" He carefully restored the notebook to his pocket.

Lane examined the writing minutely and nodded. The note read, "Believe what the bearer of this paper tells you."

"You are no longer under arrest, Mr. Saxby. I must attend to this first."

The captain ordered the sergeant to take two squads down to Teng-shan, find the telegraph night operator, and bring him at once to the audience chamber. Rejoining Saxby he found the latter standing doubtfully by the side of White Lily's pallet with the handkerchiefs in his hand. A dish of water and antiseptic stood ready by her feet.

"It has just occurred to me that I had better not touch her," Saxby explained. "My hands and these handkerchiefs may be infected. She has evidently run a long distance over flints and broken limestone practically barefoot. I can't take the risk of touching her. Not so long ago I saw a Chinaman come to a very bad end. It is just beginning to dawn on me what may have been directly responsible for his peculiar death. The circumstances of this girl's injuries are much like those of the other case. Hadn't your surgeon better attend to her?"

"He's asleep, all in. Here, I'll do it. I asked you rather than one of the ambulance men to do it because you are older than any of us, and somehow it seemed more decent. Some of these oriental women don't like young men doctors. Let me have your handkerchiefs, will you?"

Saxby hastily thrust them into his pocket.

"That's just the point. I'm convinced now that they're badly infected. So are my hands. I'll explain later. Tear off a piece of her own clothing. She's only half conscious."

Lane tore off a piece of her sleeve and did the best he could.

"That will have to do until the surgeon wakes up. I suppose she's a Christian convert. Naturally she would run to us for protection. There seems to have been a hell of a row—the Russian implied as much. We're too late to be of much use I guess."

They left her moaning. It was not physical pain that distracted her.

"I will pay," she repeated in her own tongue, believing she knew what price would be demanded of her, and not fearing it. She would suffer anything to pay her grandfather's debt and thereby win mercy for her people and eternal oblivion for herself.

"Now," Lane remarked to Saxby, "let's hear what you have to say. First, exactly how did you ever get here?"

Old Saxby, not without a ruffle of pride, recounted how he had worked upon General Maitland's nerves and how the nerves had done the rest.

"The upshot of it was that he packed me off in a bombing plane at six in the morning, Shanghai time. We should have been here two hours earlier—it's only a little over a thousand miles—if the pilot hadn't lost his way in the fog over the mountains. It was all plain sailing as long as we could see the rivers. After that it was dead reckoning. Still, he did a good job."

"He saved us. That infernal Russian would have told the Chinese to fire. We might have shot a few hundred before cashing in our chips; but we hadn't a dog's chance of routing them. And I doubt if we can hold this place if they have machine guns—which they probably have. The Russians have been arming the Chinese for the past two years. Well, we shall see. Now what about the rest of it? Why did my wife write that note?"

"First let me explain why I should prefer to hold my tongue, and why I tried to until you put me under arrest. What I have to say may disturb you about the safety of your own family. In such a mental condition you wouldn't be fit to lead the band at a Sunday School picnic, much less an expedition in a hostile country. You almost certainly would run into danger by not being able to concentrate on your job. Before going farther, I want to emphasize that there is not the slightest ground for worrying about anything in Los Angeles. It was all quiet there when I left, and I feel sure it will remain so. My theory *must* be right that far. Again I didn't want to tell you anything because it was unnecessary. The more people who know about what may happen somewhere, somehow, the worse for us all. If one lets it out prematurely the whole world will hear of it. Now, have patience with me. I'm trying to break it gently. I don't want any panic. Must you have the story, or will you let me go back to Shanghai in the morning—provided we have enough gas left?"

Lane laughed. "Let's have the story. From your hints I judge it will be exciting enough to keep me awake. I dare not turn in till daylight—if then. Shoot."

"Very well. You are sitting opposite a man who is more dangerous than a billion tons of dynamite. I may explode at any minute—how, exactly, I don't yet know. But I may. You noticed, of course, that I did not touch the girl? And have you noticed that I am very careful not to touch anything with my hands?" The captain nodded. "All right. I must ask you to lend me a pair of leather gloves. Some of the men must have a pair—any kind will do. I can't hold my hands up indefinitely. The gloves must be leather."

Thinking again that he had to do with a lunatic who needed humoring, but who might have information of some value, Lane sent an orderly to fetch a pair of leather gauntlets from his own kit. When they were brought Saxby held out his hands for Lane to put them on.

"Safety and prophylaxis first. I mustn't touch the outsides. My hands may be infected. If there is a fight and I get killed, don't bury me near sand or limestone. See that my body is burned in the hottest fire you can make, and keep the fire going for at least forty-eight hours. Don't forget. Your wife told you to believe what *I* say. The first thing I say is this: I am not crazy. The second—"

He was interrupted by a sudden disturbance at the entrance. Lane hurried to see what was happening. Saxby followed. They found two of the guards wrestling with a man apparently out of his mind.

"I must see the Commander!" the man shouted, struggling to get free. "Take me to him. Ten thousand Christians will be slaughtered if—"

"I am in command here," Lane said quietly, confronting the man. "We met you on the road late this afternoon. You were singing. Remember? What's on your mind? Is there going to be another jehad?"

"Another?" the missionary repeated in a daze. "Has there been one?"

"I don't know. A Russian told me there had. He said the dead are in here, somewhere in these caves. They may be, for all I know. We can't search till we find out how strong the enemy is. What do you know about it all? Come here and sit down."

THE gray-bearded man followed obediently. Lane passed within a few feet of the spot where White Lily lay, and went on some yards so that their talking might not disturb her. Glancing back to see if he was followed, he saw the missionary standing like a statue of haggard old age at the foot of White Lily's pallet, staring down at her. Lane joined him.

"Ever seen her before?"

"How did she get here?" the man muttered hoarsely. "I left her just before sunset and I know she did not overtake me on the way. I ran."

"Come over here and tell us about it. Things will straighten out as you talk. Now," he resumed when the dazed man had seated himself on an outcrop of ancient granite, "begin at the beginning and let us have it all."

The missionary's account was coherent and apparently straightforward as far as it went. The dates, however, were inverted. He said that two Russians, Liapanouff and Markoff, had issued an invitation to all the Christians of Kansu to seal a pact of perpetual peace with Hu the Good and his Moslem followers. He went on to relate that the Chinese girl, now lying exhausted but a few feet away, had warned him of treachery, saying that the Christians, once enticed into the caves, were to be massacred. She had told him so that very evening. The jehad, she declared, was to take place the following morning. He had come, the missionary declared, to intercede with the Moslem soldiers and to lay down his life, if necessary, to warn all converts away from the trap.

"You are sure the girl warned you?" Lane asked. "Possibly at the risk of her own life? Her people, I take it, will kill her if they hear of her treachery. That's what it is, you see, from their point of view. Sure this is the same girl?"

"How could I forget her after what she told me?" He stopped suddenly, staring into Lane's face as if he saw a spirit. "Where have I seen you?" he whispered.

"On the road. Just before sunset. Don't you remember?"

The man shook his head, struggling to pierce the black clouds that baffled his memory.

"Ask him if he speaks Chinese," Saxby suggested in a low tone. "Most probably he does, unless he has forgotten how."

"I'm coming to that," Lane replied under his breath. He addressed the missionary. "Perhaps the Chinese girl can tell us something. You speak the language, of course?"

"Like a native. I have taught the gospel fourteen years in Tengshan."

"That's fine. See what this girl has to say. Ask her what happened after she left you. By the way, you said the names of the Russians were Liapanouff and Markoff?" The man nodded. "One is a lean fellow," Lane continued, "with a sort of hawk face and a ratty mustache—brown, like his hair. Which is he?"

"Markoff."

Lane turned to Saxby.

"That's the bird behind us somewhere in these caves with an army of crazy Chinks. I think I'll act on General Maitland's orders and shoot Markoff on sight. He seems to be a pretty bad egg."

The missionary was bending over White Lily, peering into her eyes. Seeing who confronted her, and imagining that the avenger of the Christians had come to lead her to death, she sprang up with an eager cry.

"What does she say?" Lane asked quietly.

"She says she will pay."

"For what?"

In reply to the dazed old man's cross-questions White Lily told him with ghastly brevity exactly what had happened. They might kill her, she concluded, if they would spare her grandfather. He was not responsible for the jehad; he had tried to stop it when it began. He was an old man, not of strong mind. She was more to blame than he, for she had humored his childish fancy when

Markoff and Liapanouff corrupted him by months of flattery and suggestion. In exchange for her life she asked that they promise not to harm her grandfather, and that the governor of Kansu be made to prohibit any killing of Moslems in reprisal. Hu himself had said that blood cannot wipe out blood, also that he alone was guilty. She, not Hu, was guilty; let her punishment settle the score forever. They might throw her into the well of darkness at once. She was ready, and would be glad to forget it all.

When the missionary finished his translation Saxby and the captain cross-examined White Lily sharply concerning the details of the jehad, asking finally for an estimate of the number slaughtered.

"She says ten thousand."

"Clearly an exaggeration," Lane commented. "There never were that many converts in the whole of western China. The rest of her story hangs together. She hasn't contradicted herself once on cross-examination."

"Not once," Saxby agreed. "Her ten thousand is natural enough. To anyone with the instincts of a human being the number must have seemed practically infinite. If this is the sort of thing our race—for these fiends were men like ourselves—is capable of," he continued savagely, "I feel tempted to let nature take its course and wipe out our kind forever. The only excuse for not doing so is the fact that occasionally our human race does breed something better—like this Chinese girl. We must prevent these Chinamen from butchering the Moslems next. She has earned that much from us."

He was cut short by the ecstatic singing of the madman.

" 'Ten thousand times ten thousand
Are clad in robes of white—' "

"Shut up!" Lane ordered. "Tell this girl that neither she nor her grandfather will be killed. My men will permit no reprisals. Tell her we do this merely because she has shown us how."

"Are the guilty not to be punished?" the missionary demanded.

"Certainly. But not by murder, either wholesale or retail, with one possible exception. The Russian agents seem to be responsible. One is dead. The other will be captured. We shall give him all the rights of a court-martial. If he is found guilty he will be executed. If you have an ounce of common sense you will see that the girl, or her grandfather, is right. The moment the governor's men start killing the Moslems—at the very first reprisal—a religious war will break out here and it won't end till the whole of Asia, including Russia, and most of the rest of the world is drenched in blood. I'm going to use my horse sense. Never mind the law of the case. Now give the girl my message and give it straight. If I find out that you have made any mistake I'll put you under arrest. I expect another interpreter of my own here by sunrise or very shortly after."

As surly as a bear the scowling madman translated Lane's message. When she grasped its meaning White Lily flung herself at Lane's feet.

"You did it," he said. "I wish you could understand English. Don't thank me."

They left her to herself.

As they walked away, the madman began expostulating.

"I shall go to the governor myself!" he finally shouted in an insane passion.

"No you won't," Lane snapped. "Corporal! Put this man under arrest. He is not to be let out of this cave until we leave. Treat him decently. He's sick in the head."

"What will you do if the governor attacks?" Saxby asked when they were alone.

"He won't. I have other plans. But, if the worst comes to the worst, you must fly back as far as your gas will take you and make the rest of the journey any way you can. Tell General Maitland the whole story. He will know what to do. But I doubt whether the full threat of the whole American and British armies and navies will be able to put out the fire if it once starts. I'm betting that it won't, but I'll have to step lively to prevent it. You stay here and keep an eye on that missionary. If he starts making speeches, clout him. I don't want the boys to get a false view of the situation. They'll fight the Chinese better if they don't know the whole story. If those men return with the telegraph operator before I get back, take charge of him, too. Now, there's nothing to be frightened of while I'm away. This place is a natural fortress and we're on the inside. The first lieutenant will be in command. He has a level head. In case of trouble, do exactly what he tells you to do, and do it in a hurry. Well, I'm off."

"Where are you going?"

"Tell you when I see you."

Saxby watched the captain waken twenty picked men to accompany him on his hazardous mission. They marched out of the cave just as dawn streaked the sky.

VIII. LANE'S CARDS

LIKE many of the greatest commanders in history, Lane believed firmly in taking the offensive and keeping it. The Chinese outnumbered the marines at least a hundred to one. Should the governor of Kansu order an attack as soon as his men recovered from their fright, the Americans would be wiped out in half an hour. Although the captain had declared to Saxby that the position of the marines in the cave was impregnable, as a soldier he knew better. A few machine guns in the hands of strategically placed Chinese would clear the entrance in two minutes and then would keep it clear. A resolute leader who did not mind the loss of some hundreds of his men—provided his own life was not thereby endangered—could take the cave in a rush any time he cared to give the order. Lane and his twenty men were now on their desperate mission to plant a bomb under the governor's probable strategy.

On a long, smooth slope about half a mile south of Teng-shan they spied the bombing plane resting comfortably on the stubble like an enormous grasshopper. Ordering the men to proceed to the town slowly, so that he might overtake them, Lane detoured to interview the pilot. The plane had the sunny slope to itself; not a sightseer was visible.

The mechanic was on guard. He saw Lane coming and woke the pilot. Lane went straight to the point.

"How much gas have you left—how many miles?"

"Enough for seventeen hundred under good flying conditions," the pilot replied. "Less, of course, against strong headwinds."

"Fine!" Lane exclaimed. "You have plenty to fly back to Shanghai and do five hundred miles of stunts. I may want you to stage a show here. You can see the entrance to the caves. One of you keep an eye on it with your glasses all day. Take it in spells. I'll be going back in about an hour. You know how to read our wig-wag signals? All right; there will be a man with a white flag posted outside the cave. If he starts signaling get the message and act on it immediately."

"Can you give us some idea of what we shall have to do?"

"No, because I don't know myself. It may be nothing. Be prepared for anything. By the way, have you any bombs?"

"Four. But our orders were to drop none unless we were attacked by anti-aircraft fire in flying over the Chinese lines."

"Never mind that. Technically you will be attacked if I call for bombs. Most likely I shall need only some fireworks to scare the tar out of the Chinese. If I call for stunts, do your damndest and put on a real show. Scare the livers out of them. I'll send you rations and fresh water as soon as I get back to the cave. Keep the Chinese away by starting up your engine and making all the noise you know how if they get curious."

He hurried off to overtake his men. Entering the town they met the exhausted sergeant and his two squads, still searching fruitlessly for the telegraph operator. Lane explained that they now had an interpreter at the caves and ordered the men to return there and rest. As he and his twenty men marched up what seemed the main street, indifferent Chinese slouched to the doorways and followed the foreign devils with lacklustre eyes. Not a Chinese soldier was in sight. "It looks like a trap," Lane remarked to himself. Then, to a corporal, "Follow that line of telegraph poles."

Guessing that the operator would be in his place of business, Lane kept his eyes open for the telegraph office. He found it without difficulty by noting where a small cable connected a shabby building with the wires. The door was not locked. Striding in, Lane bagged his bird, or rather a brace. His own recreant interpreter was chatting with the night operator, whose "watch" lasted till ten o'clock. The captain contented himself with a single well-placed kick and turned the deserter over to his men. From the night operator he learned the location of the governor's palace.

"You come along and show us the way," Lane ordered. "You say you're a nice missionary boy. Now prove it by not getting lost, or I'll show you a short cut to Heaven."

Nearing the governor's palace on the outskirts of the town they understood why they had seen no soldiers on their search through the streets. The entire tail of the governor's army was camped around and in the palace grounds to protect his sacred person from foreign aggression. The governor had not yet recovered from his fright at the smoking dragon. He realized now, of course, that it was no supernatural monster, as the inquisitive and cultured telegraph operator, who knew all about airplanes from the missionaries, had told him so late the previous evening. But he rightly suspected it of being some devilish new kind of war bird capable of laying more infernal eggs than any that even a Chinaman has dreamed of.

The Chinese sentries promptly halted the marines. Lane played his first card. Through his interpreter he ordered—he did not make the mistake of asking—the officer in charge of the sentries to tell the governor that the commander of the American forces demanded an instant audience. The officer obeyed. He was absent fifteen minutes. During that uneasy wait Lane took time to note that the Chinese had more machine guns—evidently of Russian make—than they could possibly require, also that their rifles were of the latest pattern. Their supply of ammunition was ample, not to say prodigal. The wooden boxes containing the reserve supply were stencilled with both Chinese and Russian characters.

When the envoy returned, he informed Lane through the interpreter that the governor would receive him on two conditions. First, Lane and his interpreter alone would be admitted to the august presence provided they left all their arms with the Chinese sentries at the gate. Second, during the conference, the Americans at the gate were to surrender their arms to the Chinese sentries.

Lane accepted these terms without argument. He felt that the governor would offer no better.

"If I am not back in twenty minutes," he told the men, "walk away as if nothing had happened. Go back to the caves. I shan't be following."

The governor, attired in a loose yellow robe, gorgeously embroidered, was seated behind a long teakwood table in a large, heavily beamed room as bare as an empty barn. Behind him a fully armed guard of six men stood stiffly at attention. Taking no chance on the interpreter's nerves, the captain grabbed him by the arm and hustled him to the table.

"Tell the governor this," he ordered. To emphasize his remarks he banged his fist on the table directly under the governor's nose and began shouting in the angriest tones at his command.

"You have let your people murder American missionaries. I place you under arrest and I order you now to come with me and stand courtmartial in the cave where you butchered them."

The governor, who had jumped six inches when Lane banged the table, turned the color of his robe when the interpreter translated the bluff. His reply was a feeble attempt to prove an alibi.

"He says the Moslems killed the missionaries."

"Tell him," Lane roared, "not to argue! The Moslems who killed the Christians are Chinese. As governor of Kansu he is responsible."

The governor's color improved somewhat. He turned a purplish green. The blood was finding its way again to his brain. He pondered Lane's legal theories in silence. Then, having glanced behind him to see that the guards were still there, he put his simple, disconcerting question through the interpreter.

"Why should I go to the caves?"

With the air of a humane judge informing a murderer precisely why it was his painful duty to impose the death penalty, Lane explained in a level voice.

"Tell him this, bit by bit. Tell it slowly, so he will understand it all. First, if I am not back at the airplane within a certain time, the two men in it have orders to blow Teng-shan off the face of the earth. They will fly high and drop their bombs out of a clear sky.

The people of Teng-shan, including the governor of Kansu, won't even see the plane—it will be so high. But they will know it is somewhere in the sky when the first bomb hits this palace. Second, if I pass the plane without the governor, and if a single one of his soldiers is seen following me and my men back to the cave, the plane will at once fly back over the pass into Shen-si. We are only the advance column of a very strong American force—easily able to wipe out the Kansu army in a morning engagement. But our main army will probably not have to advance at all. There are five hundred bombing planes with it. The planes will fly back and forth over the pass for a week, or for longer if necessary, until they have bombed every farm house, village and town in Kansu into a dusty hole in the ground. That's all."

From the expression on the governor's face as he absorbed sentence after sentence of the ultimatum, Lane believed that the bluff had worked. With an air of unconcern he sauntered toward the door, expecting the governor to follow him. The governor, however, did nothing of the kind. To his horror Lane heard the governor and the interpreter exchanging a rapid cross-fire of questions and answers. What could it mean? The interpreter suddenly shot past on his way to the door.

"Halt!" Lane shouted.

Involuntarily the interpreter halted. Taking two strides forward Lane grasped him by the back of the neck and shook the wind out of him.

"Where are you going?"

"I can't tell."

"Why not? Spill it, or I'll break your neck!"

"The governor's soldiers will shoot me if I tell. Let go!"

Lane felt himself seized from behind. The governor's guards were not asleep. One banged the butt end of his rifle down hard on the captain's wrists and the interpreter bolted. The governor was not only more or less of a gentleman but also an extremely cautious man. At a word from him the guards let Lane go. It would be unwise, the governor believed, to abuse this blustering American until the exact value of his threats was ascertained.

Presently the interpreter returned, followed closely by the telegraph night operator. In a flash Lane saw what was about to happen. He played his last desperate card. If this failed to take the trick he was cleaned out. The telegraph operator had declared that he was a Christian convert. His knowledge of English, however, was not extensive. Gambling on the chance that the boy would understand, and that he was indeed on the side of the missionaries, Lane deliberately chose the simplest words he could find to phrase his plea to the operator.

"Tell this man," he pointed to the governor, "the truth. The man in Shen-si will tell you we have a big army there with five hundred airplanes. Tell him this when you come back." Lane was careful not to let his own interpreter overhear.

An all but imperceptible flicker of an eyelid is more eloquent than volumes of oratory. The operator caught Lane's. He understood exactly what he was being asked to do. Would he do it, or had the missionaries ruined his native genius for lying? Lane silently prayed that the operator might still be an artless child of China. The governor was no fool.

"What did the American say to you then?" he demanded.

A look of almost angelic piety lit up the operator's face.

"He told me to tell you the truth."

"Then ask him for me whether there is time for you to telegraph to Shen-si before the plane begins to drop bombs."

Lane replied that he thought there would be time. The governor took the chance, but told the operator to run all the way to the telegraph office and not to dally on the way back.

Either by instinct or from a Chinese sense of humor the operator took all the time he needed in the office. Lane expected him back in forty minutes. A full hour passed. The captain began to smile. He glanced suggestively at his wrist watch. The governor fidgeted. Lane believed the operator was having his little joke on the governor. The more intense the suspense the greater would be the relief with which the governor would choose courtmartial instead of bombing. But as the hour lengthened to two, Lane felt that the joke was going too far. By signs he prevailed upon the governor to send one of his guards to see what had happened to the operator. They met just outside the door.

"Is it true?" the governor demanded.

The operator, breathless from his long run, struggled to reply.

"It is true," he panted. "All western Shen-si is full of American soldiers. They have big guns and five hundred airplanes."

The governor rose hastily. With an air of well-controlled anxiety Lane pointed to his watch, then to the beamed ceiling of the room. The governor ran. At the door Lane glanced back at the operator.

"Come to the caves tonight. We'll take you back with us."

The operator's face was a beautiful mean between the Mona Lisa smile and a subtle Chinese grin. He had told the truth as he saw it, and he was pleased with himself. The big guns were his own contribution.

"You not know me," he remarked. "Other night I tell you over wire in Shen-si for God's sake hurry."

At the palace gate Lane and the shaken governor found the twenty marines hanging about and looking sheepish. Two hours had passed.

"I thought I told you to go back to the caves," Lane snapped, "if I didn't come out in twenty minutes."

"Our watches all stopped five minutes after you left, sir," the corporal informed him, offering his as evidence.

"Fall in, and march ahead of us to the caves," Lane ordered sharply. He thought it best to ignore the remarkable coincidence of twenty watches stopping simultaneously. The men grabbed their rifles from the governor's guards and obeyed.

Forty minutes later, old Saxby, anxiously scanning the slope up from the town through the lieutenant's field glasses, made out Lane's men marching rapidly toward the caves. A few paces behind the men Lane was trying to keep up. A stoutish man whose resplendent yellow robe outblazed the morning sun was leaning heavily on the captain's arm and impeding his progress, Saxby guessed.

"By Jove!" he shouted to the sentry behind him, "the captain has captured the governor of Kansu."

Old Saxby had become panicky at the long absence of Lane's party, and had left White Lily in charge of the surgeon, to go out and keep watch for the captain. In case of visible danger in the town he was to report at once to the lieutenant in the cave. Seeing that all was now rather better than well, he sprinted back to the cave to tell the lieutenant.

"They ought to make him a field marshal or something for this," he concluded enthusiastically. "That boy has a head on his shoulders. With the governor in here as hostage we can send the missionary into these black holes to tell the Chinese to come out. Then the governor can send them all home. We'll keep him till we don't need him any longer—say half way across Shen-si. And we needn't let him go until he gives us a cast-iron guarantee that he won't touch the Moslems when he gets back to Teng-shan. We—"

"Zing!" a bullet sang as it just kissed Saxby's ear and passed on.

The staccato commands of the lieutenant were drowned in the instant uproar that burst upon the silence of the audience chamber from a hundred black galleries. Mobs of yelling shouting Chinese soldiers boiled into the chamber from the caverns like a sudden eruption of vermin swarming over a carcass. The guards at the entrance to the rock caverns were swept aside like chips and hurled back against the walls. Saxby found himself isolated a few feet from White Lily. His instinctive thought was of her safety. She was small; he was strong, and his blood was up. He tucked her under one arm, seized a heavy torch with his free hand, and started to follow the main body of the marines who were retreating toward the eastern wall of the cavern. This chanced at the moment to be the nearest objective offering protection for their backs.

"Hold your fire!" The lieutenant shouted, seeing Saxby and his burden directly in the line of fire.

The front of the advancing horde parted in the middle and a flying wedge of gigantic Chinamen issued from the gap and shot like an arrow toward Saxby; a sudden surge forward of the right wing of the enemy completely cut off his retreat. Saxby found himself with his back to a thousand yelling Chinese and his face to the racing wedge. He dropped White Lily at his feet and grasped the torch with both hands. The head of the wedge misjudged its mark. The leader saw only an old man with a stick. He saw nothing more, because Saxby's torch caught him full whack on the side of his skull and broke his neck. The next got a shattered arm. The third, quick witted, and more agile than his predecessor, swooped low, grasped White Lily's tunic with one hand, snatched her to his body, and fled like a streak before Saxby could swing at him. Two more were disposed of before the torch snapped in his hands. For a sixty-year-old man he had put up a pretty good fight. He realized that it was all over. His one regret was that he did not have a revolver. For it had not escaped his notice that the flying wedge carried no arms. Their orders, therefore, were to capture, not to destroy the enemy. Saxby guessed who had given the order. From Markoff's record in the caves it was but reasonable to expect an unpleasant death.

Instinct forced him to fight to the last ounce of his strength, although reason coolly told him it was useless to struggle. Obedient to their orders, and anticipating a prolonged feast of cruelty, the Chinese took great care not to injure their captive. They produced short cords, trussed him up like a turkey about to be roasted, and carried him off swinging from a pole between two sturdy porters.

A SUDDEN lull in the pandemonium presaged the coming of the storm in all its fury. What had preceded was but a preliminary gust announcing the tornado. It broke with terrific violence from all points of the compass at once. Unable longer to restrain their hatred of their ancient enemies, who had kept them bottled up for sixteen hours in the damp and dark, the Moslems hurled themselves upon their Chinese brothers. The Moslem who dies in battle fighting for his creed goes straight to the Moslem paradise.

The vast system of caverns became the black hell of milling humanity churning itself by sheer, brute weight to pulp. The enemies were too intimately engaging for firearms to count. The Chinese soldiers dropped their rifles or had them ripped from their hands. In the half light of the vast entrance hall, where men could distinguish ally from enemy, the killing at first proceeded with some discrimination. In the other caverns each gouged whatever came to his hand. The floors of black caves that no foot had trod for a generation grew slippery under the incessant patter of innumerable feet, and the steady splash of sullen water drowned the cries of faithful and infidel alike as they plunged by hundreds into the unseen subterranean rivers.

Through it all the marines stood with their backs to the eastern wall of the entrance, not firing a shot. It was not their fight. To attack would be wanton suicide. A concerted rush from that infuriated mob would sweep them like chaff into one of the black caverns behind them, or crush them to death against the rock walls between the black holes. Retreat to the crescent exit was impossible. The Chinese soldiers had blocked that possibility at the start.

Gradually the mere numbers of the Chinese soldiers in the audience hall began to count. The indiscriminate trampling set in a definite direction like a football scrimmage gaining—or losing—headway. The whole mass moved slowly away from the entrance toward the main caverns. As the soldiers gained ground those on the outskirts of the mob picked up rifles from the floor and took up their position in the rear. They knew what was coming. Shots zipped at random over the heads of the mass. These had the intended effect. Unarmed and exhausted, the Moslems broke, became a rabble, and fled yelling into the darkest caverns.

The audience hall now belonged to the Chinese soldiers and the marines in the ratio of about four to one. The disparity would have been much greater had not the main body of the soldiers been busy elsewhere. The insane fight still raged with unabated fury in the pitch darkness of the labyrinth. Under the orders of their officers the Chinese in the audience hall retired to a line about a hundred yards from the eastern wall. One hundred yards happened to be precisely that range at which they habitually made their best score in target practice. Their officers, of course, did not withdraw to the new line by mere chance.

"Steady," said the lieutenant. He felt that the marines' turn was next.

It was. As the red tongues leapt from the rifles of the Chinese the marines dropped as if shot to the floor. A spatter of bullets rained upon them from the wall behind. The rest whined harmlessly into the black holes.

"Rush them when I say, Go." The lieutenant gave the order as coolly as if they were enjoying a Fourth of July sham battle in a city stadium. "Are you ready?"

Before he could say "go" a volley from the entrance crashed into the cave. Against the brilliant sunlight of the crescent, Lane's twenty men looked like a regiment to the imaginative Chinese. They retreated another hundred yards. Then they stood their ground. Safety, in the shape of numerous black caverns within a minute's fast run behind them, gave them courage. They also were curious to learn the exact strength of the enemy. To their surprise they saw two figures detach themselves from the thin line across the entrance and walk boldly into the cave.

"Where's the missionary?" Lane shouted.

"Here, sir. Behind us."

"Send a man forward with him."

When the madman was brought up, Lane studied his face critically. "I suppose you are rather upset by all the shooting, but pull yourself together. Who is this man?" he asked, indicating the governor.

"Pontius Pilate," the missionary replied promptly.

"Snap out of it! This is the governor of Kansu. Tell him this for me. He is to order all of the Chinese over there to come forward, ten at a time, and surrender their arms. If he does not, I will shoot him, myself. Translate!"

To emphasize the threat Lane held his revolver pressed against the governor's back while the latter shouted the order for disarmament at his men. The Chinese hesitated.

"What did the governor say?" Lane demanded of the missionary.

Before the missionary could reply the high, piping voice of a Chinese officer was heard expostulating vociferously.

"Catch everything that man says," Lane ordered. "It may cost us all our lives if you don't."

The officer was objecting to the governor's order. Why should the Chinese lay down their arms? Just give them half a chance and they would clear the cave of every American in it in two minutes. The governor began to sweat. If his men mutinied now he was a dead man.

"Tell the governor," Lane ordered, "to explain to his men how strong our main army in Shen-si is. Tell him not to forget the five hundred bombing planes."

On this wholesome advice the governor became quite eloquent. His speech evidently impressed the soldiers. The first ten marched forward, deposited their arms at the governor's feet and retired. Soon a huge stack of rifles and another of cartridge belts and bayonets rose like hastily improvised earthworks before Lane and the governor. In half an hour the Chinese in the audience chamber were disarmed. Such is the creative power of a vivid imagination working on credulity. True fighters would have seen the marines in Hades before complying with such an order.

The Chinese were to enjoy a stronger taste of discipline. At an order from Lane the marines rounded up the mob and set them at fatigue duty. First the magazines of the rifles were emptied of their shells. Then, through the governor, fifty of the vanquished were ordered to carry all of the shells and cartridge belts, under an escort of marines, into the place of massacre and pitch the lot into the black well. This done, the rifles followed. The Chinese were then ordered to police the labyrinth and round up all the followers of the governor. At his command all were to come at once to the audience chamber and bring not only their own arms but also any they might stumble over in the dark.

This, of course, was a long job, and doubtless many stragglers, firearms and all, remained in the less accessible caverns. Nevertheless, the disarmament must have been at least ninety per cent efficient. It was to be still more thorough. Lane ordered the governor to explain to twenty of the superior officers exactly why the Chinese troops were being disarmed. He added that they were under no compulsion to obey orders but if they refused, the American army would annihilate them on the following day and, on the day after that, destroy every building in Kansu by systematic bombing from the air. If, on the other hand, they chose the part of common sense and obeyed, and if, further, they gave sufficient guarantees that they would leave the Moslems in peace, the United States Army would withdraw at once without a single reprisal for the slaughtered missionaries.

It worked beautifully. The last act in the mopping up took over two hours, but it paid. Under a guard of marines the governor and the twenty officers he had instructed were hustled back to Teng-shan. There, as fast as possible, they despatched small contingents of the soldiers still camped about the palace, with all the military supplies they could stagger under, to the caves. Unopened boxes of ammunition, machine guns and hundreds of new rifles were pitched into the well of the massacre.

By four o'clock in the afternoon the disarmament was practically completed. The governor stood near the entrance, inside the cave, watching the last contingent of Chinese toiling up the slope. These men brought nothing but half a dozen machine guns and forty or fifty wooden boxes of ammunition for the guns. Lane and his first lieutenant stood beside the governor. They were tired, Lane particularly. The job was about finished and it was well done. For sheer lack of ammunition and arms the anti-Moslem Chinese would be unable for at least a year to trouble their turbulent brothers.

Lane and the lieutenant were laughing and joking over the ease with which they had worked the bluff. Bit by bit—for the captain was a modest man—the lieutenant pried out of him the whole story of his bullying of the governor and the effective myth of a huge American army with five hundred bombing planes just beyond the pass into Shen-si. At the moment the rest of the Americans were far back, supervising the Chinese in the audience hall and in the gallery leading to the pit.

"Your imaginary army," the lieutenant laughed, "has done a quicker clean up than the whole U. S. A. and U. S. N. combined could have done. And we have only lost twelve men, including Mr. Saxby." These all occurred in the first rush, when the Chinese swept the guards off their feet.

"You will lose them all in the next hour," a thin, dry voice remarked directly over their heads.

They spun round and saw nothing but a smooth, enigmatic wall of limestone. Instantly the same voice harshened and lapsed into Chinese.

"Markoff!" Lane shouted, making a grab for the governor. But the governor had heard the first Chinese sentence in the air, and it was enough.

"The Americans were lying about the army and their bombing planes in Shen-si," said that airy Chinese voice.

Before the captain could stop him the governor was racing down the slope, yelling orders at his men with the machine guns. It was too late to shoot him. The machine gunners were already bursting the ammunition boxes with the heaviest stones they could lift.

"Shall I shoot?" the lieutenant yelled.

"No!" Lane shouted back as he ripped off his tunic. "If he's killed it means war with China. Get the men out before the Chinese start firing!"

The Chinese were already feeding the first strings of cartridges into the machine guns. Lane leapt back to the entrance and, with frantic haste, signalled with his tunic a short, desperate order to the pilot in the bombing plane. Were the two in the plane watching the entrance to the cave as he had ordered? And if they were, would they be able to take his message? The first machine gun rattled into action. Before the bullets sprayed the rock ten feet to the left of where he stood, Lane saw the smoke shoot from the exhaust of the plane as the huge insect sprang forward for the takeoff.

Lane leaped back into the cave, out of reach of the machine guns, just as all six began spitting as one. He had played his last card. It looked like the joker.

IX. MARKOFF'S THEFT

UNDER the Czars, Markoff most likely would have been a chief of secret police. He was that type—cold, cowardly, and sensually cruel. Under the Moscow communists he found his true trade. As a confidential agent to China he had opportunities for betrayals and wholesale murder on a scale denied him in Moscow. The natural genius of the Chinese for inhuman forms of punishment incited him to jealous competition. They, after all, were but amateurs; he rather conceitedly classed himself as the expert professional. If such men as the infamous Letchine and certain of the bloodier czars, generals and prelates of old Russia were not commonplace, amply documented historical personages, Markoff could be dismissed as an impossibility. The historian of a thousand years hence will look back on these men and, with a superior smile, deny that they ever existed. Their common disorder seems to have been a queer type of perversion, which after all is not so rare, even outside of Holy Russia. In the prolonged infliction of pain they experienced a voluptuous pleasure. If unable to enjoy both, they preferred massacre to love in any of its more usual forms, and one and all they were physical cowards of the lowest type. Incessant brooding upon what might happen to their own hides, and imaginative exaggerations of every trivial pain, drove them over the verge of insanity and lashed them to more violent excesses. Mad dogs are shot on sight; the Markoffs and the rest achieve eminence in statecraft of a sort.

While the Chinese were engaged in sweeping one another into the subterranean rivers, Markoff was in the singularly happy position of having everything he wanted. He had enjoyed one massacre and hoped shortly to witness another, and his love was within easy reach. He might take what he had coveted for months any time the girl came out of her silly faint.

White Lily, as a matter of fact, had not fainted. She was not that kind. The brain in her was better than Markoff's vapor of brutish instincts, and she knew how to use it. So long as she lay on the limestone floor like a dead rabbit, and as uninteresting, she knew she was safe. Her captor would not pester her till she came to life. In the meantime he was getting a great deal of pleasure out of old Saxby.

Should Saxby's impotent rage pall on the insatiable Markoff, White Lily might try a trick or two which Hu the Good had taught her. She could take care of herself—for a while, anyhow. Markoff and Saxby conversed in English, so White Lily missed the gist of their remarks. Nevertheless she guessed that the old American, who somehow reminded her of her grandfather, was in a great fright.

Saxby was indeed scared half out of his wits. You may succeed in temporizing with the executioner, or you may be able to argue the inquisitor out of giving the rack an extra twist, but you cannot reason with an ignorant fool. There is but one way to reach a brain like Markoff's, and that is with a bullet. Saxby had only his eloquence. It made not the slightest impression on the void of Markoff's intelligence.

The cave where Markoff "questioned" his prisoner was one of the two which the earliest Moslems had enlarged on either side of the crescent entrance. Originally these caves were mere pockets in the limestone wall of the entrance, reached by tortuous, narrow burrows from the audience hall. When the persecuted followers of the Prophet first began using the caves as a refuge in time of massacre, they cut a peephole in the wall of each pocket so that the invisible sentry might spy on all who sought to enter the caverns. The peepholes could be closed by little slabs of limestone which fitted perfectly. Later the pockets were enlarged to capacious, airy guard rooms and liberally provided with food, torches, water and sleeping accommodations. At the same time the astute Moslems blocked the ancient waterways which were the original means of communication with the hall, and scooped out of the soft limestone an elaborate maze of narrow tunnels connecting the guard rooms with the audience chamber. The guards, of course, never lost themselves in these mazes; it was hoped that the enemies might, or at least be heard by the guards in time to be knocked on the head.

As political and spiritual advisors to Hu the Good, Markoff and Liapanouff soon learned the shortest way to each of the guard rooms. In fact the two agents believed they knew all about the caves long before they ordered the jehad. Hu told them much; personal explorations told them more. They knew of one secret exit in case of extreme danger. Hu either forgot to mention the other to them, or kept it to himself as an old man's secret to be shared with no one but his pet. Neither Liapanouff nor Markoff was told of the secret way by which White Lily left the cave when Hu told her to go and seek out the governor of Shen-si. The snakelike Markoff might easily have crawled through it; the puffy Liapanouff was too gross. The other secret exit could readily have extruded Liapanouff, had not Hu the Good shown him a broader and quicker way out.

Either of the guard rooms by the crescent entrance offered Markoff the ideal cubbyhole from which to direct operations while the marines occupied the audience chamber. The instant the marines rushed the caves when the bombing plane routed the tail end of Chinese army, Markoff, already half way down the audience chamber, hastily collected a bodyguard of three superior Chinese officers and bolted with them for an inconspicuous black hole in the north wall of the chamber. Presently he and his panting escort found themselves in the comfortable guard room at the north side of the entrance. The peephole gave them a view of the entrance, of the long, rocky slope leading up to it from Teng-shan, and of at least a part of the interior of the audience chamber. Markoff followed with interest practically everything the marines did. He witnessed the arrest of old Saxby by Lane and speculated on its significance. Were the damned capitalists divided among themselves? Before he had solved this thorny puzzle to the satisfaction of his reptilian instincts, Markoff saw White Lily arrive breathless and with bleeding feet and, a few minutes later, he observed Saxby and the captain consulting over the girl, apparently on the best of terms. At this point of his observations Markoff moistened his thin lips with his bright red tongue. He determined to possess White Lily, then and there.

Markoff's desire begot the Chinese attack that came within an ace of sweeping all the marines off their feet. At his orders the three Chinese officers departed to round up enough of their men to launch an effective offensive. The flying wedge was Markoff's conception. White Lily was to be brought to him alive. The American in civilian clothes also was to be captured, if possible. His person in any event was to be bound and carried as intact as feasible to the guard room for Markoff's inspection. Markoff's theory was that the old civilian who had come by airplane must be a figure of some weight in the councils of capitalism. Probably his clothes were rich in documents which would expose the United States as the secret enemy, not only of liberty at large the world over, but of communism in particular. And not unlikely there would be found on this person detailed plans for the invasion of Mongolia, Russia and China. The lieutenant in command of the marines was ignored. Eventually he was to be slaughtered with the rest, of course, but he probably was of no importance. Markoff had seen Lane leave the caves and, in a general way he had guessed the captain's mission. Being a one hundred per cent coward himself, Markoff could not conceive of another man taking his life in his hands for a forlorn hope. Therefore, Markoff reasoned, the American forces in China must be strong and not far from Teng-shan. He would wait until the captain's return to decide upon his further strategy. In the meantime he could pass the hours profitably with the imagined ambassador and pleasantly with White Lily.

The flying wedge of Chinese under picked officers did its work well. White Lily, unfortunately in a dead faint, and the capitalist ambassador were delivered whole at his feet. Having borrowed a bayonet from a Chinese officer, Markoff dismissed all of his faithful followers, closed the peephole and proceeded to business.

White Lily gave no trouble. Her "faint" was so deep that she scarcely seemed to breathe. She knew how to play "possum" better than the animal itself. Saxby was a tougher problem. He must be made to talk without being given a chance to make himself heard by the sentries who might march past the closed peephole. When Saxby was flung down by the guards he let out a roar that might have been heard in Teng-shan, had not the Chinese in the audience hall been raising such a prodigious racket at the moment.

Markoff easily solved the problem. He ripped off half of Saxby's shirt and stuffed most of it into the captive's mouth. Old Saxby, of course, did not open his mouth wide at Markoff's invitation to accept the gag. The agent was compelled to force the prisoner's mouth open with the bayonet. Then, to teach his captive the folly of future resistance, he heated the tip of the bayonet red hot in the flame of a torch and proceeded to use it. Saxby was so tightly bound that his struggles quickly exhausted him. When Markoff got through with his discipline, Saxby could not have shouted if he had tried. Before removing the gag Markoff cautioned the prisoner that if he raised his voice above a whisper, the bayonet, then resting with its point on Saxby's throat, would instantly cut off his remarks before he could finish them.

Markoff's first question concerned the fighting strength of the "American force" which Lane, in his parley on the slope, had told him was on the march in Shen-si. Saxby's whispered denial that he knew human being will think of to do to another would pass the belief anything about it earned him a short repetition of the third degree. Seeing that his prisoner might lose his mind if pressed too far, Markoff, like the experienced inquisitor he was, desisted. Saxby by this time was pretty much of a wreck. The things that one civilized of almost any undomesticated beast. The beasts kill their prey or their enemies and let it go at that. Markoff, heir to a more cultivated taste, enjoyed himself. Nevertheless, he got precisely nothing out of old Saxby that might give him the slightest clue to the real strength of the Americans. Therefore, he must wait till the captain returned, when the subsequent proceedings would probably enlighten him.

HAVING exhausted his ingenuity to make the prisoner talk, Markoff turned to the easier problem of picking his victim's pockets. Saxby was now but half conscious. His condition was quite genuine, not feigned as was White Lily's. Markoff therefore thieved without a protest from the thievee. Like a gorged condor he flopped down on the limestone floor beside his prey and fished for tidbits.

Markoff was not avaricious. The gold watch did not even tempt him. Greed for material goods is not one of the communist vices. The loose change he also cast aside. A sheaf of receipted club bills and a steamer ticket first claimed his attention. The incriminating letter head "Army and Navy Club, Shanghai," told the excited agent a great deal that was not so. The date of the steamer ticket also filled him to the gullet with fat, plausible lies. Finally, a typewritten circular letter announcing the date of the next meeting of the National Scientific Council in Washington, D. C., with Saxby's name typed in the proper place, completed the evidence. Saxby stood, or rather lay, convicted of being an important personal agent of the President of the United States. He had been sent to Shanghai with secret orders to capitalist generals at the Army and Navy Club, Shanghai, and possibly also to the large army of the international bankers in Shen-si. Such was the astute agent's reasonable but somewhat puerile deduction.

Here Markoff began to sweat. If the American forces from Shen-si arrived in Kansu before he escaped from the caves, he would be court-martialed and shot for having "questioned" Saxby. If, on the other hand, he destroyed the evidence against himself, he would be accused of having murdered the American. Then he would be shot, probably without a courtmartial.

Suddenly he saw a happy way out. The moment the marines left the caves—they would probably evacuate when their main force came up—he would induce the Chinese officers to take the roped prisoner and send him to join Hu. The officers, disliking the capitalist Americans as much as he, would gladly do their part and enjoy the joke. While they were laughing at their pleasantry, Markoff himself could slip out of the cave by the secret exit known to him, and leave the Chinese to settle for his little joke. Once safely on the mountainside, miles from Teng-shan, he felt that he could easily escape and make his way back to Moscow to report. What a report that would be. Flushed with proud anticipations of his chief's praise, Markoff resumed his systematic thievery with zest.

Rolling the still unconscious victim over on his side, Markoff brought the unexplored coat pocket into view. With a sibilant exclamation like a snake's hiss, he pounced upon the bulging pocket and clawed out a fat, untidy notebook blotched all over with virulent looking green stains. The evil color had soaked into the pages in half circles and long, fingering streaks, as if someone had spilled a full bottle of green ink on the half-opened book. Nearly every page had its green blob; some were completely dyed.

As he fluttered the leaves of Yang's notebook, pausing at every other page in a hopeless endeavor to understand the apparently meaningless jumbles of numerals and chemical equations, Markoff almost regretted that he was an ignorant enthusiast with but a vestigial brain. But he actually was incapable of such regret. He lacked the necessary nerve connections to beget such an emotion. He merely fluttered the leaves like an illiterate idiot. All these letters and figures must mean something, the more so as they had come out of the prisoner's pocket. But what? That was the painful question. Markoff almost laughed as the ready means of solving his puzzle presented itself. Seizing a dish of water he dashed the contents into the prisoner's face.

Saxby did not come out of his stupor at once. When at last he groaned and opened his eyes, the first thing he saw was Yang's notebook in Markoff's right hand. Instantly he forgot his pain in alarm at what the ignorant vulture before him might do with that green curse.

"Put that back in my pocket!" he shouted.

Markoff reminded him that he must not raise his voice. Saxby continued in a lower voice.

"You utter fool! Put it back where you got it, I say! You don't know what you are doing. Put it back!"

Markoff, convinced now that he had captured the enemy's most important military document, ignored the insult.

"This is important?" he taunted, fluttering the pages in Saxby's face.

The barrage of curses and abuse which he drew in reply but strengthened his superstition. He became crafty and coldly cruel. With a smile he picked up the bayonet.

"You read this for me."

He indicated a green page of chemical formulas and simple mathematical calculations. To his surprise Saxby capitulated at once. The string of names which the prisoner reeled off, of course, made no impression on Markoff's vacuum.

"You are lying," he said.

"I read you exactly what is written there. Don't you recognize a few elementary chemical names when you hear them? They can't be so very different in your own language."

"Chemistry?" Markoff snapped like a rattlesnake. He knew about explosives and poison gases, and he knew also that chemistry was at the bottom of them. That much he had gathered from the military experts during the endless round-table discussions at headquarters in Moscow. "These are military documents?"

"No. Purely scientific. No military value whatever."

"You must think I am a child," Markoff sneered. "If I cannot see the military value of this I know men in Moscow who can. As soon as your men leave this cave I am going out by another way. And I shall go straight back to Moscow. With this."

"You damned fool! You'll never get half way. That book is more dangerous than all the explosives and poison gases of all the armies of the world. Put it back in my pocket before you drop it. Look out—!"

Saxby's frenzied shout was brought out by Markoff's blundering with the book. Trying to handle the bayonet and turn the pages at the same time he had almost dropped the green abomination on the floor.

"Be quiet!" he snarled, as he slipped the book into his pocket.

Saxby closed his eyes and groaned.

"You unutterable fool. You will never know what you have done. If I told you it would do no good. You have no mind. But for your own sake, if not for the sake of the world, take that thing a thousand miles out to sea and drop it overboard if you *must* steal it. Never put it down anywhere. Leave it in your pocket. Don't touch anything with your hands after handling that book. Treat it like the plague—"

"A new poison?" the dull-witted agent queried. He was too stupid to keep his hand out of the pocket into which he had stuffed the book.

"Oh, what's the use?" Saxby groaned. "What good is it to tell you that it is probably more dangerous than a thousand Asiatic plagues? You are rotten with it already."

Markoff smiled a silly, cruel smile.

"And after I return from Moscow," he scoffed, "the United States of America will be rotten with it, too. One of the generals was talking of something like this a year ago. Diseases; they shall be our new weapons. You capitalists were coming over here, through China, to try them on us. Now I understand you. I see why the Army and Navy Club in Shanghai sent you in an airplane. You need no soldiers to invade our country. One page of this book in a lake or river that waters our people, and you have conquered them."

Markoff became almost lyrical over the imagined possibilities. In spite of himself he began to prophesy and to take a lascivious pleasure in the slaughters he predicted. Here was something that spoke directly to his cruelty, and it found him eloquent.

"But the capitalists," he concluded, "not we, shall die by millions."

"I grant you the first," Saxby flung at him. "As to the second, I doubt it. You yourself may be the first to go."

"I think not," Markoff smiled. "You shall precede me, but by another way. As I told you, I am going to Moscow. But, before I leave, you will join Hu the Good."

With brutal brevity he described to Saxby the end of Hu the Good as he had witnessed it in his futile attempt to save Liapanouff.

"You will join him," he repeated.

For some moments Saxby made no reply. His burns and the weals from the cutting ropes were about as much as any sane man could endure and keep his sanity. His excitement over, pain gained the upper hand and took a grip on his usually clear mind. His reply was not that which he would have made in his senses. Nevertheless, it may be recorded for what it may be worth.

"After seeing you," he said, "and after thinking in cold blood of what has happened in these caves, I believe it will be better for the world if nature does take the other course. You, after all, may be the greatest benefactor the human race has ever known."

"I know it," Markoff agreed, visualizing in his sublime ignorance a conquest of the world by red disease in the hands of his present friends, and later, in the happy future, their own extinction by civil strife of a similar kind. "And do not forget," he reminded Saxby, who showed signs of relapsing into unconsciousness again, "that you follow Hu."

White Lily stirred, all but imperceptibly. She had heard her grandfather's name mentioned several times by Markoff, and she could no longer control herself. Her muscles betrayed her. The slight movement did not escape Markoff's keen, reptilian eye. Instantly he was at her side, bending over her, gabbling in Chinese. The one word that she had understood so far was her grandfather's name. Now she could no longer feign unconsciousness. She knew that Markoff was aware of her deception. And less bearable than the thought of what probably would happen to herself was the agony to learn what had happened to her grandfather. Springing to her feet she confronted her tormentor.

"What have you done with him?" she cried.

Saxby swore, cursing himself for his inability to understand Chinese. The girl's distress spoke a universal tongue which any man could comprehend, and here he lay, powerless and dumb to shout her even a word of warning. For all he knew she might be swearing away her soul to the evil beast leering into her face.

Markoff found himself on the horns of a ticklish dilemma. To tell the truth might kill her on the spot and rob him of his lust. To refrain from torturing her would let slip an exquisite pleasure that could be had for the taking. A trick of memory cast the decision. He remembered her threat when he and Liapanouff had told her that the jehad was to be bloodless. And he remembered vividly the icy fear which had shot up his spine at the vagueness of that threat. So she was Hu's right hand, was she, to reward him for his share in the jehad? He jeered in her face. He would tell her where Hu's body was, and exactly how it got there. It would be the most tingling cruelty of his career.

She heard it to the end without a movement and without expression on her face. If any shred of her heart was still unbroken it broke then.

"I would have paid," she said, and turned blindly to make her way back to the audience chamber.

Markoff's talon of a hand detained her.

"Not yet," he murmured ingratiatingly. "You are too beautiful in your sorrow." He remembered the remark from a Russian drama.

Although he understood none of the words, Saxby read Markoff's intentions easily enough. To distract Markoff's attention, he began shouting. Instantly Markoff was upon him. But he had not relinquished his grip on White Lily's arm. The listless girl, already dead in spirit, was dragged after her possessor. With his free hand Markoff stuffed the gag back into Saxby's mouth. Now he was free to do what he pleased. Before doing it, however, he decided to take a look through the peephole and see how things were going with the Americans.

He removed the small slab of limestone just in time to see the Chinese, in the cleared cave, line up for their hundred yard shot at the marines. This was too good to be missed. Keeping a firm grip on his prey he abandoned himself to ecstasy. When the marines dropped to the floor in the volley he mistakenly imagined they had been shot to a man. His disappointment at seeing them rise to a crouching position lasted but a moment. He guessed that they would rush the enemy. Then there would be sport worth seeing. He licked his lips, and all but bit his tongue in two when Lane's men stepped into his field of vision and delivered their salvo that saved the minute—if not the day—for their side.

Fascinated between alternate hope for a sudden massacre and fear that the American army had arrived and was deployed on the mountainside beyond his field of vision, he stood for hours watching every incomprehensible detail of the disarmament. When White Lily struggled to get free he put a hand over her mouth and whispered that if she did not keep quiet he would kill her—horribly. He knew how.

As the day wore on and the machine guns began to follow the rifles into the pit he became almost insane with fear. The Americans must have captured the whole province. They would shoot him—or would they hang him? He couldn't live to go through that. Rather than stake his lean neck against the one chance in millions of escape he would be his own executioner. His free hand stole to his vest pocket and his numbed fingers fumbled for the slippery capsule. Then, like voices in a dream, he heard two men talking directly below him on the other side of the limestone wall. Their every word floated up to the peephole. They might have been addressing their remarks to him. Knowing that he was saved he bided his time, waiting for the strategic moment. The fewer armed Chinese abroad after the grand finale the safer his own skin. He waited till the last possible moment. Then he spoke.

Leaving the peephole he sat down by Saxby to rest. He would defer pleasure till all business was out of the way. The Chinese were already attending to that.

X. PAID

MARKOFF sat and waited, smiling at the rattle of machine guns and the crack of rifles which penetrated the thin limestone partition between the entrance and the guard room. He dared not enjoy himself at the peephole for fear of getting a wild bullet in the eye. In fact he began to perspire freely at the thought of some more energetic slug piercing the barrier of his ambush. He of course knew nothing of Lane's signal to the bombing plane. It had not even occurred to him that the plane might carry bombs. In his superstitious questioning of Saxby, he had overlooked the only practical details.

In signaling his order to the pilot Lane knew exactly what he was doing and how desperate was the chance he took. Intuition told him that where Markoff was there also would be found Saxby and White Lily. It was to be a case of kill or cure. There was no alternative.

Remembering the captain's instructions the pilot made all the noise mechanically possible. With a deafening racket he soared up the slope, flying at about twenty feet from the ground, and shot roaring directly toward the knot of machine gunners. They were on the shortest line to his objective anyway, so he took them in.

Screaming with terror the Chinese gunners bolted. One died on the spot from an overworked heart. The plane shot on; the gunners were not its meat.

The terrific roar of the plane's approach became plainly audible in the guard room. Recognizing that muffled drone as the angry voice of her dream on the mountainside, White Lily, in an access of superhuman strength, wrenched herself from Markoff's grasp and fled down the black tunnel toward the audience chamber. The instinct for self-preservation snatched her away; her lacerated feet were insensible to pain. Stunned by the rapidly increasing roar, Markoff got to his hands and knees. Slavering with fear like a mad dog he started to crawl toward the tunnel. His elbows turned to water and he collapsed like a snake with a broken back. He dreaded nothing definite, yet he believed that his end was upon him. Saxby feared nothing at all, for he had not the slightest anticipation of what was about to happen.

It happened all at once. A thundering impact on the roof directly over Markoff's head was swallowed instantly in the overwhelming rumble of an avalanche of shattered stone. Half a mountainside, jarred from its equilibrium by the simultaneous explosion of four huge T.N.T. bombs, roared down the slope, burying the crescent entrance and leaving the guard rooms open to the evening sky. Tons of splintered rock crashed to the floor and flying fragments whizzed past the heads of the two men. They escaped with only a few cuts and bruises.

Like many a costly shell explosion in the trenches the net profit was an overpowering racket that quickly died and the utter destruction of a work that had taken years, or centuries, or ages to perfect. The ruin of the crescent entrance was total; that of the guard rooms, now gaping like a couple of hollow teeth at the arch of the sky, followed as a mere corollary. Markoff lay paralyzed with fear, unable to move a muscle, gibbering like an idiot. Saxby, bound and powerless, held his tongue and wondered in his daze what it was all about.

By a natural enough combination of blunders, the shot achieved at least half a success. Lane's signal to the pilot read "Drop bombs north entrance"—meaning to drop the bombs one at a time on the slope directly over the mouth of the entrance. But, exposed as he was to the fire of the Chinese machine gunners, Lane had no time to signal more explicit orders. He intended that the pilot should drop one bomb as directed and, if lucky, shatter only the outer wall and part of the roof of the cave in which Markoff was hiding. Then, if luck still favored him, and the first bomb merely opened the cave without blowing it to bits, the pilot was to observe his hit. Lane gave him credit for that much foresight before releasing the second bomb. If the pilot saw his late passenger, Saxby, in the cave, he of course would not drop the second bomb. Saxby, according to Lane's lightning-calculated theory was to scramble out of the opened cave and be picked up somewhere by the pilot.

Unfortunately the pilot was a well-trained young man from the Navy, accustomed by tough years of rigid discipline to obeying orders on the jump and to the letter. When Lane signaled for bombs the pilot naturally assumed that he meant *bombs,* not *a* bomb. Hence he dumped the lot all at once. No one was to blame; Lane had no time to explain, the pilot no license to argue an order. The men in the plane assumed that Lane had heard of a safe back door to the caves and was signaling for them to block the front against the Chinese and their murderous machine guns. They hopped to their supposed job with a will and executed it to the President's taste.

It was thorough. The whole Chinese army would need two weeks to clear away the rubbish and force an entrance. Long before the Chinese could enter, the marines would have given their enemies in the cave the slip and be well on their way back to Shanghai. Such was the not unreasonable theory of the pilot. What Lane anticipated in case the first bomb exploded in the guard room, or merely stove in the roof, need not be dwelt upon here. He believed that Saxby would prefer such a fate to being left alive and sensitive to the mercy of Markoff.

As the plane roared back to pursue the Chinese into Teng-shan before resting to await further orders, Saxby came out of his daze. From where he lay he could see Markoff still helpless with fear. In the evening light the interior of the shattered guard room shone with a blinding brilliance after the comparative murk of the torchlight. The black entrance to the tunnel leading to the audience chamber gaped unblocked. If only he could get free of the ropes cutting his very bones he might escape before Markoff recovered control of his muscles.

Like a torpid snake thawing out on a rock in the April sunshine, Markoff began to writhe. His bony skull rolled over horribly and his glassy eyes fixed upon the bayonet. To his crazy vacuum it was now proved conclusively that the five hundred bombing planes in Shen-si were not a capitalistic myth. He had questioned, not to say tortured and robbed, the high ambassador of the United States. Therefore, if the victim escaped, he, the inquisitor, would hang. There was yet time to dispose of the evidence. He need not kill the prisoner in the guard room; he could drag him into one of the black passages and do the job there. Then he could swear to the

American officers that he had seen Saxby, crazed by fear, running from the Chinese directly into one of the corridors leading to the subterranean rivers. If only he could summon the strength to his watery muscles he might yet save his neck. But his strength ebbed as he crawled.

His fingers at last touched the handle of the bayonet. The cold contact of the murderous steel was like an electric shock to his flabby flesh. An icy current of determination flowed into his cold soul and the old lust for cruelty filled him with a new strength. He felt that he would not hang.

SUDDENLY, like a snake about to strike, he raised his bony skull and stared with maniac eyes at the wall behind him. He had heard hesitant feet feeling their way down the darkness of the tunnel. Relinquishing his grasp upon the bayonet he involuntarily clutched at his throat. Crazed beyond all memory or reason by his fear he forgot the capsule in his pocket that might save the hangman his trouble. His one instinct was the hunted animal's to seek safety in concealment. A superhuman terror put strength into his muscles and he dragged himself behind a huge fragment of the shattered roof.

Saxby recognized those footsteps, although they halted, lame with pain. A white face appeared in the darkness of the tunnel and ceased to advance. He nodded his head vigorously. Swiftly, and as noiselessly as she could, White Lily slipped into the shattered guard room and looked fearfully about her. Behind his rock Markoff was invisible. Saxby's eyes, fixed upon the bayonet, and his compressed lips were more eloquent than speech. As quietly as possible she picked up the bayonet and cut the cords. Saxby was free, but he could not move. Seeing his plight, she laid the bayonet on the floor, grasped the helpless man under the arms, and began dragging him toward the tunnel.

The noise of Saxby's body being dragged over the loose fragments acted like a douche of cold water on Markoff's cowardice. Peering round the corner of his rock he saw in a glance what was happening. Its implications for him, if successful, were obvious. And it had just struck him for the first time that White Lily could tell the American interpreter all the details of the "questioning" in the guard room. Automatically he was on his feet. His star was still high; this girl's stupid humanity had delivered her into his hand. With her and the American "ambassador" eliminated he could defy any court-martial in China. He tottered toward the bayonet.

Saxby saw his intention. Unable to stand, much less to walk or fight, he could only raise his arm and point to the bayonet. White Lily saw. In a flash she had snatched the steel. By a strange coincidence she flung at Markoff almost the identical words which Hu had addressed to Liapanouff.

"You are neither a man nor a beast. If I kill you it is not a killing."

She sprang after him like a tigress. With a strangled cry Markoff blundered into the tunnel. She followed him in a flash, as silent as a stroke of lightning. The horror of an imminent death by sharp steel, now infinitely greater than the fear of being hanged, put wings to Markoff's feet as he fled through the pitch black labyrinth.

Instinct saved him. Hearing his pursuer pass the end of his corridor he stopped dead. She raced on. Presently he heard her stop. She had lost him.

She did not search long. It may have been solicitude for the old American who reminded her of Hu, or it may have been the memory of her grandfather's command that the killing cease, that quelled her fury. It quickly died. Cold and shaken, she hurried back to the guard room.

Saxby was recovering. As the blood began to circulate through his stiffened muscles he put forth all his strength and will-power. He walked, although the effort cost him excruciating torture. When White Lily entered, he glanced involuntarily at her hands. She still grasped the bayonet. It was clean.

"Thank God!" he exclaimed. "I would rather have had my throat cut than let you do that, no matter what he has done. Your kind isn't made every day. I wish I knew Chinese—or even your name."

He took the bayonet from her hand and hobbled after her. This time he made no mistake. They did not venture unarmed into the black maze. If they passed Markoff's hiding place on their way to the audience chamber he gave no sign. Even a stupid girl and a stupider capitalist, he imagined, would learn from one such lesson as he had given them. As for himself his only safety lay in keeping strictly out of sight until the Americans left.

On emerging into the audience chamber they found it deserted by the Chinese. One and all, forgetful for the moment of their bitter feuds, had sought safety in the farthest recesses of the caverns. The terrific concussion of the exploding bombs, and the immediately following thunder of the avalanche of stone, were to them the beginning of the end of all things. The big joss of the Christian converts after all was more than a myth, and he had come, as prophesied, in wrath to judge the world and personally damn all unbelievers. Had not the gray-bearded missionary been too stunned by the concussion himself to grasp his unique opportunity, he might have followed the fleeing Chinese—Moslems, Confucians and miscellaneous infidels—into their distant caverns and converted them en masse. But he hovered like a gray ghost on the flank of the marines oblivious of time and of eternity. Of all that startled knot of men he was the one who kept his serenity. The poor fellow was too badly deranged to realize that his companions considered themselves broken beyond all possibility of patching. As they inspected the blocked exit by the dull flare of their smoky torches they said nothing. Words seemed superfluous.

Lane drew his first lieutenant aside.

"We seem to be bottled up. Unless there is another way out we may as well call it quits. It won't be long before the Chinese get over their scare and boil out on us. I am going to send you with a squad to explore for an escape."

"That Chinese girl probably knows of another exit if there is one," the lieutenant suggested.

"Yes, but where is she?"

"Probably where Saxby is. I shall try to find a way into that cave by the entrance first."

"Small chance. Saxby, Markoff and the girl are probably buried under a ton of rocks. Well, it was my only chance. I'd take it again under the same conditions. Saxby and the girl are probably better off dead. As for Markoff, I can't say."

Saxby spied the marines in the far distance by their moving torches. Just as the lieutenant was about to gather his men for the search, Saxby let out a shout.

"Captain Lane! Where's our interpreter? The Chinese girl is here."

Lane met them half way with the missionary.

"Never mind how we escaped," Saxby began. "That was a brilliant idea of yours—if it was yours—about bombing a way out. Now, I don't want to be officious and seem to be giving orders. But we must get out of this cave at once."

"Check," Lane agreed grimly. "Know a way?"

"Ask the girl here. She's on our side. She just saved my life from that Russian agent. He's alive somewhere behind us."

THROUGH the missionary, Lane put his question to White Lily. She told him at once of the two secret exits, one easily traveled by any man of only ordinary size, the other impossible to any but the slightest and most agile. There was little danger of a check from any of the Chinese then hiding in the inner caverns, as the entrances to these secret tunnels were well hidden and not likely to be stumbled upon by accident. At Lane's request she guided the marines to the easier way out. He decided that it was time to retreat, and that without delay.

As the men lined up to pass one at a time into the well concealed, small black hole, White Lily held a torch high and estimated each candidate for escape. Presently she began pulling one man after another out of the line. Lane made a gesture of protest. Saxby, standing beside him, caught his arm.

"Let her alone. She knows what she is doing. Look at that last man she jerked out. He weighs two hundred at least. The slim fellows will make it, the others may not. She's not taking any chance of blocking the tunnel at the very beginning."

When the last and fattest marine had been passed in Lane turned to the missionary.

"You're next," he said. "You refused to take your proper turn. Now you get what's left. In with you."

A fanatical gleam flickered over the madman's eyes.

"I denied my master twice. Shall I deny him thrice?"

"You can do as you please about that." Lane seized the man by the collar of his coat and the seat of his trousers. "I may need you to talk for us. After that you are your own boss. Saxby, you're next."

Saxby obeyed without comment. He might have gone earlier as far as bulk was concerned. Lane granted him his request to be one of the last as Saxby feared he might hold up the line. His burns and his general stiffness made each step a torture. There remained only White Lily. The captain motioned for her to precede him. She shook her head.

"Interpreter!" he shouted into the tunnel. "Saxby, send that missionary back."

Saxby himself had to back out in order to accommodate the interpreter.

"Tell her," Lane ordered, "that I shan't force her to come against her will, but that I think she will be safer with us than by herself. For all we know some of the enemy—or of her own people—may have found their way into the narrower tunnel."

The missionary reported that White Lily declined their protection.

"Then tell her to hurry as fast as she can to the other secret exit. I will detail a patrol to look out for her on the mountain as soon as I get out myself."

White Lily's translated reply was illuminating.

"I will stay here with my people and with those who hate them. Hu the Good said there must be no more killing. Unless these people are shown the way out they will starve, and that is slow killing. Without me they would never find this way."

Lane saluted.

"Tell her," he said, "that I respect her wish, and regret that my duty to my men prevents me from staying to help."

"I'll stay," Saxby announced quietly. "My damned feet hurt so that I can only hobble, anyway. "Lend me your revolver. Markoff is still abroad somewhere."

"But," Lane expostulated, "if any of the governor's soldiers catch sight of you they'll murder you. The girl is Chinese. She probably will know how to handle her own race much better than you or I would. If they turn on her she can bolt for the other secret tunnel and escape. I don't see what good you will be. However, I shall let you stay if the girl wants you. This is not a military matter, although technically I could order you to come with us. Put it up to her."

Saxby insisted that the missionary emphasize to White Lily her possible danger from Markoff. With an armed man accompanying her on the search of the distant caverns she would be safe until her own people assembled in sufficient numbers to protect her. Saxby avoided transmitting his private dread that her own people, blaming her and Hu for their present plight, might turn against her.

To Saxby's offer White Lily replied with evident distress. She would have none of it. She would be quite safe. There was no danger in what she proposed, either from Markoff or from her own people. In their gratitude at escaping they would protect her, and she would be safe in the caverns, which she knew far better than Markoff did. Her last request to Saxby was personal.

"Go," she said, "with your friends. When I see you I see an image of my grandfather, and I would not have him here."

She was inexorable. With a sigh Saxby turned to precede Lane into the tunnel. White Lily had earned her right to do as she thought best; it was not for him or any other man to disregard her wishes.

"Ask her what her name is," Saxby directed.

The missionary gave the Chinese.

"What does it mean in English—if anything?" Saxby asked. "I might forget the Chinese."

"White Lily."

Assured that the friend who reminded her of Hu was safely on his way—provided he and the others in front of him could squeeze through the narrow places—White Lily kindled a fresh torch from the old and left the spot, as she thought, forever. The little that must be done before she might seek and find her heart's desire would not take long. Holding the torch like a beacon light above her head she walked rapidly from cave to vaster cave in search of her people. Only the quick patter of her footfalls broke the black silence and died in the vastness without an echo. Indifferent to everything but the peace that before long would be hers, she felt no pain from her lacerated feet, and even the dull ache of her heart was swallowed up in a timeless void where there is neither joy nor sorrow.

She had never believed in the paradise of her grandfather; it was an old man's dream, a fable of his second childhood, to be tolerated but not mocked. The object of her secret contemplation was more serene than any paradise of the prophet's, and soon it would be hers as it was his even now. That he had grasped the only good thing in the very act of reaching for what he imagined was a better, was the kindest fate she could have wished him. The thing he thought he desired could never have satisfied him. Although he would never know it, he was happier than he had ever dreamed he should be. He had attained the supreme good blindly; she knew what she desired, and she would seek it with understanding.

Reaching the deepest cavern she stopped and sang her message into the darkness.

"THE crescent entrance is choked with stones. You cannot pass out that way for many weeks. Send me ten of the men you trust and I will show them a secret way out of these caves. They shall be your guides. All, the people of Hu the Good and the soldiers of the governor of Kansu, must pass out in peace. There must be no more killing. This is the command of Hu the Good to his people. He took your guilt upon himself and paid with his life. Send me ten men or you starve. You see my torch, and I feel you in the dark places about this cave."

For perhaps a minute no sound answered. Then a shrill voice screamed through the darkness.

"Is this another trap? You and your grandfather betrayed us to the governor. Why should we believe you?"

"To save your own lives."

"We are safer here, and here we stay."

"As you will. I care no longer what you do, for I heard a voice on the mountain prophesying the end of all your strife. I brought you the word of Hu the Good because I promised him that I would. Does it matter if you are as deaf as he is? Your hunger will not last long. Then you will forget and be forgotten. Does any man come with me?"

"No!"

The angry shout from a thousand throats hoarse with hatred reverberated through the vast cavern and died without an echo.

They disowned her, and would have torn her to pieces had not their fear that she was a decoy sent by the governor held them in leash.

She retraced her steps to the audience chamber. There she kindled a fresh torch, picked up a bundle of the larger ones, and hurried into the void of a vaster cave on the further side of the hall. Having promised Hu that she would avert bloodshed if possible, she kept her word to him, although she believed that he would never know she had. Yet, although he had ceased to exist, she felt his presence in those dark caves. Not till she had carried his message of mercy to the deepest of them would the memory of him be appeased.

In some of the caves she heard the stealthy stirring of men all about her beyond the narrow circle of the torchlight, but none answered her summons. Either they disbelieved her like the men in the first cave, or they were too dull-witted to forsee their inevitable end. The plentiful stores of food in the dry caverns were more eloquent than the thin whisper of a distant hunger. If what she said was true they could dig a way out before they starved. The immediate risk of a second betrayal paralyzed their imaginations and they reasoned with their bellies. In two of the smaller caves the response was similar to that in the first, but angrier.

At length, shortly after midnight, her fruitless labor came to an end. She was free now to do what she longed to do. In her joy at the serene knowledge of freedom from all obligations to the dead or the living she quickened her weary steps back to the audience chamber. Physical exhaustion all but overcame her, but her will conquered the desire to sink down on the smooth rock and sleep.

As she entered the audience chamber she broke into a run. The far eastern wall and the long corridor where ten thousand had trodden the way she was to take echoed to her coming. She heard the patter of her own feet multiplied in her ears, and it was music. Then, as from a world already forgotten in the headlong plunge to oblivion, she heard other feet racing to intercept her.

A tense, lustful face, red in the glow of the smoking torch, peered into her own. Instinctively she swung the torch at that mask of hatred and desire which froze the blood in her veins. She missed. The torch shot from her hand and the glowing coal of its tip bounded through the darkness, to expire in a constellation of crimson sparks. She felt her persecutor's claw of a hand upon her shoulder and his cold breath like a blast of death upon her cheek. Frenzied with loathing she wrenched herself free. He was between her and her heart's desire; to escape him she could only flee into the universal darkness.

But half conscious of where she was going she raced toward what she guessed was the cavern leading to the narrower secret exit. The very unconsciousness of her actions aided her. Where deliberate thought would have confused her, the lifelong habits of her unfeeling muscles took control automatically and urged her body unerringly toward its nearest safety.

Markoff did not make the mistake of immediate pursuit. He had watched and waited too long and too patiently for his opportunity to risk it in a confusion of blundering chases in the dark. Until certain of the way she was taking he could listen as coldly and as motionlessly as a dead snake. The inevitable change in the timbre of her footfalls would tell him when she entered a corridor, and the focussed sound of her flight would guide him unerringly to his prey. Every nerve of his lean body listened, as the sounds dwindled steadily in the distance, straining to detect the slight change in quality as she passed under an invisible archway. Presently he caught the change. Turning his head slowly from side to side he fixed the direction of the sound. His muscles stiffened and he leaped into pursuit.

He had watched her every movement in the audience chamber, from the moment she led the marines out of it till the instant she reappeared after her last fruitless mission to the hiding places of the Moslems. During her long absences he speculated on her mission, imagining that she was gathering her people for an assault upon the shattered exit, or to lead them to freedom by the tunnel she had shown the Americans. To attack her while still uncertain of her friends' whereabouts would be foolhardy. Her cries might well be his death warrant. Only when she was almost to the eastern wall did Markoff feel safe in accosting her. Only the forbidden caves lay that way; she could not possibly summon help from them. The ambushes of her people all lay far underground and a mile or more to her rear. Her attempt to kill him with the bayonet had inflamed his passion to the point of insanity. Love and cruelty are indistinguishable to men of Markoff's kind, and passionate hatred is their equivalent for ungovernable desire. He would possess her now in his own way.

Creeping after her into a low corridor he heard her groping along its wall. Evidently she was feeling for some entrance she knew well. The sounds ceased. Stealing forward a step at a time Markoff felt every foot of the cold hall till he touched a void. Like a rattlesnake he squeezed silently into the narrow tunnel after her.

Before long she knew that she was followed. While she still had strength to crawl she would not fall into his hands. The roof of the cramping tunnel sloped rapidly down toward the floor. Progress was possible only on hands and knees. She heard him gaining. He was was filled with an insane endurance; she, all but exhausted.

The limestone slope became as slippery as iced glass where the tunnel passed under the bed of a subterranean stream and the water dripped incessantly from the roof. Markoff slipped in the slime, cursed, and lost twenty yards. Mad with rage at his mishap he wallowed in the slimy muck till his clothing and the green notebook in his coat pocket were soaked in the ice-cold limewater. Bracing his elbows against the walls of the tunnel he dragged himself up an inch at a time like a wounded snake trying to crawl out of a gopher hole.

White Lily was now fifty yards ahead. If her strength lasted another hour she would beat him to the exit. Then she might find her friends—they had offered to wait and look for her before she refused to escape as she was now escaping. Surely they would be within hail on the mountainside, and they could destroy or hold her tormentor till she escaped forever. Her senses clouded and she struggled through the last terrible hour in an agonized dream, too exhausted to know whether Markoff still followed or whether he had suffocated in the slime.

Her dream was more vivid than any reality. With an awful immediacy she knew that it was not a dream but the shadow of a living horror that brooded on her mind. Powerless to shake off her nameless fear, even when the tunnel permitted her to straighten up and run, she resigned herself to its clutch and wondered if she must be conscious of it forever. Did Hu suffer now as she was suffering? Were the converts right? Was this the eternity they had prophesied for her and her grandfather? She stumbled up the last steep slope, crouched to pass under the shelving roof, and dragged herself up to a moonlit desolution of shattered quartz. Instantly her mind cleared in the untainted air and she knew that the damnation prophesied by the converts was a lie. Her rest would be deep and dreamless.

Until her friends found her she must stay in the vicinity of that black hole in the quartz to see what issued. She would not venture to return to the audience chamber by the broader secret way until she knew beyond all doubt that the narrower had voided its snake. For all she knew Markoff might have crawled back to the caves. If at dawn he had failed to emerge she would hasten to the other exit and ask two of her friends to see her safely back into the audience chamber.

She climbed a jagged pinnacle of quartz, found a ledge where she might rest, and scanned the moonlit mountainside for traces of her friends. Half a mile away a more massive outcrop of quartz had burst through the limestone. The tunnel she had shown Lane ended there, beneath a great rock in a small cave no larger than a panther's lair. This exit was well concealed beneath a loose jumble of huge blocks on the floor of a natural amphitheatre of quartz and limestone. It was in fact a replica on a grander scale of her own surroundings.

Half way down the moonlit slope of the farther outcrop she made out dark shadows that seemed to move. Were these her friends? Two black figures rose on the crest of the amphitheatre and dwindled down to the slope to join the others. From the build of the shorter she guessed it to be the old American who reminded her of Hu; the other might be the commander. They were safe. When Markoff emerged she could run across the intervening mountainside and soon be on her way in safety.

WHILE White Lily watched for him, Markoff labored ever more slowly up the last hundred yards toward the moonlight and the clean night air. He, too, was troubled by fitful dreams of an all but supernatural reality. In his career as a seeker of pleasure he had experimented with certain of the rarer oriental drugs, only to abandon them all after one or two trials. They intensified his morbid fear of death to such a pitch that he gladly let them alone. The dreams—if they were dreams—that tortured him now were a million times worse than the worst any drug had ever induced. He began to mutter in Russian that he must be very ill; that White Lily had poisoned the tunnel with some Chinese drug of unnatural potency, and that he would never again see the sunrise. He experienced no pain—otherwise he would have shrieked. Nevertheless he felt horribly diseased to be very marrow of his bones. The girl must have poisoned the tunnel. He could smell the stuff now. Until this moment he had not noticed the faint odor of decay that crawled with him like an aura. He stopped, panting. The smell had suddenly become a suffocating stench that made his reeling brain spin. Without the slightest premonitory twinge an infinite pain gripped every nerve of his being, and he fell instantly from the human state to a writhing thing that was neither human nor beast.

The inhuman shrieks that suddenly burst in appalling volume from the black hole in the rocks tattered the silence of the night to shreds. Half a mile away the sentries heard them and went as cold as ice. Even in battle they had never heard such sounds of agony. White Lily tumbled down the steep side of her lookout and, with her hands to her ears, fled across the slope to the Americans. No matter what the fiend had done he should not suffer like that. She must get one of the soldiers to shoot him.

Half way to her destination she met Lane and Saxby running to meet her. She could only point behind her. They raced on, hardly less fearful than she, while she fled with all her strength to outdistance those terrible sounds.

Stumbling down into the smaller amphitheatre they saw what looked like a man writhing its way out of the black hole. Freeing itself the welling thing flopped and bounded over the rocks with horrible contortions that bent its back double.

"Shoot him!" Saxby shouted.

Unnerved by those awful sounds of torment Lane fired six times and missed. Expert marksmanship and a cool head might have put an end to the agony of that thing bounding over the jagged quartz like a fish jerked from the water. Lane had neither. He tried to reload but dropped the shells. Suddenly the thing collapsed like a jellyfish. Its sounds of pain increased beyond all endurance. Before he could seize a stone, Saxby saw Markoff's right hand, limp as the flipper of a dead seal, fumbling at a vest pock. Evidently the man could still think. He still had memory, and he remembered the capsule in his pocket. The fumbling fingers crumpled and bent back double; the wrist curled up and the limp arm flowed down on the rocks, as an invisible decay progressed swiftly through the bone from finger tips to shoulder socket. The bony skull suddenly settled like a collapsing balloon; the sounds of agony ceased instantly; the whole sprawling body lost its rigidity and became a sagging bag of pulp.

Unable to move, the two men stood staring down at what had been a human being. Like a recurrent dream the next act of a tragedy older than the human race began slowly before their eyes. As if he were following a once familiar change that he had witnessed a thousand times only to forget, Saxby anticipated each event before it happened. The sequence was stark reality itself; although each individual act contradicted the accepted harmony of nature. These things, too, were natural, but in an order of nature more ancient by æons than the beginnings of evolution. Lane, knowing less than Saxby of what lay before them, felt more. It was his first experience with the older order. The foundering of the *Sheridan* was too abrupt to reveal its true significance to men battling for their lives in black waters. He felt more than Saxby now, because the changing substance of the dead man's body communicated directly with his own flesh and bone without the intermediary sophistication of thought.

The clothes of the dead man began to glisten in the moonlight as if stiff and brittle with hoar frost. Yet the night was sultry. A sleeve, rotted at the shoulder of the coat, crumbled and fell away. The frostiness of the rest thickened to a glittering fur of thousands of needlelike crystals. The rotten fabric collapsed under the increasing weight as the crystals grew, and fell with a tiny, fairy chime of tinkling glass to the quartz, exposing the shapeless arms and legs. A coat pocket collapsed. Yang's notebook, glittering with crystals; fell open, face down upon the quartz. On the bared flesh of the legs and arms, as delicately as an expert artist, an invisible worker rapidly etched the outlines of the skeleton as the completely dissolved substance of the bones sweated through the flesh. Simultaneously the flattened head became a bejewelled hemisphere of densely packed crystals that grew and multiplied visibly. Within twenty seconds the entire body was crusted over with a bristling pelt of glittering needles, whose steady growth filled the moonlit amphitheatre with a creeping, metallic rustle.

The rate of growth began doubling twice in every second. The air grew deathly cold and a slow breeze stirred among the rocks. Spears of splintering glass sprang from the quartz surrounding the body; the whole amphitheatre seemed to burst into crystalline life multiplying upon itself in explosive growth, and the rocks groaned and split asunder in travail to bring forth a new life.

"Out of it!" Saxby shouted, dragging the captain with him.

They fled for their lives back to the camp. Words were superfluous, even if they had had sufficient breath to utter them. Even Lane, who lacked Saxby's fuller knowledge, realized that Markoff, in discharging his debt to the world, had succeeded in passing his last bad check. Dead, he was infinitely more dangerous than he had ever been while living. In his crawl through the secret tunnel he had infected an entire mountain range with hellish life.

On reaching camp they were hailed by the missionary exulting like a madman.

"The Chinese girl has gone back to the accursed caves by the way we came out. She told me to tell you," he shouted at Saxby, "that she has gone to join her grandfather. 'Vengeance is mine, saith—' "

Saxby knocked him down.

XI. BURIED

For the two hours that remained till dawn the men were ordered to sleep—if they could.

"You may march far," Saxby grimly informed the sergeant, "when you do start. So make the best of what is left of this hellish night. Better obey the captain's orders. Mere noises will mean nothing unless I yell."

Saxby and Lane kept watch with the sentries, never once taking their eyes off the wall of the farther amphitheatre. They had been watching about an hour when they saw a gleaming pinnacle suddenly rear its glittering spire above the wall in the moonlight, only to totter almost instantly and disappear. Three seconds later they heard the crash of a million tons of shattering glass. The men leapt to their feet and snatched their rifles. They had not slept. That appalling sound of destruction seemed to last for centuries. Instead of diminishing it increased with an incredible crescendo till it seemed that the whole mountainside must be an avalanche of brittle crystals smashing to bits. Then, as abruptly as a thunderclap, the racket ceased absolutely.

"Well?" said the captain. "Had we better be going?"

Saxby shook his head.

"Better rest. Tell the men it's over for tonight. That's the end of the stuff we saw growing."

"How do you know?" Lane felt strangely cold.

"I started to tell you in the cave when that crazy missionary over there butted in with his prophecy of a jehad that had already taken place. How many thousand years ago was it? Do you remember? I don't. It never happened or, if it did, it was utterly unimportant compared with what may happen next. That was merely a squabble among a few thousand Chinamen about a triviality. If it ever mattered—which I doubt—I have a feeling that it will never matter again. We may be about to fight an enemy the human race has never faced. But I trust not. If that terrific conflict does materialize—as it may—we shall find it wise to forget our petty brawls for a while. For if it breaks out it will be one against all and all against one. I have seen a shadow—no more—of what may be almost upon us. That is what I started to tell you about. You wouldn't have believed me, in spite of your wife's unsigned note. And I scarcely expect you to believe me now when I tell you why she did not sign that message. She was afraid of incriminating you through me. You alone were responsible, you know, for the wreck of the *Sheridan*."

Lane stared at him.

"I don't wonder that your mind is temporarily unbalanced. Am I seeing things, too? Did I see Markoff die? Or was it just my imagination running wild after all that hell in the caves?"

"You saw that pinnacle fall a few moments ago," Saxby reminded him quietly. "So did I. And the men heard it as well as we. If you don't believe me, see what a devil of a time the noncoms are having to make the men lie down again."

"What did my wife ask you to tell me?" Lane demanded in a low tone. "Better not speak too loud. That sentry is on the jump as it is."

"Just this," Saxby began. "First, if you are questioned, to deny that you ever had anything to do with dyeing your boy's Easter eggs. That seems to have started everything—exactly how, I don't yet see. As a matter of fact I don't think you will ever be suspected. Your wife, Tom, and I are the only ones who know. Isabel has bribed the boy to forget. She says he has sense and can be trusted. Now, let me give you a bald outline, without any theorizing, of precisely what has happened since you mixed that green dye. After seeing Markoff die and hearing one crash yourself you should be able to believe the rest."

Saxby then briefly detailed the unexplained circumstances surrounding Tom's fight, the "vision" of Dan and Jake, Yang's strange death and Isabel's experience in the desert.

"Yang," he concluded, "was mercifully stupefied by gin when the disease got him. Markoff was sober, in full possession of his senses. From his end we may guess that the disease—if it is such—is extremely painful in at least one of its forms. From my analysis of what has happened so far, I deduce as a working hypothesis the existence of two distinct types, and possibly a third. Again, as a tentative guess only, I find it suggestive to imagine that those crystals we saw growing, also the others in the desert and in Los Angeles, have some form of life. This may not be a very good hypothesis. Perhaps we had better say they have proto-life. This proto-life is not the common property that all crystals have of growing in their mother liquid. It is more closely akin to animal or plant life—to life in the ordinary sense. I do not believe these growths have intelligence as we commonly understand the term. A psychologist of the extreme behaviourist school would, of course, say that they have as good a claim to "intelligence" as we have. Their actions are their minds, and their minds are nothing more than their actions. However, we can defer metaphysics till the fight is over—if we are still alive to argue.

"All I wanted to point out is this. These crystalline masses that grow at such a prodigious rate seem to be of at least two distinct species. One feeds, if I may put it so, on silicon compounds as well as on lime compounds; the other seems to require cellulose. The mineral feeders find their nourishment in sand, quartz lime—in fact in practically any kind of rock containing silica or calcium; the cellulose-feeders in such stuff as wood, clothes or fabrics containing cotton, and so on. For anything I know to the contrary either kind may be able to live, for a short time at least, on the other's proper food. Now, I take it as practically certain that there were considerable quantities of lime in some form or another in the hold of the *Sheridan?*"

"We carried several tons of chloride of lime for sanitary purposes in camp."

"Check! Calcium chloride—that's what you had. The chlorine in the compound doesn't seem to count. The calcium does. What were those rocks in the outcrop where the burros were killed? Limestone—calcium carbonate. Again you have it. What about the bones of the burros? And what about the shell of Tom's green egg? Lime again. And so in Markoff's case. The crystal brutes that overgrew the burros were silicon feeders. The sheer weight of the crystal masses, nothing more nor less than huge cutting machines of brittle glass, sliced the carcasses to ribbons.

"On Tom's Easter egg there may have been a growth of both silicon- and lime-feeders and cellulose-feeders, although the cellulose kind undoubtedly predominated—witness the total disappearance of the cotton mat. There was, however, a characteristic odor of decay in this instance, as in that of the desert. I infer, therefore, that mineral feeders were also present. Probably they fed upon the dust that is under even the most sanitary bed. What interests me is this. There must have been a third kind present, a combined mineral-cellulose feeder, which crashed when it tried to walk. Some of the same variety must obviously have come to grief over there just a few moments ago; Markoff's clothes provided the cellulose, the rose quartz, the silicon. In the case of the egg I infer that the silicon-cellulose feeders have a more durable 'heart' than the pure silicon feeders. Otherwise your cat would not have been knocked out when he first sniffed the egg. As the full sunlight worked on this thin layer of living crystals they disintegrated—just as the mineral-feeders do. The essential characteristics of all are the same; they are truly different kinds of one and the same life.

"What part the calcium compounds play in the life of these crystal brutes I don't yet see clearly. I suspect they are the necessary 'enzyme' that starts the terrific growth—the yeast, as it were. In each case so far there has been calcium present when the crystals began multiplying like a madman's nightmare. Even in the case of

Yang we have it. Those four hard-boiled eggs murdered him. Their shells were mostly limestone. It was a silicon-feeder that got him. All the glass bottles in the laboratory were gone—vanished completely."

"I still don't see how you fit Tom's egg into your theory," Lane objected. "If you can't explain that, you will have to change everything."

"The thing in your boy's bedroom was mainly a cellulose-feeder," Saxby reiterated with some heat. "The cotton mat by the side of his bed had disappeared."

"But," Lane interrupted, "you say the green egg was found under the cot where Isabel put it."

"It was. The mat, when she hid the egg, was partly under the bed. She is not sure, but she thinks she remembers putting the egg on the corner of the mat under the bed."

"If your theory that lime starts the growth is correct, that egg should not have had a shell left when the doctor found it."

"Not necessarily. I'll come to that in a minute. Only a very thin layer of the shell need have 'evaporated' to start the growth. The city chemist of course, not being told to look for anything of the sort, observed no suspicious thinness of the shell. He was concerned only with analysing the green dye. So with Yang's four crushed eggs. I had no time to examine carefully what was left of the shells."

"I think you'll find," Lane remarked, "a fourth kind of feeder among your infernal crystals. Call it a pure calcium eater."

"Not till I find it. I see certain evidence for another explanation. The calcium, I'm willing to bet, is responsible for the sex of these brutes. Oh, I know I'm crazy—have been all my life. That's why I have done some things better men couldn't do. These crystals, I suspect, have three kinds of sex—male, female and bisexual. The last correspond to certain kinds of plants or flowers. The other two are more like most animals. All this, of course, is only a crude analogy, for the crystal monsters are neither plant nor animal. They're far more ancient than either."

"What I want to know is how are we to stop them breaking out again?"

"Possibly we have seen the end of the whole story. If a certain theory of mine is correct, we have."

"Then why did you insist that we may be in for the greatest fight in history?"

"Because my optimistic theory may be wrong. Any man with a scientific training knows that even the most perfect and most logical theory is likely to be smashed at any moment by a single apparently insignificant fact. I can put mine to the test now. I believe these crystal brutes can breed and grow only in light of a certain quality. Direct sunlight is fatal to them. Total absence of light prevents them getting a start toward life. Moonlight, direct or diffused, seems to be just right. The actinic rays of the sunlight are either not present or are so diluted as to be negligible in the light reflected from the moon. You can't take much of a photograph by moonlight. The crystal brutes must have their light weak or they don't breed. If it is too diluted, they perish. In total darkness they don't even seem to begin to live. They seem to be fastidious about their light as animals and bacteria are about their temperature and humidity. Unless both lie in very narrow ranges your animal dies. Now, in all instances so far, the crystal brutes have come to birth, bred and lived only in moonlight.

"Both the quality and quantity of light present seem to determine the period of gestation of these crystal brutes or, if you prefer, the term of incubation. *When* your wife infected the rock outcrop in the desert is not known. I suspect it was *not* when she prepared supper, but early the following morning, while cleaning up to leave camp. The refuse may have been the plague spot, although Mrs. Lane thinks the rock was infected by her clothes. If so, the infection did not reach the silicon in the crack which Tom observed until some time the following day. The full sunlight held the life of the crystals in abeyance all that day; the moonlight started them breeding, and the 'rats' got the full benefit.

"Again, as to Tom's egg. Before leaving Shanghai I verified that the moon was shining into your boy's room the night all this started."

"Did you ever see Tom's cot?" Lane asked quietly.

"No. Why do you ask?"

"Because it has a heavy Mexican horsehair valance all around it clear to the floor."

"So much the better for my theory. The brute in his room cannot have been nearly so large as any of the others. It seems to have been a pretty feeble specimen; it tottered and crashed of its own weight. It was like a rickety child deprived of direct sunlight. The amount of light that could diffuse through the slit between the valance and the floor by reflection from the walls would be practically negligible. The egg was almost, but not quite, in total darkness. Its infernal offspring, generated from the cellulose of the cotton mat, was therefore a puny little devil with no stamina—luckily for Tom."

"All right," said Lane. "I won't argue with a scientist. What about the *Sheridan*?"

"You mean how did the moonlight diffuse into the hold and start things going? That's simple. Through the portholes, of course. The diffused moonlight started the spots of dye on your shirt. Your wife told me you changed it at the last moment before starting. It was in your dunnage bag, of course?"

"Suppose it was. What then?"

"It must have been in the hold, probably, although you would not know, not far from your supply of chloride of lime. Then we have simply a repetition of the essential conditions of Tom's bedroom. With hundreds of dunnage bags, themselves cotton and stuffed with clothes also mostly cotton, the cellulose-feeders had an ideal propagating place."

"And they grew at such a rate that they quickly burst the ship?"

"Precisely. A pan of dough swells to several times its initial size when the yeast gets to working well. These tons of cotton bags and clothes grew so fast into crystal masses that the effect was practically a silent explosion. From my observation of the thing in the desert, I conclude that the crystals are strong, extremely brittle, and *hollow*. Certainly some of them were filled with some substance, probably like the neon and mercury gases in these new electric signs, that glows from blue to red. The crystals at first are probably almost solid throughout. As they grow they hollow progressively and fill with gas. The gas, I take it, is the equivalent, in their kind of life, of the blood of animals or the chlorophyll of most plants. Being a mere shell when full grown, the bulk of the crystal would be thousands of times that of the compact food from which it grew. An enormous pressure would be exerted by a rapidly growing mass of such crystals before they all suddenly collapsed."

"Yes, and then what? Why didn't Isabel find any trace of the thing after it smashed? And why didn't you or those prospectors find any broken crystals in the desert?"

"Easy. One of these living crystals dies instantly if it is broken. Scratch certain kinds of glass and they fly to pieces."

"You always find the pieces."

"Of course. But suppose that condition was intensified a millionfold. There would be nothing left but a very fine dust. If colorless, as it probably is from these crystals, it would be difficult to detect. That explains, possibly, why Isabel noticed no dust on the floor of Tom's bedroom."

"It may."

"You are no more skeptical than I am. It is more probable that when a living crystal 'dies' it ceases to be a solid and sublimates instantaneously to a gas. That accounts for the terrible smell that is always present. The odor is characteristic, although unlike any with which I am familiar in chemistry. Yet, I am willing to believe almost anything about the smell of a silicon compound, and there are some pretty tough ones that can be generated from cellulose as a base. Most dabblers think the sulphur compounds are the worst. An expert in other elements knows better—or worse, according to the way you feel about such things."

"All right," Lane remarked. "Let us go back to the *Sheridan* for a moment? How did the green dye on my soiled shirt ever come in contact with the chloride of lime? You say calcium compounds are necessary to start the crystals living."

"Contact is unnecessary. See what happened to the glass bottles in Yang's laboratories. It is sufficient that the subtle gas, or emanation if you like, from the green dye shall diffuse and attack the lime—which may be a hundred feet away. The effect would be very slight, judged by any scale the layman might apply, yet chemists and physicists work habitually with traces of gases as dilute as those required by our theory, and even with quantities much smaller. It is not the size of things that is important; it is their qualities. This is a commonplace of everyday life. Seventy years ago the 'authorities' would have locked you up in an asylum if you had told them that you could wipe out a whole population with a pinprick. Yet, that is all that is necessary today, and you experts may be using just that sort of a weapon in your next human war. Your apparently clean pin may be a thriving metropolis of carefully selected disease germs. Infect one man under the right conditions and your grand offensive is launched toward a devastating victory. Only," he added with a wry smile, "nature may stop us before we can start that sort of thing."

"There is one objection to our theory," Lane remarked, ignoring the compliment to the foresight of certain leaders in his own profession. "This emanation from the green dye never got a chance at our chloride of lime. The lime was all packed in airtight cans."

"Airtight? A lot you know about cans. I'll bet the lids on half of them were as loose as ashes. Probably one or two had even slipped their covers completely in the manhandling of loading. I've watched stevedores at work. After spilling half a can over the dunnage bags the men slapped on the cover and let it go."

"Well, I can neither prove nor disprove what you say. I'm willing to accept the loose lids on those cans."

"So am I. They must have been loose. Otherwise the *Sheridan* would be afloat now."

"And you say this green dye is probably some sort of a freak that may not turn up again in chemistry for millions of years?"

"I hope so. It is probably a highly complex compound that is formed only under an extremely rare combination of circumstances—correct heat, proper concentration, and perhaps fifty more.

"When you dyed Tom's Easter eggs, you hit the right connections by accident. Yang was an expert. He was one of the most skilful technicians in the world. When he saw queer chemical reactions happening before his very eyes, he babied and encouraged them in every way to be themselves. They gave the hints; he merely followed to the best of his ability. His notebook shows that." Saxby stopped abruptly. "By the way, what has happened to that infernal notebook? Is it still in the caves?"

"I saw it fall out of Markoff's pocket when his coat rotted. Didn't you?"

"No. I couldn't take my eyes off his head. Are you sure you saw it?"

"Positive."

"Then we must go back and get it at once." He glanced at his gloved hands. "Thank Heaven Markoff let my hands alone. You mustn't touch it. The gloves may not be any real protection. Still, we know what happens when flesh that has been in contact with limestone or limewater touches the green dye. The emanation penetrates the flesh and rots the lime of the bones to liquid. If that isn't exactly what happens the fact is equally unpleasant."

"But what can you do with the infernal thing?" Lane demanded.

"I'll fly back to Shanghai with it. Then I'll take another plane and fly a thousand miles out to sea and drop it. You needn't come now. I'll get it and be back by sunrise."

"Just a word before you go. Your theory seems to be off so far as the *Sheridan* is concerned. There was no smell of decay as she sank."

"Of course not. She went down before all the crystals had time to sublimate. You smelled nothing because you were too excited trying to swim to the raft. Such gas as had already been given off in the hold of the ship dissolved in the water. Probably the gas is more soluble in water than ammonia. Anyhow, the facts indicate that it is."

"Very well. There is just one more point. You said those living crystals couldn't breed in total darkness or in full sunlight. And you supposed there was enough moonlight diffused through the portholes to start the breeding of the emanation on the lime and the cotton clothes. Again I say all right. Now for the awkward fact that demolishes your theory. The dunnage—all those clothes—and all of the chloride of lime were stored in the lower hold, far below the water line. There was not a single porthole in that hold. The very faint light required by your theory was in the sea water no doubt, even at the depth of the lower hold. But there was no possible chink or hole by which it could have filtered through to the dunnage."

"What about the hatchways between the upper and lower holds?" Saxby snapped.

"All closed tight as drums with hundreds of tons of military supplies holding them down. I guess your theory is sunk like the *Sheridan*."

"Not at all! Modified, that's all, and most beautifully. There must be a third species of crystal monsters, a cellulose-feeder, that breeds in the dark. Why, my theory is better than ever! I don't have to tinker with diffused moonlight to account for what happened under Tom's cot. Don't you see? There may be only two essential species after all—a darkness-breeding cellulose-feeder and a moonlight-loving silicon-eater. But if there is a third—"

"Wrang!"

It was not a sunrise gun from Teng-shan that cut short Saxby's rather unscientific defense of his optimistic theory. The ear splitting shot that seemed to pierce the very brain was the characteristic note emitted by the sudden fracture of a vast body of rock under tension. Those who have never enjoyed the experience of such a sound may get a faint echo of it by sticking their heads into a bathtub of water while a friend bangs two sledge hammers together, under water, within an inch of the ear. That shot was heard in Teng-shan and in all the villages within a radius of fifty miles of it. The governor, recovering slowly in his palace, had a bad relapse. The wretches imprisoned by thousands in the caves heard in it the voice of their doom. The pilot of the bombing plane stiffened his muscles and gave his bird the gas. The marines had difficulty in making their legs behave. The earth jarred slightly, but there was no earthquake. The most important consequence of that report was the conspicuous hole which it shot through the middle of Saxby's theory.

"That happened half a mile underground," he remarked when Lane could hear. "Markoff infected his tunnel thoroughly when he squeezed through it with that infernal notebook in his pocket. And it must have been pitch dark in there. I guess you're right. One kind at least of the living crystals does breed in absolute darkness. I suspected that this might prove to be so. This makes the whole situation worse than I expected. The caves will be polluted for years and Kansu will become the plague spot of the world. What I hope would not happen has happened. Nature has declared war on the human race. We had better get out of here and warn the people of Teng-shan as fast as we can."

"What about Yang's notebook?"

"It may as well stay where it is. I probably should not be able to get it before the big smash comes anyway. Keep your head and make the open plain as hard as the men can go. Don't wait for me. I'll follow at my own pace."

Lane shouted an order. The men fell in, and the column thundered by on its way to the plain. The missionary, Lane, and Saxby stood watching them pass. The sun rose, and with it the morning breeze. Almost suffocating them, a foul odor of decay drifted over from the amphitheatre. Their brains reeled.

"Take the interpreter and hurry to the governor," Saxby advised Lane. "No. Don't hang back for me. My feet are all right if I should have to run. I'm taking a professional interest in this," he called after the retreating figures. "I've been a collector all my life. See you later in Teng-shan if it's still there."

He followed as fast as he could, deliberately ignoring the pain from his burns. "Well," he remarked to himself, "if it must come, it will be worth seeing. I wouldn't sell my ticket to the show for a million dollars, even if I shall never see another sunrise for staying. Nature is greater than mere life; nature is infinite, life finite."

When, an hour or so later, Saxby hobbled down the last ten yards of the slope, he felt sorely disappointed. Nothing whatever had happened. Had he sent the marines on a fool's errand? They were to warn the governor and assist in evacuating Teng-shan of its inhabitants. For what? Perhaps nothing. Although humanely concerned about the possible fate of the Chinese, Saxby could not repress a sigh of regret that the finest specimen in his collection had failed to materialize. It remained only a hypothesis. He felt like an entomologist awakening from a dream of grabbing purple butterflies a yard square only to find a slapped mosquito in his hand. He trudged on to the village, resolved never again to theorize so long as he lived. Metaphysics is better left to the next world. It is worse than gin.

While the marines hastened to Teng-shan and Saxby trudged after them, the pilot of the bombing plane soared above the mountains searching for his fellow Americans. Never having heard the crack of snapping rock before, he interpreted the shot that altered Saxby's theory as the explosion of a huge military mine. Somehow, he thought, the marines had captured the entire store of explosives of the Chinese and were blasting their way out of the caves. Since bombing the guard room and blocking the caves, he and the mechanician had spent some pretty anxious hours. Had they done what Lane really wanted? It seemed so rash that they doubted. Worse, the Chinese gunners, headed by the governor in person, had paid a brief visit of inspection to the plane. The plane's forward and aft machine guns were observed by the visitors. They kept a respectful distance. Nevertheless their superstitious fear of the monster was rapidly evaporating. The pilot could not help feeling that, when they retired, they left merely to devise some practicable method of attack. He did not feel justified in leaving the spot until the captain sent definite word. The marines might still have need of his services. When the supposed mine explosion shattered the dawn, he shot over the mountains looking for the crater. Hoping to find it soon he planned to circle it, making all the racket he could, to scare off the Chinese till the marines escaped.

Forty minutes of criss-cross flying over the range revealed nothing remarkable. The aviators became puzzled. Surely there should have been a column of dust after the explosion? They began to fear that the explosion was of Chinese origin, deep in the caves, and that the marines were its victims.

A SUDDEN shout from the mechanician, acting as observer at the moment, caused the pilot to look down. On the floor of a natural amphitheatre directly beneath the place he saw unmistakable evidence of bloodshed. The outline of a solitary human body encrimsoned the rock. No other evidence of a conflict was visible. After a short consultation they decided to land and investigate. A mile and a half from the amphitheatre they spied a safe landing place on the slope and came down.

Revolvers in hand, although they expected no ambush, they hurried up the mountainside. Not a soul molested them. As they drew near the wall of the amphitheatre they noticed a faint odor of decay.

"There's been fighting here," the pilot remarked. "Watch your step. Take that way up—to the left, and keep your eyes peeled."

"That's no battlefield smell," the mechanician retorted, picking his way over the huge blocks of quartz. "It's different and a sight worse. It smells like rotten metal. Don't you get it?"

"Get it? I'll say I do." They were passing through the shadow of a tall pinnacle at the moment. "Makes you feel groggy, doesn't it? Do you suppose the Chinese are using a new gas?"

"Smells like it," the other agreed as they emerged into brilliant sunshine. "That's queer. It's completely gone now."

"Must be a heavy gas that evaporates in the sun," the pilot hazarded. "We had better keep out of the shade after this. I'll bet the Chinese have a new explosive, too. These are its fumes."

"Look out!" the mechanician yelled. "We're stepping slap into a bath of snakes. Well, I'm hanged! They're all dead—bushels of them."

Before them lay a deep rock basin just under the lowest point of the rim. It was full of hideous snakes of all sizes and colors, tied into still knots of frozen pain. Evidently the whole reptile population of the amphitheatre had boiled out of its dens in a futile attempt to escape a sudden peril. They had instinctively chosen the shortest way over the dip, only to writhe into the basin from which they were powerless to escape. Even a snake cannot get very far without bones.

The mechanician, who prided himself on being a hardboiled guy, grasped one of the largest snakes just behind its flat, evil head, and yanked it free of its twisted brothers.

"I guess it's dead, all right," he grinned. He cracked it like a whip. "Limp as a kelpie. Here, let's see your teeth, old boy."

For the first time he noticed that the vicious jaw, unlike the resolute firmness of the average snake's mouth, hung limply apart.

"Look here!" he exclaimed to the pilot, "it's some sort of a sucker. It has no fangs."

"Nor bones, I guess," the pilot added, pinching the horny lips together. "Snakes usually have jaw-bones, don't they?"

"Sure, to hold the fangs in place when they bite. I wonder what killed them?" He sniffed the cold skin. "Fresh as a mountain trout," he commented critically. "I guess the Chinese gassed them. We'd better look out."

Before passing over the rim they inspected twenty or more of the snakes. Not one had bone or fang in its limp body.

"Well, I'm glad they're dead," the pilot remarked, "even if they couldn't bite."

A shout of horror burst from his throat. He had seen Markoff. What looked from the air like a man lying on his back in a crimson pool appeared from a closer view as nothing that had ever been human. Only a darker pattern on the shapeless stain recalled a blurred outline of a thing with arms and legs. The living crystals had done to Markoff what they did to the burros in the desert.

The men forced themselves to investigate; the remains might be those of an American. What they first found was sufficiently puzzling to men who knew nothing of the circumstances of Markoff's death. Their find consisted of two leather boots and exactly ten metal buttons. Whoever had slashed his victim in this incredibly shocking manner had evidently first stripped the wretch of his clothes, for not a vestige of clothing remained. But why had the murderer discarded the metal buttons? Ten buttons won't hold a man's clothes together. The others had evidently taken the assassin's fancy. He seemed to have kept them. Indeed "he" had, although the men could not guess why. The remaining buttons were of bone.

They concluded that what lay before them was the work of a madman.

It was the mechanician, still subconsciously impressed by his handling of the snakes, who first observed that there were no bones under those red strands. The discovery sickened him. The supposed madman had murdered his victim for the skeleton. But, as the pilot soon discovered by looking in two of the four likeliest places, the assassin had thrown away the victim's nails. There were exactly ten. Had he looked in the grotesque leather boots he might have found ten more.

The pilot slipped. His foot kicked a small, oblong object free of the mess. The thing tinkled as fragments broke off in its skip over the uneven quartz. For all the world it looked exactly like a stone book, which is precisely what it was.

The book was open at its middle page. The pilot took out his handkerchief and picked up the book. The open stone pages wiped easily. They were as smooth as glass, evidently of pure quartz. As an object of art the thing was priceless.

At first the men thought it represented the lifelong labor of some infinitely patient Chinese artist in crystal. In the museum at Shanghai they had seen miraculous carvings in rock crystal, but this surpassed them all. Its thin pages could not be turned, of course; otherwise they were perfect, each an individual work of art. Its coloring, too, apparently natural, was exquisitely delicate. The open pages were mottled with a Chinese green like the rarest jade, and the edges of the fast shut pages showed that every one, though invisible, was equally beautiful. On the open pages a curiously regular pattern of extremely faint, metallic gray enhanced the irregular green as if it had grown there. This pattern seemed to be embedded in the thin pages.

The pilot was a college graduate with a degree in mechanical engineering. The suspiciously "human" regularity of that gray pattern fascinated him, and for a moment he forgot his surroundings. He found himself slowly deciphering what he saw.

"I'm crazy," he muttered. "Here, see if you make anything out of this."

He indicated a cloudy gray spot in the middle of the page. The mechanician had good eyes.

"243.7," he read slowly. "I'm not sure about the decimal point."

"That's what I think I see. So I'm probably right about the rest." He read aloud, a letter at a time, a short chemical equation. "Now I know," he remarked in a strained voice, "what that mess on the rocks is. It is what is left of Mr. Saxby."

"How do you know?"

"This is the book he kept pulling out of his pocket and reading when he thought we were going to crash in the fog."

"But his book was paper—just a common notebook."

"I know. This is the same book. I saw him studying it in Shanghai while you were tuning up. There's no use arguing. I don't understand what all this is about. It has happened. That's all."

"What had we better do?"

"Hanged if I know. If Mr. Saxby got out, probably the others did too. There's a hole. They may have come out that way. If they did, they weren't killed here. I suppose we had better continue the search till our gas gets too low. Then we may as well fly back and tell General Maitland."

"He'll call us liars."

"I'll take the book along. It proves something, but I don't know what. I wish we could bury that."

"There's no dirt within a mile. Come on; I'm sick."

Looking up at the cloudless blue before they took off, they saw four black shapes, wheeling slowly above the amphitheatre on motionless wings in the morning sunshine.

"He won't need burying," the mechanician remarked. "What a sight to see before breakfast! Give her the gas!"

Part III—THE PROFESSIONAL

XII. FROM THE GRAVE

It was no cynic, but one of the world's most humane poets, who observed that the evil men do lives after them, while the good is buried with their bones. For obvious reasons the scavengers of the air could not inter Markoff's good with his bones. This, however, did not nullify the first part of Shakespeare's profound theorem with respect to him. Markoff was dead, indeed; his evil was still as lusty as four vultures. In fact, as the day wore on, it almost seemed as if Markoff himself were rising from the dead. It is only a slight coloring of the sober facts to say, metaphorically, that he rose from the grave a few minutes after eight on the evening of the day following his fleshly burial.

When the bombing plane soared aloft from the place of death to reconnoiter for the marines the morning was still young. The aviators flew first toward the pass into Shen-si, thinking that the marines, if indeed they had escaped, would be getting out of Kansu as fast as possible. Their job with regard to the missionaries having evaporated, there was no reason why they should linger to tempt the touchy Chinese.

Just as the aviators flew over the pass, nature fired her second shot in the war against living things, or rather she fired a volley. In rapid succession a series of ear-splitting concussions jarred the air like titanic battering rams hammering at the steel barriers of an impregnable fortress, as stratum after stratum of the subterranean rocks suddenly split and burst asunder.

Knowing that the marines could not have marched farther than the pass, the aviators wheeled about and whizzed back toward Teng-shan. Glancing down they saw a succession of furrowed billows racing with incredible speed over the plain from the mountains of the caverns to the far horizon where they seemed to break. Farms and villages rose and fell like helpless rafts as the long furrows swept under them on their race to the northern deserts. Each volley fired by the snapping strata sent a fresh train of earth waves speeding over the plain in parallel ridges, till, without warning, the forces of nature opened their grand offensive from four fronts at once, and four furrowed tides fought to possess and destroy the battlefield. The waves in each of those tidal armies swept on in parallel regiments, but each army pursued its own direction from the base of the mountains out over the plain. As the crests of one tide reenforced those of another the heaving earth suddenly shot upward on a crest twice the height of either; as hollow met hollow, farms and villages were snatched from sight faster than they could have fallen down a void; where four crests met the brown earth was tossed high into the air in blocks of shattered spray a mile square, and where three or four hollows crashed together rocks, men, trees and cattle—everything was pulverized and ground together into paste.

The roar of the conflicting tides drowned the sharp crescendo of the snapping strata; huge fissures miles long crossed and criss-crossed the choppy sea one instant only to vanish the next, and slowly the whole mountain range of the caverns, with a shudder that shook the very sky, slipped from the core of rock to which it had been moored for a million years and began to flow over the plain. Momentarily the tides subsided. The steady roar of the advancing tidal wave of earth and rock—a whole mountain range in motion—gathered volume as the moving mass slowly gained momentum and marched upon the shattered plain to submerge it in a deluge of crumbled rock. No man-made noise could survive above the thunder of that billow curling over the wash of stone avalanches that prepared its way and made its flow smooth; the men in the bombing plane, hovering over the column of dust that had been Teng-shan, no longer were aware of their own incessant racket.

When the first shock came Saxby and the captain had just concluded their interview with the governor of Kansu. The last words of that skeptical Chinaman were addressed to Saxby through the missionary.

"Why should I warn the people of Teng-shan and the farmers of Kansu to flee? This man," meaning Lane, "has lied about the Americans in Shan-si. I questioned," here he smiled significantly, "the Christian telegraph operator. He told me everything before he died. He was a truthful boy. So when you say there is to be an earthquake that will shake Kansu from the mountains to the desert, I think you are lying. When we run away you stay behind and loot. Markoff has told me that all Americans are liars and capitalists. I believe him. You came to Kansu to rob us. The missionaries were an excuse. I am justified in executing you and all of your men, and I shall do so. You have rifles, but no machine guns. Last night my soldiers carried back their machine guns that you tried to rob them of, and strengthened the defenses of this palace. Your men are now trespassing on my grounds. They do not see the machine guns, for my men are well hidden. If Kansu is to suffer an earthquake, as you say, you will never know it."

The governor himself never knew what happened. The missionary had not quite finished translating the governor's speech—the details of Lane's and Saxby's sentence had not yet been translated—when a heavy beam from the ceiling smashed the governor's table to splinters, brained him, squashed the missionary and two of the guards, and totally disabled the remaining four.

Saxby and the Captain found themselves in the governor's private garden just as the palace collapsed. They remembered a wall that suddenly opened like a door, a leap, and nothing more. The marines, standing at ease under the mulberry trees, were not crushed by falling buildings as were the Chinese soldiers tensely waiting to open fire at the governor's order.

As for the rest of Teng-shan, it experienced all the usual freaks that accompany major earthquakes. Out of a group of twenty human beings, all apparently exposed to precisely the same hazard, nineteen would be killed outright while the twentieth escaped without a scratch. One man too terrified to run would weather the cataclysm unharmed; his more prudent friend, abandoning him to his fate, stepped instantly into a gaping chasm, not two feet away, that opened to receive him and closed immediately. One squad of marines, reeling after another to a supposedly safer spot, saw eight men vanish without ever knowing where they went.

Of Teng-shan itself not one stick of house or hovel remained in the place where the builders had put it, and, literally, not one stone or brick was left upon another. They were pulverized. Yet hundreds of human beings came through as sound as ever, or with only minor injuries.

THE great mass of the population was destroyed in the first two shocks; the succeeding waves alternately buried and disinterred the victims with a sublime cynicism as indecent as any of nature's franker brutalities. Restraint and reason are for human beings, in order that nature may drug them into a false security; she herself has no other use for either. Science would seek to put a bit in her savage mouth; she submits, to delude her dupes, and then, when they least expect it, tramples them underfoot and goes unhindered on her way.

Yet man, the incorrigible optimist and practical opportunist, discounts the worst nature can do. The major shocks of that terrific earthquake, the maddest prank that nature ever played on a superstitious race, had barely subsided before the survivors were stripping poor trifles of silver and jade from the fingers of the dead and rifling their clothes for cash. In earthquakes, in fire, and in shipwrecks the rule is the same; at least some of the survivors demonstrate their fitness to survive by plundering those who have perished. And why not, these children of nature ask; what use has a corpse for rings or money? Their logic is as irrefutable as Mother Nature's.

The marines lost a third of their force. The rest, as soon as the ground stopped heaving sufficiently to permit them to stagger, began systematically searching the ruins of the palace—for imprisoned survivors only. They found none. Lane reorganized his force with the purpose of similarly combing the ruins of the whole town. The Chinese themselves, except those engaged in looting, were incapable of any rational act. Orders had to be given by signs and shoutings into ears; the rumble of the oncoming billows of shattered rock made any other means of communicating impossible. They heard the stupendous roar, of course, and guessed that worse was to come, but they could not imagine what was happening. At the moment they were at the bottom of a vast pit that formerly had been the palace grounds. They could not see over its rim as they were too close to the steepest part of the wall.

Saxby scrambled up first and saw what was about to overwhelm the ruins of Teng-shan. By frantic signals he brought the men out of the pit in record time. They did not stop for a second look. The first was sufficient to send them fleeing from the oncoming wave, every man for himself and the devil take discipline.

Saxby himself could not run. Not that he was paralyzed with fear, or too stiff from his painfully healing burns; he simply lacked the volition to run. All his mature life he had collected and loved earthquakes, and now he saw one the like of which the world had never witnessed in historic times. The "Kansu catastrophe," as it has since been named, was unique, and Saxby, the connoisseur of earthquakes, realized instantly the rarity of the spectacle. Lane, thinking Saxby was following, pursued his routed troops.

It was a sight to make any lover of nature pause. The stupendous volume of sound, as that crashing symphony of destruction rose and fell with the periodic surge of the shattered rocks, alone would have stunned the average spectator into helpless immobility. But Saxby was not average. He stayed where he stood because he wanted to enjoy it to its last avalanche of crushed rock and its last splitting discord. It was nature at her mightiest, trampling the world like an ant hill, irresistible, ungovernable, and her admirer would witness her triumphal march if it cost him his life.

He had witnessed the puny efforts of men to destroy their own kind, and the sight had nauseated him; now he would see nature demolish herself, impartially, completely, and cleanly. As far as the eye could reach the spectacle was continuously sublime. In serried billows a whole mountain range rolled forward, toppling over upon itself when some unshattered core of rock offered a moment's futile resistance to the onrushing flood, surging forward majestically over the wash of the avalanches that fingered their way forward to feel out the terrain, leaping skyward, when the obstruction yielded, tumbling and curling forward in vaster volume, again damming up over some more obstinate resistance, and again conquering, mightier than ever. A shriller, brittle din pierced the roar of the stone billows, as if millions of tons of glass were being ground to powder beneath the flood, and Saxby knew what was coming, invisibly, before it arrived.

Nature, human, animal or other, is incomprehensible. The French peasants gathered their harvests while all the hell of the West Front girdled their fields with a sea of fire. Between Teng-shan and the marching mountains a sturdy, shaggy little Chinese pony tried courageously to keep its legs on what had once been its pasture—now a jumbled desolation of disinterred rocks and chaotic clods as big as houses. Though the jarring earth tumbled stones and clods all about it, the persistent pony stuck like a burr to the one patch of turf in all that heaving wilderness. Its legs straddling wide apart like a spider's, with determination worthy of a general resolved to hold the front line at the cost of a hundred thousand of his men if necessary; the courageous pony cropped the grass. In spite of himself Saxby admired the little beast's obstinate, natural, ignorant courage. He even felt a sympathy for it; the pony refused to run because of the hunger of its belly; he, the man, was risking his life to appease the cravings of his æsthetic nature. Suddenly the pony collapsed as if pole-axed. It did not even kick. If not done for it was at least knocked out—cold.

Saxby felt that it was time to retreat. The pony's collapse was exactly like that of the firemen and the doctor when they stuck their heads under Tom's cot. A heavy gas, colorless and lethal, was creeping forward in advance of the tide. Thus far there had been no odor; the sun had not yet volatized the corruption that seeped from the base of the rotting mountains. The gas of course was only a hypothesis. Saxby, however, believed in it sufficiently to turn his back on the grandest of all the avalanches he had so far witnessed, and run as hard as he could in the opposite direction. When he noticed also that a cold breeze, colder than the wind from an ice floe, was blowing in his face, he doubled his speed.

"Gad!" he panted, "what a fool I've been. I guess I'm dished this time."

Doubtless he deserved the worst, but he did not get it. The pilot of the bombing plane had early located the Americans with his field glasses and had followed their precipitate retreat from the pit. He had also observed that one of their number, possibly because too scared to move, stayed behind. For forty minutes the pilot had been endeavoring to attract the laggard's attention by all the noises at his command, as he wheeled in a narrow circle a thousand feet above the loiterer's head. His noise was nothing in competition with nature's and Saxby, with no eyes for anything but the greatest earthquake in history, never thought of looking up at the zenith. Seeing that the loiterer had at last found his legs, the pilot swooped low and flew in front of him, guiding Saxby to his invisible companions floundering in a vast crater two miles away.

SAXBY's best was not quite good enough. Glancing back the pilot saw him stumble and fall just as a fresh avalanche roared down from the main mass to within a hundred yards of the fallen man. From his observations on the progress of the tide the pilot estimated that it would be only about four minutes till the tottering crest followed the wash of the avalanche to sweep clean over it and gain a quarter of a mile in a single surge.

Saxby was on his feet again, but not running. He could not; even his iron endurance had almost reached its limit. The pilot had to act instantly or abandon the man to his doom. He acted. By the kind of miracle that favors the courageous, he brought the careening plane to rest on the hummocky ground all cluttered with ruins, just ten feet short of a crevasse that would have swallowed it, and within running distance of Saxby. The mechanician was over the side and on his way before the plane stopped. The pilot climbed out and by brute force, exerted on the tail of his bird, slewed it round for the take-off. A quarter turn brought it into position for a start that might not end in a smashed propeller or a plunge into a fissure—if they were lucky.

When the mechanician saw who it was that he was rescuing, he yelled.

"You're dead!" he shouted.

Saxby didn't hear, and the mechanician, ready to believe that this too was merely an incident in the general nightmare, did not stop to argue. He hustled Saxby to the plane and into it. One shock more to the pilot's nerves meant little. He accepted Saxby as a fact and took off, mentally balancing the probability of a smash from the rear against an equally likely crash ahead. The tide roared after them just as the plane moved forward; half a ton of shattered rock burst like a bomb against the fuselage and jagged fragments shot past their heads as they ducked or dodged, but they made it—how, they never knew. Take a chance and win is the airman's motto.

They could not land in the marines' new crater; one miracle a day is enough. Flying on at a low speed they found a practicable stretch of alluvial dirt, not too violently furrowed and fissured by the earthquake, about five miles beyond the crater. Landing, they waited for the others to overtake them. Eventually only Saxby waited; the aviators departed in haste ten minutes after they stopped.

At this distance from the stone tide it was possible to carry on a conversation by shouting. The first thing the pilot wished to know was who the dead man was.

"What dead man?" Saxby shouted.

The pilot described the place where they had found the mess. Saxby informed the aviators that it was a Russian agent—the man responsible for all the trouble with the Chinese.

"The Chinese got even with him. They cut him up and boned him like a chicken tamale," the mechanician bellowed. "Made me sick."

Saxby recognized the symptoms.

"It's a new disease," he shouted. It would have taken hours to state the facts adequately. To his intense astonishment the pilot broke the startling news that they had thought the remains were Saxby's.

"Why?"

"Because we found your book—or one just like it—made of glass or crystal. See here."

The pilot led Saxby back to the plane and produced Yang's crystallized notebook. Saxby got the shock of his life.

"Don't drop it!" he yelled. "Keep it away from any kind of earth—put it back in the plane! That's the cause of all this. Put it back, I say !"

Somewhat bewildered the pilot obeyed. So many insane things had happened already that one more might be accepted as part of the nightmare. Saxby continued, speaking rapidly.

"I was going to wait for Captain Lane to give you your flying orders. General Maitland ordered you to do as I directed; I'll not wait for Lane. Don't think I'm crazy—I'm not. Lane would order you to do exactly as I say. I predicted the earthquake from my knowledge of that book. We were warning the governor when the first shock verified my prediction. If that infernal book comes in contact with lime and silicon dioxide—common sand, quartz, granite—almost any mineral—it may start another earthquake worse than this. I don't know whether it will or not, but I'll take no chances. This terrific earthquake is only the least of what may be coming. Fly back to Shanghai with that thing, and don't stop till you get there. Don't touch anything but your plane, and don't take the book out of it. You must not get out of the plane. Send for General Maitland and tell him that I advise this.

"First, your plane is to be refueled for a flight to the most convenient American war vessel that is not less than five hundred miles from the nearest land. You are to fly at once to it—you can do it as an endurance test if you must. When you see the war vessel, relieve one another while you both strip to the skin and pitch your clothes overboard. Then drop the book in the sea—to be sure it sinks and does not float with the plane. Come down in the water. Hang on to your plane as long as you can, and souse every part of your bodies, particularly your hands. If you can't manage a thorough job that way, don't let the sailors lug you aboard till you are exhausted. Get them to tow you for an hour or more. Your plane is to be blown to bits and sent to the bottom. General Maitland will give all the necessary orders if you tell him what you have seen and say that I back my advice with my scientific reputation. I gave him one straight steer; this is a straighter. Tell him that, and tell him that the Russian agents beat us to our objective.

"Finally, he is to cable at once to the United States for the ten best geological chemists in the country. The National Scientific Council will select them and send them at once if he gives my name and says it is to avert a world disaster. In the meantime he is to send me all the chemists and geologists he can collect in the foreign concessions in China and rush them here by air. He must communicate with me daily by air until the danger is past—if it ever is. Now, beat the record back to Shanghai!"

Ten hours later Kansu had stopped shaking, except spasmodically, and the shattered mountains had apparently flowed their limit. The marines, officers and men, slept the sleep of exhaustion in a large plantation of stunted firs, whose fallen needles made the ideal bed for weary bones. Saxby alone kept watch, although there was no necessity for him to do so, as there was not a hostile human being within miles. After a short foraging expedition through the ruined and deserted farms to salvage dead pigs, hens and cattle for their supper, the marines turned in to the last man. Even the captain could not have kept his eyes open to see the greatest bombardment in history. Saxby volunteered to act as sentry and they accepted. He wished to keep his eye on the expiring earthquake. The characteristic odor of decay that had followed them all day while the sun was up had gradually dissipated. Saxby felt, however, that the danger was not yet past.

Events so far had confirmed his theory in the main, although modifying it in some details. The thing, or more accurately one of the things, that destroyed Markoff was evidently a cellulose feeder. The transformation of Yang's notebook from wood-pulp paper to rock crystal threw a flood of light on the habits of at least one species of the living crystals. Anxious to observe further evidence in support of his theory Saxby could not have slept had he tried. His lonely vigil was no hardship, especially as the intense, unnatural cold forewarned him that nature had not yet done her utmost.

JUST as the night began to grow interesting from a scientific point of view for Saxby, it developed, hundreds of miles away, an unexpected human interest for the aviators. It was now about half an hour before midnight. The mechanician was taking his turn flying while the pilot slept. At the moment they were speeding eastward less than a hundred and fifty miles from Shanghai, and were some two thousand feet above the bloodiest battlefield of the Chinese revolution. So stubborn and sanguinary had been that long-drawn-out butchery, that its aura tainted the air about the plane to the point of nausea and woke the pilot. It is unpleasant to have to record such facts, but they are essential to an understanding of nature's attack; moreover they are a part of our common heritage from the war that was to end war, and there is no good reason for strewing roses on human stupidity or sophisticating it under a yellow or a red flag. Both the pilot and the mechanician became violently ill.

"Here's where I quit the service," the mechanician remarked, trying hard to swallow his disgust. "You saw the West Front; I didn't. You're hardboiled; I've still got a stomach. Watch me cash in and get out when we get to Shanghai."

"It won't be much longer now—less than two hours. You'll recover after you've had a bath."

"In salt water. Yes, like hell I'll recover. I don't give a damn if I drown. Say, did it smell this bad on the West Front?"

"Worse. Cheer up, we'll soon be there."

On the moonlit battlefield beneath them all was quiet—from a military point of view—with a ghastly serenity that mocked the dead and jeered at the living who were yet to slaughter and be slaughtered. China at last had awakened from her sleep of two thousand years; she was westernized, civilized, and this portion of her at least smelt like it.

The false peace of the night was not due to any formal armistice, but to one of those tense lulls that sometimes supervene in times of madness when, by tacit consent, the opposing armies stop fighting one another to fight their common enemy before she can steal a march on them all and impartially obliterate friend and foe alike. If there is one thing that Asiatic soldiers dread worse than death, dysentery or the devil, it is the bubonic plague. The medical corps of neither army would as yet admit an indisputable case of death by plague, but both acknowledged an alarming number that looked suspiciously like the real thing.

Neither side had fired a shot for the past thirty-six hours; both were engaged in burying their dead as fast as they could scratch the shallow ditches in the rocky soil. Mere burial in this case was insufficient. The transports of both armies were straining every nerve to rush vast quantities of quicklime and disinfectants from the cities to the battlefield. The congested roads, the wretched inefficiency of the transport service, and the keen competition for the fast diminishing supplies of sanitary materials all indicated an overwhelming victory for nature in the immediate future. The faster the diggers worked the more they had to do, and no man could say that he would finish his particular bit before the grinding cramp seized him by the middle and tumbled him headlong into his half-completed job.

Naturally the nerves of both armies were on edge. The least hint of a check in its necessary work might well send either army into a Chinese berserker rage and incidentally end the revolution in its favor. The side that fired the first shot would probably get it in the neck; the victors might celebrate by infecting the entire civilian population.

The course of the bombing plane lay directly over the main defenses of the army holding the southern edge of the battlefield. Both armies were thoroughly westernized. They had all the approved weapons, and lots of them, including machine-guns, flame-throwers, gas, tear and smoke bombs, field artillery of the latest French pattern, American and European airplanes, trench mortars, blimps—one apiece, and anti-aircraft guns. In fact, their equipment would have been a credit to any nation on earth, for they had bought it with their own money, a treasure at a time, from most of the nations on earth. The cheaper truck, such as rifles and shells, they manufactured themselves under the expert direction of European technicians. They were quite proud, poor devils, of their aptitude.

The combination of a bombing plane in the moonlight and a general on the verge of hysteria made a highly explosive mixture. The general quickly verified the fact that no plane on his own side was aloft that night. He did not act in haste. Although he felt morally certain that his side was playing the game straight, he took pains to ascertain the truth by telephone. Since it was not one of his own birds, it must be one of his rival's. Practical soldier though he was, he cursed his enemies for a pack of inhuman blackguards, technically within their rights as laid down by the laws of civilized warfare, but beyond the pale of human decency in their sneaking disregard of an unwritten agreement. He personally telephoned to the anti-aircraft batteries to open fire.

"What the hell!" the mechanician shouted as the first shell burst like a white mushroom in the moonlight.

"What the hell" was right. The second shot brought them down—two thousand feet. Perhaps it was lucky in more ways than one. If the second shot hadn't got them the two hundredth would. They escaped the suspense.

The plane crashed directly astraddle of a long, shallow ditch packed like a box of sardines with the victims of a sudden sickness. The loose gravel had not yet been thrown over them, but the quicklime had. As the fuselage of the plane burst, the fragments of Yang's petrified notebook shot out and buried themselves in the quicklime. The bodies of the aviators followed.

The burial squad removed what they could of the plane and mechanically went on with their work, shoveling gravel.

An officer inspected the wreck. It was not worth salvaging. He abandoned it and finally ordered his squad of shovel men to get to work on the next ditch.

The general's nerves had snapped. His Oriental calm vanished in a blazing, occidental, homicidal fury. The field batteries were ordered to lay down a barrage to prepare the way for an infantry attack by moonlight. From a military point of view it was sheer insanity; but the general was beyond reason. Burial parties broke up and raced to join their companies. Thinking like the general that they had been spied upon by the enemy as a preliminary to a night attack, they seized their rifles and machine-guns with a will, inspired, as they were, by a sort of courage of panicky desperation.

The first salvo of the barrage roused the opposing army to the pitch of madness. Their nerves too had snapped. The officers had difficulty in holding the infuriated men back. They did not wait to be attacked. With fixed bayonets they plunged forward to burst through the red curtains of the barrage and attack.

Half of them never reached their objective. The other half, however, made up in spirit what they had lost in their number.

The field gunners of the attacked saw them coming, became confused, shortened the range, and drummed a devil's tattoo upon their own front-line trenches. The maddest battle in the history of the Orient was on. There was no doubt about that.

It raged twenty hours—all that night and all the next day till eight o'clock in the evening, when the full moon rose on a shambles that was silent, save for the cries of the wounded, only because both armies had run out of ammunition. Exploding dumps, deliberately touched off by the Russian advisors of the Chinese in more than one instance, had hastened the end. The Russian agents were strictly impartial. They did what lay to their hands, whether it benefited friend or foe. As in diplomacy, so in war; to double-cross is to win the day—for yourself, if not for your allies. From the red point of view the melée had proved a glorious victory; from the Chinese it was a draw. Both armies were out of the war for good. They had ceased to exist as armies; their remains would be absorbed into less butchered organizations. By that much the communists were nearer their goal of an Asia regenerated by the new faith.

Every yard of the battlefield had been trampled over fifty or a hundred times by the frenzied combatants. If indeed the ground was infected the plague was now thoroughly disseminated. Nature, however, did not have to rely upon a mere plague of buboes, of swelling lymphatic glands, to demonstrate her superiority in the art of war. She chose a weapon almost infinitely older than the most ancient disease germ.

The sword she grasped was forged in geologic stone, ages before organic life began, and she had not forgotten in all that time how to use it.

The general whose order had initiated the madness lay moaning on the loose gravel, mortally wounded. Like a captain of old he had lost his head in the heat of battle and had risked his own life to rally his wavering troops.

Under his personal leadership the battered army had pulled itself together for a last supreme assault that swept the enemy from his feet—for half an hour.

Then the tide turned and the dead of the enemy were duly avenged.

Again and again that fluctuating tide took up the quarrel, first of one side, then of the other, with the foe of the moment, in order that its temporary friend might sleep in peace on fields too barren to support a white poppy.

The dead of both sides slept soundly, too weary to dream that the victorious fortune that avenged them was a deceiving harlot.

As the dying general's eyes clouded he had a strange vision of death. From the bloody charnel before his eyes he saw a transparent sword shoot into the moonlight and glitter icily as if crusted with diamonds. The sword seemed to live; flickering bands of purple and green light pulsed along its axis in the substance of the crystal, and myriads of spicules, bright as sparks of electricity, budded along its brittle edges. Suddenly two arms, like those of a cross, shot from the sword a third of the way down from the tip and began to grow. The vision may have comforted the dying man, for he was a convert of the missionaries. It is possible that he closed his eyes in peace on a symbol of mercy conquering the world.

If he did so, he died happy, for what he saw was Markoff rising from the dead.

A wounded infantryman by the general's side also saw nature's apparent miracle and tried to crawl away. The grave where the sword grew burst and hurled the wounded man free. Screaming with terror he clapped his hands over his stomach and fled. He had seen the enemy.

He stumbled over the propeller of an airplane, picked himself up and ran with the rest. All had seen it now.

Those who had legs ran.

XIII. CONFLICT

WHILE Saxby watched, and under the same bright moonlight the maddened Chinese were annihilating one another hundreds of miles away, the marines slept. But they did not rest. The unnatural cold chilled them to the bone, and a specific poison, odorless as clean air, tainted the night. They began to toss and groan in their sleep, unable to shake off the dreams that defied reason and yet were more credible than any human experience.

"I had better waken them," Saxby muttered to himself. "They are having the same dream that I had the night Yang died. Gad! I begin to feel it myself. Something's going to happen; I can feel it coming, and I think it is coming pretty soon."

He tried to move and discovered that he could not. He seemed to be paralyzed.

"Something new," he remarked. "Well, let it come. I can't stop it."

Unable to move a muscle he sat staring straight ahead over the moonlit desolation of the shattered mountains. To test the strange paralysis he tried to shout, only to find he had lost control of his throat. The automatic functions of his body continued normally. His heart did not lose a beat, he breathed regularly, and he saw and heard as clearly as ever. Then he became aware that his hands and feet were losing all sensation. The numbness rapidly spread over his whole body, and he sat as rigid as a rock, without sensation, yet fully conscious of what he saw.

His condition was precisely that of a patient submitting to a surgical operation under one of the newer wonderfully effective local anæsthetics.

Naturally he wondered what the nature of the operation was to be.

It began with a tremendous roaring swish like the simulanteous ascent of thousands of gigantic skyrockets. The wilderness of shattered rock that had overflowed the plain for a distance of fifteen miles or more began to boil. Its surface rose and fell tumultuously in huge bubbles of rock and earth that puffed up suddenly, burst, and collapsed with a brittle din that shook the sky.

This phase lasted but a few seconds.

First one bubble survived, then another, until the whole desolation became a city of bleak, colossal domes. The domes began to glitter icily in the moonlight, and almost instantly the imprisoned life that was in them burst forth and multiplied. Jostling one another to ruin, the furiously increasing masses of crystal flashed out gleaming arms that branched and begot new colonies of glittering crystal; these fed for a moment on their generative substance, then instantly burst out in explosive growth in all directions, repeating the conquest of space. As yet they had no mode of locomotion; their sole power over distance was growth. In their urgency to survive, the opposing masses shot their gleaming progeny at one another, devouring the diminishing distances between them.

Their one instinct, if they had any, was to exterminate their competitors by seizing and absorbing all of the food by which they might increase.

Before the last alley closed and became a dense mass of furiously growing crystals like the rest, the mountain range that had flowed over the plain was a vast concourse of gigantic crystal shapes, towering and flashing in the moonlight, that shot upward with an accelerated growth that menaced the sky. Each glittering pinnacle budded at a thousand sparkling points into living spears of crystal; these shot into the night, themselves to become the sources of explosive life. Neither upward nor lateral growth apparently had any natural limit, and the huger the vast bulks became the faster they grew. The whole mass pulsed and flickered with striæ of green and purple light deep within the hollow crystal masses, and from the brittle, spearlike points streamed steadily upward innumerable brushes of clear, cold blue light. The loftiest pinnacles, leaping skyward with an ever greater speed, bristled with electricity whose sharp, dry hiss all but drowned in volume the creeping rustle of an incessant growth.

With a succession of pealing clashes of crystal masses the last lanes closed and instantly became new foci of fecundity. For perhaps a second the densely packed mass withstood the internal pressure of its own lateral expansion. Then with a transcendent crash thousands of irregular chasms were instantly created, radiating in all directions through the still growing mass, as the hollow crystals collapsed along the planes of greatest pressure.

As the crushed crystals released the purple and green luminescence which was the source of their life, they instantly lost their solid structure and sublimated into a heavy, invisible gas. Where one crystal volatized, the impact of its destruction set free the imprisoned energy to shatter the densely packed crystal matrix in which it was embedded; the wave of destruction thus started stopped only at the densest cores, isolating them as prolific centers of unabated vitality.

Again the merciless contest for possession of the nutritive rocks was fought out, but with diminishing speed, and again the resultant deadlock was suddenly broken by waves of destruction that cleft the solid unit into thousands of isolated enemies. The terrific speed of the encounters became less as the nutrition in the rocks was drawn into successive generations, to be dissipated into gas as enemy clashed against enemy, till, after the hundredth assault the lanes ceased to close, and the towering victors grew slowly and silently upward, starving on their exhausted rocks. The food they had battled for no longer existed. Ten thousand conquerors towered in the moonlight to await the trivial accidents that would destroy them as they had destroyed their enemies.

The whole conflict lasted but an incredibly short time as men measure events. From the instant when the first gleaming spire rose from the rocks to the last clash but thirty or forty seconds had elapsed. Yet every detail of it was fixed distinctly and indelibly on the consciousness of the one human being who saw it all from beginning to end.

Saxby would have closed his eyes and stopped his ears if he could, but he had lost control of his body. By a sense more ancient than either sight or hearing he experienced a torture less endurable than either the sights or the sounds of that conflict between things which lived, and yet were neither animal nor plant, for the cells of his whole body were aware of the combatants' agony as parts of their substance died.

Each wave of destruction that cleft the warring masses asunder rocked the very atoms of his own flesh and bone with a pang that was not mortal pain, but the after-shock of an immemorial dissolution. The stuff of his own body had suffered in forgotten ages as those things were suffering now; before the first life started on the millions of years of upward evolution that had culminated in his own body and in his mind, the substances of his body had lived as these things were living, and had died in agony such as theirs.

It was not a dream. The men who slept, drugged by the same poi-
its creatures by reason alone, nor through the haze of ideas that
son as he, also experienced it. Nature does not communicate with
reason evolves to explain nature, for it is insensible to reason, but directly, thing to thing. Because we have existed, thought and reasoned for at most a few million years—which are less than a pulse beat in the life of the stuff of which we are made—we assume that nature has but one mode of expression and but one way of communicating with its creatures. When the last man has ceased to think, the universe will still be evolving as if our race had never existed, and possibly the shadow of our own passing may fall upon the life that is to follow us, chilling our successors with the memory of a pain that only their atoms remember. May no accident precipitate us into their age as the living crystals were hurled into our own. With all their insensate ferocity, according to the lonely watcher who saw their war and who suffered in their death, those crystals were less terrible than some whose nostrils are filled with the breath of life.

The discharge of millions of volts of electricity from the warring crystals, and the escape of vast quantities of ionized gases as the dying bled out their purple or green lifeblood, incurred its inevitable reaction. Even as the clashing Titans warred, grinding themselves and their opposing kind to dust that sublimated instantly, the suspended moisture of the chilly air condensed into black thunder clouds above their splintering pinnacles.

When the conflict ended, and the victors towered up in solitary might awaiting starvation and the dawn, a vast canopy, black as anger, sagged down from the sky above them, shutting them from the moonlight and penning them up in all but total darkness. All about their sombre isolation a soft radiance flooded the plain, and it became the dream, the unsubstantial vision of an infinite ocean from another life; the black island of the Titans awaiting the lightning was the reality, the substance, and the familiar dwelling place. The lucent calm, glowing like a milky opal about the black cliffs at the base of the island, and receding with diminishing brilliance to infinity, was the incredible memory; the stark island; the vivid present.

The sooty shadow, under that black canopy instinct with lightning, was the natural habitat and fecund breeding place of the living crystals that had bred and multiplied in sunless caverns to burst asunder the mountains; in total darkness they increased without restraint; in sunlight they ceased to multiply. Injured in darkness they still lived; the most trivial wound inflicted in full daylight slew them progressively and swiftly from pinnacle to root. In one last effort to increase in their fostering darkness, the living crystals drew from the impoverished rocks the last traces of their silicon, absorbed and digested it into the compounds that gave them life, grew explosively for a fraction of a second, and ceased absolutely to grow. Unless transplanted to fresh feeding grounds the ravenous Titans must stand where they were rooted, and starve till the accident of a thrown missile should break a fragment from the brittle armor of one, releasing the prisoned life and letting the famished thing perish utterly.

The black island leaped into stark relief as the lightning struck the highest pinnacle, demolished it, and sent the towering crystal crashing down in a wave of progressive ruin to fragments that volatilized instantly. The following crash of thunder, sharp as a pistol shot, was the signal for the sagging canopy to release all of its forked darts. Under the volleying thunders that jarred the plain like a rapid earthquake, the stabbing lightnings etched every glittering detail of the motionless Titans in glaring relief, playing harmlessly about a group of fifty or a hundred, only to leap suddenly away and strike down a solitary martyr. As a colossal crystal expired, the man watching its extinction suffered its infinite pain, and the sleepers dreamed of its agony with every atom of their bodies. The vast army of the victorious crystals that had survived by annihilating their kind dwindled rapidly to half its numbers, then to a quarter, and then more slowly, till but a scant dozen of Titans stood where they had grown, powerless to flee, awaiting their doom. A single spurt of blue fire from above destroyed all but three; the clouds burst, and with a roar that might have been heard fifty miles let down their deluge.

The three survivors toppled slowly over on the dissolving earth and came gently to rest on their sides in the flood, exposing their matted roots of crystal to the rain.

The lightnings did not cease with the coming of the rain, but continued to strike viciously at the last of their fallen enemies. In falling the three had exposed their secret places, the very hearts and fountains of their life. Through the crystal curtains of the rain it was not possible to see precisely what happened to the exposed roots about which the lightnings concentrated their attack; yet the quality of the flickering light which they emitted changed visibly. It was in the roots that the purple and green light, the lifeblood of the living crystals, first generated as the monsters grew. Passing into the hollow crystals that budded from the roots, the light gave life to the branching mass, and carried with it the principle of life and generation to the farthest tips. As the glancing lightnings played all about the roots the quality of the light underwent a gradual change. The purple separated from the green and darted through the limbs of the recumbent masses, while the green, its brilliance intensified, remained in the roots. As if repelled by the green, the lightnings followed the purple, stabbing viciously. Simultaneously the recumbent purple branches of all three were struck. The stricken branches withered instantly, and the same bolts which destroyed them fused the ends of the huge stumps, sealing up the green light in the roots. The lightnings ceased, and a pall of darkness descended with the flood. Through the black torrent three misty green embers glowed and flickered evilly, waiting the accidental missile which would liberate their prisoned life to ravage the world.

A sleeping man stirred in his dream and groaned. Saxby felt sensation steal into his nerves once more. The man who had groaned staggered to his feet in six inches of water, cursed, and shouted to rouse his companions before they drowned.

"What a hellish night!" It was the captain's voice. "Where's Mr. Saxby?"

"Here. I'm beginning to move again."

"Why the devil didn't you waken us?"

"I couldn't. You were drugged into paralysis. So was I. But I saw everything."

"I dreamed it," a man muttered. "Why can't I move my legs?"

"Gassed," Saxby informed him. "Lie still. You'll find your legs in a minute. This downpour is dissolving the poison like salt and soaking it into the ground."

"There will be a flood if this keeps up another ten minutes," Lane remarked. "Give us a hand in rousing the men. We must move higher up the slope at once."

It was a half an hour before they were on the march uphill, slushing through a torrent of gravel and muddy water that almost swept them from their feet. At length they reached a place of safety and stood about miserably in the dark and the rain waiting for daylight.

On comparing notes Saxby and Lane found a remarkable similarity between their awareness of pain during the battle of the living crystals, although one had been stupefied in sleep and the other intensely awake. Questioning his men Lane found that they, too, had distinct recollections of the same thing, although only three or four had the skill to express graphically what they had "dreamed." On being assured by Saxby that the rain was disposing of the poisonous gas for good, the men brightened. The downpour continued to within an hour of daybreak.

The sun rose red upon a welter of white mud—the sticky paste of crushed rock from which every particle of silicon compounds had been absorbed by the living crystals. Most of this stuff was pulverized limestone. The living crystals, it appeared, needed only a small amount of lime or other calcium compounds to start their explosive growth; their food, so far as they obtained it from rocks, was silicon dioxide. From the fate of Tom's cotton mat and Yang's woodpulp notebook, it was clear, as Saxby had already deduced, that some at least of the crystals could draw nourishment from cellulose. An equally probable theory suggested was that at some stage of their development the crystals in which both the purple and the green luminescence played the part of blood or chlorophyll, could live and multiply on both kinds of food, silicon and cellulose, but that they preferred silicon and thrived best on it. In fact some of the phenomena indicated that these dual monsters could absorb only a limited amount of cellulose, no matter how huge they became. When the lightning which must have been electricity of some kind, positive or negative, played about the roots of the three survivors, it repelled the oppositely electrified gas, the green, into the roots and pursued the purple into the farthest tips before striking the branches of hollow crystal and sealing off the green in the roots. Such was Saxby's tentative explanation to Lane as they stood staring out over the mass of white mud that buried the ruins of Teng-shan. The deluge had one good thing; it had effectively sluiced the earthquake fissures full of gravel from the undestroyed hills.

THE men gathered in silent knots viewing the three enormous roots, towering up in the cold morning air, like the wrecks of colossal icebergs, which were all that remained of the vast forest of monsters that perished in the night. Saxby was uneasy.

"I can't understand," he said, "why those infernal things don't melt into gas as the sun strikes them. They must be a new breed."

"Let's walk—or swim—over and take a look," Lane suggested.

"Not yet. Give the sun an hour. If they're not dead then, I'll go with you. What about sending the men off on a foraging expedition in these hills? There must be dead pigs or chickens in the ruins of the farm. I'm starving."

"So am I. We shall have to get over the pass into Shen-si today. I'll send the men off to see what they can do."

"That's the stuff. Tell them to bring back a cow or something for me. I've got to stay and see the end of this."

When, at the end of an hour, the three bergs of crystal showed no sign of melting in the hot sunshine, Lane and Saxby made their way down to the white, sticky, steaming mess. As they slipped and floundered through the mire stretching for miles between them and their goal they regretted their early start. The deluge had washed the lethal gas of the crystals' destruction from the air thoroughly enough, but the stuff still poisoned the soil. Under the sun's rays it was now decomposing in the paste which it impregnated. Every step released a sickening puff of the repulsive gas. Although it was not definitely poisonous in this advanced state of decay, its indescribable odor was all but unendurable. Only an insatiable curiosity on Saxby's part held Lane to his intention.

Presently splintered timbers, fragments of copper waterspouts, and the remains of three machine guns sticking up from the mire, announced that they were walking over the churned-up ruins of the governor's palace. They were now rapidly nearing the smallest of the crystal "bergs." Saxby walked warily ahead, glancing sharply from side to side.

"I say," he called back, "do you notice anything?"

Lane, trained as a soldier to observe the minutest details of the enemy's territory, replied that he did. The metal scraps were more plentiful than ever, and two twisted copper spouts showed that they were still walking over the ruins of important buildings. There was, however, a total and suspicious absence of wood. Not a splinter was to be found.

"Evidently that green devil squatting there like a tame iceberg is a cellulose feeder," Saxby remarked.

"Squatting" was rather a contemptuous term to apply to the huge shape that towered above them like a skyscraper, shadowing the mire with its distorted limbs of hollow crystal for a radius of a quarter of a mile. Through the vast bulk of its main mass, and along the jagged "roots" that sprawled in all directions, a dull green light pulsed slowly as if the creature had a living heart. Watching it in awed silence the men almost heard the steady beat of the life flowing and ebbing through the crystal arteries of the thing. They could not doubt that it lived. Saxby broke the silence.

"After last night nothing surprises me. Yet this beats them all. You can see it live, or rather you can see it starving to death. There's not a stick of wood or any other cellulose material within half a mile of the infernal brute, and that, I'll wager, is the only sort of stuff it can absorb. It must be a cellulose feeder. What would happen, do you suppose, if I were to go back and get one of those posts and offer it to the brute?"

"You might try it and see," Lane suggested. "I'll wait here."

Saxby was as good as his challenge. He started back to get a stick of wood. Lane stopped him.

"Don't be a fool! You haven't the ghost of an idea how that green devil eats its food when it gets the chance. We saw how the purple and green got at Markoff's bones. Once is enough."

"All right," Saxby laughed. "I'll have to wait till you're gone. Shall we go up and take a look at him at close quarters? I want to see how brittle he is."

"I'm game." He suddenly remembered what had happened to Tom's mat. "Take off your clothes," he ordered, proceeding to set the example.

"What the devil for?" Saxby demanded.

"You say it is a cellulose feeder. There's a lot of cotton in our clothes. I have a wife and kid in Los Angeles. Want any more reasons?"

Under protest Saxby stripped to the skin. Lane would not even permit him to put his shoes on to protect his bare feet.

"The fact that Markoff's boots and nails were not destroyed doesn't prove anything," he objected. "Nor does the fact that the hoofs of the burros came through unchanged have anything to do with us. Neither you nor I ever saw an all-green brute like this. Ours all had a dash of purple. This fellow may relish leather and horn and stuff like that as much as Markoff's seemed to enjoy bones and cotton. You make your inspection in a state of nature or you don't make it."

Grumbling at Lane's "militarism," Saxby submitted. Naked as worms the two men passed into the cold shadow of the colossus. Though neither admitted it till long afterwards, both were so stiff with fright that they had difficulty in making their legs move. Had either been alone he would never have dreamed of going forward. Afraid of acting the poltroon before his companion, each made a fool of himself, for it was nothing less than ignorant bravado to tempt the devil of whose habits they knew precisely nothing, except that they were probably evil.

On close inspection the towering buttresses of the creature appeared as nothing more ominous than huge, hollow crystals, packed solidly together, and filled with a moving green light. The whole structure gave an impression of massive strength, and somehow, for the feeling it induced was undefinable, a sullen threat of immense stores of creative energy locked up within the crystal cavities.

"I wonder how brittle this rock crystal is?" Saxby speculated. He glanced up at the tremendous root three hundred feet above them, zig-zagging far out over the site of Teng-shan like a forked dart of green lightning. "If that thing up there should break away now and fall on us, we should be cut to ribbons before we could yell. Feel how sharp these edges are where the crystals twin. Damn it! I've cut my finger."

"Don't do that!" the captain yelled.

Before Lane could stop him, Saxby had dealt the crystal wall a resounding blow. The hollow crystal vibrated, emitting a deep, bell-like note that was inexpressibly mournful. The sound died away in the vitals of the thing and the wall ceased to shudder.

"You could almost imagine the brute had nerves," Saxby remarked. "But, of course, that's rot."

"What did you hit it for?" Lane expostulated, his own nerves on edge.

"To get some idea of its elasticity. I wanted to find out what are the chances of killing it with a judiciously thrown stone. From the way the crystal vibrates I infer that it is extremely brittle." He looked up at the hanging root. "Before the breeze grows into a full-sized wind and snaps that thing off, I think we had better retreat. I don't like the way the gusts eddy about the base of this berg."

As they put on their sodden clothes they held a council of war.

"These infernal things have got to be destroyed before you leave," Saxby declared. "There's no telling what a sudden storm may blow up. These are cellulose feeders, pure and simple, I'm convinced of that. Suppose there is another storm and a high wind. Those roots will be blown down and smashed into millions of bits. They are exceedingly brittle. When they do smash, they will go all to pieces, and vast quantities of pulverized glass will blow all over western China. What if some of that dust settles on a forest, or even on a grove like the one we camped in last night? Although I am not sure of my deduction, I believe that it is certain that something bad would start.

"With abundant nourishment the germs of life in the dust might well generate a plague of the huge brutes that would sweep the world and denude it of all growing things—trees, grass, shrubs and all. We saw how the silicon feeders stop growing when they have exhausted their food. They can't budge an inch, except by growing laterally, from the place where they take root. The slightest impact jars them to pieces; the breaking of the brittle crystals starts a physical reaction that dissolves the solids instantly into heavy gases. Then, when the sun rises, it finishes the killing by decomposing the gases into lighter, unstable ones that are perfectly harmless, apparently, and don't seem to retain their composition long. That they smell like the very devil while they are disintegrating is merely an unpleasant detail of no significance. Now, I vote that we act on these obvious hints and try our luck against these three green devils before you leave. I've got to stay here till General Maitland sends me some word and a geologist or two."

AFTER much argument Lane finally agreed. The point which decided him was not made by Saxby. That intrepid collector of earthquakes thought nothing of his personal danger. He never even mentioned it. Lane simply could not leave him, even with a squad or two for protection, to his own devices. To do so would expose him and his insatiable curiosity to almost certain destruction, for Saxby would never be content, with Lane out of the way, until he had explored every crystal of those evil bergs. With the devils destroyed before he left with the main body of his men, as he must do owing to the scarcity of food, Lane felt that Saxby might safely stay a year in Kansu if he liked, and enjoy himself after his own fashion. The decision was a human one. It offered, perhaps, the only solution of a difficult problem. Neither could foresee what would happen. The only way to find out was to experiment, which they did. "There can't be any danger," Saxby repeated. "These brutes have consumed every stick of wood within reach. They were the outposts of the army that destroyed itself last night. What can they live on if we smash them where they stand? Nothing. They'll die, half an hour after we let their blood out. But destruction in a high wind would be another matter. At least some of the spores—if you can call them that—would blow into trees before they were dead. To make everything safe for the future, you can collect an army of Chinese in Shen-si and bring them back with you to bury all the fragments under six feet of this paste. There's not an atom of silicon or a splinter of wood in it, so the disease will be buried forever. Here's where we get the better of nature. Our kind of evolution shall survive, not her antique brand that would make the silicon compounds masters, and the carbon compounds—ourselves among the rest—slaves and food for these brainless abominations."

The battle of "carbon against silicon," as Saxby called the assault of the human beings against their primeval rivals, began at twelve o'clock sharp. On returning to the camp in the fir grove, Saxby and the captain found the men roasting the sad remains of half a dozen fowls, nine pigs, and two marmots—all victims of the earthquake. The ration was inadequate for the ravenous men, but it would eke out what they carried in their knapsacks and make a forced march into Shen-si possible.

Believing in safety first, Lane organized the attack against the smallest of the crystal bergs—the one he and Saxby had inspected. If they conquered that one they would proceed to demolish its two gigantic brothers. The baby was not much taller than the tallest New York skyscraper; its brothers made it look like a pigmy.

At a quarter to twelve the marines lined up just opposite the zone which the voracious infant had licked clean of the last splinter of wood. The jagged projection shadowing the plain, three hundred feet from the ground, under which Lane and Saxby had conducted their investigation, was selected as the most vulnerable point. If that forked streak of crystal lightning could be severed at its base, it would crash against the main body in its fall and probably bring the whole huge berg crashing down in shattered crystal. Such was the mechanical theory of the attack. By chipping off chunks of the jagged root at the highest point of its thickest part, where it branched from the exposed core, the desired end would follow with eclat. It was as easy, the sergeant asserted, as shooting fish with dynamite. The captain's voice rang out.

"Are you ready? Fire!"

Most of the steel-nosed bullets made clean hits. A shower of crystal chips leaped into the sunlight; the brittle support cracked, and very slowly for a fraction of a second the huge root began to wheel inward toward the main mass. Then, with a terrific impact it struck the crystal berg at its weakest part, and the whole cracked asunder and began collapsing in a thousand cascades of glittering crystal.

The men's cheers were lost in the brittle thunder that filled the sky. So also was Saxby's warning shout. Unable to make himself heard he ploughed through the puddles and sticky mud and grasped the sergeant by the arm. By signs he conveyed his warning and the sergeant passed it on. It was a slow process, as the men were reluctant to turn their backs on a spectacle that beat a hundred Niagaras.

What sent the cold shivers up Saxby's back was this. He noticed as the green gas escaped from the broken crystals that it flowed down, not up. Moreover, as the sunlight played upon the gas it rapidly bleached. The hollow crystals evidently were filters for the actinic rays of the sun. Now that the sunlight played directly upon the gas, chemical changes set in, transforming it into a colorless compound. Was the new gas as heavy as the old? Was it heavier than air? If so, it would continue to stream downward, invisibly, and pile up for a moment as it fell about the crumbling base of the berg. Then, when the whole berg collapsed, the wind of its fall would shoot the colorless gas out over the plain in a huge, ever-expanding vortex.

If the gas was poisonous the shattered berg would be avenged on the men who had destroyed it.

It was every man for himself. Saxby and the captain found themselves floundering in white mud up to their knees. They had stumbled into a shallow earthquake fissure which the deluge had filled with sticky slime. The premonitory puff of air, being shoved forward in a huge wave before the oncoming gas, knocked them flat on their faces in the white mess and ducked them completely. Saxby stuck his head up, wiped his eyes as best he could, and saw the captain's head just reappearing. He also saw a rabble of men trying to run. They were having about as much success as flies on fly-paper, but they had made progress. They were now bogged in one of the worst places where splintered timbers from the governor's palace protruded through the mire. Saxby found his attention riveted by one stout post, evidently part of a roof beam, which stuck up in solitary desolation between the men and the shattered berg. It was covered with a glittering crust of large scales which looked like bright green barnacles, but which were in fact young living crystals. Saxby grabbed Lane's arms and pulled them under the slime.

"Keep under, except enough to breathe with," he shouted. "It's coming!"

Lane did not see it come, as he was unable to wipe the white paste off his eyelids. Saxby did, and he regretted his ability to see. Yet he could not have closed his eyes; horror forced them open. First he saw the fur of green crystals on the post add a second coat on top of the first. What happened, of course, was that the first coat was thrust out from the decomposing wood by a more vigorous growth of crystals that absorbed the first as they grew. He remembered a third coat being laid on in a fraction of a second. Then instantly the mass attained the maximum growth and exploded into a motionless dome of green crystal, bristling like a mace, forty feet in diameter. The entire substance of the post had been devoured by the monster. Its hollow crystal cells, thin as paper yet strong as granite, were the offspring of an invisible gas breeding on the cellulose of the wood. In its explosion to maturity the brute cut one bogged man to pieces with its razor-edged knives of crystal.

What happened next was repeated until the shattered berg had achieved a complete and barren victory over its destroyers. One man, bogged to his boots in the white paste, suddenly disappeared. The invisible gas flowing over the quagmire had isolated him like an island in hell. Instantly the life in the gas seized upon the cotton in his uniform, devoured it, and burst into a living crystal that reached its maturity in less than a second and ceased to grow. A pillar of densely packed green crystals, ten feet in diameter and six feet high, squatted in the mire where, less than a second since, a living man had stood. The white of his naked body gleamed mistily at the core of his living tomb.

In less than ten seconds the last man was dead. The victors, except the two cowering in the mudhole, were wiped out by the fiend they had conquered. Some fell victims to the knives of the living crystals, that burst from every stick or splinter, before the gas overtook them a second or two later and crystallized their clothes, but most were entombed as was the first. That these men had come to Kansu on a mission of mercy counted for nothing with nature, whose motto seemed to be, "Who taketh the sword shall fall by the sword."

THE two survivors did not dare to venture from their mudhole till sunset. When at last Saxby decided to risk it, he managed to tear off a piece of his cotton undershirt without getting it completely smeared with white paste. This was brought to the surface in his clenched fist and hastily dropped. It was not attacked. The men crawled out of the mess that had saved their lives and reeled off toward the pass into Shen-si.

"I must report as soon as possible to General Maitland," Lane muttered. "We can do nothing here."

"No," Saxby agreed. "We made a ghastly mistake. We shall have to get back somehow to Shanghai and return with the proper weapons for destroying these infernal things."

"How can they be destroyed? Your last guess was a bad one."

"After what has happened I won't insult you by prophesying. Still, I have an idea. Stay here while I go over and look at one of these new brutes. No! Don't you come. Remember you have a family; I haven't."

Saxby's latest idea was a natural outgrowth of his previous theories. His main contentions still survived, although each successive assault of nature modified the details. These new crystals were of a different kind from any of the others. This much was obvious from their habits. They were pure cellulose feeders like the two Titans still looming undestroyed above the ruined mountains; but their contours were utterly different from those of the giants. Saxby still maintained that his initial strategy was sound. He had merely blundered in carrying it out. Before firing, the men should have stripped to the skin and they should have burned every stick of wood in the vicinity of the bergs.

Approaching one of the squat pillars Saxby suffered a mishap which nearly cost him his life. He learned that the living crystals were not quite so immobile as they seemed. Human beings and other animals walk by advancing their feet. The object of lifting the feet and walking is to cover distance, to move from one place to another—in short, not to be chained a prisoner to one spot. It probably has never occurred to most human beings or animals that other natural ways of breaking their bondage to space are available. Yet such an alternative escape without machines is not only feasible but also ridiculously simple. This is exactly what Saxby almost lost his life to discover.

The crystals had devoured every stick of wood in their vicinity that showed so much as a splinter through the protective paste. It was Saxby's misfortune to stumble elaborately over the submerged barrel of a Chinese rifle and kick the stock violently against one of the razor edges of the brute before him.

There is a lot of good solid wood in a rifle stock. The cutting edge of the crystal bit into its prey and instantly began to feed. Saxby was stabbed in the calf of the left leg by an evil green sword that shot from the stock. A difference in aim of a few degrees would have cut his leg off. That was the one accident that befell him; the other crystals shot away from him. Within two seconds the green devil had acquired a huge protuberance on its side that shifted its center of gravity. Then it walked.

Lane came to Saxby's rescue just as the unbalanced brute heaved slowly over in the slime to regain its equilibrium. As they floundered through the sticky mud the thing seemed to pursue them. In whichever way they turned, trying to shake it off, it followed. In horror they began to believe that it had intelligence. But, as they subsequently discovered, it had none. It was merely a blind devil that walked in spite of itself. As its keen swords of crystal swished through the slime they bit into submerged rifle butts and splintered beams. These became new masses of crystal, like tumors on the old, and again shifted the balance. Occasionally the green brute stood rocking uncertainly for a few minutes, as if undecided which way to roll, when the slight, inevitable fluctuations of the law of chance swerved some crystal knife against a submerged splinter, and immediately the new growth tipped the monster forward. It walked by toppling as it fed and grew irregularly, a pure sport of nature. Where its food chanced to lie plentifully it advanced rapidly; where sustenance was scarce, it tottered; with a whole forest but ten feet away it would stand and starve till a chance storm should strew the ground before it with twigs and hurl a broken branch against its terrible knives. Then it and its voracious progeny would devour the forest.

The last hundred yards of their flight was a nightmare. Exhausted by the loss of blood from his wound, Saxby had to be dragged. He begged Lane to leave him, reminding the captain that he had a family. Lane, of course, refused. When at last they reached comparative safety Lane was all in.

"Let's rest a minute," he panted, "and see if we can't stop your leg from bleeding."

While they were binding up the wound with rags torn from their shirts they saw the last of their pursuer. In its wallowing lurch through the mire in search of food it collided with one of the squat, well balanced pillars. The impact shattered both, and their green blood gushed out in the twilight.

"Watch that stuff," Saxby whispered. "If it doesn't lose color and turn white my theory is wrecked."

Almost before he had stopped talking the green gas vanished.

"That settles it!" he exulted. "They're only a species of cellulose-feeders after all. If there were any wood around here now you'd see something."

"What about my clothes?"

"Great Scott! I clean forgot. Beat it, before the stuff spreads. Up on that higher ground!"

They spent the night marooned on a hillock of harder paste. The first few hours till the moon rose were the hardest. Gazing at the two undestroyed Titans that loomed through the fading light, and imagining the worst of the insignificant green devils their own foolhardiness had created, they sat silently dreading what the moonlight might bring forth. Was the malignant fecundity of the ruined mountains indeed exhausted? Were those crystal demons slowly starving where they stood, or were they merely waiting for their generative light to give them strength to march blindly over the plain?

The east brightened; the underside of a fleecy cloud became silver, and the first level rays of the full moon struck the highest pinnacles of the Titans. The two men held their breath and waited for the flooding light to bathe the whole infernal brood. The moon cleared the undestroyed hills, and the vast desolation, like a memory from a forgotten life, lay still as death under a cold, unearthly brilliance. Not a vestige of life stirred.

"We had better take no chances," Saxby advised, venting his relief in a prodigious sigh. "If the moonlight isn't strong enough to take the vice out of that hellish gas the sunlight may be."

"It wasn't this afternoon," Lane reminded him. "The men were killed in the blazing sunshine."

"I know," Saxby admitted. "But I believe the stuff can live only a short time in the full sunlight. The men were all killed within five minutes of our crazy attack."

"Yes," Lane argued, "but the gas stopped crystallizing things only because its food ran out. When it died there was not a stick of wood or a rag of cotton above ground. If there had been, the gas would have attacked it in short order."

"That's obvious. And like most obvious things it is obviously only half true. What happened when we crawled out of the mud to inspect? Were our clothes attacked? They were not. That disposes of your pessimism. When I kicked up that damned rifle it came into direct contact with one of the razor edges of the crystal. The crystal was still living—you saw what happened. It was the living crystal that attacked the wood, not a concealed pocket of undissipated gas. My optimism, as usual, comes out top dog. We shall walk away from here tomorrow morning as sound as a couple of bright new pennies. Then, after we get to Shanghai, we shall come back and lay those devils out for good. Your boys will be avenged. Maitland will give us whatever we ask."

"Much good it will do them," Lane responded bitterly. "They're dead."

"Could they have died better? They were not here to kill and pillage. If they are the means of ending the reign of terror quickly and forever, they will have died like soldiers."

"Do you remember what the Chinese girl told us her grandfather said? 'There shall be no killing.' I wonder if she would extend that order to cover the enemy over there? They are just as much alive as you or I, and if last night is any criterion, they can feel more pain than a woman. Why should we kill them?"

"In order that we may survive. Our kind of evolution is better than theirs."

"Sure?" Lane quizzed.

"Shut up! You're just arguing to keep awake. You think as I do. Nature blundered when she made those brutes. Take it from me, it is not mere chance that gave the carbon compounds a long lead over their competitors—these silicon and cellulose feeders among others—in the race toward evolution and a higher form of life. Whatever we may be we are less fiendish than they are. There must be something more than insane chance behind it all."

"What, for instance?"

"Oh, shut up! How the devil should I know?"

"I think you may have said it," Lane chuckled. "Just one more question. How do you propose to demolish our fellow creatures over there?"

"No bragging till we do it. We may never beat them. Still, I think there is rather more than a hint in a fine line I remember from one of the poets—who wrote it I forget:

"'A stone is hurled; the giant falls.' Now, for Heaven's sake shut up and let me try to get some sleep. This has been a hell of a day."

While they slept, dreaming of victory, the enemy marched in triumph over the battlefield, hundreds of miles to the east, which two human enemies had consecrated with their futile bloodshed. Nature was showing those who could still see what war is. It beggared their best.

XIV. VICTORY

MARKOFF'S resurrection accomplished at least one good thing. When the survivors on the battlefield saw what was upon them, they temporarily forgot the distinction between ally and enemy. They became merely human beings in a panic to escape.

It chanced that exactly two of the motor trucks that had been hauling quicklime to the battlefield remained intact when the armies ran out of ammunition. The rest were destroyed by inefficient artillery fire and exploding shell dumps. One of these, packed with thirty-five officers and men from both armies, succeeded in getting away. The other was cut to pieces with its cargo, because not one of the soldiers swarming over it knew how to start it. Disregarding the frenzied appeals of the men running after the luckier truck, the officer at the wheel stepped on the gas and headed for Shanghai. He could not possibly have carried another man. Looking back the refugees saw enough to make them yell for more speed. They got it; two of the thirty-five men were jolted overboard. Twenty minutes later the thirty-three in the truck might have boasted that they were the sole survivors of the battle.

One ludicrous incident of that retreat merits immortality. Fifty miles west of Shanghai the thirty-three in the truck began wrangling bitterly over who had won the battle—the army of General X or the opposing army of General Y. Unfortunately the debate could not be decided by single combat between the generals, as it was General X who saw the first sword of crystal flash from the grave, and General Y was slain by a similar sword while attempting to board the truck which stayed behind. The driver of the lucky truck was a major in the late army of General X. Being an intelligent man he used his eyes—it was moonlight, and he had halted the truck to facilitate debate. He immediately saw a fair way of settling the dispute. As the men had flung away their arms on quitting the field of honor, the major's proposal struck them as being both just and practical. Moreover it was seasoned with a spice of chance, and if there is one thing that a Chinese cannot resist it is a fair opportunity to gamble. They agreed to count noses, or rather uniforms.

The soldiers wearing the uniforms of General X squeezed over to one side of the truck, those of General Y to the other. All agreed to abide by the decision of arithmetic, the losers to become prisoners of the winners. The major, acting as referee, did the counting. There were exactly sixteen on each side, till he cast the deciding vote in favor of General X and won the battle by a majority of one.

The victory was extremely fortunate for the losers as well as the winners, as Shanghai was the great headquarters of the winners' side. It would have been awkward, to say the least, to be forced to take one's prisoners through their own territory. The late General Y's great headquarters were in Manchuria. If it did nothing else, this incident demonstrated the blithe courage of the Chinese soldier in the face of overwhelming natural odds against him. It also earned the major his promotion to the rank of colonel. He had won the battle.

The truck made good time, as the roads had recently been reballasted to hasten the transport of disinfectants to the battlefield. At a quarter past four the following morning it delivered its sixteen prisoners of war to the guard at great headquarters. By six o'clock every Chinese in Shanghai was celebrating the victory. General Y's sixth army, the adherents of General X were informed, had been totally destroyed except for sixteen prisoners. This was, of course, the literal truth—so far as it went.

While Shanghai as a whole celebrated with squealing bands and sputtering firecrackers, the staff officers at Great Headquarters were patiently trying to get at the facts. All thirty-three survivors were being grilled. The one credible detail in their singularly concordant testimony was the story of the bombing plane which precipitated the battle. For the first time the survivors of each side learned that the plane did not belong to their enemies. It was not the property of either General X or General Y. Therefore, the staff officers concluded rather unreasonably, the whole battle was a stupid blunder. The incomprehensible tales of huge crystal devils suddenly leaping out of the ground and racing over the battlefield with swords that slashed like razors, and the equally fantastic accounts of the devils fighting among themselves till they smashed one another to nothing, were dismissed as the fevered fancies of men who had lived for weeks in constant peril of death by gas, flames, bombs, bullets, shells, bayonets and the bubonic plague. The witnesses, protesting like magpies, were hustled off to the pest house.

With the chattering thirty-three disposed of, the staff officers quickly solved the problem of the bombing plane. The chief of the intelligence department, after consulting his records, made a probable guess in three minutes. The only foreign plane within five hundred miles of Shanghai that had been granted a permit to fly at any time during the past two weeks was an American bombing plane. Permission was granted at General Maitland's request for the plane to fly with one passenger, Dr. Saxby, to the Christian missions in Kansu. General Maitland made the request, he declared at the time, because he had learned through private sources that the mission stations were threatened with an epidemic of typhoid. Dr. Saxby wished to fly to Kansu with a supply of antitoxin. As a matter of course the Chinese granted the request—not that they believed General Maitland for an instant. The story of Saxby's flight over the Chinese lines, and the humane conduct of the Chinese in permitting the flight, would win all the sentimentalists in America to their side at one swoop, and it wouldn't cost a soy bean. They didn't give a damn what Saxby might be up to in Kansu. The staff officers had perfect confidence in their friend the governor.

It was with a smile of regretful satisfaction that the chief of staff now called General Maitland on the telephone and informed him that his bombing plane had met with a serious accident while flying over the trenches of General X. Was anyone injured? Yes, unfortunately; the chief feared that all in the plane had lost their lives. It fell from a great height. The cause of the accident? It was impossible to say. Several soldiers, on sick leave from the victorious army of General X, agreed in reporting that the gasoline tanks must have exploded. The plane suddenly burst into flame and crashed from a height of two thousand feet—some said three thousand. The chief of staff tendered his personal condolences and those of his entire army. He trusted that General Maitland would convey these to the people of America. The accident was but the more tragic in that Dr. Saxby perished in the cause of mercy and humanity.

"Amen!" said General Maitland, banging the receiver back on the hook. "And to think that we sold those damned scoundrels their anti-aircraft guns."

"What are you going to do about it?" his aide asked cynically.

"Do? Watch me and you'll see."

HE reached for the private telephone connecting him with the American Air Force in Shanghai. Five minutes later fifty of the fastest bombing planes in the world were roaring over the city on their way to Teng-shan. They were under orders to support Captain Lane and to keep in constant touch with General Maitland by wireless. If necessary they were to cruise back and forth until Lane and the rescued missionaries were safely escorted through the Chinese lines to Shanghai. And further, at the first hostile demonstration from the Chinese, the latter were to have hell bombed out of them and be raked with machine gun fire from above.

"I guess that's plain enough for our Chinese friends and sympathizers," the general remarked to his aide.

"The planes won't be allowed to carry their wireless, you know," the aide archly reminded him.

"Like hell they won't," the general snapped. "If anything happens —no matter what—I'll return the Chinese staff's 'regrets' with thanks."

General Maitland was an impulsive, excitable man. He lacked the great Papa Joffre's ability to sleep ten hours a day while the fate of his army was up in the air. Maitland should never have been made a general. He lived with his men, even when they were fighting a hundred and fifty miles away. As the quarter hours dragged by, the general fought hundreds of imaginary battles with the men in his bombing planes, sometimes achieving brilliant victories, but more frequently suffering the humiliation of disastrous defeats. Why the devil didn't they send him some message? Their orders were explicit, and they surely knew him well enough to realize the penalty for disobedience. They were to keep in constant touch with headquarters by wireless. Why didn't they? The aide stood silently by, as uneasy as his chief.

At last, an hour and twenty minutes after the planes started, the telephone bell jingled. It was a message from the wireless station. The general brushed his aide aside and snatched the telephone.

"General Maitland talking, yes?"

"The colonel wants to send a man back, sir."

"What for? He's got his orders! Send him this—."

"The message says he has sent one plane back to report."

"Report what? Speak up! I can't hear."

"The colonel says he has seen something this side of the battlefield you should know about."

"What has he seen?"

"The message didn't say. The colonel thinks you should know—"

"Yes?"

"I'm sorry, sir. We lost the rest of the message. The static is quite bad."

The general's jaw set. He anticipated the worst.

"Those damned Chinese are firing on them and bringing them down like partridges."

Till the unauthorized courier from the bombers arrived, the general held himself as tense as a steel spring. The aide wisely held his tongue. This was no time for fatuously making the best of things. Maitland brooded in silence. His impetuosity, he imagined, had precipitated a stupid disaster. What could he tell Congress to pacify it for the loss of fifty of its pet bombing planes? Probably nothing. They would insist that he be demoted and disgraced. Their spiteful anger would hit him alone, for he was responsible for the great "air program"; it was his sensational disclosures that had caused the inspired press to howl for planes, more planes, and yet more planes. And now that the country had given him his precious planes, what had he done with them? Sent fifty of the finest to a certain scrap-heap death. Worse, fifty of the bravest air crews of the world had probably perished with their planes. It never occurred to the general that the courier might be returning to report a devastating victory. Having acted in haste, he could only repent.

When at last the pilot of the returned bomber entered the general's office, Maitland rose slowly, white-faced and silent.

"What has happened?" he asked.

"We don't know," the pilot replied. His face was a greenish white.

"Where are the other planes?"

"Half way to Teng-shan by now."

The general made an instant recovery. He was himself, cold, precise and shrewd.

"Then why aren't you with them?"

The pilot took his life in his hands. He looked his very superior officer in the eye, spread his legs wide apart, jammed his muscular fists against his belt, and deliberately spat on the Chinese carpet directly in front of the general's feet. Maitland eyed him curiously, but said nothing. It was not the first time he had seen a man crack and reveal his true color under the stress of war.

"General Maitland," the pilot retorted coolly, "this is no time for military etiquette. I've got to do something drastic to make you notice me." The general was noticing. "Courtmartial me if you like after the fight. But the fight ahead of us won't be with the Chinese. Their war is over—at least for a year or two. How can I make you understand?" The general nodded encouragement.

"Their armies aren't there any more," the pilot continued. "We flew all over their bloody battlefield. They've been wiped clean out. And we saw what did it. They're still at it—coming this way. Toward Shanghai. Are you following me? They're rolling over forests and rivers and villages like a flock of crazy steam rollers, getting bigger with every yard they make. And they leave nothing—absolutely nothing—behind them. Like a fool I dropped a bomb on one of the biggest of the green devils just as it rolled into a village. I hit it, all right. It smashed to nothing. Before the dust settled there were fifty new ones, just as big as the first, rolling away from it. Now, you've got to think up a way of stopping them before they roll in on Shanghai."

The general sidled to his desk and unobtrusively pressed a button.

"What do you think they are?" he asked suavely.

"Something the Chinese have invented—some new kind of tank, or a new sort of gas that turns solid and grows in the air when it bursts from the shell. I don't know. But I guess whatever the things are, they can't stop them. Can we? Some of them are the size of five city blocks and taller than skyscrapers."

"I think we can," the general replied soothingly, keeping an eye on the door, "no matter how big they are. The colonel sent your plane back alone?"

"Yes. He wanted to turn the whole flock back."

"Why didn't he?"

"Well, he said you're hardboiled, and would court-martial the lot of us for disobeying orders if he did. I volunteered to come back alone. I know you can stop them!"

"You weren't afraid of me, were you?" The general laughed boyishly, like the good fellow he was at bottom—when he wasn't nervous.

"Nor of any other soldier," the pilot retorted. "I've seen what's going to happen to us. These new things put all our equipment out of date. Better warn everybody to take to the water."

The door opened and two tough-looking orderlies entered.

"Arrest this man and take him to the hospital. He's crazy," the general snapped. "He is under arrest till further orders."

At the door the prisoner looked back and laughed.

"The colonel bet me a month's pay you would court-martial me. Do I win or lose? It's all the same to me. But get the civilians out of the city!"

THE aide's insight into human nature was much sharper than the general's. Otherwise he could never have been an aide. The pilot's report, fantastic though it was, somehow had a ring of truth.

"Why not send out a scout plane," he suggested, "to see what has really happened to those armies?"

The general pondered this plan in silence.

"The pilot was drunk, or crazy, or both. That's what we get by taking the riffraff of the colleges into the service. A West Point man doesn't go yellow the first time he sees a little blood."

The aide discreetly held his tongue. Presently the general made up his mind. He telephoned an order to the air force. In two minutes the scout plane was on it way. It never came back, and to this day its fate is not know. Probably it flew too low and was cut in two by the sudden upthrust of a sword of green crystal. Its continued absence, hour after tenser hour, again grew unendurable. Maitland hazarded the guess that the Chinese had shot it down. On calling up the Chinese chief of staff about three o'clock that afternoon to protest, the aide received a polite assurance that if a mistake had been made by the anti-aircraft gunners the staff would indemnify the United States.

The Chinese staff saw no reason for telling the Americans that their army could not have shot down the scout for the simple reason that General Y had annihilated the forces of General X, and conversely. Not believing the green-devil yarns of the survivors, the Chinese staff concluded that the scout plane had foolishly crashed into a tree. The bewildered staff itself was waiting for solid information. Before the fifty bombers left for Teng-shan, Chinese intelligence officers were on their way to the battlefield to learn exactly how badly their side was cut up. But they did not confide their anxieties to General Maitland's sympathetic ear. They waited a long time for their information. The intelligence officers never reported.

Between four and five o'clock that afternoon two footsore and weary men halted midway on the pass from Kansu to Shen-si and sat down to rest before limping on to find a village. Lane scarcely recognized the pass as that down which he and his column had hastened to the rescue of the missionaries. This spur of the mountains was merely shattered by the earthquake, not burst asunder and strewn over the plain as was the range of limestone caverns. Yet even here there was abundant evidence of what nature can do when irritated. And far to the west, gleaming in the sun, two turreted and pinnacled bergs of crystal flashed like cities of emeralds and diamonds above the white wilderness of an utter desolation, which they and their progenitors had created.

"How on earth are we ever going to destroy those monsters?" Lane asked.

"I won't prophesy," Saxby replied, "but I think it will be easy. We must choose a day when the air is perfectly calm. This evening would be ideal. Hark! Do you hear what I do?"

They listened intently to a sound that was not yet audible, feeling rather than hearing it. A distant hum began to drone on the air far to the east.

"Planes!" Lane exclaimed, springing to his feet. "Good old Maitland guessed we were hard pressed from what your pilot told him. Do you see them yet?"

"No. But we shall in a minute." Saxby was frantically collecting sticks and leaves. "They've got to see us. Lend me your revolver. My matches were all ruined in that mudhole."

Before the forty-nine bombers pricked the sky like a fleet of midgets flying in battle formation, the men had a thick pillar of white smoke streaming up in the motionless air. As the midgets grew rapidly from mosquitoes to wasps, then to droning hornets, and finally to a roaring flock of low-flying battle cruisers, the men fanned the smoke with their coats to attract the aviators' attention. They were seen; the fleet shot over them, wheeled, and turned again and dived in search of a landing place far down the slope. The one that came down nearest the pass was about three miles away; the farthest fifteen. What looked like smooth ground from above turned out to be either a sticky quagmire or a trap of earthquake fissures. The fleet scattered when it saw what was beneath it. Each pilot was now on his own in spite of the general order to stick together.

Saxby and the captain met the first pilot a little better than half way down the slope.

"What's been happening here?" the pilot bawled.

"Earthquake," Saxby shouted.

No further remarks were exchanged till the panting men joined them.

"Earthquake," he puffed, "be damned. I meant what are those green things like icebergs standing up out there?"

"A new kind of crystal," Saxby informed him, thinking the indefinite reply sufficient for the moment. To his astonishment the man asked if they were alive.

"Yes. How did you guess?"

"I didn't."

"You have seen them before?"

"Not these. Others just like them. Much bigger."

"Where?" Saxby demanded.

"About a hundred and thirty miles east of Shanghai. Hundreds of them. They were walking all over the woods and trampling down villages like match-boxes. Headed for Shanghai is my guess. Know anything about them?"

"Lots," Lane cut in. "General Maitland ordered you fellows to come and fetch us?"

"Just about."

"Well, we two are the lot. The rest of my outfit was killed in the earthquake and by what happened afterwards. Maitland sent forty-eight planes too many."

"Our orders were to support you. What's first? Here's the boss coming up the slope now."

"The pilot I sent back," Saxby resumed, "told General Maitland what happened here?"

"No. I guess it must have been your pilot that was shot down by the Chinese a hundred and fifty miles west of Shanghai. Ask the boss?"

Saxby guessed the whole story without asking. Details were of no moment. The commander briefly confirmed the pilot's account of the march of the living crystals toward Shanghai.

"One of our crowd flew back to warn the general of what was coming. The man bombed one and made things worse than ever—fifty at least took its place."

"Why didn't you all turn back?" Lane demanded.

"Orders. You know how touchy and how bullheaded Maitland is. Well, where do we go from here?"

"Ask Mr. Saxby. I don't know."

"Shall we take orders from him?"

"Yes. If anyone knows he does. If he doesn't know we may as well fly on as long as the gas lasts. What's first, Saxby?"

"Drop bombs from five thousand feet on those two bergs out there. "I'll go up with the pilot. The outcome of our shots will determine what is to be done next. By the way, have you an extra coat with you?"

"You'll be warm enough as you are."

"I guess not," Saxby retorted, stripping his coat and shirt off. "Give me your clothes, Lane. Come on, all of them! I'll drop them when the pilot drops the bombs."

"What's the idea?" the commander asked.

"Plague of some sort," Saxby explained sufficiently. "Our clothes may be infected. You will have to dig up spares for us from your men. We can crawl into the insides of our planes and keep warm somehow." He turned to Lane. "If I have an accident, you tell the rest what happened. Watch the effect of our shots. If they turn out O. K.—you know what I mean—fly back to Shanghai at once. Wait half an hour for all the gas to disperse. When you see Maitland tell him to do this."

He gave the captain the necessary brief instructions and followed the commander down to the plane.

"You can signal somehow to your men?" he asked. The commander replied that they could receive radio messages from his own plane, and Saxby continued. "Then order them to get a thousand feet above the ground and fly around until we finish. Tell them to take their orders from Lane if we come a cropper."

The commander included in his general order a special one for ten of his men to contribute toward clothing the captain while he and Saxby were up. They were to drop their duds from the air. Before the plane took off, Saxby removed his boots and socks, wadded them up with his clothes, and included them with the captain's bundle of discards. He then borrowed the pilot's leather coat and wrapped it, leather side in, around the possibly infected clothes. The mechanician donated an outer coat, the commander a sweater, and Saxby crawled in where it was warm. They were off like a rocket.

"Up as fast as it will climb," Saxby bawled in the pilot's ear. "We must have at least a half an hour of sunshine after the shots. Lend me your glasses."

The desolation beneath them seemed to flatten out at the center and rise like a vast bowl toward the horizon. At the bottom of the bowl two glittering jewels flashed and sparkled in the sun. Saxby crawled out of his refuge and dropped the bundle of clothes. Then he shook the commander's shoulder and nodded. The plane circled slowly above its mark and laid a big black egg.

The men in the wheeling planes four thousand feet below the attackers let out a shout of involuntary joy at the sheer beauty of the spectacle; a peak of pure crystal burst into a cloud of flashing emerald and diamond and showered down on the plain in a scintillating rain. Saxby, peering down through his field glasses, saw the green ring shoot out from the shattered base and spin over the plain. Before it had traveled two miles, it was bleached colorless. In its wake, and for five miles after it became invisible, an army of green pillars leapt from the ground as the gas spread over half submerged splinters from the ruins of the suburbs of Teng-shan and farmhouses. Then, suddenly, as if a gigantic sword in one circling swish had severed the rushing vortex and cut it clean out of space, the invisible gas ceased to devour its prey. Less than twenty feet beyond the outmost pillar of crystal, uprooted trees remained mere uprooted trees. Either the sticks already devoured and transformed to living crystals had absorbed all the gas as it rushed past, like a charcoal filter on common gases, or the continued action of the dying sunlight had destroyed the baleful vitality of the shattered crystal.

"We know how to kill them!" Saxby shouted. "Now for the biggest devil of them all!"

In four minutes the monarch of the wilderness was a ruin. There remained only three rings of squat green pillars to be destroyed. Bombing them would take too long. By radio the air fleet was ordered to fly low and rake them with machine-gun fire.

As the sun set, the last low dome of green crystal burst into a shower of fragments and vanished. No progeny sprang from this brood. By letting out the life-blood of the giants first, Saxby had robbed the lesser devils of the food by which they might have lived again and bred.

The victors rose from the strangest battlefield in history and soared over the pass in battle formation to consolidate their victory.

XV. SHOPPING

Hours before the returning planes swooped down upon Shanghai to refuel for the conflict, the grand offensive against the living crystals was well launched. Shortly after the fleet soared over the pass into Shen-si the sun set, atmospheric conditions instantly improved, and radio communication with American headquarters in Shanghai became possible. From that moment to the last minute before they landed, the fleet was in constant communication with General Maitland and Admiral Bligh, in command of the battleships in the harbor.

The unanimous testimony of ninety-eight trained experts—the pilots and mechanicians of the bombing planes—was not to be disregarded or pooh-poohed as the sudden evidence of a yellow streak. If General Maitland did not credit the first or the second message from the returning planes, he was forced to believe the twenty-second. They were all so curiously similar, so consistent in an insane way, that the general broke into a profuse perspiration. When to the unanimous testimony of the fliers was added a brief account—by radio—of what Saxby and Lane had seen, with the fact thrown in for good measure, that the major part of Lane's troops had been wiped out by the living crystals, the truth at last percolated through the general's hardboiled skepticism. Messages began to flicker back and forth through the twilight.

"Do this, do that," was the tenor of Saxby's curt sparks: "What shall we do next?" that of the general's. Among the orders which Maitland executed like a lamb was a forcible command that he cooperate immediately with the Chinese staffs—of all factions—and with all British, French and other foreign legions within two hundred miles of Shanghai, also with the fleets of all powers.

Like many soldiers of the higher ranks, general Maitland hated that word "cooperate." It always seemed to mean "play the second fiddle, or, if you don't like that, try a tin whistle." Before nine o'clock that evening he was cooperating with Chinese, French, and British at such a high pitch of proficiency that he threatened soon to beat the band. By ten o'clock he had induced all of the oil corporations in China to cooperate with the Chinese and foreign forces to the full limit of their resources. In fact, failing to meet with as prompt and as hearty a response as he had anticipated half an hour earlier, he confiscated their property at one swoop, justifying his high-handed action by that rude phrase "military necessity."

By ten-fifteen all the oil trucks within two hundred miles of Shanghai, loaded to capacity, were headed full speed for the battlefield. The hint that any reluctant cooperator might find his tanks bombed in the morning, if his trucks failed to start as ordered, may have had something to do with the remarkable demonstration of efficiency. With a pressing, real job in front of him, Maitland forgot his nerves and showed what he was made of.

Scout planes, swifter than swallows, skimmed through the night to spy out the enemy and report by radio his latest advances. At eleven o'clock it was learned that the nearest of the oncoming green devils was toppling and trundling toward Shanghai over a village less than sixty miles from the city. The main army of crystal giants was some ten miles further back, advancing on a two-hundred-mile front. Behind them, glittering for mile after mile in the moonlight, stretched broad bands of sheer desolation populated by squat domes and pillars of stationary, living crystal. Flying further west to the human battlefield where the monsters first seized life, the scouts reported in response to a request from Saxby, relayed by Maitland, that the battlefield for miles was a gleaming lake of white mud densely packed with regiments of low domes and stunted pillars. Evidently here, as in Kansu, the lightning growth of the bisexual crystals, with the purple and green bloods, had been attended by strong electrical discharges. The vast uprush of electricity had induced the storm which here, as in Kansu, had severed the purple from the green—or male from female; the males had perished, completely sterilized, in the sunlight, while the females with the green blood had devoured every stick and cotton rag on the battlefield. Then, sinking in the mire they had found fresh food, consumed it, "walked" and toppled from the battlefield, which sloped toward Shanghai, to trundle over woods and villages, breeding a new race independently of the males.

Wherever one of the blind brutes blundered into an obstruction of stone or metal it was instantly shattered, and its yet living blood bathed every fragment of wood in the vicinity with malignant life; from the death of the mother sprang a whole brood of monsters as prolific as she. Where the food was sparse—here and there a few sticks or a handful of straw—the living crystals rooted where they stood, or toppled aimlessly but a few yards to come to equilibrium. Those that ceased to grow were doomed to stand indefinitely, consumed by their own hunger, till some chance wind might blow them a twig or a straw, and possibly start them walking and growing explosively for miles.

If ever an army marched on its belly, this one did. The accident of an exposed root frequently determined the impact of an entire campaign, and more than once the headlong rush of a whole toppling battalion of monsters, any one of which might have crushed a village in its forward lurchings, was halted in abrupt starvation by a strip of gravel two yards wide at the bottom of a dry river bed. Occasionally one of a host thus suddenly stopped would be urged forward once more by the settling of a single handful of gravel beneath it, and in half an hour the fair countryside beyond the immobile army would be ravaged and as desolate as the territory it had conquered.

WITH sublime impartiality blind nature did not always destroy. To her the life of plant, animal or man, and all their laboriously acquired wealth of age-old habits that had fitted them to survive—their beauty, their cunning, their poor treasures—were nothing. In her supreme indifference to them and their fate she stumbled like a drunken imbecile all about them, utterly careless whether she destroyed or did not destroy. The accident of where chance had thrown the best food for her latest brutes alone determined her course, and for these youngest and yet most ancient of all living things she had neither hatred nor shadow nor mercy. To her it was the same whether she led them to plenty in the destruction of the works of her other spawns, or abandoned them to dumb anguish on the barren stones. She who could not feel let her creatures suffer for her. She was neither their friend nor their enemy, merely their creator.

It was decided to make a stand on a two-hundred-mile front fifty miles west of Shanghai. By drawing in the lines so close to the city, Maitland and those cooperating with him hoped to have ample time for the deployment of the effective fighting force on the human side. Between this line and the nearest enemy lay a band now less than ten miles wide of thickly settled, heavily wooded, rolling hills and farm lands. Immediately after the oil trucks were despatched, vast quantities of war material of practically all kinds began streaming along all but two of the available roads and railroads toward the front. Tanks trundled and clanked in the van, or clattered along short cuts to the battlefield, crashing fences and farmyards, shanties and pigstys with a serene disregard of everything but haste. The crews inside these rattling fortresses gave such of the terrified Chinese farmers as saw them the scare of their lives. Except for their leather shoes the men were stark naked. These were the shock troops until the bombing planes should arrive.

The first to reach no man's land were the oil trucks and their supporting troops—Chinese regulars, French and British sailors from the battleships, and American marines. By two o'clock in the morning the counter-attack of human beings was well launched. A front twenty miles long burst into billowing red flames, and huge, tumbling clouds of velvety soot rolled skyward, blotting out the stars and the moon. The empty oil trucks were already bumping back at top speed along the two open roads to the bases of supplies. Farms, villages and woods, drenched in oil, flared up in one thundering conflagration. The wind rose with outraged violence, hurled itself upon the bellying flames, and swept them volleying back over the enemy's territory. As attack after attack opened along the two-hundred-mile front, the sooty sky flickered and throbbed with dull crimson, till the astonished ships, a hundred miles at sea, thought they were witnessing the Armageddon of all Asia. Where the oil failed, incendiary shells burst and rained down fire; the surging groan of the bombardment rose and fell monotonously over the seaports, getting the timid out of their beds in the cheerless dawn to flee from an imagined invitation of Mongols.

As dawn turned the murky air to the color of dry blood, the returning planes roared over the battlefield on their way to Shanghai, and the first of the tanks clattered into action. Withering flames had bleached the vanguard of the advancing hordes, but had not killed the life in their green cores. As far as the human fighters could see, and towering above the horizon where they had been halted by the starvation, colossal bergs of crystal loomed through the dun air as motionless as an army of Gibraltars.

The crews of the tanks donned their gas masks and charged across the devastated strip in their clattering fortresses. The first was within a hundred yards of crashing its berg when one of the returned planes veered, roared back to the battlefield, swooped almost to the ground in front of the tank to attract the attention of the crew, and circled it three times before landing. The signal was sufficient; the tank men were not without brains. They brought their clanking monsters to an instant halt.

"Don't attack till the sun is well up!" Saxby shouted, tumbling out of the bomber. "I know what I'm talking about. The wave of gas from a brute the size of this one will travel five miles. Unless there is full sunlight to sterilize the gas before it reaches the edge of the burned area, you men will start the war all over again."

"All right," a voice shouted.

"All right, is it? What's that gas mask of yours made of? There's canvas in it, isn't there?"

The man sheepishly admitted that there was.

"Your attack is off, young man," Saxby snorted. "Hasn't any man in your headquarters a brain in his head? I told you *no cotton, no cellulose*. You got our messages, I know, because you repeated them by radio."

"Can't we try it if we leave these masks behind?"

"That's up to you. The gas may not be poisonous in the usual way."

"Do you think it is?"

"No. It passed over my head; I breathed it by the cubic yard, and I rather liked it. Send a man out of each tank back with the masks, and then you can have your fun. You can't start for an hour yet, anyway. And it won't be fun when you do start."

When the cheer which hailed this verdict died, old Saxby's face was a study of disillusioned pessimism.

"Ten dollars to five cents your rattletrap is stuffed with cotton waste. What do you wipe your machinery with?"

They were guilty. Old Saxby became eloquent on the subject of military efficiency.

"If every wisp of cotton is not out of your tanks before you attack," he concluded sourly, "they will swell up suddenly and burst like glass bombs. And you'll be inside the glass like flies in amber. Good-bye; I'll see you later—if you use common sense. If not, you are just as well crystallized."

Two hours later, as a reward for their fine night march, the tanks were given the honor of starting the grand assault. In full sunlight, on a front of twenty miles, the ungainly tanks hurled themselves upon the motionless enemy. The air was filled with the brittle din of their ruin, and the minds of the attacking army with the mute agony of their enemies' death.

Half an hour later the entire fleet of planes, refueled and carrying all the ammunition they could lift, soared out over the vast territory conquered by the living crystals.

All that day, all the following day and into the late afternoon, while blazing oil inundated the bays of the battlefield, the planes bombed the huge bergs that stood motionless to receive their death, and raked the standing regiments of crystal pillars and squat, evil domes with machine-gun fire. As the slaughter of the helpless offspring of a blind chance increased to its peak, the fliers tried to forget that they had nerves and to remember only that if one kind of life is to survive, another must perish.

The indefinable sense of agony was no illusion. In distant cities, where the rumor of the battle had not yet penetrated, the inhabitants eyed one another suspiciously, apprehensive that their neighbors carried the strange new plague which, they could swear, was feeling with a hand of ice for the marrows of their own bones. Those who had the means stupefied themselves with opium.

Only when the sun set on the final day of that battle, and the last green dome of living crystal gave up the crushed thing at its heart, did the echo of that distant pain from a forgotten age become a memory.

* * *

ABOUT ten months later, Isabel took Tom shopping on a Saturday afternoon. He was to receive a real rabbit—a live one—to solace him for his great loss. For his mother had suddenly announced that a boy of five should put such childish things as Easter eggs behind him forever. Worse, appeal to his father, carried over his mother's head, had but confirmed the stern decision.

"Is it because of what happened to Hoot with that green egg last year?" Tom persisted as they entered the entrancing shop where guinea-pigs, young bulldogs, kittens, canaries and horned toads were sold.

"I thought you promised me to forget all about Hoot and that green egg," his mother reminded him.

Tom was floored. Diplomacy came to his rescue.

"I can't forget Hoot," he said.

Sorrow for the forbidden eggs vanished in the resplendent vision of an enormous black rabbit with a long face as decorously mournful as a prosperous bishop's.

While Tom was concluding his purchase of the Bishop—Isabel christened him on the spot—old Saxby was on a shopping tour of his own in a romantic quarter of the city not far from the railway station. He was to have Easter breakfast with the Lanes, and he wished to take them some small gift, also to get some decoration for his earthquake cabinets. A flower shop, its windows jammed with waxy Easter lilies swathed in green oiled paper at a dollar a blossom, caught his eye for a moment, but he passed on.

Passing a news-stand he unconsciously took in the headlines, but did not stop. Presently, what he had read registered on his absent mind and he turned back.

HERO BOMBS TWO HUNDRED

the headline yelled. Old Saxby bought a paper, and read how one man in a bombing plane had killed, with a single bomb, two hundred

Nicaraguan rebels who were about to slaughter a handful of American marines. He dropped the paper into the nearest "Help Keep Our City Clean" can, wiped his hands, and marched into a small grocery store.

"Give me two packages of dyes for Easter eggs," he said to the clerk. "One blue and one yellow."

He put down ten cents, slipped the packages into his pocket, and started for the interurban station, his shopping forgotten.

The problem in his mind absorbed him. Was it by more than a sheer accident that Yang succeeded in concocting the specific compound that caused silicon dioxide to take on at least the semblance of life? Almost certainly not. Yet, of all the billions of unstable compounds existing for infinitesimal fractions of a second in the almost instantaneous rush to stability, only a few, perhaps only one, under the exact conditions necessary, had the power of making silicon colloids self-perpetuating and self-feeding. What was the probability of hitting this once chance? Practically nil, unless one had genius to read the slight variations of innumerable failures, and from their mazes discern the one, infinitely crooked, path to the hidden goal.

Yang had had such genius. Saxby knew that he himself lacked it. Yet, if he were lucky, he might stumble upon the fortunate combination of circumstances before he died. With reasonable care of his health he might live to be a hundred. That would give him nearly forty years. But what if, after all, it was not the green dye that was the essential "priming" of the explosion, but some rarer accident? Isabel told him the first afternoon they talked together that the waterglass which she had thrown away was foul with milk blue spots and was "stringy." Were those evil threads and blue spots the secret principle of the life in the living crystals? If so, how many millions of years must elapse before chance would again turn up the lucky number which called them into being? In the absence of luck in either event—green dye or stringy waterglass—it might well be millions of millions of years before another crystal relearned the forgotten secret of life.

This much he saw by the simple rules of arithmetic and the iron laws of chance, laws less flexible than any ever devised by man. Yet, he might live forty years, and in one year thousands of routine experiments can be carried out. Only one need be the lucky one.

Mathematics does not tell us everything. Saxby realized this. The rest of his problem was the hardest, and here arithmetic failed him. Which way was better? The present order of nature, where the finest flower of evolution dies or inflicts death to be free to grow, or the older order, where brute killed brute blindly, without purpose and without the sanction of reason? Was either way better than the other? What had ethics to do with a problem that was a mere puzzle in the laws of chance? How escape it? Was not a revolution to achieve liberty and a less brutish life—the sort of thing these unfortunate Nicaraguans were always pulling off—a contradiction in itself?

"At any rate," Saxby muttered to a helpless lamppost, "those crystals didn't say they were killing one another for the victims' good. Fundamentally they were lesser humbugs than we are. Red-blooded men; blue blood; fists across the sea; green-blooded crystals; true blood; which shall it be? I'll try for the green! Forty years . . . I'll do it!"

He savagely kicked the lamp-post and discovered to his dismay that he was lost. A poker-faced Chinaman stood in the doorway of his shop smoking a long pipe.

"Is this Chinatown?" Saxby asked, rather fatuously.

The imperturbable merchant nodded, a slight, Chinese nod. It was Chinatown, the very heart of it. Saxby stood staring at the dingy shop window. Unlike an American shop window, the Chinese merchant's gave no indication of what the proprietor sold. It was bare of everything except one small bowl of pebbles and water in which a single Chinese lily bloomed in white purity.

"How much for the lily? Bowl and all?"

"Him not for sale."

Saxby fished out a twenty-dollar bill and flashed it in the Chinaman's face.

"I guess you'll sell it for twenty dollars."

Without a word the merchant reached for the lily, bowl and all, handed it to Saxby, and pocketed the bill in silence.

As he walked away, carrying his purchase tenderly, old Saxby fumbled in his pocket. He found the two packets of dyes, the blue and the yellow.

With a gesture of shame he tossed them into the gutter.

"White Lily!"

THE END

CATALOGUE OF DOVER BOOKS

Puzzles, Mathematical Recreations

SYMBOLIC LOGIC and THE GAME OF LOGIC, Lewis Carroll. "Symbolic Logic" is not concerned with modern symbolic logic, but is instead a collection of over 380 problems posed with charm and imagination, using the syllogism, and a fascinating diagrammatic method of drawing conclusions. In "The Game of Logic" Carroll's whimsical imagination devises a logical game played with 2 diagrams and counters (included) to manipulate hundreds of tricky syllogisms. The final section, "Hit or Miss" is a lagniappe of 101 additional puzzles in the delightful Carroll manner. Until this reprint edition, both of these books were rarities costing up to $15 each. Symbolic Logic: Index. xxxi + 199pp. The Game of Logic: 96pp. 2 vols. bound as one. 5⅜ x 8. T492 Paperbound **$1.50**

PILLOW PROBLEMS and A TANGLED TALE, Lewis Carroll. One of the rarest of all Carroll's works, "Pillow Problems" contains 72 original math puzzles, all typically ingenious. Particularly fascinating are Carroll's answers which remain exactly as he thought them out, reflecting his actual mental process. The problems in "A Tangled Tale" are in story form, originally appearing as a monthly magazine serial. Carroll not only gives the solutions, but uses answers sent in by readers to discuss wrong approaches and misleading paths, and grades them for insight. Both of these books were rarities until this edition, "Pillow Problems" costing up to $25, and "A Tangled Tale" $15. Pillow Problems: Preface and Introduction by Lewis Carroll. xx + 109pp. A Tangled Tale: 6 illustrations. 152pp. Two vols. bound as one. 5⅜ x 8. T493 Paperbound **$1.50**

AMUSEMENTS IN MATHEMATICS, Henry Ernest Dudeney. The foremost British originator of mathematical puzzles is always intriguing, witty, and paradoxical in this classic, one of the largest collections of mathematical amusements. More than 430 puzzles, problems, and paradoxes. Mazes and games, problems on number manipulation, unicursal and other route problems, puzzles on measuring, weighing, packing, age, kinship, chessboards, joiners', crossing river, plane figure dissection, and many others. Solutions. More than 450 illustrations. vii + 258pp. 5⅜ x 8. T473 Paperbound **$1.25**

THE CANTERBURY PUZZLES, Henry Dudeney. Chaucer's pilgrims set one another problems in story form. Also Adventures of the Puzzle Club, the Strange Escape of the King's Jester, the Monks of Riddlewell, the Squire's Christmas Puzzle Party, and others. All puzzles are original, based on dissecting plane figures, arithmetic, algebra, elementary calculus and other branches of mathematics, and purely logical ingenuity. "The limit of ingenuity and intricacy," The Observer. Over 110 puzzles. Full Solutions. 150 illustrations. vii + 225pp. 5⅜ x 8. T474 Paperbound **$1.25**

MATHEMATICAL EXCURSIONS, H. A. Merrill. Even if you hardly remember your high school math, you'll enjoy the 90 stimulating problems contained in this book and you will come to understand a great many mathematical principles with surprisingly little effort. Many useful shortcuts and diversions not generally known are included: division by inspection, Russian peasant multiplication, memory systems for pi, building odd and even magic squares, square roots by geometry, dyadic systems, and many more. Solutions to difficult problems. 50 illustrations. 145pp. 5⅜ x 8. T350 Paperbound **$1.00**

MAGIC SQUARES AND CUBES, W. S. Andrews. Only book-length treatment in English, a thorough non-technical description and analysis. Here are nasik, overlapping, pandiagonal, serrated squares; magic circles, cubes, spheres, rhombuses. Try your hand at 4-dimensional magical figures! Much unusual folklore and tradition included. High school algebra is sufficient. 754 diagrams and illustrations. viii + 419pp. 5⅜ x 8. T658 Paperbound **$1.85**

CALIBAN'S PROBLEM BOOK: MATHEMATICAL, INFERENTIAL AND CRYPTOGRAPHIC PUZZLES, H. Phillips (Caliban), S. T. Shovelton, G. S. Marshall. 105 ingenious problems by the greatest living creator of puzzles based on logic and inference. Rigorous, modern, piquant; reflecting their author's unusual personality, these intermediate and advanced puzzles all involve the ability to reason clearly through complex situations; some call for mathematical knowledge, ranging from algebra to number theory. Solutions. xi + 180pp. 5⅜ x 8. T736 Paperbound **$1.25**

MATHEMATICAL PUZZLES FOR BEGINNERS AND ENTHUSIASTS, G. Mott-Smith. 188 mathematical puzzles based on algebra, dissection of plane figures, permutations, and probability, that will test and improve your powers of inference and interpretation. The Odic Force, The Spider's Cousin, Ellipse Drawing, theory and strategy of card and board games like tit-tat-toe, go moku, salvo, and many others. 100 pages of detailed mathematical explanations. Appendix of primes, square roots, etc. 135 illustrations. 2nd revised edition. 248pp. 5⅜ x 8. T198 Paperbound **$1.00**

MATHEMAGIC, MAGIC PUZZLES, AND GAMES WITH NUMBERS, R. V. Heath. More than 60 new puzzles and stunts based on the properties of numbers. Easy techniques for multiplying large numbers mentally, revealing hidden numbers magically, finding the date of any day in any year, and dozens more. Over 30 pages devoted to magic squares, triangles, cubes, circles, etc. Edited by J. S. Meyer. 76 illustrations. 128pp. 5⅜ x 8. T110 Paperbound **$1.00**

MATHEMATICAL RECREATIONS, M. Kraitchik. One of the most thorough compilations of unusual mathematical problems for beginners and advanced mathematicians. Historical problems from Greek, Medieval, Arabic, Hindu sources. 50 pages devoted to pastimes derived from figurate numbers, Mersenne numbers, Fermat numbers, primes and probability. 40 pages of magic, Euler, Latin, panmagic squares. 25 new positional and permutational games of permanent value: fairy chess, latruncles, reversi, jinx, ruma, lasca, tricolor, tetrachrome, etc. Complete rigorous solutions. Revised second edition. 181 illustrations. 333pp. 5⅜ x 8.
T163 Paperbound **$1.75**

MATHEMATICAL PUZZLES OF SAM LOYD, selected and edited by M. Gardner. Choice puzzles by the greatest American puzzle creator and innovator. Selected from his famous collection, "Cyclopedia of Puzzles," they retain the unique style and historical flavor of the originals. There are posers based on arithmetic, algebra, probability, game theory, route tracing, topology, counter, sliding block, operations research, geometrical dissection. Includes the famous "14-15" puzzle which was a national craze, and his "Horse of a Different Color" which sold millions of copies. 117 of his most ingenious puzzles in all, 120 line drawings and diagrams. Solutions. Selected references. xx + 167pp. 5⅜ x 8. T498 Paperbound **$1.00**

MATHEMATICAL PUZZLES OF SAM LOYD, Vol. II, selected and edited by Martin Gardner. The outstanding 2nd selection from the great American innovator's "Cyclopedia of Puzzles": speed and distance problems, clock problems, plane and solid geometry, calculus problems, etc. Analytical table of contents that groups the puzzles according to the type of mathematics necessary to solve them. 166 puzzles, 150 original line drawings and diagrams. Selected references. xiv + 177pp. 5⅜ x 8. T709 Paperbound **$1.00**

ARITHMETICAL EXCURSIONS: AN ENRICHMENT OF ELEMENTARY MATHEMATICS, H. Bowers and J. Bowers. A lively and lighthearted collection of facts and entertainments for anyone who enjoys manipulating numbers or solving arithmetical puzzles: methods of arithmetic never taught in school, little-known facts about the most simple numbers, and clear explanations of more sophisticated topics; mysteries and folklore of numbers, the "Hin-dog-abic" number system, etc. First publication. Index. 529 numbered problems and diversions, all with answers. Bibliography. 60 figures. xiv + 320pp. 5⅜ x 8. T770 Paperbound **$1.65**

CRYPTANALYSIS, H. F. Gaines. Formerly entitled ELEMENTARY CRYPTANALYSIS, this introductory-intermediate level text is the best book in print on cryptograms and their solution. It covers all major techniques of the past, and contains much that is not generally known except to experts. Full details about concealment, substitution, and transposition ciphers; periodic mixed alphabets, multafid, Kasiski and Vigenere methods, Ohaver patterns, Playfair, and scores of other topics. 6 language letter and word frequency appendix. 167 problems, now furnished with solutions. Index. 173 figures. vi + 230pp. 5⅜ x 8.
T97 Paperbound **$2.00**

CRYPTOGRAPHY, L. D. Smith. An excellent introductory work on ciphers and their solution, the history of secret writing, and actual methods and problems in such techniques as transposition and substitution. Appendices describe the enciphering of Japanese, the Baconian biliteral cipher, and contain frequency tables and a bibliography for further study. Over 150 problems with solutions. 160pp. 5⅜ x 8. T247 Paperbound **$1.00**

PUZZLE QUIZ AND STUNT FUN, J. Meyer. The solution to party doldrums. 238 challenging puzzles, stunts and tricks. Mathematical puzzles like The Clever Carpenter, Atom Bomb; mysteries and deductions like The Bridge of Sighs, The Nine Pearls, Dog Logic; observation puzzles like Cigarette Smokers, Telephone Dial; over 200 others including magic squares, tongue twisters, puns, anagrams, and many others. All problems solved fully. 250pp. 5⅜ x 8.
T337 Paperbound **$1.00**

101 PUZZLES IN THOUGHT AND LOGIC, C. R. Wylie, Jr. Brand new problems you need no special knowledge to solve! Take the kinks out of your mental "muscles" and enjoy solving murder problems, the detection of lying fishermen, the logical identification of color by a blindman, and dozens more. Introduction with simplified explanation of general scientific method and puzzle solving. 128pp. 5⅜ x 8. T367 Paperbound **$1.00**

MY BEST PROBLEMS IN MATHEMATICS, Hubert Phillips ("Caliban"). Only elementary mathematics needed to solve these 100 witty, catchy problems by a master problem creator. Problems on the odds in cards and dice, problems in geometry, algebra, permutations, even problems that require no math at all—just a logical mind, clear thinking. Solutions completely worked out. If you enjoy mysteries, alerting your perceptive powers and exercising your detective's eye, you'll find these cryptic puzzles a challenging delight. Original 1961 publication. 100 puzzles, solutions. x + 107pp. 5⅝ x 8. T91 Paperbound **$1.00**

MY BEST PUZZLES IN LOGIC AND REASONING, Hubert Phillips ("Caliban"). A new collection of 100 inferential and logical puzzles chosen from the best that have appeared in England, available for first time in U.S. By the most endlessly resourceful puzzle creator now living. All data presented are both necessary and sufficient to allow a single unambiguous answer. No special knowledge is required for problems ranging from relatively simple to completely original one-of-a-kinds. Guaranteed to please beginners and experts of all ages. Original publication. 100 puzzles, full solutions. x + 107pp. 5⅜ x 8. T119 Paperbound **$1.00**

THE BOOK OF MODERN PUZZLES, G. L. Kaufman. A completely new series of puzzles as fascinating as crossword and deduction puzzles but based upon different principles and techniques. Simple 2-minute teasers, word labyrinths, design and pattern puzzles, logic and observation puzzles — over 150 braincrackers. Answers to all problems. 116 illustrations. 192pp. 5⅜ x 8.
T143 Paperbound **$1.00**

NEW WORD PUZZLES, G. L. Kaufman. 100 ENTIRELY NEW puzzles based on words and their combinations that will delight crossword puzzle, Scrabble and Jotto fans. Chess words, based on the moves of the chess king; design-onyms, symmetrical designs made of synonyms; rhymed double-crostics; syllable sentences; addle letter anagrams; alphagrams; linkograms; and many others all brand new. Full solutions. Space to work problems. 196 figures. vi + 122pp. 5⅜ x 8.
T344 Paperbound **$1.00**

MAZES AND LABYRINTHS: A BOOK OF PUZZLES, W. Shepherd. Mazes, formerly associated with mystery and ritual, are still among the most intriguing of intellectual puzzles. This is a novel and different collection of 50 amusements that embody the principle of the maze: mazes in the classical tradition; 3-dimensional, ribbon, and Möbius-strip mazes; hidden messages; spatial arrangements; etc.—almost all built on amusing story situations. 84 illustrations. Essay on maze psychology. Solutions. xv + 122pp. 5⅜ x 8.
T731 Paperbound **$1.00**

MAGIC TRICKS & CARD TRICKS, W. Jonson. Two books bound as one. 52 tricks with cards, 37 tricks with coins, bills, eggs, smoke, ribbons, slates, etc. Details on presentation, misdirection, and routining will help you master such famous tricks as the Changing Card, Card in the Pocket, Four Aces, Coin Through the Hand, Bill in the Egg, Afghan Bands, and over 75 others. If you follow the lucid exposition and key diagrams carefully, you will finish these two books with an astonishing mastery of magic. 106 figures. 224pp. 5⅜ x 8.
T909 Paperbound **$1.00**

PANORAMA OF MAGIC, Milbourne Christopher. A profusely illustrated history of stage magic, a unique selection of prints and engravings from the author's private collection of magic memorabilia, the largest of its kind. Apparatus, stage settings and costumes; ingenious ads distributed by the performers and satiric broadsides passed around in the streets ridiculing pompous showmen; programs; decorative souvenirs. The lively text, by one of America's foremost professional magicians, is full of anecdotes about almost legendary wizards: Dede, the Egyptian; Philadelphia, the wonder-worker; Robert-Houdin, "the father of modern magic;" Harry Houdini; scores more. Altogether a pleasure package for anyone interested in magic, stage setting and design, ethnology, psychology, or simply in unusual people. A Dover original. 295 illustrations; 8 in full color. Index. viii + 216pp. 8⅜ x 11¼.
T774 Paperbound **$2.25**

HOUDINI ON MAGIC, Harry Houdini. One of the greatest magicians of modern times explains his most prized secrets. How locks are picked, with illustrated picks and skeleton keys; how a girl is sawed into twins; how to walk through a brick wall — Houdini's explanations of 44 stage tricks with many diagrams. Also included is a fascinating discussion of great magicians of the past and the story of his fight against fraudulent mediums and spiritualists. Edited by W.B. Gibson and M.N. Young. Bibliography. 155 figures, photos. xv + 280pp. 5⅜ x 8.
T384 Paperbound **$1.35**

MATHEMATICS, MAGIC AND MYSTERY, Martin Gardner. Why do card tricks work? How do magicians perform astonishing mathematical feats? How is stage mind-reading possible? This is the first book length study explaining the application of probability, set theory, theory of numbers, topology, etc., to achieve many startling tricks. Non-technical, accurate, detailed! 115 sections discuss tricks with cards, dice, coins, knots, geometrical vanishing illusions, how a Curry square "demonstrates" that the sum of the parts may be greater than the whole, and dozens of others. No sleight of hand necessary! 135 illustrations. xii + 174pp. 5⅜ x 8.
T335 Paperbound **$1.00**

EASY-TO-DO ENTERTAINMENTS AND DIVERSIONS WITH COINS, CARDS, STRING, PAPER AND MATCHES, R. M. Abraham. Over 300 tricks, games and puzzles will provide young readers with absorbing fun. Sections on card games; paper-folding; tricks with coins, matches and pieces of string; games for the agile; toy-making from common household objects; mathematical recreations; and 50 miscellaneous pastimes. Anyone in charge of groups of youngsters, including hard-pressed parents, and in need of suggestions on how to keep children sensibly amused and quietly content will find this book indispensable. Clear, simple text, copious number of delightful line drawings and illustrative diagrams. Originally titled "Winter Nights Entertainments." Introduction by Lord Baden Powell. 329 illustrations. v + 186pp. 5⅜ x 8½.
T921 Paperbound **$1.00**

STRING FIGURES AND HOW TO MAKE THEM, Caroline Furness Jayne. 107 string figures plus variations selected from the best primitive and modern examples developed by Navajo, Apache, pygmies of Africa, Eskimo, in Europe, Australia, China, etc. The most readily understandable, easy-to-follow book in English on perennially popular recreation. Crystal-clear exposition; step-by-step diagrams. Everyone from kindergarten children to adults looking for unusual diversion will be endlessly amused. Index. Bibliography. Introduction by A. C. Haddon. 17 full-page plates. 960 illustrations. xxiii + 401pp. 5⅜ x 8½.
T152 Paperbound **$2.00**

Fiction

FLATLAND, E. A. Abbott. A science-fiction classic of life in a 2-dimensional world that is also a first-rate introduction to such aspects of modern science as relativity and hyperspace. Political, moral, satirical, and humorous overtones have made FLATLAND fascinating reading for thousands. 7th edition. New introduction by Banesh Hoffmann. 16 illustrations. 128pp. 5⅜ x 8. T1 Paperbound **$1.00**

THE WONDERFUL WIZARD OF OZ, L. F. Baum. Only edition in print with all the original W. W. Denslow illustrations in full color—as much a part of "The Wizard" as Tenniel's drawings are of "Alice in Wonderland." "The Wizard" is still America's best-loved fairy tale, in which, as the author expresses it, "The wonderment and joy are retained and the heartaches and nightmares left out." Now today's young readers can enjoy every word and wonderful picture of the original book. New introduction by Martin Gardner. A Baum bibliography. 23 full-page color plates. viii + 268pp. 5⅜ x 8. T691 Paperbound **$1.50**

THE MARVELOUS LAND OF OZ, L. F. Baum. This is the equally enchanting sequel to the "Wizard," continuing the adventures of the Scarecrow and the Tin Woodman. The hero this time is a little boy named Tip, and all the delightful Oz magic is still present. This is the Oz book with the Animated Saw-Horse, the Woggle-Bug, and Jack Pumpkinhead. All the original John R. Neill illustrations, 10 in full color. 287 pp. 5⅜ x 8. T692 Paperbound **$1.50**

28 SCIENCE FICTION STORIES OF H. G. WELLS. Two full unabridged novels, MEN LIKE GODS and STAR BEGOTTEN, plus 26 short stories by the master science-fiction writer of all time! Stories of space, time, invention, exploration, future adventure—an indispensable part of the library of everyone interested in science and adventure. PARTIAL CONTENTS: Men Like Gods, The Country of the Blind, In the Abyss, The Crystal Egg, The Man Who Could Work Miracles, A Story of the Days to Come, The Valley of Spiders, and 21 more! 928pp. 5⅜ x 8.
T265 Clothbound **$4.50**

THREE MARTIAN NOVELS, Edgar Rice Burroughs. Contains: Thuvia, Maid of Mars; The Chessmen of Mars; and The Master Mind of Mars. High adventure set in an imaginative and intricate conception of the Red Planet. Mars is peopled with an intelligent, heroic human race which lives in densely populated cities and with fierce barbarians who inhabit dead sea bottoms. Other exciting creatures abound amidst an inventive framework of Martian history and geography. Complete unabridged reprintings of the first edition. 16 illustrations by J. Allen St. John. vi + 499pp. 5⅜ x 8½. T39 Paperbound **$1.85**

SEVEN SCIENCE FICTION NOVELS, H. G. Wells. Full unabridged texts of 7 science-fiction novels of the master. Ranging from biology, physics, chemistry, astronomy to sociology and other studies, Mr. Wells extrapolates whole worlds of strange and intriguing character. "One will have to go far to match this for entertainment, excitement, and sheer pleasure . . . ," NEW YORK TIMES. Contents: The Time Machine, The Island of Dr. Moreau, First Men in the Moon, The Invisible Man, The War of the Worlds, The Food of the Gods, In the Days of the Comet. 1015pp. 5⅜ x 8. T264 Clothbound **$4.50**

THE LAND THAT TIME FORGOT and THE MOON MAID, Edgar Rice Burroughs. In the opinion of many, Burroughs' best work. The first concerns a strange island where evolution is individual rather than phylogenetic. Speechless anthropoids develop into intelligent human beings within a single generation. The second projects the reader far into the future and describes the first voyage to the Moon (in the year 2025), the conquest of the Earth by the Moon, and years of violence and adventure as the enslaved Earthmen try to regain possession of their planet. "An imaginative tour de force that keeps the reader keyed up and expectant," NEW YORK TIMES. Complete, unabridged text of the original two novels (three parts in each). 5 illustrations by J. Allen St. John. vi + 552pp. 5⅜ x 8½.
T1020 Clothbound **$3.75**
T358 Paperbound **$2.00**

3 ADVENTURE NOVELS by H. Rider Haggard. Complete texts of "She," "King Solomon's Mines," "Allan Quatermain." Qualities of discovery; desire for immortality; search for primitive, for what is unadorned by civilization, have kept these novels of African adventure exciting, alive to readers from R. L. Stevenson to George Orwell. 636pp. 5⅜ x 8.
T584 Paperbound **$2.00**

A PRINCESS OF MARS and A FIGHTING MAN OF MARS: TWO MARTIAN NOVELS BY EDGAR RICE BURROUGHS. "Princess of Mars" is the very first of the great Martian novels written by Burroughs, and it is probably the best of them all; it set the pattern for all of his later fantasy novels and contains a thrilling cast of strange peoples and creatures and the formula of Olympian heroism amidst ever-fluctuating fortunes which Burroughs carries off so successfully. "Fighting Man" returns to the same scenes and cities—many years later. A mad scientist, a degenerate dictator, and an indomitable defender of the right clash—with the fate of the Red Planet at stake! Complete, unabridged reprinting of original editions. Illustrations by F. E. Schoonover and Hugh Hutton. v + 356pp. 5⅜ x 8½.
T1140 Paperbound **$1.75**

THE PIRATES OF VENUS and LOST ON VENUS: TWO VENUS NOVELS BY EDGAR RICE BURROUGHS. Two related novels, complete and unabridged. Exciting adventure on the planet Venus with Earthman Carson Napier broken-field running through one dangerous episode after another. All lovers of swashbuckling science fiction will enjoy these two stories set in a world of fascinating societies, fierce beasts, 5000-ft. trees, lush vegetation, and wide seas. Illustrations by Fortunino Matania. Total of vi + 340pp. 5⅜ x 8½. T1053 Paperbound **$1.75**

RURITANIA COMPLETE: THE PRISONER OF ZENDA and RUPERT OF HENTZAU, Anthony Hope. The first edition to include in one volume both the continually-popular "Prisoner of Zenda" and its equally-absorbing sequel. Hope's mythical country of Ruritania has become a household word and the activities of its inhabitants almost a common heritage. Unabridged reprinting. 14 illustrations by Charles Dana Gibson. vi + 414pp. 5⅜ x 8. T69 Paperbound **$1.35**

GHOST AND HORROR STORIES OF AMBROSE BIERCE, Selected and introduced by E. F. Bleiler. 24 morbid, eerie tales—the cream of Bierce's fiction output. Contains such memorable pieces as "The Moonlit Road," "The Damned Thing," "An Inhabitant of Carcosa," "The Eyes of the Panther," "The Famous Gilson Bequest," "The Middle Toe of the Right Foot," and other chilling stories, plus the essay, "Visions of the Night" in which Bierce gives us a kind of rationale for his aesthetic of horror. New collection (1964). xxii + 199pp. 5⅜ x 8⅜. T767 Paperbound **$1.00**

BEST GHOST STORIES OF J. S. LE FANU, Selected and introduced by E. F. Bleiler. LeFanu is deemed the greatest name in Victorian supernatural fiction. Here are 16 of his best horror stories, including 2 nouvelles: "Carmilla," a classic vampire tale couched in a perverse eroticism, and "The Haunted Baronet." Also: "Sir Toby's Will," "Green Tea," "Schalken the Painter," "Ultor de Lacy," "The Familiar," etc. The first American publication of about half of this material: a long-overdue opportunity to get a choice sampling of LeFanu's work. New selection (1964). 8 illustrations. 5⅜ x 8⅜. T415 Paperbound **$1.85**

FIVE GREAT DOG NOVELS, edited by Blanche Cirker. The complete original texts of five classic dog novels that have delighted and thrilled millions of children and adults throughout the world with stories of loyalty, adventure, and courage. Full texts of Jack London's "The Call of the Wild"; John Brown's "Rab and His Friends"; Alfred Ollivant's "Bob, Son of Battle"; Marshall Saunders' "Beautiful Joe"; and Ouida's "A Dog of Flanders." 21 illustrations from the original editions. 495pp. 5⅜ x 8. T777 Paperbound **$1.75**

THE CASTING AWAY OF MRS. LECKS AND MRS. ALESHINE, F. R. Stockton. A charming light novel by Frank Stockton, one of America's finest humorists (and author of "The Lady, or the Tiger?"). This book has made millions of Americans laugh at the reflection of themselves in two middle-aged American women involved in some of the strangest adventures on record. You will laugh, too, as they endure shipwreck, desert island, and blizzard with maddening tranquility. Also contains complete text of "The Dusantes," sequel to "The Casting Away." 49 original illustrations by F. D. Steele. vii + 142pp. 5⅜ x 8. T743 Paperbound **$1.00**

AT THE EARTH'S CORE, PELLUCIDAR, TANAR OF PELLUCIDAR: THREE SCIENCE FICTION NOVELS BY EDGAR RICE BURROUGHS. Complete, unabridged texts of the first three Pellucidar novels. Tales of derring-do by the famous master of science fiction. The locale for these three related stories is the inner surface of the hollow Earth where we discover the world of Pellucidar, complete with all types of bizarre, menacing creatures, strange peoples, and alluring maidens—guaranteed to delight all Burroughs fans and a wide circle of advenutre lovers. Illustrated by J. Allen St. John and P. F. Berdanier. vi + 433pp. 5⅜ x 8½. T1051 Paperbound **$2.00**

THE WAR IN THE AIR, IN THE DAYS OF THE COMET, THE FOOD OF THE GODS: THREE SCIENCE FICTION NOVELS BY H. G. WELLS. Three exciting Wells offerings bearing on vital social and philosophical issues of his and our own day. Here are tales of air power, strategic bombing, East vs. West, the potential miracles of science, the potential disasters from outer space, the relationship between scientific advancement and moral progress, etc. First reprinting of "War in the Air" in almost 50 years. An excellent sampling of Wells at his storytelling best. Complete, unabridged reprintings. 16 illustrations. 645pp. 5⅜ x 8½. T1135 Paperbound **$2.00**

DAVID HARUM, E. N. Westcott. This novel of one of the most lovable, humorous characters in American literature is a prime example of regional humor. It continues to delight people who like their humor dry, their characters quaint, and their plots ingenuous. First book edition to contain complete novel plus chapter found after author's death. Illustrations from first illustrated edition. 192pp. 5⅜ x 8. T580 Paperbound **$1.15**

TO THE SUN? and OFF ON A COMET!, Jules Verne. Complete texts of two of the most imaginative flights into fancy in world literature display the high adventure that have kept Verne's novels read for nearly a century. Only unabridged edition of the best translation, by Edward Roth. Large, easily readable type. 50 illustrations selected from first editions. 462pp. 5⅜ x 8. T634 Paperbound **$1.75**

FROM THE EARTH TO THE MOON and ALL AROUND THE MOON, Jules Verne. Complete editions of two of Verne's most successful novels, in finest Edward Roth translations, now available after many years out of print. Verne's visions of submarines, airplanes, television, rockets, interplanetary travel; of scientific and not-so-scientific beliefs; of peculiarities of Americans; all delight and engross us today as much as when they first appeared. Large, easily readable type. 42 illus. from first French edition. 476pp. 5⅜ x 8. T633 Paperbound **$1.75**

THREE PROPHETIC NOVELS BY H. G. WELLS, edited by E. F. Bleiler. Complete texts of "When the Sleeper Wakes" (1st book printing in 50 years), "A Story of the Days to Come," "The Time Machine" (1st complete printing in book form). Exciting adventures in the future are as enjoyable today as 50 years ago when first printed. Predict TV, movies, intercontinental airplanes, prefabricated houses, air-conditioned cities, etc. First important author to foresee problems of mind control, technological dictatorships. "Absolute best of imaginative fiction," N. Y. Times. Introduction. 335pp. 5⅜ x 8. T605 Paperbound **$1.50**

GESTA ROMANORUM, trans. by Charles Swan, ed. by Wynnard Hooper. 181 tales of Greeks, Romans, Britons, Biblical characters, comprise one of greatest medieval story collections, source of plots for writers including Shakespeare, Chaucer, Gower, etc. Imaginative tales of wars, incest, thwarted love, magic, fantasy, allegory, humor, tell about kings, prostitutes, philosophers, fair damsels, knights, Noah, pirates, all walks, stations of life. Introduction. Notes. 500pp. 5⅜ x 8. T535 Paperbound **$1.85**

Prices subject to change without notice.

Dover publishes books on art, music, philosophy, literature, languages, history, social sciences, psychology, handcrafts, orientalia, puzzles and entertainments, chess, pets and gardens, books explaining science, intermediate and higher mathematics, mathematical physics, engineering, biological sciences, earth sciences, classics of science, etc. Write to:

Dept. catrr.
Dover Publications, Inc.
180 Varick Street, N.Y. 14, N.Y.